HARRY'S
WAY

The Twelve Steps Without God

MARK LAGES

authorHOUSE®

AuthorHouse™
1663 Liberty Drive
Bloomington, IN 47403
www.authorhouse.com
Phone: 1 (800) 839-8640

Published by AuthorHouse 06/27/2016

ISBN: 978-1-5246-1627-4 (sc)
ISBN: 978-1-5246-1626-7 (e)

Library of Congress Control Number: 2016910516

Print information available on the last page.

This is a work of fiction. All of the characters, names, incidents,
organizations, and dialogue in this novel are either the products
of the author's imagination or are used fictitiously.

Any people depicted in stock imagery provided by Thinkstock are models,
and such images are being used for illustrative purposes only.
Certain stock imagery © Thinkstock.

This book is printed on acid-free paper.

CONTENTS

About the Author

Mark Lages is an award-winning author who has published both short stories and novels over his writing career. He takes a special interest in the subject of alcoholism, being an alcoholic himself and having lived with the problem in his family for years. He currently lives with his wife in Orange County, California, where he continues to live sober and enjoy all the great things life has to offer without drinking.

Preface

A Warning

The story you are about to read is not a true story, nor is it roughly based on true events. Yet while this is a work of fiction, it has been inspired by my own actual life experiences. It is the result of my lifelong struggle with alcoholism and my many attempts to find a viable means of treatment. I have learned a great deal about this subject over the years. Much of this story is presented as conversations between two fictional characters, Harry and Lester. These dialogues are completely invented. The purpose of this book isn't to memorialize events that have actually taken place, but rather to share with you through a work of fiction how I have finally achieved my own sobriety. With this in mind, I turn the narrative over to the main character.

CHAPTER 1

The Twelve Steps of AA

My name is Lester Madison. Before I list the twelve steps of Alcoholics Anonymous for you, let me tell you something about myself. I am many things; I am a father, husband, building contractor, taxpayer, home owner, writer, and avid cigar smoker. But for the purposes of this story, the most important thing for you to know is that I am an alcoholic. It's a role that has shaped a good deal of my life. I have struggled with drinking ever since I was a teenager; it was in my teens that, as they say in AA, the tail began wagging the dog. Also, you should know I don't believe in God. Sorry if this upsets you, but I have some very good reasons for my skepticism. I am not an evil person; I just don't happen to believe in God.

The first time I tried to quit drinking, I was in my twenties and desperate to get alcohol out of my life. I found myself in AA just like so many others who had the same problem. I swallowed my pride and sought their help, not realizing what I was getting myself into. Yes, I bought their book, reading it faithfully from cover to cover and studying the steps like I was preparing for a college exam. Are you familiar with the twelve steps of AA? Just in case you haven't read them before, they're listed below:

1. We admitted we were powerless over alcohol, that our lives had become unmanageable.
2. Came to believe that a Power greater than ourselves could restore us to sanity.
3. Made a decision to turn our will and our lives over to the care of God as we understood Him.
4. Made a searching and fearless moral inventory of ourselves.

5. Admitted to God, to ourselves, and to another human being the exact nature of our wrongs.
6. Were entirely ready to have God remove all these defects of character.
7. Humbly asked him to remove our shortcomings.
8. Made a list of all persons we had harmed, and became willing to make amends to them all.
9. Made direct amends to such people wherever possible, except when to do so would injure them or others.
10. Continued to take personal inventory and when we were wrong promptly admitted it.
11. Sought through prayer and meditation to improve our conscious contact with God, as we understood him, praying only for knowledge of His will for us and the power to carry that out.
12. Having had a spiritual awakening as a result of these Steps, we tried to carry this message to alcoholics, and to practice these principals in all our affairs.

I still go to AA meetings when I feel I need them. If it weren't for Harry, who knows where I'd be now? I wish I'd met Harry when I was younger, for I could've saved myself a lot of grief. But I didn't meet Harry until I was sixty, around two years ago.

CHAPTER 2

How I Met Harry

Before I tell you how I met Harry, let me talk a little more about myself. I should give you a rundown of my drinking life, for it's important to this story. In AA they refer to this sort of rundown as a drunkalog. Even having gone to AA as long as I have, I find such recollections are seldom dull. They're like grand adventures, in a way. And they're important for a number of reasons. First, they provide newly arrived members of AA with stories to which they can relate. They also provide a means for alcoholics to put into words what happened to them. A lot of denial is involved with alcoholism, and to put the stories into words helps make everything more obvious. Lastly, for alcoholics who have some sobriety under their belts, these drunkalogs are useful reminders of where they once were, and most importantly, where they don't want to find themselves again.

So where do I start? Let's begin with my very first drink, for I can remember it clearly. I was fourteen, and my best friend, Eddie Montgomery, and I decided we were going to give alcohol a try. I lived with my parents in Northern California, and Eddie lived just a few houses up the street, where his dad had a well-stocked bar. One afternoon while Eddie's parents were gone, we got an empty mayonnaise jar from the trash and cleaned it out. One by one we went through his father's booze bottles and poured a little of each into the jar, taking enough to fill the jar, but not enough from any one bottle that anyone would notice. We then grabbed a few willing friends and took the jar to the basement of a nearby construction project.

It was a Sunday afternoon, and no one was working at the construction site, so we had the place to ourselves. We sat on a pile of dirt in the musky basement, passing around the jar. It was cool and dank in the unfinished room, and it smelled of freshly turned soil. And I remember the way the alcohol smelled when I lifted the jar to my lips. It had a strong, queer odor that was powerful and overbearing. It literally gave me the shivers. When I drank, it burned in my heart with a glorious heat. It was astonishing. We finished off the jar, and I stepped out of the basement and into the bright light of day. The world outside sparkled and glowed with color, and everything seemed to be in its proper place. I was strangely lucid and clearheaded, and for the first time in my life I felt truly comfortable with myself.

That was my first high. Ever since that day, I found myself chasing that exciting feeling, and a weekend didn't go by when my friends and I didn't find a way to get our hands on more alcohol. We'd steal it from our parents or from neighbors, or we'd shoplift it from the local convenience store. Some of us had older siblings of legal age who would buy it for us. Often we'd sit at the curb in front of the liquor store downtown, asking its customers to buy some for us on their way in. It was amazing how many said yes.

I could write an entire book just about my drinking days when I was a teenager, but I'll try to keep this brief. I was obsessed. I'd try to behave myself, but often I'd drink way too much; for if a six-pack of beer made me feel all warm and fuzzy, then why not another can, and then another? I can't tell you how many times I found myself falling-down drunk, eventually on my knees in someone's bathroom, my face staring at a toilet full of water and vomit. It never crossed my mind that I was out of control. I did stupid things, some stupid and harmful things, and I often made a fool of myself. But I figured this just came with the territory. On the whole, it was all well worth it.

When I turned twenty-one, everything changed. Now I was of legal age to buy all the booze I wanted, and I did so. I got married then to my nineteen-year-old bride, Amy, and the two of us moved into a small one-bedroom apartment near my school. I went to college, and both of us worked to pay our bills. But my drinking was no longer just a weekend activity. I made sure there was enough booze in the house for me to drink whenever I pleased, and I did so every night. I'd begin at about five and continue on until the wee hours, watching talk shows and old movies on TV. By the time I was ready for bed, I'd be completely smashed. The following day I'd feel horrible, but the next night I'd go and do it again.

I had a routine, and I loved my nights. It's hard to explain in words just how perfect the alcohol made me feel when I was drunk. I began to live for these evenings, and my daylight hours just became an overture for the main show. Oh, I had a good excuse for all this. I told Amy that I suffered from insomnia, that the drinking was necessary for me to fall asleep. But I knew the truth, that alcohol was becoming my best friend, and that I'd grown to need its company. I didn't quite realize the severity of it then, but I was addicted.

This ritual of nighttime drinking went on through college and continued a few years after that. Then it was during my late twenties that my drinking exploded into something horrific. These were the years right after Amy and I packed up our things and moved to Southern California so I could start up my own construction company. At first I was drinking every night as usual, taking care of my business during the day. But somehow things quickly got out of hand, and I found myself drinking at lunch, then in the mornings, and then all day long. I'm not sure when exactly it happened, or how it happened, or why. It seemed to have crept up on me so rapidly. The quantity of alcohol I was suddenly consuming was unbelievable, and I remember I'd look at my bloated countenance in the mirror and wonder what the heck was happening.

I'd look at the whites of my eyes, which were now sickly yellow, and I'd wonder who exactly I was. Each morning I'd wake with shakes that could be calmed only by my drinking more booze, and I kept a bottle of vodka under the bathroom sink. Yes, I was physically ill, but this was only a part of it. The construction business I had started was now a daily nightmare; all my jobs were behind schedule and riddled with problems. And I owed large sums of money to a growing number of people, so I was being called by debt collectors, sued in court, and even taken to the police for bad checks. It was amazing that in just three short years I had turned my entire life upside down.

It would require hours to describe everything that happened during those years, and I'll refrain from telling all the gory details. What I will tell you is that during all of this I never once considered myself to be an alcoholic. The idea of quitting drinking was never even on the table. I honestly thought that the difficult circumstances of my life were causing me to drink excessively, not that the circumstances of my life were being caused by my drinking. For the alcoholic, this is a huge distinction. I was blind to everything. I'd been hopelessly perverted by my boozing. All this madness finally came to a head on a Christmas Eve, when Amy was in Albuquerque with her parents preparing things for Christmas Day. I was still in California, presumably taking care of some business, and I was to catch a flight to New Mexico that afternoon. I remember a lot about that day.

I remember getting up in the morning to shave and shower. I turned on the water and spread the shaving cream over my face, but when I lifted the razor to my skin, I couldn't hold it still for a single stroke. I set the razor down and looked under the sink for my vodka, but the bottle was gone. I rummaged through our liquor cabinet, but there were nothing but empties. I had to get something to drink, so I wiped off the shaving cream and put on a T-shirt and sweats, grabbed my keys, and went to the car. I drove to the liquor store and bought a fifth of vodka, returning to our apartment. Jesus, I felt like I was going to shake right out of my clothes. The vodka quickly got rid of the shakes, but now I started sweating profusely. I plopped on the sofa and turned on the TV for a minute to see if I could stop sweating. A game show was on, and I watched it with my bottle in my lap. The next thing I knew I was staring at a soap opera and the bottle was completely empty. Yes, I wanted more.

Oh, how I wanted more. They say one drink is never enough, and I say one bottle was not enough. I had to go back to the liquor store, and I stumbled out of the apartment and back to my car. I have no idea what I was thinking, since I was very drunk. The last thing I needed was another bottle, but I drove toward the store with one thing in mind. About halfway there I heard a siren behind me, and I looked in my rearview mirror. It was a police car, so I pulled over to the shoulder of the road. "Where are you headed?" the lady officer asked. She was not very feminine, and she seemed too young to be a cop.

"I was driving to the store," I replied. I could hear my words slurring as they left my mouth.

"You were swerving back and forth between lanes."

"I was?" I asked incredulously.

"License and registration, please."

I handed the cop my license and registration. She walked over to her police car for a minute and then returned.

"Can you step out of the car, please?"

"What for?" I asked.

"I'm going to give you a field sobriety test."

"I won't pass it," I said. The booze was now hitting me pretty hard. I was having difficulty keeping my eyes trained on her face.

"Please, just step out of the car. I have to give you the test."

I did what she said. It was terribly embarrassing, performing this test at the shoulder of the road in front of my car. What if one of my neighbors saw this? What if someone I knew happened to drive by? Even worse was the fact that I failed the test miserably, every single portion. I could not count backward, I couldn't touch my nose with my finger, and when I was asked to walk a straight line, I completely lost my balance and tumbled to the ground.

The cop told me she was placing me under arrest, and she handcuffed my wrists and led me to her car. "Did you know you have four warrants out for your arrest?" she asked. I told her I was unaware of the warrants. The officer drove me to the Orange County Jail in Santa Ana, and there I was booked and processed.

I was led from one secured room to the other until I finally wound up in a large room full of forlorn men sitting on several benches. There were open tiled showers at the opposite end of the room. The deputies began to call names and hand out slips to those who were to be released on their own recognizance. I was not to be released. Instead, I was told to remove my clothes and take a shower; then I was handed a foul-smelling jumpsuit and sneakers. I put the ill-fitting clothes on, and they led me through another series of secure rooms to my cell block, where I was then put in my cell. Five of us were in the cell and only four bunks, so I wound up lying on the floor.

I missed my flight to Albuquerque and spent Christmas in this awful place rather than with Amy. I'd go into detail describing for you what life is like in jail, but it's very depressing. In AA they refer to one hitting bottom, and I think I had done just that. I was locked up in jail on Christmas Day, my car was impounded, and my business was in ruins. I was bankrupt morally, emotionally, and financially.

So enter Aunt Agnes, the chain-smoking, AA-touting older sister of my mom. When my parents learned I was in jail, they called Agnes to help out. My parents were unable to do anything, since they lived up in Northern California. Amy's parents lived clear over in Albuquerque, so there wasn't much they could do from there. Agnes bailed me out of jail by putting her little Long Beach house up as security, and she picked me up at the Orange County Jail at five o'clock in the morning the day after Christmas. She drove me to our apartment in Mission Viejo, smoking her cigarettes, weaving in and out of traffic, and telling me how much trouble she gone through to post my bail.

When we arrived at the apartment, she came in with me and surveyed the mess. Amy had been gone for several days, and I had been living there alone. There were empty booze bottles everywhere, empty pizza boxes, dirty coffee cups, and overflowing ashtrays. There were papers from my business strewn all over the floor and a pile of dirty pots and dishes in the sink. "You'll have to pardon the mess," I said.

"I've seen worse," Agnes replied.

"I guess I need help."

"You think so?"

"I guess I need to stop drinking."

Agnes held my hand and squeezed it. "I can help with that," she said.

"Mom says you're in AA."

"For twenty-three years."

"You haven't had a drink in twenty-three years?"

"Nope," she said. "Not a drop."

"Can you get me into AA?"

"I can take you to a meeting."

"So tell me," I said. "What's the big secret? How do I stop drinking?"

"It's simple," Agnes said. She lit a cigarette and blew the smoke up toward the ceiling. "You don't take the first drink."

This made no sense to me. I had asked how to stop drinking, and she told me not to drink. Clearly I was missing something, but I was intrigued. I agreed to attend a meeting with her that night, and we went to one of her gatherings in Long Beach. Agnes bought me a Big Book (the "Big Book" of AA) and gave me a handful of brochures. We sat and listened to other alcoholics speak, and at the end of the meeting we all stood in a circle holding hands and said the Lord's Prayer. This wasn't for me, and yet it was. How do I explain this contradiction? I felt very uncomfortable at this meeting, and yet I felt like I belonged there. I didn't like what the people were saying, and yet I felt like I needed to hear every word. After Agnes took me home that night, I stayed up until the early hours reading every page of the Big Book from cover to cover. Could I do this? Could I actually believe in a God?

About a year went by while I continued to attend AA meetings with Agnes. I filed bankruptcy to get all my creditors off our backs, and we moved to a different and less expensive apartment. I was in and out of court, sorting out criminal and civil cases against me; it took me a full year to get everything settled down. I started jogging and dieting to get rid of all the weight I'd gained, and by the end of the year I was back to my old self. Amy was still working, and with her money I bought a used truck. It was a rust bucket, but it got me from here to there, and at the end of the year I began looking for construction work. I remember my first job, doing some minor home repairs for which I needed a power drill to complete the job. I wrote a hot check for the drill, hurried to complete the job, and covered the check with my payment just in time to keep it from bouncing.

It wasn't easy, starting my business back up with such limited funds and resources, but I did it. Within several years, I was running a successful and good-sized operation, making a good deal of money ... and most importantly, not drinking. In fact, I stayed sober for over sixteen years, living well and enjoying life. I no longer had to go to AA meetings. Amy and I had two boys, Danny and Miles, and we bought our own house. These were pretty good years; then something happened when I turned forty-five that would turn everything on its ear—which is to say I started drinking again.

People have asked me why I started drinking after sixteen years of sobriety, and I've given my excuses. I told Amy it was because I was depressed, or maybe it was because I was just too happy, or maybe it was a little of both. I'm serious about this; I could not seem to make up my mind. The excuses alcoholics give for drinking are phenomenal. Unfortunately for me, whatever the excuse, I had made a decision to drink, and it seemed impossible to stop. Once one starts that ball rolling, it's like it just rolls on forever.

I have to say my most recent drinking has been worse than ever. I've gone off on boozing binges for three to four days at a time away from Amy and the boys, off to other cities with strange people, sleeping in strange places, blacking out, and winding up in hospitals and jails. I needed to stop. It was only a matter of time before something serious and irreversible would happen, so I checked myself into a rehab program, then another, and then another after that. I went to scores of therapy sessions and psychiatrists and sober-living houses. I also went to hundreds of AA meetings, but nothing seemed to work. I'd stay sober a few months, and then, wham, it would happen again.

Then I met Harry. It was several weeks following the incident in Tijuana. Yes, I'll tell you what happened in Tijuana. You should know that there was nothing extraordinary about that day. Things were going pretty well in both my business and personal life; I hadn't been drinking for several months. My construction jobs were cruising along smoothly, and for the most part my life with Amy and the boys was in order. It occurred to me that I deserved some kind of reward for this good fortune, so I stopped at a bar on the way home from work and ordered a couple of drinks. That was all I intended to have that afternoon, a couple of drinks. I drank them slowly, talked to the bartender for a while, and watched a soccer game on TV. Then I left, and as I drove home from the bar I decided to stop at a liquor store to buy some more booze, just to keep the good feeling going. I bought a pint of vodka and took it to my truck. I twisted the top off the bottle and drank. Within a couple minutes I had finished the entire thing, and I stepped out of my truck to discard the empty bottle. I felt great! I felt so happy. My eyes were watering, and my chest was warm. I looked over at Buster on the passenger seat and said, "Oh yeah, Buster. This is so nice."

I haven't mentioned Buster. He is our family dog, a four-year-old Boston terrier we originally purchased for our younger son, Miles, at his insistence and promise to take care of it. Of course, the novelty of owning a dog wore off fast, and Miles lost much of his interest in Buster. Amy and I were now taking care of the dog, and I took him with me in my truck to visit my construction sites and run errands. Buster was with me when I drank the pint of vodka. Was I drunk? I wasn't drunk, but I was under the influence. And when I am under the influence of alcohol, I do the strangest things ... and rather than go home that evening, I decided to make a run to Tijuana.

I sped from the liquor store parking lot to the freeway. I called Amy and left a message on our home phone. I knew she wouldn't be home, and that's why I called the house. I knew if I called her cell phone she would answer, and I didn't want to talk to her. I just wanted to leave her a message. I said, "This is Lester. Yes, I've been drinking again. Buster and I are going to Mexico to let off a little steam. Don't worry about us. We'll be home soon." What a joke.

When I arrived in Tijuana it was nearly dark. I parked and, leaving Buster in the truck, walked to the nearest bar. I must have blacked out in the bar, for I don't have any memory of what took place, but I do remember leaving and walking to the nearest liquor store, where I purchased a quart of mescal. I returned to the truck to drink, and that's when I blacked out again. When I came to I was stopped in the middle of a busy Tijuana street, horns were honking, and a Mexican police officer was knocking at my window, motioning for me to roll it down.

I opened the window, and he asked if I'd been drinking. I told him yes, and he asked me to step out of my truck. He leaned in and found my half-empty mescal bottle between the seats. They hooked me up to a tow truck, and the cop took Buster and me to their police station, where they locked us up. We sat on the cell floor and waited. I think I fell asleep, for the officer who had arrested me was suddenly shaking my shoulder. "Wake up," he said. "Come with me, and let me hold your dog. You need to talk to the judge."

I handed over the leash, and the cop led me into their courtroom, a dismal little space with some assorted tables and chairs. An older guy was seated at one of the tables with an official-looking document in his hand. I tried to stand up straight, but I lost my balance and fell headfirst into a wooden chair, cutting my forehead just above my eye. Blood was now trickling into my eye and down my cheek as the judge spoke. He asked me several questions, and I did my best to answer, wiping at the blood with the back of my hand. He then said something to the arresting officer in Spanish, and I was escorted out of the room. I was required to sign some papers, and then Buster was returned to me along with my wallet. Apparently, they were going to let me go.

I was upset about losing my truck but glad to be going home. They drove me to the border and let me loose. I wound up walking along a sidewalk lined with run-down retail storefronts and gas stations. I had no idea where I was, so I just walked for a while and checked the area out, looking for a phone. I didn't feel very good, and I tried to make myself puke in some bushes beside a parking lot, but I couldn't get anything to come up. So I continued to walk. I suddenly caught a glimpse of myself in a window; my forehead and face were covered with dried blood, my hair was a mess, and my shirttails were hanging out. I looked like an old derelict.

I tucked in my shirt and combed my hair with my fingers, trying to make myself look presentable. Buster and I then stopped at a gas station where they appeared to have a working pay phone. I was still quite drunk, and a little shell-shocked over what had happened. I called Amy on the pay phone, hoping she would be able to come rescue me. She was furious and told me to find my own way home. She had an important meeting that morning, and there was no way she could drive all the way to the border and get back in time for her meeting. "And I was up all night worrying about you. I didn't get any sleep."

"Okay," I said.

She was not in a good place and was fed up with my drinking. In order to get home, I would have to find a taxi driver that would take me on the two-hour trip home. Unfortunately, there wasn't a taxi in sight, for it was just after three in the morning and the streets were virtually empty. The gas station I was at was open twenty-four hours a day, so I got some coffee and cigarettes. When I opened my wallet, I noticed that the Mexican police had taken all my cash except for a twenty dollar bill. I had had several hundred dollars in the wallet earlier that evening, but I guess it was nice of them to leave me a twenty. I found a place to sit out by the street and smoked cigarettes and drank coffee, waiting for a cab to appear. Buster sat beside me, not sleeping but looking up, wondering what we were doing there in the middle of the night. At about six, I was finally able to find a cab to drive me home.

When I arrived home, Amy had already gone to work. I took a shower and changed my clothes, but it didn't make me feel any better. I was stunned and disappointed in myself over what had happened. I had no truck to drive to work. I didn't have my cell phone, because I had left it in my glove box. There were also some important papers on the backseat that I'd lost for the time being, and I wasn't sure what to do without them. It was overwhelming.

It's hard to explain the feelings one has after such an incident, and my words here probably don't do it justice. It took months to finally sort this fiasco out. I had to hire a Mexican attorney to handle the drunk-driving charges, and they had to contact a special transport service to get my truck. It was a very confusing and complicated process, and it cost me a small fortune just to make things right.

I marked it on my calendar. It took exactly ninety-three days to get my truck back from Tijuana. The inside had been ransacked, and everything of value was gone. But I did get it back, and it was now time to get back to business.

I tell you, the day after the truck was returned, I drove it to a noon AA meeting in Mission Viejo. I hated AA meetings, but I needed to show Amy I was taking proactive measures to prevent another drinking disaster. I sat through the meeting patiently and listened to everyone talk. I clapped when it was appropriate, poured myself a cup of weak coffee, and put a couple dollars in the donation basket. When the gathering was over, everyone stood up and formed their big circle, holding hands and getting ready to say the Lord's Prayer. I quickly made my way to the exit so I wouldn't have to participate. I've never been big on the God stuff, and saying the prayer made no sense to me. Just as I reached my precious truck in the parking lot, I felt someone's hand on the back of my shoulder, and I turned around.

"Hello," the man said.

"Hi," I replied.

"Skipping the Lord's Prayer?"

"Not really a believer," I explained.

"My name is Harry."

"I'm Lester," I said. "Lester Madison."

"Are you an atheist?"

"I guess you could say that."

"You and I should talk."

CHAPTER 3

The Test

The day I met Harry, I thought I recognized him from past meetings. I didn't remember him talking, and he seemed to be the sort who was content to just sit and listen. Harry had the kind of face that immediately put one at ease. He was probably in his seventies, with thick gray hair and slightly weathered skin, but he did not appear at all feeble or elderly. He seemed quite healthy for his age, alert and firm-bodied. He reached for a friendly handshake, and I obliged. His hand was warm and soft, and his grip was not overpowering. As we stood there in the parking lot, I suddenly realized I'd been staring at him. "What did you say?" I asked.

"I said you and I should talk."

"What would we talk about?"

"About this AA thing," Harry said. "Do you have a sponsor?"

"No," I said.

"Have you ever had a sponsor?"

"Not ever."

"Have you ever worked the steps?"

"I guess not. I mean, I started to work the steps in rehab, but I didn't finish them. I had a hard time with them."

"How many times have you been to rehab?"

"Three," I said, a little ashamed.

"And now here you are."

"Here I am."

"When's the last time you drank?"

"Several months ago. I ended up in Tijuana, and it turned into quite an ordeal. That's why I'm here today, just to appease my wife."

"I think I can help you."

"As a sponsor?" I asked.

"Yes, as a sponsor. I've managed to stay sober for fourteen years, and I'm an atheist. You don't have to believe in God."

"I don't?"

"Here's my number." Harry handed me a business card. All that was on it was his first name and phone number. "Call me anytime."

"Okay," I said.

Harry then put his hand on my shoulder and said, "I think I can help you. Just give it some thought. And I mean it when I say you can call anytime."

"Okay," I said. With that, Harry removed his hand from my shoulder and gave me a friendly smile. I smiled back, and he walked away. I climbed into my truck and put his business card on the passenger seat. When I arrived home that night, Amy greeted me at the door. She wanted to know how the meeting had gone. I told her it was like any other meeting, with the exception of my encounter with Harry. I told her how Harry offered to be my sponsor, and how he gave me a business card with his name and number.

"Are you going to call him?" Amy asked.

"I don't know," I said.

"I think you should."

"I might," I said, and I meant this. Harry did intrigue me, and he seemed like a nice enough guy. I told Amy a little about him, but I didn't tell her he was an atheist. I don't know why I didn't tell her. It wasn't like she'd be alarmed, for she wasn't particularly religious herself. We had no Bible in our household, and we never went to church. Would Amy be bothered to know that I might be coached by a self-professed atheist? Some people aren't religious, but they still believe in God. It's funny, but I'd been married to Amy for over thirty-seven years, and I don't remember ever asking her if she believed in God. She knew my opinion on the matter, but she never expressed her own, and for some reason the subject of her own beliefs never came up. It's true that she sometimes talks like she believes in God; for example, she will tell me that Agnes, who died several years ago, is looking down at me from above every time I take a drink and do something foolish. Where else would Agnes be but in heaven?

Does Amy actually believe in heaven, or is she just talking that way out of convenience?

Atheist is such a strong word, and it has so many negative connotations that I usually try to avoid using it. Agnostic is such a nicer word. It implies that the person is basically good, maybe just a little misguided, and that he or she may someday see the light before it's too late. No, I didn't tell Amy that Harry was an atheist, even though he said he was. But I did tell her that Harry said he could help me work around the God issue, something that had always been an obstacle for me in AA.

"Isn't that what you've been looking for?"

"I don't know that I've been exactly looking for it, but it sounds interesting." If I was to be completely honest with Amy, I would have said I hadn't been looking for this at all. What I was looking for was a way to avoid AA completely and still quit drinking. I really disliked AA.

"I think you should call this man. What's his name again?"

"Harry," I said.

"Yes, I think you should call Harry. You should call him right now."

"Okay," I said. "I'll give him a call." I needed to do as Amy asked, given all that had recently happened in Tijuana, so I went to the study and picked up the phone. I had no idea what I was getting myself into. Harry picked up the phone on the second ring, and he said he was glad that I called. He asked if I wanted him to be my sponsor, and I said yes. We then agreed to meet at Harry's house the following night, and he gave me his address. "It's in a gated community, so you'll have to give your name to the guard; I'll call you in."

The next night I drove to Harry's house. The guard at the gate let me in, and I drove to the house. He lived in a nice neighborhood filled with large custom homes and spacious yards. Harry's home was an English Tudor structure with a high roofline and lots of leaded glass windows, and the front yard was packed with shrubs and flowers. The driveway was a fake cobblestone expanse, and on the driveway was Harry's car, a shiny black Mercedes. I had parked my truck in the street alongside the curb, and walked up the fake cobblestone path to the front door, where I rapped the large knocker several times.

Harry appeared immediately, sporting a friendly smile. I stepped into the foyer, a spacious room with high ceilings and marble floors, and an amazing chandelier suspended from the ceiling. The chandelier probably cost him as much as all the furniture in our house combined. Harry then led me to the library, a good-sized room just off the foyer, with double French doors and bookshelves from floor to ceiling. Two leather chairs sat in the middle of the library, and Harry motioned for me to take a seat. I plopped myself into one of the chairs, and Harry sat in the other. I looked around for a moment. The bookshelves in the room were stuffed with books, and there was a ladder to help one reach the higher shelves. "You like to read?" I asked.

Harry laughed. "Reading is my passion. Ever since I quit drinking, I've been reading."

"Have you read all these books?"

"Many of them. Not all of them."

"Wow," I said.

"The book is man's most fantastic invention. The book is more formidable than electricity, greater than the gas-powered motor, more useful than the telephone, more powerful than the home computer. Books promulgate ideas, and there is nothing more profound in the world than a timely idea. Just think about it, Lester."

"Yes, I see what you mean."

"They say people don't read anymore, and I guess for the time being they're right. People these days want their information broadcast to them, but nothing has the thoroughness and convenience of a good book. The novelty of TVs and movie theaters and computer monitors will eventually wear off, and we'll be back to reading books. I say the book will be back in vogue. Nothing stirs the imagination like a good book. Nothing beats its portability, its ease of use, its complete independence from any device or power source to enjoy. You can take a book with you anywhere and hold the world in the palm of your hand. With the simple turn of a page, you can summon up the thoughts of a genius, go backward or forward in time, travel the planet, experience other cultures, learn in exquisite detail all the accomplishments of mankind. It can all be right there in your sweaty little human hands. Do you like to read?"

"Yes, I like to read."

"If you take the time to read, you become a student of the world rather than one of its victims. Mark my words on this." What was becoming clear to me was that not only did Harry like to read, but he also liked to talk. And I wanted to hear what he had to say. I wanted him to keep talking, but he suddenly turned the tables on me and asked me to speak. "Enough about my books," he said. "Tell me about yourself."

"Where do I start?"

"Start at the beginning, of course. I'll give you all the time you need. Let's begin with your first drink. Nearly every alcoholic remembers his first drink. Do you remember your first?"

"Yes, I do," I said.

"How old were you?"

"I was fourteen. I was living with my parents in Northern California, and I was a freshman in high school."

"Go on," Harry said.

I went on to tell Harry about Eddie Montgomery and the mayonnaise jar, and the way the alcohol made me feel that day. I told Harry all about my drinking habits in high school, then in college, and then after I graduated and went to work. I recalled a handful of incidents that were indicative of my behavior those years. You should know that in AA they conduct speaker meetings where one person stands before the group and spends the good part of an hour recalling his personal drunkalog. Yes, I knew the drill. I was so used to this procedure that I could have done it blindfolded. I went on and on, telling Harry how my life spun out of control, how I'd moved to Southern California and started my own construction company, and how I drank the company into the ground. I told Harry how I hit bottom when I spent that Christmas Day in jail, how Agnes rescued me with her AA meetings and made me sober. I then explained that I'd been sober for sixteen years, only to start drinking again when I was in my midforties.

I described some of my recent binges and the problems they caused, how I sought all sorts of treatments, and how I just didn't seem capable of staying sober for an extended period of time. Finally, I described my fiasco in Tijuana in some detail, since that was my most recent drinking episode. Harry listened to my story patiently, sometimes closing his eyes while he sat in his big leather chair, sometimes opening his eyes and nodding his head and agreeing with my conclusions. When I was done, Harry stared at me with his legs crossed, and for a moment he said nothing. Then he spoke. "Are you done?" he asked.

"Yeah, I guess so."

"What have you left out?"

"Probably lots of things. If I included everything, we'd be here for hours."

"So tell me, what do you expect me to do as your sponsor?"

"Help me work a program?"

"Yes," Harry said.

"Work the steps, I suppose."

"We can do that."

"I've never had a sponsor. I'm not sure exactly what a sponsor does."

"I can help you with the steps," Harry said; then he stood up suddenly. "Come with me."

"Okay," I said. Harry walked out of the room, and I followed him. We stepped outside and went to his car, and he opened the passenger door and motioned for me to enter. Harry then hopped in the driver's side and started the engine. "Where are we going?" I asked.

He smiled. "Oh, you'll see." He backed the car out of the driveway, and we sped down the road. As he maneuvered the car through traffic, he talked to me. In fact, he talked the entire duration of the trip, keeping his eyes on the road and his hands on the steering wheel. He didn't turn his head to look at me once while he talked.

He said, "When I was in your shoes fourteen years ago, I was about your age and had been going to AA meetings for several years. Like you, I had trouble with the God thing, but more than anything I wanted to stay sober. I went to AA meetings every night, and I watched all those AA people sharing bits and pieces of their lives, applauding each other, and drinking coffee. I watched them smoking their cigarettes in the parking lot, shaking each other's hands, and hugging each other. God, how I hated the hugging. I felt like a complete outsider, but I truly wanted what those people had.

"I wanted to be sober. I wanted to escape the madness and misery that had come to define my life. But how would I do it? I didn't believe in God any more than a microbiologist believes in Santa Claus. So I picked out a sponsor, a crusty old-timer who was nearly in his eighties. Lots of younger guys were available as sponsors, but I needed someone substantially older than me. I couldn't see myself taking advice and orders from someone my junior. Perhaps you feel the same way. My sponsor's name was Ralph. He told me to keep going to meetings, at least one a day, and he told me to read the Big Book several times. 'It's all in the book,' he liked to say. Ralph also said he would help me work the steps, and the two of us met at his house. He had me memorize the steps, and in no time I could recite all twelve of them word for word. But memorizing the steps is a lot different than actually carrying them out.

"I was an atheist, and I just couldn't get over the God thing, no matter what kind of spin Ralph put on it. After a few months, I found myself getting nowhere, and I decided I would have to find a sponsor who was an atheist. It was a simple solution, but it proved to be impossible. Since the entire foundation of AA involved turning your will and life over to God, no such sponsor existed, at least not at any of the meetings I attended. I decided I would have to find my own way."

"So what did you do?" I asked.

"Do you know the first step?"

"Yes, I think I do."

"Can you recite it for me?"

"You accept you're powerless over alcohol, that your life has become unmanageable."

"Very good."

"Weren't you able to do step one?" I asked.

"I split it up."

"What do you mean?" I asked.

"The first step states two things: one, that you are powerless, and two, that your life is unmanageable. I took these one at a time."

"I see."

"First, I asked if my life was unmanageable. Did I ever tell you what I did before retiring?"

"No, you didn't."

"I was an attorney."

"Okay."

"I was very good at what I did. I was a trial lawyer. When I was in my thirties, my whole life was ahead of me. I married my wife, Janice, and we had a daughter we named Alice. I'd started my law practice, and business was booming, for there seemed to be no end to the number of criminals willing to pay for a good defense. As time went by, I developed an excellent reputation, and I took on partners and a very competent staff. We moved into a prestigious office and drove nice cars, and I built my home here in Newport Beach. Janice made lots of friends and flourished nicely in Newport's society circles. Alice brought home good grades and accolades from her teachers. I never drank during those years, because my father was a heavy drinker and I saw what booze did to him. I did not want the same thing to happen to me, but sometime in my forties, alcohol crept into my life. I say crept, because I'm still not sure exactly what happened.

"I guess it began with lunches out with clients and other attorneys, where I began ordering drinks to fit in with everyone else. It seemed like everyone did this, and it didn't seem to be causing them problems. I remember the way I felt during those lunches—that I felt so good and so in control. I fancied myself as one of Southern California's preeminent trial lawyers; people seemed to like me, and I felt the same way about them. I was so comfortable with things. I then began drinking at home in the evenings, not a lot, but just enough to unwind. No one was complaining about this either, and Janice certainly didn't seem to care. Then it all happened so quickly, like a hurricane blowing in from the ocean; it landed on my shore like some crazy, hell-bent storm and seized control of my life. The next thing I knew, I was drinking all the time.

"This happened during a period of only about two years, and it was just long enough for me to turn my life upside down. I honestly didn't understand what was happening to me, and I remember looking at myself in the mirror, truly wondering what had become of that promising young attorney who once stood tall and looked forward to the challenges of each day. Now I dreaded each day, and I dreaded even waking up. I dreaded facing the nightmare I had created.

Everything finally came to a head when my associates at the law firm forced me into early retirement. It was either leave the firm or face possible disbarment, or perhaps even face prison time for some of the things I had done. I had hired all of them, and now they were giving me the boot. I was humiliated and depressed, yet I continued to drink. I sought solace from prostitutes and advice from bartenders. I was completely out of control. I took out my frustrations on Janice and Alice. I racked up three DUIs and now had to appear in court, not as an attorney, but as an accused criminal to be tried and judged.

"This went on for several years until Janice and Alice packed up and left me. Janice said they couldn't take it anymore. I tried calling old friends, but everyone was weary of me. One of the last nights I drank, I drained a quart of Scotch and took a steak knife from the kitchen drawer and tried to slash my wrists. The cuts were deep enough to produce a lot of blood, and I panicked and called 911. It turned out they required only a handful of stitches, but they locked me in a mental hospital for observation.

I remember sitting in that hospital, a pathetic slob who had lost complete control of his life. For the first time I'd been institutionalized. They had a file on me, and doctors and therapists were now prying and asking me all sorts of personal questions. They spoke gently, treating me like a five-year-old who had just lost his mother. When I was released from the mental hospital, I swore to myself I would never drink again. It was a horrible experience."

"So you stopped?"

"Not right away. It took me a few years to become completely sober. I would stop for a few weeks and then try it again. I would stop for a few months, and then the urge would hit me, and I'd find myself at home, drunk as hell and watching TV. Because of the DUIs, I was required by the court to attend AA meetings. At these meetings I listened to people who were struggling as I was. They all arrived by different roads, but the destination seemed the same for each of them. It was a place of lost businesses, car accidents, court dates, jail time, suicide attempts, and divorces. There seemed to be no end to the tragedies and difficulties alcoholism caused. I didn't want to admit it then, but I belonged there with all of them. I belonged in those dismal meeting rooms with all those fold-up chairs and open boxes of donuts, with all those whining, advice-giving freaks who seemed never to be at a loss for words. After all that had happened in my life, I had finally found a home in AA. It was so depressing, I wanted to cry."

"That's exactly how AA makes me feel," I said.

"In any event, that's my answer to the question."

"I forgot what the question was."

"Was my life unmanageable?"

"Oh, yes," I said. "I remember now."

"My life was certainly unmanageable. That brings me to the second question, the even more important half of step one. Was I powerless over alcohol?"

"Were you?"

Harry drove his car into the parking lot of a little retail center. He pulled into a space and shut off the engine. We were right in front of a liquor store. "What are we doing here?" I asked.

"We'll get to that in a minute. Let's talk first about power. What does power mean to you? How would you define it?"

"I don't know. I suppose power is when you have to ability to cause something to happen. Does that make sense?"

"That works for me. Now, how would you define powerlessness?"

"It would be just the opposite, that there's nothing you can do."

"Do you consider yourself to be powerless over alcohol?"

"Yes, I do."

"What about the weather—would you say there's nothing you can do about it, that you're powerless over the weather?"

"Yes, I would say so. There's not much one can do to change the weather."

"So what is the purpose of a house?"

"Are you changing the subject?"

"Not at all. What's the purpose of a house?"

I thought about this a moment and then said, "A house serves many purposes, don't you think? It's a place to keep your things. It has closets, shelves, and furniture with drawers and places to put possessions. A house is also a place to raise a family ... home sweet home and all that good stuff. And it gives one privacy, for it has walls, doors, and window coverings to prevent others from seeing in. It has bedrooms and blankets and pillows so one can sleep, and it has bathrooms for all your bodily functions. A house can also be a status symbol, and for the architect, a house can be a work of art. So how'd I do?"

"That's all fine, but what's the primary purpose? What prompted early humans to create homes?"

"To shelter themselves from the elements?"

"Yes, exactly. They were looking for shade from the sun, a dry place during the rain, and warmth from the chilling winds of winter. Shelters and homes are all examples of humans exerting power over their environment. Nowadays it's a lot more sophisticated, but it's the same idea. We are definitely not powerless over the weather."

"Okay, I'll grant you that."

"Now I will actually change the subject. If a man who can't swim jumps into a swimming pool and drowns, would you say he was powerless over water?"

"I don't know."

"Didn't he have a choice to make?"

"Yes, I think he did."

"And he made a decision to jump into the pool?"

"Yes, I suppose so."

"He had the power to choose between staying dry or getting wet, did he not?"

"Yes," I said.

"So making the right decisions is a form of power?"

"Yes, I can see that."

"Good," Harry said.

"So are we ever powerless?"

"Of course we are. We can be powerless over tornados and floods. We can be powerless over earthquakes. And it's not just natural disasters that can bring us to our knees. I'd say those poor people who were trapped in the World Trade Center were powerless against their predicament. I would say that if a robber aimed a gun at your head and demanded your watch and wallet, that you would be powerless. I'll bet I could come up with a thousand different kinds of powerlessness, but I can probably come up with just as many situations where people thought they were powerless when in fact they weren't.

"Power can be an illusion. There is the illusion of having power when no power exists, and there is the illusion of powerlessness when one does in fact have power. Many alcoholics fall into the latter category, suffering from an illusion of powerlessness. They think their drinking is completely beyond their personal control, when in fact sobriety is a matter of choice.

"I've been sober now for fourteen years, and do you want to know how I do it? I don't take the first drink, and it's just as simple as that. I know what happens when I do drink, for I spent years proving to myself the sort of misery that comes with my drinking. I'd have to be an idiot not to see this, and, trust me, I'm not an idiot. I'm a pretty smart guy. I don't drink, because I choose not to drink, and if I ever do decide to drink again, it will not be because I'm powerless. It will be because I choose to ignore my own power. You know, Lester, there is such a thing as free will, and it is a powerful force. And we all have it. I may not believe in God, but I do believe in free will. Hang on a minute." Harry opened his car door to get out. "I'll be right back."

"Okay," I said.

I watched Harry enter the liquor store. Beer advertisement posters were taped all over the storefront, blocking my view, so I couldn't see what Harry was doing. He didn't take long. He returned with a brown paper bag, and after getting himself situated, he removed the contents of the bag. It was a pint bottle of vodka. Harry crumpled the paper bag and tossed it over his shoulder, and he then unscrewed the cap.

"What's that for?" I asked.

"It's for you."

"For me?"

"One last drink before you swear off the booze completely. One last drink for you, Lester. Your last hurrah."

"I don't know," I said skeptically.

"Go ahead and take a swig. One last drink isn't going to kill you. And I won't tell anyone."

I looked at the bottle Harry was offering. "I don't think I should. I mean, I'd like to, but I know I shouldn't."

"Are you going to ignore the advice of your sponsor?"

"I don't know."

"So what's it going to be? Is it yes or no?"

"I guess it's a no. I'm sorry."

"You're sorry?"

"Well, maybe not sorry."

"Congratulations."

"For what?" I asked.

"You passed the test."

"So you were testing me?" I was a little miffed, and the tone of my voice reflected it.

"You need to understand something."

"Like what?"

"Like that being a sponsor is a big-time commitment. It's a time-consuming and emotionally draining experience, and I don't like to commit to someone unless I'm sure that the person is truly serious about his sobriety. You refused the vodka. I think you're serious about staying sober; would you agree?"

"Yes," I said.

"Here, screw the cap back on, and throw it away." I did as Harry instructed, dropping the bottle in a waste can near the liquor store door. I then got back in the car, and Harry looked at me. He said, "You're not so powerless after all, are you? I offered you a drink, and you turned it down. You weighed your options, and you made a wise decision using your own free will. If there's one thing I want you to get out of this evening, it's that Lester Madison isn't powerless. No matter what you hear to the contrary, no matter what you hear from some of those dopes in AA, you must always remember this."

"Okay," I said.

"Which brings us back to step one. How should we rewrite step one?"

"I don't know."

"We'll write it to say that because of our drinking our lives became unmanageable, but we won't say that we're powerless. Instead, we'll acknowledge that we do have power over alcohol."

Harry backed out of the parking stall, and we drove back to his house. We didn't talk much during the trip, and Harry turned on the radio. I thought about Amy and what I was going to tell her about my sponsor, Harry, and this strange first evening we had spent together, going to the liquor store and rewriting step one.

CHAPTER 4

Wives and Children

I hated lying to Amy, but I didn't tell her the truth. She asked how my meeting with Harry had gone, and I told her everything went fine, which it did. But I still didn't tell her Harry was an atheist, and I certainly didn't tell her about the vodka he had offered me. I didn't explain how Harry had rewritten the first step. Everything Harry had said during our first meeting made perfect sense, yet I didn't tell any of this to Amy.

My next meeting with Harry took place again in his library. It was only two days after our first meeting, and we met this time on a Saturday afternoon. Harry had brewed a pot of coffee in the kitchen, and he offered me a cup, which I accepted. The two of us sat on his leather chairs surrounded by Harry's amazing collection of books. I started our conversation by bringing up Amy. I said, "Something's bothering me. It's about my wife."

"What about her?"

"I didn't tell her the truth about our first meeting. She has no idea what we're doing here. I told her so many lies when I was drinking, and I promised her the lying would stop."

"Did you lie to her, or did you just withhold some of the truth?"

"I guess I withheld the truth. But isn't that the same as a lie?"

"Not necessarily."

"How do you figure?"

"Working with a sponsor is like seeing a doctor or psychologist. Your conversations are private. They have to be private, and there are some very good reasons for this. Did Amy ask you what we talked about?"

"Not really."

"Did she ask what we did?"

"No, she didn't. She just asked how things went, and I said they went well."

"Well, then, you didn't lie."

"But what if she starts asking more questions? She's bound to get curious."

"Tell her what happens between us is confidential."

"She'll feel left out."

"Maybe she will. But you'd be telling her the truth. What we do and talk about here is a private matter."

"I don't know …" I said skeptically.

"After everything she's been through, don't you think she'd be willing to make some concessions to keep you sober? Don't you think she'd be willing to help out by respecting your privacy? My experience is that wives of alcoholics are ready, willing, and able to put up with just about anything if it means keeping their husbands sober. When you stay sober, it's unlikely she'll insist on looking a gift horse in the mouth."

"Maybe you're right."

"You need to agree with me on this. You're going to need to be honest with me, but I'm also going to tell you some things about myself that are very confidential. I don't necessarily want you blabbing about all the things I've done—about my feelings, about my transgressions—to any other people you may happen to talk to, not even your wife. I'm putting myself out on a limb for you, Lester. Our conversations need to remain private, not just for your sake, but for mine as well."

"I understand."

"Have you ever put yourself in Amy's shoes?"

"I think I have."

"Have you?"

"I don't know."

"Have you put yourself in your sons' shoes?"

"Probably not the way you mean."

"You're acting like you're so concerned about Amy's feelings, about being honest with her, but the truth is alcoholics are extraordinarily selfish people. If you ask an alcoholic about his drinking years, he will inevitably tell you about all the horrible things that happened to him. But this is where his insight ends. He'll tell you every gruesome detail about every bad event and feeling that came his way, but he'll tell you very little about the way his wife felt, the way his children felt, or the awful way their lives were affected.

"He'll describe his wife and children like they're background music in a movie. They are there, and yet they aren't. Only once in a while does the background music rise up and become noticeable. If I look back honestly to my heaviest drinking years, I can barely remember Janice and Alice at all. They were there living in the same house with me, and yet I have very few memories of them.

"Only once in a while did they become noticeable. I can give you an example. I recall when Janice came into the room where I was watching TV and told me she had a present for me. There was no special occasion, and it seemed like such a nice thought. I followed her into the dining room, where sitting on the table was a large cardboard box wrapped in colorful paper and tied up neatly with a big red ribbon. "Open it," she said. I untied the ribbon and tore off the paper. I then opened the top of the box, and my heart sank. It wasn't a gift at all. The box was filled with empty booze bottles. They were the bottles I had hidden around the house and garage, thinking I'd get rid of them before they were discovered. 'You told me you were going to stop drinking,' she said angrily. I was hurt and embarrassed. I still can recall the way I felt. And most of all I recall the look on Janice's face, the way she was looking at me. But that brief moment was the proverbial exception that proved the rule. Like I said earlier, for the most part I recall very little of her."

"I think I understand."

"Amy is still not that important to you. If Amy played an important role in your life, you would not have so much difficulty staying sober; you would not have been going to rehabs and sober-living houses and group therapy sessions and psychiatrists. You would not be going to AA meetings, and you would not be here talking to me now."

"Don't my efforts show I care?"

"If you cared, an effort of this magnitude would not be required. It would be a no-brainer. And it's not just your wife. The same thing holds true with your sons. Your sons, whom I assume you claim to love, actually mean very little to you when compared to your desire to drink."

"Wow," I said.

"Let me tell you a few things about my relationship with my own child. When Alice was first born, she was the absolute light of our lives. Janice and I loved her and doted over her during her first few years, up until the time I started drinking. Then not only did my relationship with Janice begin to suffer, but Alice also fell into the distance. I don't remember much about Alice at all during the years I was drinking heavily. I was not anywhere in Alice's life, and I didn't go to birthday parties, school functions, or soccer games. I don't remember talking to her, and I couldn't tell you a thing about her dreams or ambitions. She was just some kid who lived in the house with us, eating at our dinner table, and sleeping in her room. Her name was Alice, and she had blond hair.

"There are a few things I do recall, and most of them are rather unpleasant. Perhaps the worst was when she was in high school, when she was over at Kaleb's house. Kaleb was a widower Janice had met at Alice's soccer games. He was a psychiatrist who lived just a half mile from our house, and Janice would sometimes take Alice over to visit with Kaleb's daughter. I was very jealous of Kaleb and the time he was spending with my wife.

"One night when I was very drunk, I drove over to Kaleb's house to give the guy a piece of my mind, and when I rang the doorbell, Kaleb answered. I immediately shoved him backward, and he fell to the floor. As he picked himself up, I began ranting and raving, spewing out a profanity-laced tirade. He was afraid of me, and it gave me a sense of power, knowing that he was afraid. I assumed it was because I was so righteous and manly, not understanding that he was just afraid of having this drunken lunatic invading his peaceful home.

"I stepped toward Kaleb, and he remained standing in front of me. I took a wild swing at his jaw, but he ducked and I completely missed. Frustrated, I then tackled him and got myself positioned so that I was sitting on his chest. I reached for his throat with both hands to strangle him—not to kill him, mind you, but just to give him a good scare and release my pent-up anger.

"Suddenly, I heard a loud crash and felt a sharp pain at the back of my head, and I fell from Kaleb's chest to the floor. Standing over me was Alice, who had just whacked me with one of Kaleb's antique vases. There were bits of broken vase on the floor and in my hair, and warm blood began to spread from the cut in my scalp. But the thing I remember most from that night wasn't Kaleb, and it wasn't the blow to my head. It was me looking at my daughter's face as she stood looming over me. She was like a stranger, and I could barely recognize her. Her eyes were wide, and her young face was contorted with fear and hatred. I had forced her to choose between her friend's dad and her own, and she chose to defend Kaleb. The vision of her face that evening is still etched upon my mind. I'll never forget that night. But it too was the exception. For the most part I don't remember Alice."

"So what did Kaleb do?"

"You mean after Alice saved him from me? He did nothing. He got up off the floor and walked to the other side of the room. Janice offered to help me with my bloody wound, and then Alice started bawling and ran out and down the hall, presumably to her friend's bedroom. I left the house holding my head with one hand and digging into my pocket for my car keys with the other. I drove home feeling sorry for myself. I think I cried the whole way back to the house. Looking back on it now, I realize I was right to feel jealous. When Janice and Alice left me, they moved into Kaleb's house. Janice and Kaleb were married just two years later, and Kaleb became Alice's stepfather.

"When I did finally get sober, Janice agreed to see me now and again, but when I tried to stoke up a relationship with Alice, she would have nothing to do with me. She went on to college, and then she got out and married a guy named George. They moved to Vermont and had two children, whom they named Robbie and Pamela. I haven't seen either of my own grandchildren, not ever. I send Christmas and birthday presents to them every year, but I have no idea of whether Alice bothers to give the gifts to them. I've sent Alice several letters, but she doesn't write back. Janice shows me pictures of Alice and George and the grandkids, and she lets me know what they've been up to. That's as close to them as I ever get."

"That's too bad."

"Yes, it's too bad. You don't know how lucky you are, to still have your family."

"I think I understand what you mean about background music. I've tried to recall things about Amy during my worst drinking years, when we first moved to Southern California, and I just can't remember her at all. It's like she wasn't even there for my whole ordeal … like you say, living with me in the same house and sleeping in the same bed, but not really there. I was so deep into my drinking that I never even stopped to think about what I was doing to her, what she was thinking, or how she was feeling."

"I don't think much has changed."

"You don't?"

"Tell me about your rehabs."

"I went to three of them. Two of the rehabs were voluntary, but one of them was required by the court in order to avoid jail time for a DUI accident."

"Did they have family programs?"

"Yes, all three of them did."

"Tell me about the most recent one. Did they have you apologize to Amy?"

"Yes, I remember they put us all in a big circle of chairs, and in the center they placed several chairs facing each other. Amy and I had to sit in the center chairs and talk to each other in front of the group."

"What did they have you say?"

"I was supposed to acknowledge to Amy what I'd done wrong and accept responsibility for it. Then I was supposed to apologize."

"And how did it go?"

"It went terribly. Everyone in the group said I sounded insincere. If they were handing out grades for our efforts, I would have gotten an F."

"Why do you think it went so badly?"

"I don't know. I guess I don't do well in group therapy. It's not my thing."

"How did Amy feel about this?"

"I'm not exactly sure."

"Did you even stop to think about her feelings?"

"No, I suppose not."

"Did you ask her how she felt?"

"No, I didn't."

"When I say the following, I mean it with the best intentions, that you're not much of a husband. When I said you were lucky, I meant it. You have no idea how lucky you are that your wife and children are still in your life."

"I suppose that's true."

"You already gave me a pretty detailed rundown of your escapade to Tijuana. You got drunk and were arrested, and they took your car away?"

"That's it, in a nutshell."

"I'd like you to tell this story from a different perspective."

"What do you mean?"

"I'd like you to tell it to me from Amy's viewpoint. Do you think you can do that?"

"I don't know."

"Give it a try. Start with that afternoon. What was Amy doing?"

"She was at work."

"And what were you doing?"

"I was having a couple drinks at that bar."

"And what did Amy think you were doing?"

"She probably thought I was working."

"When she got home at night, she would have noticed that your truck was gone. What do you think she thought when she discovered you weren't home?"

"I usually get home before her, so she was likely wondering where I was."

"Was either of your sons at home?"

"The younger one was. He still lives at home. Our older boy has his own place in Laguna."

"When do you think Amy checked the voice mail?"

"She always checks it right when she gets home. It would've been one of the first things she did."

"And so she heard your message?"

"Yes," I said.

"How do you suppose she felt?"

"Probably a little angry."

"A little angry?"

"Maybe a lot angry. I don't know."

"You haven't thought about it, have you?"

"No, I guess not."

"How about this? I'll see if I can do this for you. She listens to your message and slowly hangs up the phone. Her stomach is tied up in knots. *Damn it, you've done this so many times before, running off and drinking. Sometimes you come home late at night, sometimes the next morning, and sometimes you don't come home for days.* She has no idea when you're coming home or what you're doing while you're gone. And her mind travels to the worst possible scenarios, many of which have a good chance of being correct. Her hands are starting to shake, and she's beginning to panic. She has no idea what to do. How am I doing so far?"

"You're probably accurate."

"So she checks your son's bedroom to make sure he's home. She confirms this and tells him not to go out anywhere—that she might need him, that Dad is off drinking again, and she might want his company. He says okay and goes back to what he was doing, and she goes back to the phone in the kitchen, where she calls your cell phone number hoping you might answer. She might be able to convince you to come home before something terrible happens, but you won't answer the phone. Either you are deliberately avoiding her call, or you are already in Mexico, where your cell phone doesn't work. She calls again and again, but there is still no answer. She is powerless. Like those people in the World Trade Center, all she can do is let the events unfold.

"She imagines the sort of phone call she could get—a call from the highway patrol saying you've been in an accident, or a call from you locked up in a San Diego jail saying you've been arrested for drunk driving and you need her to bail you out. Or perhaps you are in Mexico, and she'll get a call from the Mexican police saying you've hit and killed a pedestrian. Her mind is now reeling. How would she ever be able to get you out of trouble with the Mexican authorities? She's heard horror stories about Mexico's legal system. Why in the world would you choose to go to Mexico? Perhaps it's even worse than this, and perhaps she'll get that most dreaded call … that you've been killed.

"She calls her parents. Or maybe she calls a girlfriend she can talk to. She needs to speak with someone about her predicament, but she finds that this doesn't make the situation any better. Talking to others only confirms that the rest of the world isn't as crazy as hers. Why in the world does she stay married to you and subject herself to this never-ending ritual of trauma? You promised this wouldn't happen again, and yet here she is, suffering, worried and sick, unable to concentrate.

"It is dinnertime, and she makes herself something to eat, thinking that cooking will help distract her, but all she can think of is what you're doing at the moment. Are you at a bar, buying everyone drinks, or are on top of some Mexican prostitute, groaning and sweating and having unprotected sex? Or maybe you're just driving around, drunk and dangerous, a tragedy just waiting to happen.

"She suddenly remembers the dog, how you took Buster with you. Why in the world would you take the family dog with you on one of these horrible binges? Would you lose the dog in Mexico? Or would you leave him in your unlocked truck, and would someone steal him? What if you were arrested? Would Buster wind up in a Mexican pound? Do they even have animal control services in Mexico? Why has she stayed married to you after all these drinking episodes? Any woman in her right mind would have left you years ago, and it's not like she wasn't still a good catch. She's sure there are plenty of men out there who'd love to have an attractive, devoted companion like her, men that didn't drink and run off to Mexico. What was the point? Was it love, or was it just foolishness? Or was it just the inertia of making a change? How many times was she going to let herself be duped?

"These are the questions she's asking herself as she sits down to eat dinner, but she isn't hungry at all. Her stomach is still in knots, and so she turns on the TV. She watches the evening news as they report on all the horrible events of the day. Is she going to see your face broadcast on the news? She turns off the TV, because it's only making things worse. What is she supposed to do with her time?

"It could be hours before she gets a call. Hell, it could be days. Will she have to go to work tomorrow not knowing where you are? The evening goes by slowly and tortuously. Every minute seems like an hour, every hour like a day. She turns on the TV again, this time to one of her favorite sitcoms, but it doesn't seem at all funny. So she reads from a book but finds it impossible to concentrate. She reads the same page five times before she finally gives up. When her bedtime finally comes around, she says good-night to your son. 'Have you heard from Dad?' he asks, and she says, 'No, nothing yet.'

"She then climbs in her bed and tries to sleep alone with no one beside her. You are now so noticeably gone. She sits up and checks for the dial tone on the bedroom phone, just to make sure the phone is working, just to make sure she hasn't missed your call. While she has the phone in her hand, she makes another call to your cell phone, just on the long shot that you might answer. But you do not pick up. Of course not. She rests her head on her pillow and pulls the blankets up to her chin with her eyes wide open. She is wondering to herself what else can be done to put an end to your drinking.

"It seems you've tried everything, and nothing has worked. She then wonders whether you love her, if you're so willing to keep upsetting her like this. Yes, she's finally beginning to question your love for her. And rightly so. What kind of husband puts his wife through this misery over and over with no hope in sight? What kind of husband, indeed?! She remembers that she has an important meeting first thing tomorrow at work and needs to be well-rested, but good luck with that. She tosses and turns, and falls in and out of a tense substitute for sleep. She can't get comfortable, and she still has that knot in her stomach.

Then finally—yes, finally—the phone rings early in the morning. It's you, completely oblivious to what the evening has been for her. You tell her you were arrested in Mexico for drunk driving, and they impounded your truck. The Mexican police took you to the border, and you hoofed it to some gas station with a pay phone. But you don't even know what city you're in, let alone the street address. You don't even bother to apologize. All you want is for her to hop in her car and come get you. She asks about the dog, and you tell her he's fine. Suddenly her fear turns to anger, and she tells you to find your own way home, that she has an important meeting in the morning and needs to get her sleep.

"So you agree to find a cab. She hangs up the phone and closes her eyes. You are still alive, and for that she is grateful. But she's still tense and angry, and she's convinced that something has to change. Then it hits her, the very thought she's been trying to avoid, the fact that she's truly sorry she ever married you." Harry stopped talking, and he leaned forward in his chair and stared at me. He was looking at my face as though looking for something specific.

"What are you looking at?" I asked.

"I'm looking for some sort of reaction."

"Like what?"

"Like an expression of remorse or empathy. Maybe even a tear."

"And what do you see?"

"I see nothing."

"But I love Amy."

"So you say."

"I'm sorry for what I did."

"But you keep on doing it."

I thought about this, and I had to admit it was true. "I don't know what to say."

"She's going to leave you."

"I don't think so."

"A person can take only so much. She's going to leave you if you don't stop drinking."

"Can I get myself another cup of coffee?"

"Sure, it's in the kitchen."

I stood up with my empty coffee cup and went to Harry's kitchen. I filled my cup and returned to the library.

"Have you read the Big Book?" Harry asked. He had been thumbing through the pages of his own Big Book while I was gone.

"Yes," I said. "Several times."

"Have you read it recently?"

"No," I said.

"Read the Big Book, cover to cover. Then give me a call, and we'll meet again. Don't call me until you've read the book."

"Okay."

"And when you get home tonight, tell Amy you love her. She'll probably be wondering why you're saying it, but tell her anyway."

When I got home that night, Amy was reading a novel on the family room sofa. When she saw me, she set the book on the coffee table. She took off her reading glasses and placed them on top of the book. "So how'd it go?" she asked.

"It went fine."

"What do you guys talk about?"

"Alcoholism."

"I figured that."

"It's kind of personal," I said.

"Is he helping you?"

"I love you," I said, and Amy gave me the strangest look. Then the look went away.

"I love you too, Lester."

CHAPTER 5

In God We Trust

I read the AA Big Book in its entirety over the course of the next few days. As I read, I realized I hadn't so much as looked at the book for years. It brought back memories of the day Agnes had bailed me out of jail, and that night when I read the book for the first time. It made me realize just how long I'd been struggling with this problem, and I was disappointed in myself for not having found a solution years ago. Worse yet was the fact that Amy was still suffering from my drinking. Harry was right; I was very lucky Amy had never left.

I called Harry and told him I had read the book, and we set up a date to meet again. This time he wanted to meet for coffee at Starbucks, and we decided to get together on a Sunday morning. I arrived at the place on time, and Harry was waiting for me. He had found an outdoor table in a remote part of the patio, and he had already ordered and received his drink. I went to the counter and purchased a coffee and then joined Harry at his table. I had brought my book with me and set it down. Harry smiled and then took a sip from his cup.

"You brought your book."

"Yes," I said.

"That's good."

"I read the whole thing. I haven't read it for years, and it brought back memories."

"I haven't read it for years either. My sponsor made me read it when I was first getting sober. It has way too many references to God for my taste. He made me memorize each of the steps word for word."

"Will I have to do that?"

"No, let's forget the book for now. Have you ever heard the story about the religious man caught in the flood?"

"I don't think so."

"I'll tell you the story. I heard this at an AA meeting years ago. So, there's a terrible flood, and the people in the area all flee their homes for safety. One man gets trapped and finds himself surrounded by water. The water is rising rapidly, and the man goes up the stairs to the second story. He opens a second-floor window and looks out across the rising water. He is a deeply religious man, and he closes his eyes and says a prayer. He knows he's a good Christian, and he's sure that God will save him from the flood. Time passes, and a man swimming with a life preserver wades to the window and offers his help. 'We can share this life preserver,' he says. The man in the window declines the offer and says, 'I have said my prayers, and God will save me.' The man with the life preserver shakes his head and goes away. More time passes, and the water continues to rise.

"The water is now in the second floor of the house, and the religious man climbs out the window and pulls himself atop the roof to stay dry. Again he closes his eyes and prays to God, and no sooner is he done than a powerboat motors past his house. The motorboat driver notices the man on his roof, and he steers the boat over to save him. 'Jump down into my boat, and I'll take you to safety,' the driver shouts. 'No, thanks,' says the religious man. 'I've said my prayers, and God is going to rescue me.' The motorboat driver shakes his head and chugs off into the distance.

"Time passes and the floodwaters continue to rise, and now the man is stranded at the very peak of his roof. Again he closes his eyes and prays. 'Please, God,' he says. 'Please rescue me from this flood.' He hears a helicopter overhead, and a guy in the helicopter dangles a rope down to the man. 'Grab onto the rope,' says the man in the helicopter, 'and we'll fly you to safety.' The man looks at the rope and then up at the helicopter. 'Go help someone else who needs it,' the man says. 'God is coming to save me.' So the helicopter flies away, and the man is now left alone. The water is now up to the top of the roof.

"The man closes his eyes and prays again, and he waits for God to save him from the flood. Within minutes the floodwaters continue to rise rapidly, and the flood overtakes the roof and the religious man. He does not know how to swim, and he drowns in the filthy water. Everything goes black, and the next thing he knows he's up in heaven, meeting with his maker. God sits on his throne before the man, and the man complains, 'I can't believe you let me die! Why didn't you answer my prayers?' God shakes his head and speaks. He says, 'I sent you a life preserver, and you turned it away. I sent you a powerboat, and you refused to jump in. I even sent you a helicopter at the last minute, and you told him to fly away and help someone else. What exactly were you expecting of me?'" Harry leaned forward in his chair. "Have you heard this story before?"

"No, I haven't," I said.

"When I first heard this story, I remember thinking that maybe I could believe in God—the story seemed so convincing on its face. God helps those who help themselves, right? I could believe in this kind of God. But then I thought about it, and the more I thought, the less sense the story made. For example, what about the flood?"

"What about it?" I asked.

"Isn't a flood an act of God?"

"I suppose so."

"You're a building contractor, right? Don't you have a clause somewhere in your contracts that keeps you from being responsible for acts of God?"

"Yes, I do."

"Aren't weather disasters acts of God? And if they are, why would God have created the flood? Why would God have made it rain and put this devout man in his predicament in the first place? Why would he put his life at risk? Why would he destroy his home? It doesn't make any sense."

"No, I guess not."

"And if God wanted the man's life saved, why didn't he have the first fellow with the life preserver tell the poor guy that he'd been sent by God to save him? Why all the mystery? Why not just come out and make it clear?"

"I don't know."

"And on top of all that, what's even the point of being saved?"

"I don't understand."

"Now the guy is in heaven. Who wouldn't want to be in heaven? Why would the man want to be back on earth with all its floods and tornados and hurricanes and earthquakes? Why would the man want to live in a society riddled with greed and violence and crime and deception? And for that matter, why would anyone want to remain living on our crazy planet? Why is death such a tragedy, when we supposedly get to go to heaven and be reunited with all our loved ones, and bask in the warmth and goodness of the kingdom of God? When you think about this stuff, it becomes very confusing, and God shouldn't be confusing, should he? Shouldn't God's truth enlighten us?"

"You would think so. But I think the point of the story is as you said, that God helps those who help themselves."

"In other words, God does nothing. Isn't that the logical extension of that thought? God does nothing, and it's all up to us."

"Seems to be," I said.

"Do you read the paper?"

"Sometimes."

"Did you happen to read it this morning?"

"No," I replied.

"There was a horrible article about a lady in Iowa who accidentally left her seven-month-old daughter in her minivan while she was at work. The child's name was Clare. Ordinarily, the father dropped Clare off each morning at the babysitter's house on the way to his job, but for some reason he was unable to take Clare this particular morning, and the mother did it instead. She strapped Clare into her car seat and drove off. She was thinking about work as she drove, completely preoccupied with some meetings she had first thing in the morning, and she forgot she had Clare with her. She didn't drop Clare off at the babysitter's house; instead, she drove straight to work, parked her car, and went to her office.

"The woman never did remember Clare, and at the end of the workday she went back to her minivan. She stopped by a day-care center on the way home to pick up her elder son, and that's when the boy finally found Clare's dead body, strapped to the backseat of the van. Can you imagine that? Now the DA is trying to decide whether to press charges against her for the death of her own daughter."

"Wow," I said.

"They say that on a hot day, the temperature inside a parked car can reach a 130 degrees. They say that within fifteen minutes a child can die."

"I've heard that."

"So where's the outrage?"

"I'm sure there are people who are outraged."

"Sure, they're outraged at the woman's negligence, but that's not the outrage I'm talking about."

"What outrage are you talking about?"

"I'm talking about outrage at God."

"At God?"

"Why aren't they angry with him? Why don't they charge God with negligence? Why don't they put him on trial? I mean, think about it. Here is a guy with the power to create the entire world, and he couldn't take time out of his schedule to make little Clare sneeze or cough or even whimper so that her mother would be reminded she was in the backseat of her minivan? Seriously? He would have barely had to lift his little finger to change the course of events. Instead, he let that innocent seven-month-old girl bake to death in her mother's car. People believe God pays attention to everything, every time of the day and night. God is always watching, right? Why wouldn't he pay attention to something as important as a seven-month-old child about to be roasted alive in a minivan?"

"I don't know."

"In God we trust, indeed. I haven't always been an atheist. When I was a youngster, I believed in God. But the more I began to look around, the more I began to read, the more I became convinced that either God didn't exist, or that he was very cruel."

"Yes, I've felt the same way myself."

"Did you ever believe in God?"

"No, I don't think I did. Maybe I tried for some short periods of time, but I just couldn't get serious about it. And my family isn't religious."

"My mom and dad were pretty religious. We went to church every Sunday, we said grace each night before dinner, and when I was a kid, they made me say my prayers at night.

"Prayers are certainly a queer thing, aren't they? The way otherwise sane people kneel down and try to talk to a supernatural power, try to convince him to look after them and their loved ones, try to convince him to ensure the outcomes of certain events? The child prays the school bully will leave him alone, and the student prays for a passing grade. The abused wife prays her husband will come home in a good mood. Worried parents pray the doctors will cure their children's maladies, and grandparents pray for their grandchildren. Criminals pray their sentences will be reversed, and victims pray the criminals will stay in jail. Even football teams pray to win their next games, while opposing teams pray for the same. It's crazy, isn't it, all these people praying to someone who doesn't even exist? Even if he did exist, how could he possibly sort all these demands out? There are over seven billion people in the world. If God doesn't have time to save a seven-month-old girl from dying in a parked car, how can he possibly be expected to consider seven billion needy prayers?"

"It does seem crazy."

"Do you like science fiction?"

"It's okay," I said.

"Imagine that a spaceship full of aliens from outer space lands here on earth. Imagine they're able to look just like humans and mingle unnoticed in our population, and that they see all these people on their knees praying to an invisible supernatural power. What do you think they'd report to their home?"

"I don't know."

"That they'd discovered a primitive and superstitious culture?"

"Probably."

"They'd probably look at us the same way as we look down upon early man—filthy, flea-bitten creatures living in caves and huts, sharpening stones for tools and weapons, praying to the many gods they had dreamed up to explain the phenomena of the world around them. We've come so far, and yet we still pray. Someday all of this will change. I'm sure of this. Someday, maybe ten years from now, maybe a hundred years from now, maybe thousands of years from now a baby will be born to a mother, a baby that grows into a charismatic young man or woman who is wise beyond years, who is a genius of sorts, who speaks and convinces the world that God does not exist. People will follow this new messiah's teachings in droves, and the entire complexion of mankind will change. Religions will be abandoned, churches will become museums, and men of the cloth will become financial planners and doctors. The pointless chatter of prayer will be replaced with the healthy murmur of intelligent people talking, asking themselves what is best. It will become an age of self-responsibility, of ownership of individual thoughts, actions, and morals. *Atheist* will no longer be a dirty word."

Harry sat silent for a moment, probably still thinking about what he had just said. I then asked, "Why did you have me read the book?"

"Pardon me?" Harry asked.

"Why did you have me read the Big Book?"

"Oh, that. Yes, I did have you read the book. And you brought it with you."

"Yes, I did."

"Whenever I get into a discussion with AA members, they're always ready to admit that there are many who have a little difficulty with the God issue. But it's more than just a little difficulty, isn't it? You're putting these people into an impossible situation. You're telling them they need to change their very core belief system in order to stay sober. I think everyone deserves the chance to be sober, even atheists."

"And this book?"

"Open it up, and read step two."

I picked my book up and thumbed through the pages to the chapter. I read the step from the book. "We came to believe that a Power greater than ourselves could restore us to sanity."

"Very good."

"They capitalize the word *power*."

"Of course they do. They're setting the table. I need to tell you about Jerry."

"Jerry who?"

"Jerry was an atheist. I met Jerry when I was first getting sober, when I first started going to meetings. He was in his twenties, and he wasn't afraid to share. He'd always raise his hand to speak, and he always talked about his atheistic beliefs. I could relate to a lot of what he had to say. I was about sixty at the time. He was three months sober when we met, and I knew this because I'd watched him get his ninety-day chip. Everyone applauded when he went up to get his chip, and he sat down in his fold-up chair with a big smile on his face.

"I was about a year sober, give or take a few weeks. I never did keep track of my last drinking date the way others did. I was pretty skeptical of AA, and I didn't participate much at the meetings. I just sat there, listening patiently and hoping the miracle of sobriety would somehow sink into my atheistic soul. My problem with AA back then was that I didn't believe in God. I'd read the book over and over, and I just didn't see how a program that was so tightly wound around the concept of a God could ever help someone like me.

"Then along came Jerry, and finally there was someone I could relate to. When he spoke to the group, it seemed like he was speaking for me. He made it clear he planned to stay sober one way or the other, and people in the room offered their silly suggestions. One man wanted Jerry to pray. He told Jerry to keep his car keys under his bed so that he'd have to get on his knees each time he wanted to use his car. While on his knees, he was supposed say a quick prayer, and somehow after doing this day after day he'd eventually come to believe in God. This was the sort of advice they gave, gimmicks and ridiculous ideas."

"I've heard some of those," I said.

"Following the meeting when Jerry took his ninety-day chip, I approached him and introduced myself. I told him I liked hearing him share, and he said thanks. I then asked if he wanted to get coffee with me somewhere, and he said yes. We walked to a coffee shop not far from the meeting place and took seats in a booth. We ordered our coffees from the waitress, and she promptly brought them out. Jerry started the conversation by asking how long I'd been sober, and I told him it had been a year, give or take a few weeks. He asked me if I believed in God, and I told him no, that this was why I wanted to talk with him. I'd found very few people in AA who actually had the guts to admit they were atheists. 'You're old enough to be my dad,' he said, and I replied, 'You're young enough to be my son.' We both laughed, and then he said, 'I guess us atheists have to stick together.'

"I didn't feel like talking much about myself, so I asked Jerry how he wound up in AA, asking for a brief version of his drunkalog.

Being young and a little self-centered, as young people often are, he was more than happy to spend the evening talking about himself. He began with his first drink in elementary school."

"Elementary school?"

"Yes, he started early."

"I'll say."

"He told me about his parents. His father was a teacher at a community college, and his mother was an administrator at the same school. He said his father taught biology and had done so for as long as Jerry could remember. His mother worked in admissions, in charge of student finances, tuitions, and scholarships. Jerry's parents were big on academics, and they always pushed him to study hard and get good grades. They had Jerry's IQ tested early on, and he scored very high, to their delight. They signed Jerry up for Mensa and bought him a lifetime membership in the society for his ninth birthday. They were so proud of him during those years, showing him off to their friends, saving all his papers and report cards in boxes they stored in a closet.

"Jerry remembered how his parents would throw parties and introduce him to their adult friends, engaging him in sophisticated adult conversations where his precociousness and intelligence were impressive. The grown-ups at these parties were always drinking alcohol it seemed, and one evening after his parents had gone to bed, Jerry went to the kitchen, where they'd been mixing drinks. He poured himself a little bit of liquor out of each bottle, knowing they'd never miss the booze. Bracing himself with one hand on the edge of the countertop, he downed the pilfered glass of alcohol. Within seconds, his entire world would change. He'd never felt such a feeling all his young life."

"I know that feeling. This reminds me of my mayonnaise jar story."

"Except Jerry was younger than you. He was only in the sixth grade. He wasn't even a teenager. For the next couple years, he continued to do well in school, and he dreamed of someday becoming a literature professor at a famous university. He loved to read, and he loved to read about writers. He had high hopes for himself, especially when he drank. He knew he was especially smart and that anything was possible. The alcohol made him feel even smarter than he actually was, and everything seemed within his reach when he drank. He said it was like standing at the top of a mountain, the whole world at his feet. He began to seek out opportunities to drink, often after his parents' parties, and he tried to talk them into having guests over often. He befriended kids at school who he knew drank and who he knew could secure liquor readily.

"All these boys became a group of good friends, and he liked being around them. And they liked him because he was smart and going places. None of them had any real ambitions, but they liked to live vicariously through Jerry's potential for success. By the time Jerry was in middle school, he was drinking every weekend, not just enough to get high, but often getting falling-down drunk. He'd puke and pass out, and his friends thought this was hilarious.

"By the time he was in high school, he was drinking during the week. He explained to me that this was when things began to get out of control. He'd go to school drunk, and he'd come home drunk in the evenings. It was a constant effort, getting enough booze to meet his needs, and securing the alcohol became an obsession. His grades began to falter, and his parents became worried about the boys Jerry was hanging around with, thinking they were a bad influence. And it wasn't just his parents. One of his teachers had Jerry stay after class to discuss his behavior, and the school counselor called Jerry into her office, suggesting he find new friends who were more on his own level. All the advice given to him fell on deaf ears.

"By the time he was a junior in high school, he was barely passing his classes. He tried to run away from home twice, and when he was a senior in high school, he ran away for good. He never did get his high school diploma. He thumbed a ride to LA and lied about his age, getting a job working as a laborer for a construction company where they paid him minimum wage in cash every Friday. For three years Jerry worked at this job and shared a dismal room downtown with one of his buddies from work. They'd work during the day and drink all night, puke and shower, and go to work again. It was a horrible existence, but it wasn't until Jerry lost his job that he came to realize just how low he'd fallen. He began to steal and beg for money, and he and his pal were kicked out of their place for not paying the rent.

Finally, he was arrested for shoplifting a bottle of vodka from a liquor store, and he was locked up in jail for the offense. He went before the judge, and rather than give jail time, the judge required Jerry to attend AA meetings and perform community service. He didn't perform any of the community service, but he did go to a few of the AA meetings.

"Jerry told me he hated the meetings but that he kept going back to them out of curiosity. Then he gave up on them, unable to reconcile himself with the God issue, and he went back to his old life for a year or so, living on the streets. He stole and begged for money, did odd jobs for cash here and there, and spent every dime he could get on fast food and bottles of vodka. He was finally arrested again for shoplifting, this time from a grocery store, and he landed back in jail.

"This was enough for him. When they gave him his one call at the jail, he phoned his parents and told them he wanted to come home. He told them he was an alcoholic and that he needed help. To their credit, within an hour or so they showed up at the doorstep of the jail to bail him out. They brought him home to clean and feed him, and they gave him his old room back and hired an attorney to handle his legal issues. Jerry told his parents he needed to go to AA, and since Jerry had no car, his father went out and bought him one so he could get to his meetings. Jerry told me it was rough going, but he somehow managed to get three months of sobriety under his belt."

"And that's when you met him?"

"Yes, that's when we went to the coffee shop. He'd just received his three-month chip."

"How did he seem?"

"Like someone who was scared to death. He was trying not to show it, but I could tell he was scared."

"What was he afraid of?"

Harry didn't answer my question. I wasn't sure if he'd heard me, but if he had, he didn't acknowledge it. He went on with his story. "Over the next several months, Jerry and I became good friends, meeting in the coffee shop after every Thursday-night meeting, usually at the same table. The waitress there got to know us and brought us our coffee without our even having to order. He was a remarkably intelligent young man, and I enjoyed listening to him talk. Like I said, he was young enough to be my son, but I didn't treat him like my junior. We spoke to each other like two adults and shared our thoughts and experiences like equals.

"I learned more and more about Jerry as the weeks went by, and he learned a lot about me. I told him all about my drinking, about how I was forced out of my own law firm, about how Janice divorced me, and about how my own daughter, Alice, refused to have anything to do with me. We talked about our mutual disbelief in God, and then we chuckled over our unlikely involvement in AA. 'Just keep coming back!' Jerry would say enthusiastically, mocking the members.

"It was Jerry who got me interested in reading and collecting books, for it was remarkable how well-read he was for a kid in his twenties, and I admired this. Each time we met, he'd tell me which book he'd recently picked up, and I'd read it too so that we could discuss it. These were such good times, and the fear I first saw in Jerry's eyes gradually gave way to a youthful optimism that was rubbing off on me. At times I almost forgot why we were friends, the awful circumstances that had brought us together. This all took place fifteen years ago. Jerry would be in his forties now, and I miss him."

"What happened to him?"

"One week after Jerry took his six-month chip, he didn't show up for the Thursday-night meeting, and so we didn't go to the coffee shop. At first I figured he must have felt ill and stayed at home, but I thought about it and was a little surprised that he hadn't called. We had each other's phone numbers. Jerry had the phone number to my house, and I had the number to Jerry's parents' house, where he'd been living. We called each other often, so it didn't make sense that he wouldn't have given me a ring that night to tell me he'd miss coffee. When I returned home that evening, I picked up the phone and called him. His dad answered, and I asked if I could speak to Jerry. 'We thought he was with you,' he said. 'Don't you two have coffee around this time?' I told Jerry's father I hadn't seen him all night."

"Where was he?"

"Nobody knew."

"Did you find him?"

"The cops found him on Harbor Boulevard."

"Was he okay?"

"They were called to the scene at around four in the morning. They found Jerry's wallet and driver's license in his back pocket and sent two officers to his parents' home to break the news. Jerry had been hit by a car, and he was pronounced dead by the paramedics. The driver of the car was a woman in her thirties on her way home from a night shift. She was given a sobriety test by the officers in charge, and they determined she was sober. She told them Jerry had just stepped right out in front of her car without any warning, and that she had tried to hit the brakes, but there was nothing she could do to avoid him. The officers believed her.

"When they checked Jerry's blood later that morning, they determined he had a blood alcohol level that was through the roof. They said it was surprising Jerry was able to walk at all, given his condition, and they decided that his death had been a terrible accident. Jerry was either trying to cross the road illegally or had stumbled off the sidewalk and into the path of the woman's vehicle. There was a third scenario they didn't mention—that the death may have been a suicide. Jerry may have stepped in front of the car on purpose; he may have got drunk and become so filled with guilt and remorse that he just decided to end it all. You know, this idea wasn't so far-fetched.

"When I learned of the accident, I was shocked and overwhelmed with grief. We're all going to die eventually, and it's a sad fact of life. But for Jerry to have been taken away at this particular time was especially disconcerting. I felt so sorry for Jerry, but I felt even sorrier for his poor parents. They had had their precious son back in their lives for just a little over six months, and then the boy had been abruptly taken away from them—just like that, with one crazy relapse. It's true what they say in AA, that you're only one drink away from your next drunk, and it's also true that you're just one drunk away from death. So I was still asking myself, was Jerry's death an accident or a suicide? I guess we'll never know. But in either case it was a tragedy.

"I imagined what death was for this friend of mine. I did not imagine his soul soaring up to its divine perch in heaven. Instead, I imagined him as he was, bloody roadkill, his atheist's body lying in the middle of Harbor Boulevard, just another dead mammal curled up in a heap on the dirty asphalt. His heart no longer pounded, and warm blood no longer flowed to his remarkable brain. He was cold, empty, and stiffening. He was no longer Jerry. He was Jerry's remains."

"Wow," I said.

"I told the Thursday-night AA group what had happened."

"What did they do?"

"They said a prayer for him."

"A prayer?"

"It's the last thing Jerry would have wanted. I thought to myself that these people just didn't have a clue."

"Did you keep going to that meeting?"

"Yes, I did. I still go to it today."

"Why?" I asked.

"I go to lots of meetings. I like being a sponsor. For me it's an issue of paying it forward and making the world a better place. The big question when I started as a sponsor was, being an atheist, what sort of role could I play?"

"It's a good question."

Harry reached into his pants pocket and removed a handful of coins, spreading them out on the table. He turned them all faceup, and he pushed them toward me. "What do these coins all have in common?"

"They're all round," I said.

"What else?"

"They all have presidents' heads."

"And?"

I looked closely at the coins, and I picked one of them up and held it closer to my face. "Oh, of course. They all say, 'In God We Trust.'"

"Exactly."

CHAPTER 6

Harry's Dad

My fourth meeting with Harry took place at Harry's house again, but this time it was in his front room. We sat on two sofas that faced each other. In the room, in addition to some other things, there was a fireplace, a grandfather clock, more bookshelves stuffed with books, and a grand piano near the windows. On the piano were framed photographs I assumed to be of Harry's family. "Do you play the piano?" I asked.

"Not even a little. We bought the piano for Alice and gave her lessons from age eight up. She was rather good at it. No one has played the thing since she moved out of the house. Do you play the piano?"

"No," I said.

"I thought of selling it, but I couldn't get myself to part with it. It reminds me of Alice. There's so little I have to remember her by."

"What are all these photographs?"

"They're all of family. Many of them are old pictures I've kept over the years. Some of them are more recent photos, pictures Janice gave me of Alice and the grandkids in Vermont. There are a few current shots of Janice that Kaleb took." I stood up from the sofa and walked to the piano, picking up one of the photos.

"Who are these people?" It was an old black-and-white picture of three people posing in front of a fireplace. The frame was old and fragile.

"That's my family. That's me with my parents, back when I was ten years old. I didn't have any brothers or sisters. I remember that picture was taken just a couple years before Mom died of cancer. I think I told you my dad drank a lot, and I'm pretty sure he was drunk in that picture. I remember when my uncle took it. My uncle, who was my dad's brother, always said my dad didn't start drinking heavily until after Mom died, but he was wrong. My father drank for as long as I can remember."

"That's too bad," I said.

"Yes. He was a handsome man, wasn't he?"

I looked at the photo and agreed. "Yes, he was a good-looking guy. What did he do for a living?"

"He was a steelworker. Except for his drinking, I have no complaints. He was a good man who worked hard and loved his family. I remember sitting in his lap when I was a small boy, playing with his large calloused hands and rubbing the tips of my fingers against the beard stubble on his jaw. He was like a god to me. I remember the way he smelled, that acrid aroma of body odor and whiskey. I didn't think much of this smell when I was a small boy, just assuming it was the way that all fathers smelled, the way adult men smelled. It began to bother me as I grew older and realized what I was smelling, but as a boy I sort of liked it. I enjoyed being around my dad."

"His drinking didn't bother you?"

"Yes, it bothered me."

"Was his life unmanageable?"

"That's a good question. In all the years I lived with him, my father rarely missed a day of work, and there was always food on the table and a roof over our heads. He never raised a hand to my mom or me; in fact, I don't remember him ever even raising his voice. He never went bankrupt or went to jail. Our bills were always paid on time so far as I knew, and he kept the front yard manicured and the house painted. It was the little idyllic home in the Southern California suburbs, basking in the sun and repelling the rain, keeping us safe from the weather. Dad had a rule about his drinking, that he'd never drink during work, and he drank only in the evenings or on weekends after his chores were done. I'm sure he had hangovers, but he never showed them. His head could be pounding like a timpani drum, and he'd carry on like nothing was wrong with him, going about his business and taking care of his responsibilities."

"Did he believe in God?"

"Both he and my mom were religious, and they took me to church every Sunday. Dad said grace at the dinner table before every meal, and although he stopped going to church after Mom died, he continued the tradition of saying grace. He'd always say the same thing, thanking the Lord for all the food we were about to eat. My dad had an interesting relationship with God, for he wasn't big on being read to from the Bible or listening to sermons at church.

"When he said grace before dinner, I think he knew where the food came from; it came from the grocery store, from money he earned from all his hard work. It was Dad with his big hands and strong back that provided for our family, not God, not some supernatural power. My dad was a firm believer that God helped those who helped themselves, and my dad was one who helped himself.

"I remember when mom was still alive, how we'd all pile into the old Buick and go to church, and how Dad would sit politely beside her listening quietly to the minister go on and on about sin and redemption and all the other topics ministers carry on about. Sometimes Dad would get a glazed look in his eyes and fall asleep, and Mom would have to nudge him to wake him up. But he definitely believed in God, although if he'd ever made it to AA, I think he would have had just as much trouble with the steps as you and I."

"It sounds like he was a good man."

"He was a good man, but was also a drunk. He'd stop at the local bar and drink with his buddies every evening after work. Often he'd come home just tipsy, but many times he'd be completely plastered. It was just the way things were. Mom and I would watch TV, or she'd watch TV while I did homework, waiting for him to return and wondering what condition he'd be in. Sometimes he'd be so drunk that we'd have to stand at each side of him and guide him to the bedroom. We'd plop him down on the bed, and Mom would undress him and get him under the covers. Sometimes his head would be spinning, and he'd stagger into the bathroom where, leaving the door wide open, he'd kneel down and groan and puke into the toilet over and over. I can still remember those awful sounds, and the way they made me feel as a small boy.

"I used to wish that Dad would stop drinking, but I didn't know what to do. There must have been something I could do, no?

I remember once he came home so drunk that he'd wet his pants. There was a sopping-wet spot on the crotch of his work trousers. Mom tossed the soiled pants in the laundry hamper with all their other clothes, and I remember hoping she wouldn't throw his pants in with my own clothes when she did the wash. Those are the kinds of things a kid thinks about."

"What happened when your mom passed away?"

"Dad hired a lady to come live with us. Her name was Miss Strawberry. I remember thinking she had a funny name. She was in her thirties, a little overweight, and not very attractive, but she had a very mothering disposition. She stayed in the spare bedroom, and during the day she did the things Mom used to do—cleaning the house, doing the laundry, and preparing meals. She'd help me with my homework and babysit while Dad was gone. Miss Strawberry was very kind, and I liked it that she didn't try to boss me around. My dad liked her because she put up with his drinking. Miss Strawberry and I took care of him, just as I'd done with my mom.

"Now that I look back, it's hard to believe this woman put up with all Dad's nonsense. When I moved out to go to college, Miss Strawberry left my father for a job she found in Arizona. I haven't seen or heard from her since, and sometimes I wonder what became of her. It's kind of a shame we didn't stay in touch, and I wonder if she ever got married. She's probably passed away by now."

"It's like you had two different fathers."

"That's a good way of putting it. I did have two fathers, like you say. One was responsible, loving, and hardworking, and the other was a drunken slob. I loved my father dearly, but I can't say his behavior didn't affect me. When he came home drunk, it gave me a knot in my stomach the size of a basketball. I would feel physically ill. I was repulsed by his behavior, and when Mom was still alive I'd daydream about us leaving and moving to another town. We'd be able to live such a happier life without him, just the two of us. These daydreams caused me a lot of guilt, for like I said, I loved my father. It was difficult to reconcile these opposing feelings."

"When did your dad die?"

"He died when I was thirty-four. He was diagnosed with cirrhosis of the liver, and he suffered a prolonged and painful death. It was not a good way to go. Dad had no health insurance, so I paid the doctor and hospital bills. It was very expensive, and he was fortunate I was making a lot of money. Business at my law firm was booming, and I owed my dad the best possible care. Without him I would never have made it through law school.

"I remember when I first told Dad I wanted to be an attorney, he said he wanted to pay my way, and he began working overtime to earn the cash. He also took out a second mortgage on his house to provide me with the needed funds. There wasn't anything my father wouldn't do when it came to giving me a better life, and he never once complained or tried to make me feel guilty for taking the money. He told me he was just doing what any good father would do."

All this time Harry had been speaking, I was standing by the piano and holding his old photograph. Harry stopped talking, and I set the picture down. I picked up another and looked at it. It was of a young Harry with his bride. Harry was dressed in a tuxedo, and Janice had flowers in her hair. She was a very pretty woman. "Is this you and Janice?" I asked.

"Yes, from the wedding."

"How old were you?"

"I was twenty-five, and Janice was twenty-four. We met in college. My dad liked Janice a lot."

"What did she think of him?"

"Before they met, I told her lots of good things about Dad, but I also told her about his drinking, about how difficult it had been growing up with him. So Janice knew a lot about my father before they even met, and when Janice and I started to get serious about our relationship, I decided she should meet him in person. This was a huge step for me. You have to understand that all through my childhood and early adulthood I kept my friends and girlfriends away from home. I never knew if my father would be in the house, and if he was there, I never knew what sort of condition he'd be in. I just didn't want to take any chances. When I decided it was time for Janice to meet my father, I called him to arrange a date. I told him to be sure to be sober, that I wanted the meeting to go well, that Janice was probably the girl I was going to marry, and I didn't want him scaring her off. He seemed a little hurt, but Dad agreed to the terms.

"When I brought Janice to the house a week or so later, Dad was sober and charming as promised, and later that night on our way back to the college, Janice said he seemed very nice. When I called Dad the next day, he couldn't say enough good things about the girl. He really liked her. I took Janice over to the house several times after that for dinner, and the meals always went well. Dad and Janice got along fine. I always wondered if Janice had ever seen my father drunk, whether she would have agreed to marry me. No one in her family drank like my dad, and she didn't know what a nightmare living with an alcoholic could be.

"Anyway, when we did decide to marry, we spent months making preparations. It was quite a ceremony. I made Dad promise to stay away from the champagne during the reception, and he agreed and behaved himself marvelously, making small talk with all the guests, politely accepting their congratulations. He probably got drunk when he went home that night, but he was on his best behavior at the reception."

I set the wedding picture back on the piano. I then stepped over to the sofa, sat down, and crossed my legs. Harry stood up and asked me if I wanted something to drink. "All this talking makes me thirsty," he said. I told him I didn't need anything, so Harry stepped to the kitchen for a Coke and then returned to his seat.

"When did you become an atheist?" I asked.

"It was in college."

"Did your dad ever know?"

"We never talked about it."

"Do you think it would've upset him?"

"I don't know," Harry said.

"What happened in college that made you believe there was no God?"

"Nothing actually happened. I can't say it was a specific event. I remember we'd stay up all hours of the night, arguing about what we were learning in our classes, and the subject of God often came up. One kid named Martin Flower brought up an old childhood conundrum, asking, 'If God is all-powerful, can he create a rock so heavy that even he can't lift it?' I'd heard this question before, but what was once just amusing to me as a kid now took on much importance. And it wasn't just this question that disturbed me. For example, if God made man in his own image, was God a sinner? And if God was such a good and benevolent being, why all the wars and diseases and hatred in the world? Why would God go through the trouble to create such a maelstrom of despair and violence? All my life I'd heard adults claiming that God did this, and God did that, using his name to explain nearly everything. But isn't it odd how these people pick and choose which situations and events are influenced by God, and which are not?

"A little boy develops cancer, and his parents pray to God for remission or a cure, but didn't God cripple the kid with the cancer to begin with? Asking God to help us is like asking a rattlesnake to help with a snakebite or asking a thief to protect your valuables. You can't pick and choose God's involvement in order to best suit your need to explain what's going on. Either he's responsible for the events that occur in this world, or he's not. By my junior year in college, I was a full-fledged atheist. I believed God was no more relevant to my life than a witch doctor dancing about to drumbeats and shaking his rattles."

"Did you drink at all in college?"

"Not a drop," Harry said.

"That's so hard to believe. I thought everyone drank in college."

"I never did. As a young boy, I saw what booze did to my father, and I promised myself that I would never drink. For years I was able to keep that promise. I honestly never touched the stuff. I didn't hang around with kids who drank in high school, and college was no different. I chose my friends wisely, even if they were the most boring kids on campus. I didn't go to parties or football games, and I avoided placing myself in any compromising positions. When I did find myself in certain social situations, I was sure to turn down even the most innocuous offers of a glass of wine or a friendly bottle of beer. I was very serious about this. The last thing in the world I wanted was to be a college-educated clone of my father, puking up bile and whiskey in the dorm toilet, or pissing my pants at the end of an evening. My dad was a wonderful man, but I didn't want to be anything like him."

"I guess I can understand that."

"When my dad was on his deathbed, it broke my heart. Do you want to know exactly what he told me? First, he said he loved me, and then he gave me the strangest piece of advice. He told me to keep my nose clean. That was it—keep my nose clean. Now isn't that an odd thing for a father to say with his last breath? Maybe it isn't, and maybe it is. But it certainly seemed weird to me at the time. Now that I look back, I feel as if it was like some ominous premonition, and I wonder what my dad saw in my future to prompt him to say those words. Did he know something I didn't?"

"That is kind of weird."

"Was he talking about what I did for a living, or was he talking about my future struggle with alcohol? Or was he just repeating something he had heard on TV or had seen in a movie?"

"I guess only he knows."

"You know, I think if he were alive today he'd be disappointed. Not angry, but very disappointed." Harry stopped talking a minute. He seemed to be thinking about what he'd just said. He then stood up and grabbed his Big Book. He handed the book to me and asked me to read step two again. I turned to the chapter.

"We came to believe that a Power greater than ourselves could restore us to sanity," I said, reading from the book.

"Power with a capital *P*?"

"Yes, they capitalize *power*."

"Meaning?"

"I assume they mean that the power is God."

"Yes, they're talking about God. Can you think of any other entity they might mean?"

"Not really."

"But we agree God doesn't exist?"

"Yes," I said. "On that we agree."

"Then there's only one thing that can keep an alcoholic sober. Let's go back to the man and the swimming pool I talked about earlier. Do you remember this man? He can't swim, but he jumps into a pool and drowns. We agreed he isn't powerless over water, right? He just made a bad choice. He had free will, but he blew it. No matter how hot a day it was, how weary he was of the heat, or how inviting and cool the water looked, he could have reminded himself that he couldn't swim. Sure, he might have wished he could swim, but that doesn't change the fact that he couldn't. In order to stay alive, he had to stay out of the pool. Likewise, Lester, you can't drink. What is it that they say in the Big Book—that we're like men who've lost their legs? Once you drink, you're doomed. It's that simple. You just have to be a man and say no while you're still sober."

"You make it sound so easy."

"I said it was simple; I didn't say it was easy."

"Okay," I said.

"We're going to rewrite step 2. I say we state that we came to believe that we and we alone could restore ourselves to sanity."

"That's it?"

"Simple as that."

"Doesn't that go against everything they teach in AA?"

"Do you believe in God? Do you think he can get you out of this?"

"No, I don't."

"Then you have no other options. You need to empower yourself. You need to stop looking for supernatural tricks and miracles. You just need to grow up."

"Grow up?"

"Yes, grow up. I know this is difficult to swallow as a sixty-year-old man, but you need to stop acting like a helpless child."

CHAPTER 7

Gobbledygook

For the next two weeks, Harry and I didn't meet. He told me to go to AA meetings at least once a day. He told me to listen carefully to what people were saying and to compare what I heard with the things we'd been talking about. I wasn't sure what the point of this was, since Harry was rewriting the steps and thus we were out of sync. I sat through the meetings, and I daydreamed through many of them. A few things, however, caught my attention, and one was the idea that alcoholism is a disease. I had come to accept this idea over the years, and it seemed everyone in the meetings took this for granted. But I was curious to get Harry's thoughts. I was sure he'd have something to say.

When Harry and I met again, we decided to attend an AA meeting beforehand. When the meeting was over, we drove to a coffee shop near Harry's house. We ordered coffee, and Harry ordered some French fries. "You want something to eat?" he asked, and I said no. While we were waiting for the order, Harry looked at me quizzically. "So?" he asked.

"So what?" I said.

"So what did you get out of the meetings?"

"Actually, I have a question."

"Okay," Harry said.

"Do you think alcoholism is a disease?"

"Do they still have door-to-door salesmen?"

"Do they what?" I asked.

The waitress brought our order, and Harry scooted the fries into the center of the table just in case I wanted some. "Help yourself," he said.

"Thanks."

"I don't know if they still have these guys around, because I now live in a gated community, but when I was young these salesmen used to roam the neighborhoods ringing doorbells and pestering housewives. I remember when I was about eight years old, my mom let a vacuum cleaner salesman into our home. It was hot outside, and the poor fellow was sweating profusely. He had a handkerchief that he used to wipe the perspiration from his face, and he had a vacuum and a case full of parts and demonstration props that he lugged into the front room. It was a sight just watching this guy in action, carrying all this stuff and wiping his forehead at the same time. He was short and overweight, and his clothes were a size too small, and he looked very hot and uncomfortable. It was decades ago, but I can still remember exactly what he looked like.

"The salesman took a seat and began to explain all the workings of his vacuum, taking it apart and putting it back together, running its motor, flipping switches, and hooking up all the different attachments and explaining their purposes. He pointed out the whirligigs and whatchamacallits, and identified them with a lot of impressive jargon. In just fifteen minutes he had turned the simple vacuum cleaner into something it would require a degree in engineering to fully appreciate. My head was spinning, and I wondered how my dear mother would ever get up the nerve to purchase such a sophisticated piece of machinery and put herself at the helm of it. If it had been up to me, I would have bought the thing right then and there. I was young and naïve, and I was sold by the demonstration.

"But when the man was done talking, my mom told him she would have to talk to my dad. She asked for the man's business card. I could tell by my mom's demeanor that she was just being polite. I knew she was fine with the old vacuum cleaner she had, for I'd never heard her complain about it or ask my dad for a new one. I don't know why she let the salesman in our house—perhaps just to break the monotony, to provide her with a break from her daily chores. The man gave my mom his card and then lugged all his merchandise back to the front door and out to the porch. Mom shut the door after him and locked the latch, and then she looked down at me and smiled. 'Gobbledygook,' she said. I had never heard her use this word before.

I thought it was just a silly expression she made up on the spot, but I learned later that it was an actual word."

"What does it mean?"

"Nonsense. Pointless blather. A lot of meaningless jargon—that's what gobbledygook means."

"Okay."

"Lester, a lot of what you hear in AA meetings is gobbledygook. There's enough going around to fill an encyclopedia. So what was your question again … is alcoholism a disease?"

"Yes," I said.

"How would you define a disease?"

"I've never thought about it in precise terms. I guess it's where there's something wrong with you, some kind of disorder. It would manifest itself in a negative way. It would be something physical or even mental, something that needs to be treated."

"Yes, that's close enough."

"So is alcoholism a disease?"

Harry picked up several fries, stuffing them into his mouth. He waited until he swallowed before he started talking. "Let's go back again to the man and the swimming pool. I like that analogy. Is jumping into the pool a disease?"

"Probably not."

"It was a bad decision, wasn't it? But a bad decision isn't a disease. When I think of a disease, I think of shingles or smallpox, or even the common cold. When I think of mental diseases, I think of something like schizophrenia. It's true that you can contract a disease from making a bad decision. You can get lung cancer from smoking, but the act of smoking itself is not a disease. You can get the flu by attending a large gathering where people are coughing, sneezing, and breathing the same germ-infested air, but the act of going to the gathering isn't a disease. Have you ever heard of people going to the doctor or a hospital to cure their compulsion to attend large gatherings?"

"No," I said.

"You've been to rehab three times?"

"Yes, that's right."

"I went once. It was a facility here in Newport Beach. I went voluntarily, hoping they would provide me with a cure. Rehabs view alcoholism as a disease, don't they? And they do their best to treat it as such; they don't claim to have a cure, but they do attempt to put the disease into remission. Do you remember much of your rehabs? Do you remember how they'd spend countless hours lecturing you about biology, chemistry, and psychology? They'd bring in all sorts of experts, and they'd scribble terms and diagrams on whiteboards and distribute handouts by the reams. You'd learn about how alcohol affects the brain and nervous system, how family dynamics determine personalities, and how childhood traumas influence adult behaviors. Then they'd shoo you off to therapy sessions. All the while, you'd be reminded over and over how you'd picked a state-of-the-art treatment center, that your money hadn't been wasted.

"They'd say if you'd just pay attention to all this gobbledygook, you might find yourself getting well. I remember these experts scampering about my own rehab facility like a colorized version of the Keystone Cops. And what did they do when my thirty-day stint was over? They told me to attend AA meetings, to go find God. They told me that if I didn't believe in God, that I'd wind up right where I started, drunk and miserable.

"It's absurd, isn't it? Can you imagine any other disease being treated this way? Say you go to the doctor with an upset stomach or a painful rash on your arm, and he spends the next thirty days lecturing you on everything he can think of that might relate to your condition. He then has you reveal your deepest secrets to a room full of strangers. Then he sends you off to a religious self-help group where you're expected to seek salvation from some supernatural power. This doctor would be laughed right out of the medical profession, don't you think? Am I making any sense to you?"

"Yes, you are."

"The reason doctors have such a hard time with alcoholism is because it's not a disease. It's a powerful obsession. Life is full of obsessions. Being head over heels in love with someone who doesn't love you back can be an obsession. Having a burning and irreconcilable hatred of those annoying neighbors down the street can be an obsession. Having an overwhelming desire to drive to the grocery store for a gallon of chocolate ice cream when you're on a diet can be an obsession. Being in love, hating neighbors, and wanting to eat ice cream are not diseases, and just because it's convenient to call them such, it doesn't make it so."

"Then what exactly is an obsession?"

"It's just a part of human nature. All of us experience obsessions of one kind or another. It's how we act on them that defines us. This is an important point, and you'd do well to remember it—that how we chose to deal with an obsession is more important than the obsession itself." Harry stopped talking a moment and stuffed some more French fries into his mouth. "Are you sure you don't want any of these?"

"No, thanks," I said.

"Did you go to a meeting each day like I told you?"

"Yes, for the past two weeks."

"And what did you get out of them?"

"I can't say for sure. I've gone to so many meetings in my lifetime that they all sort of seem the same. They all run together. The meeting I went to tonight with you could just as easily have been a meeting I went to when I was in my twenties."

"Then you should stop going to meetings."

"But you told me to go."

"I wanted to see if you're getting anything out of them. Obviously you're not. It's a waste of time."

"Don't they say you have to keep going to meetings for the rest of your life?"

"Some people say that."

"And?"

"I don't say that," Harry said. "I think you should stop going."

"But don't you still go to meetings?"

"I've been going to them for seventeen years."

"And you don't get tired of them?"

"I don't go to meetings because I like them."

"Then why go?" I asked.

"I go to help others. I go to provide my services as a sponsor."

"And doesn't that help you stay sober?"

"Sure, it does. Helping others is a good thing to do, and it helps one stay sober. But there are lots of ways to help others besides being an AA sponsor. You don't have to set your sights on alcoholism. And you certainly don't have to go to meetings. Listen, I think meetings are a good thing if you like them. If you like sharing your story and feelings with others, a meeting is a great place to go. If you're not sure whether you're an alcoholic, meetings are the perfect place to listen to other alcoholics speak about their lives so you can decide if you're in the same boat. If you're confused about passages you've read in the Big Book, meetings are perfect for getting other alcoholics' opinions and advice; believe me, there's no shortage of advice or opinions at meetings. If you're an alcoholic who's been sober for several years, and you want to be reminded about what a nightmare drinking can be, meetings are a terrific place to hear fresh horror stories. I can think of all sorts of good reasons to go to AA meetings, but unless you're getting something positive out of them, I just don't see any reason to keep going."

"Then what am I supposed to do?"

"We'll keep working the steps."

"Okay," I said.

"Have you ever heard the story about the drunken judge?"

"I don't think so," I said.

"I heard this story years ago at a meeting, and I haven't heard it since. It's the story of a judge who had a terrible drinking problem and kept his booze hidden in his chambers. He'd sneak drinks every so often when the courtroom was in recess, and usually no one was the wiser. But one day he got carried away with the drinking, and he found himself getting drunk. He did his best to maintain his composure on the bench, but he couldn't wait for the day to be over.

"On his way home that night, he stopped at a bar to have a few drinks, thinking the booze would help clear his head. In less than an hour he was plastered, and he climbed into his car to drive home. On the way home his head spun and his mouth started salivating, and the next thing he knew he had puked all over his lap. 'Damn,' the judge said to himself, 'How am I going to explain this to my wife?'

"Thinking he was clever, the judge came up with the perfect explanation. He would tell his wife that a kid who came before the court that afternoon for shoplifting was pathetically drunk. The kid was only seventeen years old, and his parents knew nothing of the court date, so they weren't there with him. The judge felt sorry for the boy, so rather than proceed in court without the parents, he postponed the appearance to the next morning and offered to give the kid a ride home. On their way to the house the kid got sick and puked all over the judge's lap. The judge decided the story was perfect, and when he got home he told it to his wife. He did his best during the story to maintain his composure and not let on that he was drunk. 'Tomorrow in court I won't be so nice,' he said. "I'll teach that kid a lesson.'

"After giving the wife his story, the judge went to the bedroom to change clothes, and he dropped the soiled pants in the hamper. The next morning while the judge was getting ready for work, his wife grabbed the hamper. She took it to the laundry room to wash the clothes. When she returned to the bedroom, she told the judge he'd better do more than just teach the kid a little lesson, that he'd better throw the book at that awful boy. When the judge asked why, she said angrily, 'Not only did that troublemaker vomit all over your lap, he also crapped in your pants.'"

I laughed at this. "I haven't heard that one before, and I thought I'd heard them all."

"It is funny isn't it? I mean, not funny-funny, but odd funny, no?"

"How is it odd?"

"The way we laugh at ourselves."

"I suppose so."

"We laugh at stories about ourselves, and we laugh at stories about others. You'd think that the life of an alcoholic was a comedy. Yet wasn't it just about the most horrible experience of your life? Do you remember all the depravity, humiliation, and sadness you suffered? I'm as guilty as the next guy, telling bits or pieces of my drinking life as though they were fodder for a good laugh. Many times I've told about how I was kicked out of my law firm as though the story was amusing, how the very firm I founded and men I had hired turned around and gave me the boot. It's an absurd and ironic story, and absurdity and irony can always elicit a laugh. And I guess it's a good thing to have a sense of humor, but in reality my story isn't funny at all. And I'm not sure laughing about it now is such a good thing. If I concentrate and remember those years, I realize they were truly the most awful times in my life.

"My life then was in the toilet, and there was nothing I could do about it. Friends and family wanted nothing to do with me, and each day I was racked with loneliness and a sense of isolation that is hard now to put into words. I remember I just wanted to die, and there's nothing funny about that, is there? There was nothing funny about being transported by ambulance to a mental hospital with those big gauze bandages wrapped around my wrists, my shirt and pants still wet with blood. Do you remember I told you about the steak knife? I'm lucky to be alive today, of that I'm certain. Alcoholism is a very serious matter, one that should not be taken lightly. Do you agree with me?"

"Yes," I said. "I do agree."

"And it is doubly difficult for us atheists."

"How so?"

"All said and done, there's nowhere for us to go but the rooms of AA. It's our last chance at sobriety, and instead of getting a proper helping hand, we're told to believe in God and seek his love. We're told our only means for survival is to reach out for something that goes against everything we believe."

"Yes," I said.

"I am not changing the steps because I think I know more than others. It's not hubris or obstinacy that motivates me. It's a life-or-death matter of survival. I change the steps to save my life."

"That makes sense."

"Can you recite step three?"

"Not without my book," I said.

"Okay, I'll recite it for you. Step three says that we made a decision to turn our will and our lives over to the care of God as we understood him."

"Yes, that sounds familiar."

"Can you even do this?"

"No, I suppose not. I can't turn my will and life over to something I don't even believe in."

Harry reached for another fry, stuffing it in his mouth. He made a face but chewed on it anyway. "They're cold," he said. "Nothing worse than a cold French fry. You said you're a building contractor, didn't you? What kind of stuff have you built?"

"All sorts of projects," I said. "I've been doing it for over thirty years."

"Ever built a custom house?"

"Sure," I said. "I've built several of them."

"Building a life is like building a custom house, don't you think? You plan and scheme and calculate. You work your tail off, trying to keep the project moving smoothly. It requires drive, creativity, intelligence, and energy, all of which you must muster up from your own limited resources. You don't just sign a contract with the home owner and then turn the project over to God."

"No, I don't."

"You have to take the bull by the horns and get the job done on your own. God has nothing to do with it. And it's a lot of work, isn't it? I don't think most people appreciate the effort that goes into building a house.

"The house I live in now, Janice and I had built thirty-three years ago. I remember everything our contractor went through putting it together for us. His name was Edward. At the beginning of the job, he encountered problems with the soil, and the foundations had to be redesigned. It took the structural engineer weeks to resolve the issue, and so right off the bat it seemed we were behind schedule. Then the foundation subcontractor tried to overcharge us for the additional work required, and Edward had to negotiate a new deal with a different subcontractor. It was weeks before we were even able to start work. Once the foundation was installed, the carpenter went to work, and his job moved along rather nicely until Janice walked through the rooms and decided many of the walls needed to be reconfigured to meet her needs. You should've seen the look on the carpenter's face.

"The carpenter did his best to accommodate her at a reasonable extra price. His name was Sonny, and I liked the guy. Carpenters are a pretty agreeable lot, but then along came the rest of the trades. They descended upon our little wood-framed project like a swarm of bees. I'd never seen such a thing in my entire life. They damaged each other's work and stole each other's tools. They called in sick at critical times, and they showed up to work late, hungover and worthless. Some of them smoked weed during their lunch breaks, while others drank beer.

"They never picked up after themselves, and the job site was a constant pigsty of construction debris, fast-food wrappers, ant-covered soda cups, beer cans, bottles, empty cigarette packs, and cigarette butts. Edward did his best to keep everything under control, but I began to realize just what an overwhelming task this was. The plumber and the air-conditioning subcontractor argued, and the electrician and our alarm company couldn't agree on anything. The stucco guy complained about the framer's work, and all the subcontractors complained in unison about the building inspector, who, code book in hand, picked apart their workmanship and refused day after day to sign off on the inspection card. 'I've been doing this all my life,' one of the workers complained to me. 'I think I ought to know what I'm doing by now.' I've only touched upon the tip of the iceberg here, for these conflicts and annoyances went on for months.

"Finally, after a full year of bickering and antler banging, our project was actually completed. Don't ask me how he did it, but Edward got the project done on time. The results were outstanding, and I can't think of a single complaint Janice or I had over the end product. The house was everything we'd dreamed of.

"On the day Edward came over to get his final payment, I found him standing in the street in front of the house. He was clicking pictures with his camera. 'You must be proud of yourself,' I said, and Edward smiled. I truly meant this, that he must be proud. He'd signed a contract with me, and he'd completed his end of the deal. He faced all the obstacles and found a way to get the job done. This is what life's all about, isn't it? Pitting one's wits and energy against the powers that be, finding a way to achieve one's goals? This sort of struggle gives life meaning. I say it's the essence of the human experience. You shouldn't let anyone take this away from you, Lester. And you certainly shouldn't give it away. Not ever."

"I like what you're saying."

"I thought you would."

"So?" I asked.

"So what?"

"So, how do we rewrite the third step?"

"I say step three is that we make a commitment to take responsibility for our lives."

"It changes the step completely," I said.

"The change is for the better. God is now out of the equation. We face the powers that be on our own, with our own wits and fortitude. It's essential if we're to get anywhere with this program."

"I can see that."

"Let's talk about something else. I'm a little tired of all this AA talk."

"What do you want to talk about?"

"Let's talk about your boys."

"My boys?"

"Tell me about them. It's seems like I've been talking a lot about myself. I'd like to learn more about your family."

"Well," I said, "as I've already told you, I have two sons. The younger, Miles, is nineteen years old and still lives with us at home. My older son, Danny, is twenty-seven and lives in Laguna Beach. Both of them are taller than Amy but shorter than me, and I'd say they both got Amy's good looks. They don't look the same, but each boy is handsome in his own way.

"Danny is an artist who lives in a little studio attached to a beach house where he paints and draws. During the day he works for a sandwich shop downtown for minimum wage, where he earns his spending money. Amy and I pay the rest of his bills, including his rent, car payments, insurance premiums, and cable TV. He did go to college for one year, with no particular major in mind, but nothing they were teaching caught his fancy. He felt the calling to become an artist, and he dropped out of college to pursue his dream.

"It's interesting, but just recently Danny said he's going back to school, and now he plans to become a computer programmer. He says he's tired of being a poor artist and wants to pursue an actual career. I have no idea how he made the jump from artist to computer programmer, and I guess this will always be a mystery. He hasn't offered any explanation, and I haven't asked for one. His abandoning his dream makes me a little sad, and I'm not sure I want to hear all the details. Amy and I told him we'd be happy to pay his tuition at the college of his choice, and that if he wanted to become a computer programmer, his mom and I would stand behind him. I've always supported my boys in pursuing their ambitions. I think it's a reaction I have to the fact that my own father was something of a stick-in-the-mud when it came to cheerleading my own pursuits."

"Do your boys drink?"

"Perhaps a little. Danny got thrown in the drunk tank once in Huntington Beach when he was a teenager for some rowdy Saturday-night behavior. But for the most part, my boys stick to marijuana. I think they smoke more weed than Amy or I realize, but I don't think they take any harder drugs. They're probably pretty tame, all things considered."

"Their marijuana use doesn't bother you?"

"Not really. They're good kids. I don't see any reason to make a big deal out of it."

"Tell me about Miles. Is he in college?"

"No, he hates school. He never applied to college, and he never went."

"What's he doing?"

"He wants to be a rap musician. He spends all his time working on his hip-hop music, and he turned Danny's empty bedroom into a recording studio. Every birthday we buy him a new piece of equipment, and he now has a pretty good setup. His friends are over at the house all the time, and our home has become the place they all gather. They don't even bother to knock anymore; they just come right in through the rear door.

"I know you only had a daughter, but there's something you ought to know about teenage boys, and that is that they eat. I don't just mean three meals a day; I mean like all the time. They're never sated, no matter how much food passes their lips. Amy is constantly coming home from the store with boxes of donuts, cookies, muffins, and cupcakes. She brings home bags of potato chips, corn chips, cheese puffs, and weird flavored popcorns. She buys frozen pizzas, macaroni and cheese, and cold fried chicken, and she fills the refrigerator drawers with hot dogs, cheeses, and lunch meats. She carries in soft drinks by the case, like she's filling a giant hotel vending machine. By the end of the week our trash cans are filled with empty containers and crumpled aluminum cans and sticky bottles and bags.

"It's like we're running some sort of bizarre residential restaurant where everything on the menu is free, where the sky's the limit. The boys, of course, are always very polite, and they thank us for everything. It's at least nice to know that they're appreciative. But I wonder why they're so hungry. Perhaps their own parents chase them away from their own pantries and refrigerators, refusing to be a party to their marauding appetites. Perhaps we're the only parents who break down and actually feed the poor creatures. Maybe that's why they keep coming back to our house. Maybe it's not because they like Miles or us, and maybe it's just because of the food."

"Does Miles have a job?"

"No, not yet. We're letting him pursue his music. It takes up a lot of his time."

"You're pretty easy on your kids, paying their bills the way you do."

"I love my boys. But it isn't a matter of being easy."

"What would you call it?"

"You have to understand that when I was a teenager, more than anything I wanted to become a writer. I had no idea what I was going to write about, but I knew I wanted to be a writer. Books fascinated me, much the way they fascinate you now. It seemed to me there was no more exciting way to make a living than to pen words on blank sheets of paper and turn them into glorious tales. I was convinced that before the age of thirty, I would be writing the great American novel, right up there with Hemmingway, Faulkner, and Dreiser. This fantasy of mine persisted from high school and right into college.

"My dad was aware of my ambition, but he didn't say anything until my twentieth birthday. I remember we were at his house after dinner, and while Mom and Amy were in the kitchen doing dishes, my dad and I sat at the dining room table having coffee and nibbling on the remnants of my birthday cake. Dad was talking about his work, about how this manager or that was driving him crazy, and he sighed and said, 'Lester, it's a dog-eat-dog world.' Then he said, 'We need to talk about this writing obsession of yours. You're twenty years old now, and someone needs to make you aware of the facts of life.'

"Dad went on to tell me what a struggle life was, even for those who were bright and ambitious. He told me it was time to look life in the eye. He explained that the majority of those who wanted to be writers never got published, and that most of those who did get published made little money. He said he was telling me this for my own good, that someone had to shine some light on the truth. He said I'd been going to college for two years without declaring a major, and it was time for me to be pragmatic. Mom used to say at times Dad could suck the life right out of a room, and often she was right.

"After that conversation with him, a pall fell over my boyhood dream. Self-doubt and visions of an unfulfilled life crept into my psyche. Amy and I were about to be married, weren't we? I didn't want to lead her into a life of empty vodka bottles, rejection slips, and unpaid bills. No one would be happy with that. I decided to drop the book-writing dream and declare a major in business administration.

"Everyone was now optimistic about our future, and when I graduated I went into the construction business. Don't get me wrong … I've enjoyed being a contractor, and the money has been more than adequate. Our bills are paid, the lights are burning, and there is always food on the table. We go on lots of costly vacations, and we can afford some nice things. But every now and again I'll sit and wonder what sort of writer I could have been. I read others' books, but not a lot. I find myself feeling jealous every time I see some new novel on the best-seller list, jealous that mine never got there.

"So, you see, this is how it is with my two boys. I don't want them to ever feel that they didn't at least get a good shot at their dreams. If they're successful, that's great, but if they're not, I want them to decide when to call it quits, not me. I don't want it to be my decision. I want them to feel like I've always been there, behind them a hundred percent, cheering them on and wishing them success at whatever they decide to do."

"It's nice to be young," Harry said. "I envy your boys."

"They have their whole lives ahead of them."

"For what it's worth, I think you're a pretty good father. Your boys are lucky to have you."

"Thanks," I said.

Both of us yawned despite all the coffee we'd consumed. It was getting late, and we decided to call it a night. Harry left some cash on the table for the waitress, and the two of us left the coffee shop. Harry said he was busy the next day, but he wanted to meet me the day after that. We decided to meet at his house again.

I climbed into my car and drove home, and the streets were dark and quiet. It was about a forty-minute drive from Newport to my house, and I spent the time thinking about my conversation with Harry. When I arrived home, Amy was in the kitchen with Miles and three of his friends. They were baking chocolate chip cookies, and the kitchen was a mess. The TV was blaring from the family room, and the windows were all open.

"How'd your meeting go?"

"Fine," I said.

"How's your friend Harry?"

"He's doing good."

"What'd you two talk about?"

I thought it was kind of odd for Amy to ask me this, since Miles and his friends were right there with us. I just smiled at Amy and said, "Gobbledygook." She gave me the weirdest look.

CHAPTER 8

Pillow Talk

Amy and I went to bed at about eleven. We climbed under the covers and turned out the lights. I liked sleeping with Amy, next to her warm body and beating heart. I lay there on my back with my eyes wide open, thinking. Amy was on her side, facing away from me. "Are you asleep?" I asked, and she said no. "Do you think we're too easy on our boys?"

"Why do you ask that?"

"Because of what we do. Because we're paying half of Danny's bills when he's already a grown man. Because we let Miles live in our house without requiring him to get a job. Do you think we're being too easy on them?"

"Danny is going back to college. He seems to want to be financially independent."

"That's true," I said.

Miles is another story."

"You know, he thinks he's going to be rich and famous soon. He's going to bring all his friends with him as his loyal entourage. He's going to live in a Beverly Hills mansion and drive around in a Rolls Royce."

"I know. He's told me."

"Do you remember when I was going to be a famous writer?"

"Yes, Lester. I remember that."

"Do you ever wonder what sort of life we'd be living if I'd stuck with my writing?"

"Not really."

"Harry says I'm a good father."

"Yes, you're a good father," Amy said.

"You think the boys will be okay?"

"The boys will be fine. So why all this talk about them?"

"Harry asked about them tonight. He said he wanted to know more about our family. I told him all about the boys and what they were doing. I came to realize that they could probably be doing a lot better, and I began to wonder whether we had made the best decisions raising them, about whether we should have required them to be more self-sufficient. I was just wondering, that's all. You're probably right, that they're going to be fine."

There was a full moon outside, and its light poured through the window and filled our bedroom. I saw Amy turn her head so she was now facing me. The moonlight lit up the curious expression on her face, and she asked, "Do you and Harry talk about me?"

"Yes," I said.

"What have you told him?"

"Actually, Harry's told me more about you than I told him."

"What does that mean?"

"It means we talked about my recent run to Tijuana, about how it made you feel. He wanted me to understand what I did to you." Amy did not respond. "I'm sorry," I said, because I knew she was now angry. Every time I brought up Tijuana, she immediately got mad at me. Mentioning the trip stirred up a lot of negative emotion, and I wished I hadn't said anything at all. "I really am sorry," I said.

"You should be," Amy replied.

"Harry thinks I need to grow up."

"He's right about that."

We were both quiet for a moment, and Amy rolled over so she was facing away from me again. "Do you believe in God?" I asked.

"Honestly, Lester, let's go to sleep."

"Can't you answer me?"

"You want to know if I believe in God?"

"Yes," I said. "Do you?"

"I don't know, Lester. I suppose I do. I suppose there's something out there, a force of one kind or another. It's hard to believe everything we see in the world just happened without a purpose. Are you thinking of changing your mind? Are you now thinking of believing in God?"

"No," I said. "I was just curious where you stood."

"Does Harry believe in God?"

"No," I said. "Harry is an atheist." I expected Amy to turn and look at me, but she didn't. I had finally said it, that Harry was an atheist. I don't know why this was so difficult to say.

"No wonder you two get along so well."

"We agree on a lot of things."

"I don't know if that's good or bad."

"Harry says I don't have to believe in God to stay sober. He doesn't believe in God, and he's been sober for fourteen years."

"Good for him."

"It's funny, Amy, but all this time I've thought of my drinking as my own personal problem, worried about how it affected my life. But Harry's given me a view into my soul. You do believe we all have a soul, don't you? I'm not talking about a religious soul, the kind that floats up to heaven when one dies. I'm talking about that biological miracle between our ears and in our rib cages, that living, breathing, pulsating sense of self-awareness. Each of us has a soul, and some souls are just plain selfish. An alcoholic's soul is one of those particularly selfish souls. I realized all this while I was talking to Harry. He asked me to describe my trip to Tijuana from your viewpoint, rather than from mine, and you know what? I actually couldn't do it.

"I was surprised to learn that I had never even considered how you felt while I was gone. Harry says you're going to leave me if I drink again, and he was right to say this. It hurt my feelings, but it was true. So where did all this selfishness come from? Have I always been this way, and so I drank? Or did the drinking make me selfish? It's like the chicken and the egg thing, isn't it? Which came first, the selfishness or the drinking?

"I can't even begin to count the number of times I've hurt you, the number of times I've let alcohol twist my thinking and behavior into something ugly in your life. Do you remember when we got married, how I wrote our vows? Wasn't there something in there about loving you always and being good to you? I'm sure there was. What in the world have I been thinking?

"And the Tijuana trip was nothing compared to the others, when I'd be gone for days at a time without even bothering to call you.

I'd be off carousing in my blackout nightmares, doing God knows what to whom, never giving a second thought to the harm I was inflicting on you. I'd come home with my tail between my legs, my head throbbing and stomach churning, expecting you to feel sorry for me and take me back into your loving arms. I'd stink of sweat, alcohol, and stale cigarette smoke. There'd be cuts and scrapes on my arms, and vomit stains on my shirt and pants. I was disgusting. I was rotten to the core. Certainly you'd never signed up for this; it was not something we'd ever agreed to. Harry thinks he can help me, and I'm hoping you'll please be patient. I guess what I'm trying to say is that I'm truly sorry, and that I hope you haven't given up on me. You haven't given up on me, have you? Amy?"

She didn't respond to my question, and I leaned over and looked at her face. She was sound asleep. I put my hand on her shoulder and shook it gently to wake her. "What do you want?" she mumbled.

"I've been talking to you. Have you heard anything I said?"

"Are you still awake?" she asked.

"Yes, I'm awake."

"I'm so tired. Can't you just go to sleep?"

I left her alone. She quickly fell back asleep, and I rolled over to my side and tried to do the same. But I could not sleep. I just lay there on my side, stewing in my thoughts.

I was being selfish again, expecting Amy to stay awake and listen to my ramblings. When would this end? When would I stop talking about myself? I always seemed to be so self-centered. I remembered that during one of my drunken runs to Las Vegas I hired a prostitute and paid for a room. We went inside and sat on the edge of the bed, where I talked and talked about my pathetic life. My deal with the prostitute was that she would listen to me for an hour, paid in advance. She was a pretty girl but dressed like a Las Vegas hooker. She wore a high skirt and low-cut top, and had a glittery sort of wig on her head. I paid for the hour, and she stuffed the cash into her small leather purse.

Although everything I talked about that night seemed of great importance at the time, I can't remember anything I said. I do remember crying a lot. I remember the girl going to the bathroom to get me a large wad of toilet paper to dry my eyes and face. But why was I crying? And what was I talking about? To this day, I don't know. The girl kept checking her watch to see when we would be done, and when the hour was up she let me know she was going to leave. I asked her if I could pay for another hour, and she said, "It's your money." I never told Amy about this evening. I didn't have sex with the girl, but it has seemed to me since that night that talking and baring my soul to another woman was maybe even a worse transgression. Sex is intimate, but there's nothing more intimate than talking to someone. I mean really talking.

I wished Amy were awake. I felt like talking to her, but I didn't want to disturb her sleep. I had a good feeling about my meetings with Harry, and I wanted to share my optimism. I had never felt comfortable with all the God talk in AA, yet that was all I'd ever experienced. I'd been going to AA meetings on and off for over thirty years, and not once did I run into a character like Harry who was willing to sit down and rewrite the steps and come up with a program that made sense. It was so encouraging! I know AA regulars would cringe at the thought of what Harry was doing, and they would probably call it an example of an alcoholic's ego run amok. But who wrote the steps to begin with but a handful of imperfect human beings who were just trying to survive their alcoholism?

"You won't be able to do it!" That's the mantra of the defeatist. That's the naysayer and the cynic. I now choose not to listen to them. Harry was right, that I wasn't powerless over alcohol. When I was arrested in Tijuana, the judge asked me a question no American judge had ever asked me. As I stood there wiping blood from my eye, he said, "Why were you drinking and driving on our streets?" The question took me by surprise, and I didn't have an immediate answer for him. Then he asked me the question again, and I told him I was an alcoholic. That was my answer, that I was an alcoholic. I figured if the judge knew anything about alcoholism, he'd understand that I just couldn't have helped myself. But now I saw I wasn't answering the judge's question at all; I was just palming off a lame alcoholic's excuse. I wasn't drunk earlier that afternoon when I drove my truck into the parking lot of that bar, and I knew exactly what I was doing when I ordered my drink. I had a choice, and I chose poorly. The problem wasn't that I was powerless over alcohol. I was sober earlier that afternoon, and whether I chose to drink was completely up to me.

If only Amy had been awake. I'd have told her all this, and I would have convinced her Harry was leading me in the right direction. Then I thought of Agnes and the day she bailed me out of jail when I was in my twenties, and I remembered asking her how to stop drinking. She answered, "You just don't take the first drink," she said. It had made no sense to me at the time, but now in light of what I'd learned from Harry, it made perfect sense. I wondered what Agnes would think of Harry's way of doing things, rewriting the steps the way he did. I remembered when Agnes died; she was eighty-five and suffering from congestive heart failure. She wound up in the hospital, and the doctors said she didn't have much longer to live. Her son Henry called me and told me I ought to come pay her a visit, that she'd been asking about me.

I've never handled the death very well, and rather than go straight to the hospital, I stopped at a liquor store and purchased a pint of vodka, which I drank in my car. One thing led to another, and the next thing I knew I was seated on a bar stool downing doubles one after the other.

I got hammered that night, and I don't remember much of what happened. I remember being asked to leave the bar by a large well-dressed man who I assumed was the bouncer. I walked down the sidewalk to find my truck, and I tripped over a curb, landing on the palms of my hands. People were staring at me, and one fellow came over to see if I was okay. Then I remember getting in my truck and driving. This was a big mistake, for the next thing I knew, I was in the emergency room of a hospital, restrained by leather straps to a gurney. A security guard stood at the door, a short friendly-looking fellow in uniform. My T-shirt was covered with blood, and my head was throbbing something awful. I asked the security guard what I was doing there, and he said I'd been in an accident, that I'd run into a streetlight. It was terrifying, that I'd blacked out through the whole event. I'd missed the accident, the fight I put up with the cops when they tried to arrest me, and the ambulance ride to the hospital. I didn't even remember the doctor sewing stitches into my forehead.

Worst of all, I'd missed my opportunity to see Agnes before she died. She had passed that evening, and I'd never even said good-bye. I thought if anyone could understand my behavior that day, it would be Agnes, but that didn't make things any better. They say in AA that if you feel guilty, you probably are, and about this I think they're right. Was I truly powerless over alcohol, or was I just a jerk? No one had twisted my arm and forced me to drink that night, for it was a calculated and sober decision. I had pulled into the parking lot, opened the liquor store door, put the bottle on the counter, and paid for it. At any point in time I could have stopped and turned around.

I looked at Amy, lying there asleep. I wondered if she was dreaming, and I wondered what sort of things she dreamed about. Did she dream about her job? Or maybe about Miles and Danny? Or even about our dog, Buster? Or maybe she dreamed about our life years ago, the days we were first together, when we were crazy in love. Sometimes I think about those days. One should be able to look back to those kinds of memories with a lot of fondness, and I do. But they also make me sad at times, not because I'll never have them back, but because of what I'd let our lives become.

Instead of looking forward to seeing me at the end of each workday, now Amy wondered if I'd even be home. For years I'd believed all this was the result of my powerlessness, but now I saw things differently, thanks to Harry. It was all up to me. The gauntlet was at my feet, and I was being challenged.

CHAPTER 9

Fear and Loathing

"Are you a W. C. Fields fan?" Harry asked, and I laughed and said yes. We were sitting in his library again in the early afternoon, and it had been two days since our last meeting. "I remember in one of his movies he steps into a bar and asks the bartender, 'Did I spend a hundred-dollar bill here last night?' The bartender says yes, and Fields says, 'Thank God, I thought I lost it.'"

"I remember that scene," I said.

"It was funny, no?"

"Yes, it was very funny."

"Fields was a notorious alcoholic, yet he made us feel comfortable with his alcoholism. He made it funny to be a drunk. He had completely given in to his condition, and he made it a way of life worthy of laughter and emulation. I adored this guy during my drinking years, and I would watch and rewatch his old movies.

"But if drinking was so much fun, why was I growing so miserable? Why was I losing all my friends, and why were my law partners conspiring against me? Why were my wife and daughter so angry? No one I knew seemed to be laughing at my antics, and the joy in my life was all but gone. I felt ill, despondent, and lonely. Once I sobered up, these feelings gradually went away, but I still found myself laughing at W. C. Fields movies, sometimes wishing I'd never stopped, longing for the good old days when I could polish off a bottle of whiskey before the night even began. As we get into our sobriety, and as the distance from our drinking increases, it becomes so easy for us to forget just what disasters we were. It's strange, isn't it, the way we forget?"

"Yes, it is."

"I have a feeling that Fields's real life wasn't so great, that it was not as charmingly amusing as he would have liked us to believe. I have no way of proving this, but I'm guessing he was a miserable soul right up until the time he died in a sanatorium of a stomach rupture brought on by his chronic drinking. He was in his sixties, like you. Are you ready to die at your age?"

"No, I'm not."

"Alcoholism can be deadly."

"I know," I said.

"You know, I'm trying to save your life."

"I appreciate that."

"I no longer watch W. C. Fields movies. They don't make me laugh; in fact, they make me feel sorry for the guy. It's like the story I told you about the drunken judge. It made you laugh, didn't it? But the truth is that alcoholism isn't very funny."

"No," I agreed.

"We're about ready for the fourth step, and I see you didn't bring your book."

"No, I didn't."

"You can borrow mine," Harry said.

Harry stood up and retrieved his copy of the Big Book from a shelf. He handed the book to me and asked me to read step four. I thumbed through the pages until I found the chapter. Then I cleared my throat and said, "We made a searching and fearless inventory of ourselves." I asked, "Are we going to rewrite this step?"

"No, we're going to leave it exactly as it is. It's an excellent step, and there's no reason to change a single word."

"Okay."

"What does this step mean to you?"

I thought for a moment. I was a sixty-year-old man, yet I felt like such a neophyte in Harry's presence. I said, "It means we analyze our character."

"You forgot to include the word *moral*."

"So I did."

"What does moral mean to you?"

"Knowing the difference between right and wrong?"

"And how do we know what's moral and what's immoral?"

"I'm not sure."

"Is it moral to kill another human being?"

"No, of course not."

"What if you're a soldier? Is a soldier immoral?"

"Well, now you're talking about war. It's okay to kill the enemy when you're in a war."

"So killing can be moral?"

"I'm not sure I would call it moral."

"Well, either it's moral or it's immoral. You can't be just a little bit pregnant."

"Okay, I guess it's moral for a soldier to kill an enemy."

"And which side are we talking about?"

"What do you mean?"

"If two countries are at war, which one of them is good and which is bad?"

"I would have to know more about them."

"Don't you think both countries think they're in the right?"

"Probably."

"Only probably?"

"Well, yes for sure. Both countries would think they're in the right, or they wouldn't be going to war."

"So the soldiers on each side are acting morally?"

"I guess you would have to say so."

"Then according to you war is moral, since we've agreed that the participants are all acting morally. You're saying that the organized slaughter and maiming of thousands of human beings over an issue of political contention is a moral act, since the soldiers on each side of the conflict are moral. That's what you've agreed to. It's preposterous, isn't it?"

"Yes, it actually is."

"Are you aware that over 84 percent of citizens in this country identify themselves as Christian?"

"That sounds about right."

"Don't most morals in the country come from Christianity?"

"Yes," I said. "I think that's fair to say."

"And Jesus taught his followers the difference between right and wrong?"

"Yes, I'd agree."

"What did Jesus say about getting slapped in the face?"

"He said to turn the other cheek."

"Do you know anyone who actually does this?"

"Very few, if any."

"I worked as a lawyer in the justice system for many years. What do you think the purpose of the system is? What exactly is justice?"

"Meting out punishment for crimes?"

"It's much more than that. I've defended lots of criminals, and I can tell you what justice means to the victims of this country. It's their way of getting even with those who've wronged them. People want to retaliate. If you're violated, the perpetrator must be made to pay for what he's done. If a news reporter slanders you, you can't just go punch him in the face. If a thief makes off with all your money, you can't settle the score by robbing something of value to him. If a rapist attacks your daughter, you can't exact revenge by pinning him down and cutting off his private parts.

"We have a legal system, and you're expected to use it. So what exactly is this legal system? It's a gigantic organization of lawyers and judges and paralegals and secretaries and bailiffs and bondsmen and police officers charged with the task of making sure criminals get their just desserts. When someone slaps you in the face, the justice system affords a civilized way to slap him back. Make no mistake about it, that's exactly how people see our legal system. It's completely unchristian. There's no turning of the other cheek. If you believe in the teachings of Jesus, our justice system is an immoral institution."

"I can see that."

"So now I've shown you that war is moral and justice is immoral. Confusing, isn't it? Where exactly does that leave us?"

"I don't know."

"How are you going to make a searching and fearless moral inventory of yourself?"

"I don't know."

"You're going to be like the man who tells the art dealer at his gallery, 'I don't know much about art, but I know what I like.'"

"Okay."

"I once defended a man named Ernest Handley for the robbery of a gas station in Anaheim. Ernest was thirty-eight years old, married with three children. He lived in a modest home in Santa Ana, and he had worked for years at a company in Irvine that manufactured parts for pool tables. The company Ernest worked for suddenly found itself competing with the Chinese, whose cheap labor and lax regulations allowed them to manufacture the same pool table parts at half the price. There was no way Ernest's company could compete, and they shut the doors and let all their workers go.

"Ernest found himself without a job. He had worked for the pool table company for years, and all he had learned to do was to make leather pockets to hold pool balls. When he searched for a new job, he found that no one needed a worker who knew how to make pool ball pockets, and the jobs that were available to him would never pay enough to cover his bills. He hadn't accumulated any sort of nest egg in case of such an emergency. It wasn't like he'd been blowing money on expensive cars or other possessions, for he was a simple family man who lived within his means. When he was let go from the plant, he had nothing to fall back on.

"Several months went by, and both Ernest and his wife had been looking for work. His wife found a night job cleaning office spaces for a janitorial company. It didn't pay enough money to cover the family expenses, but it helped put food on the table while Ernest continued to look for a job.

"Ernest borrowed money from family and friends until he wore out his welcome, and his past-due bills continued to mount. Finally, the bank sent Ernest a notice that they were going to foreclose on his house. Ernest panicked, for his house payment was far less than what they'd have to pay in rent. Besides, his credit had already been ruined, and qualifying for a decent rental would be a virtual impossibility. What could he do? Surely, he would eventually find a job, but in the meantime, he was facing an ugly financial crisis. Unless you've been in this position yourself, it's difficult to empathize with Ernest and the severity of the situation. Ernest grew consumed with fear over what was going to happen to his family, and he took the only option available to him.

"Ernest took a handgun that he'd kept in the house for protection, and he drove the streets of Orange County, trying to work up the nerve to do what he had to do. He drove the streets for three hours, until his car was low on gas. He had only ten dollars in his wallet, and he stopped at a gas station. He gave the cashier the ten dollars and went to pump the gas into his car. When he was done, he grabbed his handgun and went back to the cashier. Pointing his gun at the woman, he demanded all her money, and she handed over several hundred dollars.

"Then suddenly and without warning, a man from behind grabbed Ernest's gun and tackled him. Ernest was neither large nor particularly strong, and struggling was pointless. Ernest was now facedown on the floor, and the man was sitting on his back. Ernest began to cry. He was desperate, frustrated, and scared. The cashier called 911. The cops showed up promptly, and they arrested Ernest and took him downtown. It was his wife who came to see me a couple weeks later, asking if I would defend him. They obviously didn't have any money, but I agreed to take the case regardless. Every now and again I took on cases just for the challenge."

"So what happened to Ernest?" I asked.

"How do you think the jury found him?"

"I don't know."

"The trial went very fast. There wasn't anything we could do to create even the smallest degree of doubt that Ernest had robbed the gas station. They had him dead to rights."

"Yes," I said.

"So the trick here was to play to the jury's empathy for Ernest. Everything rested on my summation."

"What'd you say?"

"I told them all about Ernest and his situation, telling them about how he had lost his job, how he'd been looking for a new one, how his wife was laboring nights cleaning up after people for a pitiful wage, how Ernest and his wife had done everything they could to pay their bills, including borrowing from relatives and friends until their welcome was exhausted. Then I asked the jurors to put themselves in Ernest's shoes. I'm very good at what I do, and I have to say, this was one of my more eloquent closing arguments. Several of the women jurors looked to be on the verge of tears. Even the men appeared sympathetic. It took the jury just two hours to reach a verdict. They found Ernest innocent of all charges, and Ernest's wife broke out in tears."

"So what happened to Ernest?"

"The papers ran a story on the trial. There were a couple of subsequent opinion pieces and a whole page full of letters to the editor. The consensus was almost unanimous, that a man had a moral obligation to feed and protect his family. You asked what happened to Ernest? During the weeks after the trial, he was still without a job, and the bank began the foreclosure proceedings. Then it happened."

"What happened?"

"The owner of a furniture manufacturing company had read the stories and letters about Ernest in his morning paper, and he called my office to get Ernest's phone number. I gave it to him, and the man called Ernest and offered him a job. He said he would pay off arrears on Ernest's mortgage to stop the foreclosure proceedings, and that he would take these amounts in installments from Ernest's future paychecks at the company."

"Wow," I said.

"To this day, I get a Christmas card from Ernest's family every year."

"So you did good."

"Did I really? I got a letter from the gas station owner complaining about what I'd done, railing about the future safety of his employees and customers, worrying about the security of his gas station. His point was that if the courts let every holdup guy go free just because of some hard-luck story, that it would become open season on honest businesses. He had a good point, and I wonder what you think."

"About hard-luck stories as a defense?"

"Yes," Harry said.

"I don't know."

"Was the holdup moral or immoral? Was it right or wrong?"

"Well, it was the wrong thing to do, but I understand why Ernest did it."

"Was the jury's decision moral?"

"That's a tough question."

"Step four asks you to take a moral inventory, but how are you going to do this? What's moral, and what's not? Sometimes this question isn't so easy to answer. How should you handle this?"

"I don't know."

"I say it isn't that complicated."

"It isn't?"

"Like I said, the man doesn't know much about art, but he knows what he likes."

"I still don't get that."

"You go with your gut."

"With my gut?"

"You know, Christians have a much easier time with this. Follow the simple teachings of Jesus Christ, and you will be on a moral road, no? Don't kill others, and don't slap people back in the face. Do unto others as you would have them do unto you, and don't take the Lord's name in vain. Christians have a very difficult time staying moral, but at least the rules are written down, readable, and relatively simple to follow. But for the atheist, it's a whole different story. The atheist needs to come up with morals on his own. He needs to follow his gut."

"That's it?"

"Unless you're mentally ill, I think you'll have a pretty good feeling for it, sorting out right from wrong. Don't you think you have a pretty good feeling for knowing the difference?"

"I suppose so."

"When you do something right, don't you feel good about yourself and want to pat yourself on the back? And when you do something wrong, don't you feel guilty?"

"Yes, that's true."

"And when you see other people doing something wrong, don't you feel shocked or incensed, but just the opposite holds true when you see them doing something right?"

"Yes," I said.

"Morality comes to us naturally."

"It seems so."

"Which brings us back to step four, making a searching and fearless moral inventory of ourselves. We're being asked to sort out rights from wrongs. Some people feel this step is all about describing everything they've done wrong in their lives, but the step says a moral inventory, implying that we look at both the good and the bad. Just as detailed as this inventory should be about all the wrong things we have done, so it should be equally inclusive of all the right directions we've gone."

"Okay."

"To thine own self be true, no?"

"Yes, I can see that."

"I want you to go with your gut. You won't be concerned with the written laws of our judicial system or with the Bible, Koran, or Buddhist Tripitaka. You'll have faith in your ability to discern these things correctly by going with your gut."

"Okay," I said.

"Did you ever do a step four in rehab?"

"Not really."

"Let me get you a paper and pen."

"We're going to do this now?"

"There's no time like the present." Harry stood up and walked out of the room. He came back with a pad of paper and a ballpoint pen. He handed the items to me and sat down.

"I don't know where to start," I said.

"Do you love your wife?"

"Of course I do."

"Write it down," Harry said. I wrote down that I loved my wife.

"What's next?"

"Do you love your sons?" Harry asked. I said yes, and he told me to write that down.

He continued, "Let's make this simple. Have you done anything to your wife or sons over the past several days that makes you feel guilty?"

"Actually, yes."

"Such as?"

"I didn't tell Amy that I'm no longer going to AA meetings. I lied to her. I told her I was going to a meeting last night, and instead I went to Starbucks and hung out for a couple hours, drinking coffee and working on my laptop."

"Why didn't you tell her the truth?"

"I thought it might cause her to worry."

"What do you think she's going to feel like if she finds out you're going to Starbucks?"

"She's going to worry. She's going to be angry that I lied to her."

"She'll find out eventually."

"Yes, she probably will."

"Write it down. Write down that you lied to her."

"Okay," I said.

"Do you need any more help from me, or can you handle this on your own?"

"I can probably handle it."

"Have at it then. I'll be in the family room if you need me. I'll give you an hour. That should give you enough time to get a lot down. Remember to be searching and fearless. And don't forget the good stuff, the right things you've done. Everyone has good stuff they can write about. If you need me, just come get me. Are we good?"

"We're good," I said.

Harry stood up and left the room.

I began to write. It was slow going at first. I had never been given an assignment like this, put on the spot to write so truthfully about myself. I was proud of my abilities as a writer, and I took care to use complete sentences, proper punctuation, and correctly spelled words. It seemed easier to come up with my immoral behavior, so I used it as a starting point.

I decided to write down an incident that occurred several months ago that was still fresh on my conscience. It had occurred with one of my nicer customers. The woman liked me and was very trusting. Her project was going along smoothly, and I was having very little difficulty with my workers and subcontractors. I was building a restaurant for her in an old section of Santa Ana, in an aged building she had purchased for the purpose of opening her first eating establishment. She was an extraordinary chef but wasn't too familiar with construction, and when we were almost done with the project, she asked me how much it would cost to put a new roof on the building. That was her mistake.

The woman figured we may as well do the work while we were there, that the old roof would probably need replacement soon. I called up my roofing subcontractor, and he gave me a price for the work. The price was exorbitant, and I knew it was out of line, but I quoted the price to my customer anyway, telling her my subcontractor did excellent work. The lady accepted the price, but then rather than have the subcontractor do the work, I shopped the job around to other roofing contractors in the area and found someone willing to install the roof for half the price. We put on the new roof, and I charged the lady the originally quoted price and pocketed the windfall profit for myself. I never told her about the deal I was getting, never offering to lower the price. This sort of thing goes on all the time in the construction business, but that didn't make me feel any better about what I'd done. The woman trusted me and liked me, and I took advantage of her. What I did to her bothered me, and I knew it.

I wrote down this little roofing story on the pad of paper Harry had given me. I then thought further about immoral things I had done in my business, and I came up with quite a few. I then wrote about how I'd recently mistreated Amy, and I wrote about the bad example I'd been setting for our boys. I then wrote about the sixteen years I'd been sober. It was amazing how many immoral things I'd done even during those years, especially in my business dealings. I was taking advantage of people in ways that were perfectly legal on their face, but that were also perfectly wrong. There are lots of legal ways to get over on subcontractors and customers in the construction business, and I knew about all of them. I'd always put on an air of fairness and integrity, when deep down I knew exactly what I was doing.

I then went back to the drinking years of my twenties, when I was completely out of control. I wrote about how the jobs I had going were a total disaster, and how I was driving my poor customers crazy. I wrote about how I was signing on new projects and taking illegal deposits from these new clients, not telling them the trouble I was in and using their money to pay past-due bills on other jobs. It was like some wild Ponzi scheme. When I was twenty-nine, I filed for bankruptcy and wiped the slate completely clean. It was clean for me, but not for the people who received my notices. Filing bankruptcy is legal, yes, but it's a completely immoral act. I wrote this down.

I then thought back further, back to school and during the years I was in college. I remembered how I befriended a boy named Aaron Harris. Aaron was in our dormitory several rooms down from mine, and he had a difficult time making friends. He was a short, skinny boy with thick glasses and a face full of painful-looking acne. Aaron had the most annoying habit of picking his nose when he thought you weren't looking, and when you caught him at it, he'd pretend to be scratching his face.

But the main thing about Aaron was that he was smart. He studied diligently and got good grades while the rest of us were drinking and horsing around, and despite the fact that he was very friendly, he didn't participate in much of what we did. But I found a use for him. I took advantage of his loneliness and discovered Aaron was thrilled to have me as a friend, so thrilled that he'd write my history papers for me and let me turn them in under my name. I didn't care for the boy, but in private I became his best pal. I used the poor kid in the worst way, feigning friendship for those well-researched history papers. After the school year was over, he sent letters to my parents' house, trying to maintain our friendship, but I never wrote him back. Eventually he stopped writing, and I have no idea whatever became of him.

I wrote down the story about Aaron in college. I then went even further back, turning to my behavior in high school. By now I was on my eighth page on the notepad. It was weird thinking back like this, as I'd put most of these memories out of my mind, but now they were coming back to me readily. Most of my high school antics had to do with my drinking, cutting school classes, lying to my parents, and vandalizing property. We vandalized a lot of property when we were in high school, my group of friends and I. We'd get drunk on Friday and Saturday nights, and having nowhere productive to go, we'd roam the streets like a pack of wild animals breaking antennas off cars, throwing rocks through windows, and peeing and defecating on people's front yards. Once in a while the police would give us chase, but we always managed to get away.

I do remember one incident that occurred when I was sober. It had nothing to do with my weekend drinking. My friend and I were asked by his mom to pick her up a Christmas tree, and she gave us twenty dollars to make the purchase. We hopped into my friend's car and devised what we thought was a most clever scheme. Rather than spend the money buying a tree from a Christmas tree lot, we'd keep the money and drive up in the mountains to find a tree to cut down for free. We stopped by my house and borrowed my dad's saw, and off we went to complete our mission. It took us about thirty minutes to get up into the mountains, and we drove along a windy road looking for an appropriate tree.

Then my friend slammed on the brakes. "That's it!" he said, and he pointed across the street. There in the very middle of a nicely manicured front yard of a home stood the perfect little Christmas tree. It was healthy and symmetrical, and stood just the right height. Next to the tree was a wheelbarrow and a shovel, and a half-full sack of manure. The tree was obviously the home owner's pride and joy. He probably spent every weekend fertilizing and watering it.

My friend and I jumped out of the car. We looked around to be sure no one was watching, and then we ran to the tree and cut it down with my father's saw. We carried the tree back to my friend's car, laughing and out of breath. When we arrived at my friend's house that evening, we brought the tree inside for his mom to see. She said, "I didn't know they sold sequoia Christmas trees!" "Oh, yes," my friend said. "It was the best one on the lot." I always did feel bad about that, wondering how the poor guy felt when he came out of his house to see a bare stump where his precious sequoia once stood. It gave me guilt pangs, and I tried not to think about it.

Now I was on my fourteenth page, and I still hadn't written anything good about myself except for the fact that I loved my wife and sons. Why was it so hard to come up with the good stuff, as Harry had called it? My hour was nearly up. I was running out of time. Well, perhaps I wasn't much of a husband, but I was a good father, wasn't I? Could I write about that? But what about the times I was drunk, the times I had left Amy and the boys alone for days on end while I was off binging, the bad example I was setting, and all the trauma I was causing? Did the boys worry about me while I was gone? They'd never shown it, and I'd never talked to them about it. That didn't mean they didn't have feelings about it, and surely having an alcoholic father was not a good thing.

So what else? What about the fact that I was a good provider? That could be some of Harry's good stuff. I worked hard and made a decent amount of money for the family to live on, didn't I? Of course, Amy worked as well and brought home a good-sized paycheck. It's not like she didn't contribute to the family budget. In fact, there had been recession years when my business was slow, when I wasn't the real breadwinner, and when without Amy's income we would have been in serious trouble. Perhaps I wasn't such a great provider after all. Perhaps I wasn't such a great anything.

"How's it going?" Harry asked. He had stepped into the room holding a cup of coffee. "I made a fresh pot of coffee if you want some."

"No, thanks," I said.

"How many pages did you fill?" Harry sat down.

"Fourteen," I said.

"Do you think you could keep going?"

"Probably."

"It's weird, isn't it?"

"What's weird?" I asked.

"How easy it is to find the bad, and how hard it is to find the good."

"Yes, I noticed that."

"You're not unusual."

"I'm not?"

"Alcoholics are not very moral people. They think they're moral, until they actually sit down and think about what they've done."

"Do I need to keep working on this?"

"I think you've done enough."

"Are you going to read it?"

"Most sponsors read fourth steps, or they have the alcoholic read them aloud. To be honest with you, none of what you've written is any of my business. It's all between you and yourself. And you're the one who has to live with what you've done, not me."

"So what do I do with this?"

"Burn it."

"Burn it?" I asked.

"You don't want anyone reading it, do you?"

"Not really."

"Then let's go burn it in the fireplace." Harry stood up, and I followed him to the front room. Harry picked up a pack of matches from the mantel and handed them to me. I lit the pages on fire, one by one, and dropped them atop the grate. "Sit down," Harry said.

I took a seat on one of the sofas, and Harry sat across from me. "So what now?" I asked.

"How do you feel about yourself?"

"Not that great."

"Do you feel like drinking?"

"Not really."

"If I drove you to the liquor store and bought you a pint of vodka, would you drink it?"

"No, I wouldn't," I said.

"Have you ever read any Hunter Thompson books?"

"Yes, I have. When I was in college, he was very popular."

"I read his stuff after I got sober. My friend Jerry recommended them to me. Do you remember me telling you about Jerry?"

"Oh, yes," I said.

"I read Thompson's books with a lot of interest at first, and I have to admit I enjoyed them. He was a very talented writer. But I grew to have the same trouble with Thompson as I have with W. C. Fields. He glorified a lifestyle that was no longer interesting to me. It actually was just pitiful the way he carried on. And just as I felt about Fields, it was hard for me to imagine that Thompson was a very happy man. Do you know how Hunter Thompson died?"

"I think so."

"He shot himself in the head at age sixty-seven."

"Yes, that's what I thought."

"He liked the title *Fear and Loathing* for a couple of his books, and some of his articles, but out of honesty to his readers, I feel he should have taken this a step further. He should have titled his works Fear and Loathing and Desperation and Loneliness and Guilt and Self-Hatred and Irresponsibility and Depression and Humiliation and Selfishness. It would have been a cumbersome title, but it would have been more accurate. People like Thompson and Fields, with all their talent, have done very little to help the alcoholic. If anything, they've only made things worse by romanticizing a lifestyle that ends badly."

CHAPTER 10

Moon River

Harry told me that the worst consequence of a lie isn't the revelation of the truth, but rather the revelation that you've been telling a lie. A week went by since Harry told me to stop going to AA meetings, and still I hadn't told Amy about it. I was still making my nightly trips to Starbucks. I would sneak my laptop into my truck and drive off to the coffee shop for an hour and a half, and then I would come home pretending I had gone to a meeting. This had to stop, and I decided to tell Amy the truth before she caught me. I wasn't going to tell her about the crazy Starbucks routine, but I was going to tell her that I was no longer going to any more meetings.

At breakfast one morning, the two of us were seated at the table, Amy eating her granola and I munching on my Captain Crunch. I tried to bring the topic up as nonchalantly as possible. I chewed and swallowed a spoonful of my cereal, and then I softly blurted out the news. "I'm not going to any more AA meetings," I said.

"What do you mean?"

"I mean just what I said."

"Why would you want to stop going to meetings?"

"I'm not getting anything out of them. Harry said if I'm not getting anything out of them, that I don't have to go."

"Are you sure that's what he said?"

"Yes," I replied.

"Are you sure this guy knows what he's doing?"

"He's my sponsor, Amy. We're working the steps. That's the important thing."

"I guess no one can force you to go," Amy said. "But it worries me a little. I thought you were supposed to be going to meetings all the time."

"I'll still be working with Harry."

"Okay, I think it's very important for you to have a sponsor."

Doing the math, I figured I'd been to six or seven hundred AA meetings in my lifetime. Amy had been to three or four. She'd never read the Big Book, and she had no idea of what AA entails. She had it in her mind, like many people do, that if you want to stop drinking you need to be a member of AA. She didn't understand that no one is literally a member, that you just show up for meetings, listen and talk, put a dollar in the basket if you're so inclined, and then stand in a circle at the end of the meeting and say the Lord's Prayer. The counselor at my last rehab told Amy that I needed to get a sponsor, so she'd had this sponsorship business on her mind ever since. She seemed to be accepting my work with Harry, and I was glad she didn't put her foot down about meetings. I was a little surprised but very glad.

"I'm seeing Harry again tonight."

"Miles and I will be clothes shopping after I get home from work. We need to buy the boy some clothes. He looks like a vagabond."

"We're on the fourth step."

"That's good, Lester."

"Harry has taught me a lot."

"And they say you can't teach an old dog new tricks." Amy winked at me.

I liked it when Amy winked at me, but what was she actually thinking? Was she truly as lighthearted as she was acting? It was hard to say. I'd been married to Amy for thirty-seven years, and I still had a difficult time reading her. She seemed pleased with the progress I was making with Harry, but what was actually going through her mind? Was it that one more of my drinking episodes and she was out the door, packing her bags and taking Miles and all her belongings with her? Was this playful demeanor of hers at the breakfast table just the calm before a storm?

I met with Harry that night at his home. To my surprise, he was dressed in an old pair of swimming trunks, a T-shirt, and flip-flops.

His hair was uncombed, and his face appeared a little red, as though he was sunburned.

"Excuse my appearance," Harry said. "Please come on in."

"You look like you've been to the beach," I said, and Harry smiled.

I entered the house and followed Harry to the library, where we took our usual seats on the chairs. Harry leaned back and crossed his legs, and I could see sand caked on his bare ankles and feet.

"I went to the peninsula this afternoon. Took a long walk on the beach. I really enjoyed myself."

"Sounds nice," I said.

He looked so strange in swimming trunks and a T-shirt, and I tried to imagine Harry at the beach on a weekday afternoon, this seventy-three-year-old gray-haired man in his shorts strolling along among the noisy children, moms, and teenagers. It's funny how you can get used to seeing someone only in a certain context. For a moment he didn't seem like the Harry I knew, but then he began to speak with his familiar voice, and his attire seemed irrelevant.

"So what's new?" he asked.

"I told Amy about the meetings. I told her I wasn't going to any more AA meetings. I said it was okay with you."

"What'd she say?"

"She asked me if you knew what you were doing."

"And how'd you reply?"

"I said you did."

"Good," Harry said.

"No more secret trips to Starbucks."

"Yes," Harry said. "That was sort of a ridiculous idea."

"So what's on tonight's agenda?" I asked.

"I want to talk to you about consequences."

"Okay."

"For years I made a living helping criminals avoid the consequences of their crimes. When most people think of a trial lawyer, they think of TV lawyers like Perry Mason or Matlock, guys who take on clients who are wrongly charged, innocents who need a competent attorney and private investigator to help find the real culprits. But the truth is that the folks who work on the government's side of the legal system do a pretty good job charging the correct people for their crimes, and most of the people I defended were guilty as hell. My job was to help them avoid paying the consequences for what they'd done. Like it or not, that was most of what I did. The money was great, but this sort of work takes its toll on a man.

"I think that the legal system should require that criminal defense attorneys be allowed to practice their craft for only a few years, and then move on to some other legal endeavor. It would be like serving combat tours; this sort of activity should be allowed for only limited periods of time. It makes one callous and cynical, and it twists one's perspective of the world. I'm not saying that being a criminal defense attorney caused me to drink, but it did make it difficult to stop. But this is all beside the point."

"It is?"

"I'd like to talk about consequences. Your wife is going to leave you, Lester."

"You've said that before."

"Your predicament is dire. It's not something you'll be able to talk your way out of, or something you can hire an attorney like me to negotiate in your favor. It will become a real consequence if you continue to drink. This happened to me when Janice and Alice left, and I've seen it happen to others in AA. Believe me when I say that it happens all the time."

"It's not what I want."

"Of course it isn't. But sometimes consequences are unavoidable. Years ago I defended a boy named Stan Dryer. He was nineteen years old, the same age as your younger son, and his father was an executive of a local pharmaceutical company. They had plenty of money, and they lived here in Newport Beach. Stan was a student at USC, and while he lived up in Los Angeles at one of the frat houses, he often came home to his parents' place on weekends.

"One Saturday he brought home a girl while his parents were off vacationing in France, and the two of them had the house to themselves. Stan invited his friends over, and the kids threw a party. Lots of alcohol, marijuana, and other drugs were available, and according to the interviews the police later conducted with the kids, everyone was having a good time, staying up late and making lots of noise, doing what kids do at parties.

"It was early Sunday morning when the police were called. The name of the girl Stan brought home was Cynthia, and she had called the police to report a rape. Cynthia was no longer at the house; instead, she was at a gas station on Coast Highway. The police came to her immediately, and she told them how Stan had raped her in his bedroom, how she'd tried to say no, but that he'd pulled off her jeans and panties and forced himself on her. She said she put her clothes back on and ran away from the house just as soon as she had the chance, and then she called 911 from her cell phone."

"Was she telling the truth?"

"She was checked out by the cops. There were some minor vaginal injuries and bruises on her arms consistent with rough sex, but no semen in the vagina. But they did find some semen on Cynthia's thigh. Stan had apparently not been careful with his used condom, and the evidence had been transferred to the girl's leg. When they checked Stan's DNA with the semen, they came up with a match. At first Stan denied having sex with the girl, and he said she must have had intercourse with one of the other boys at the party. But when the match came in, he changed his story. He said he did in fact have sex with Cynthia but that the sex was consensual. Changing his story like this looked bad for him, and the cops arrested him for rape. Later on the police were able to find a witness, another nineteen-year-old boy, named Jason Anderson, who heard Stan bragging about the rape to another boy at the party. He was willing to testify to the fact that he had heard the conversation."

"So it sounds like he was guilty. Did you get him off?"

"His father came to me with the case. He said he was desperate to get his son cleared. Having the rape charges filed against his son was bad enough, but a conviction would be unacceptable. The father said he couldn't believe his son could have done such a thing, that he'd been raised to respect women, and that he certainly knew right from wrong. I interviewed Stan and then told the father what my fee would be; he said money was no object. I didn't like the kid, for I felt he was a typical narcissistic Newport Beach teenager, the sort of kid who thought only about himself and who always seemed to evade having to take responsibility for his actions. I knew in my heart of hearts that this boy was guilty, but I agreed to defend him. After all, that's what I did for a living, right? I had enthusiastically defended a lot worse people than Stan in my time.

"We finally went to trial several months later, and I employed every tactic possible to secure a not-guilty verdict for this kid. I explained that he told the police that he didn't have sex with the girl because he was afraid of being wrongfully charged. I explained away the vaginal injuries and bruising as the result of two teenagers getting carried away in the heat of the moment. I brought in witnesses to testify that the girl was no saint, that she'd lied about her relationships with boys before. I argued that the conversation Jason Anderson overheard was misinterpreted, that Stan was merely bragging that he had had sex with the girl, as boys are inclined to do. I pointed out that Jason had been drinking and smoking marijuana, that his faculties were most likely impaired. In short, I tried to make Jason look unbelievable and Stan look like a victim, and I tried to make Cynthia look like a compulsive liar. When the testimony was over, it was time for our summations."

"How'd you do?"

"I thought I did pretty well."

"So, what was the verdict?"

"They found Stan guilty. He was sitting next to me when they read their decision, and I turned to look at him. All through the trial he had been sure he'd be let off the hook and had a smug look on his face, but now the harsh reality of the matter set in. At first he had a look of shock, and then he had a look of intense anger. 'This can't be!' he said to me, and I said I was sorry. But I wasn't really sorry. Like I said, I didn't like this kid, and he was getting exactly what he deserved. It's very tough facing consequences for what you've done, but consequences are a fact of life. You can dodge them for a while, but eventually they'll catch up to you. When I look at you, I see Stan Dryer."

"You see a rapist?"

"I see someone about to face consequences."

"If I don't stop drinking."

"Yes, if you don't stop drinking. In AA they talk about the yets. You still have lots of yets in your life. Amy hasn't walked out on you yet, and your boys aren't estranged from you. You haven't killed anyone in a car accident, and you haven't been sent to prison. You haven't been locked up in a mental hospital, not that I know of. I could go on with this."

"I get the point."

"Do you play chess?"

"Sometimes."

"Is the point to win the game or to lose the game?"

"The point is to win, of course."

"It's a microcosm, isn't it?"

"A microcosm of what?"

"It's a microcosm of life. Aren't all games a microcosm of life?"

"I don't know."

"You have your board, thirty-two chess pieces, and all the rules of the game. There are consequences for making foolish moves, and there are rewards for making smart ones. Your goal is to entrap the opponent's king, and you can win or lose, just like in real life."

"But there are so many more things to life than winning or losing," I replied.

"Are there really?"

"There's love, art, and music, to name just a few."

"They're all just chess games."

"You think so?"

"Think about it, Lester. What happens when you fall in love? You want the girl for your own, and you want her to love you in return. Quite simply, you want her to adore you just as much as you adore her. This is your goal, and you set out on your board with all your chess pieces to win her heart. There are rules you must follow, an environment you must contend with, and people and things that will be involved. You make your moves to the best of your ability, and you cross your fingers that your skill and luck will be sufficient to be competitive. If you win, you take the cherished prize. If you lose, you gather up the pieces and reset them on the board, living to fight for someone else, on another day.

"You mentioned art, didn't you? Art too is like a chess game. You have a blank canvas, which is your chessboard, and you have your men—several tubes of paint, some brushes, an artist's palate, and a bottle of turpentine. You begin the game with a goal in mind, to create something of beauty. You apply the first brushstroke of paint to your canvas, moving the first pawn forward. There are rules to follow, rules for color and proportion and perspective. And you do win or lose in art, for not all paintings are winners. Some of them wind up being admired on gallery walls, while many of them go unnoticed in closets and storage rooms, lonely and collecting dust.

"And how about music? What is music, Lester, but another chess game? Musical instruments are your game pieces. The game is governed by rules of harmony and rhythm and tone and loudness and timbre. You have your goal—to create moods, to impress others, to elicit emotion, and maybe even to make money. And there are winners and losers. Some compositions dominate the airwaves, while others are never heard by anyone but their author.

"There are winners and losers in all facets of life, and you have to ask yourself, do you want to be the player to proudly proclaim checkmate to his opponent, or do you want to be the one who's always sighing and tilting over his defeated king?"

"I guess I want to win," I answered.

"Then you've got to stop making bonehead moves, saying the wrong things, playing the wrong notes, using the wrong paint colors. You've got to stop repeating the same mistakes."

"I can agree with that."

"You know how they define insanity in AA?"

"How?" I asked.

"It's doing the same thing over and over, and expecting different consequences."

"Yes, I've heard that."

"In life there are consequences for every move you make. You need to understand this."

"You're probably right."

"The human brain is a miraculous thing."

"Pardon me?"

"The human brain," Harry said. "It's a miraculous thing, but it's highly undervalued in AA. The problem starts with step one, where alcoholics errantly believe they're powerless over alcohol. Is there any question what an amazingly useful piece of anatomy the human brain is? It doesn't just process air and blood, or bile and food, or solid waste and urine. It processes something you can't pour into a test tube or drop on a glass slide. It processes thoughts. We like some things, and we hate others. We have opinions and attitudes and emotions, and we can motivate our corporeal bodies to act on them. We dream up goals and destinations, and we invent the means to reach them. We perform complex calculations in our heads, and we create machines to perform even more complex calculations. We build skyscrapers and bridges and tunnels, and we assemble modes of transportation to move us from city to city, from continent to continent, and from earth to its moon. We cure diseases, create paintings, compose music, write books, and perform dances and plays.

"The human brain is stupendous. I can't think of anything known in the universe that is more impressive ... or more powerful. Yet everyone in AA is hung up on the first step, acquiescing to the idea that they're powerless. They have the most impressive piece of equipment known to humanity between their very ears, yet they seem so willing to give in to their addiction. I believe they're selling themselves short."

"I can see that."

"It's dangerous to think you're powerless."

"How so?"

"You've acquiesced to a loss before the game has even begun. It's absurd, isn't it? You've identified yourself as someone who has no control. Can you think of a single game where this strategy works, admitting that you're powerless?"

"Not really."

"Neither can I," Harry said. "I need a cup of coffee."

We were done for the day. Harry asked me if I wanted a cup before I left, and I said I was fine. He walked to the kitchen, where he turned on the coffee maker, and then he returned to the foyer to see me off.

Two weeks would go by before we'd meet again. During those weeks I gave a great deal of thought to what Harry had said. It all made so much sense and was so simple, that there had to be something wrong with it. But if there was, I couldn't find it. I found myself thinking often about the consequences of my drinking. And I thought about Amy. And what about Miles and Danny? I'd never noticed my drinking taking a toll on my sons' behavior, but was I wrong? How could a child live with an alcoholic and not be adversely affected? There had to be consequences. Perhaps they just hadn't manifested themselves, or perhaps I was just too blinded by my own obsession to see what was actually taking place. Maybe my support of them and their dreams wasn't support at all. Maybe I was just letting them have their way with me out of guilt, not because I loved them, but because I felt I owed them something to compensate for my bad behavior.

I didn't know a single other parent who was paying the way for their twenty-seven-year-old son, paying his rent, car payments, insurance, and cable TV bills, and I didn't know anyone who would condone letting their nineteen-year-old son live at home, eating their food and having his mom do his laundry without at least requiring that he get some kind of job. Why was I allowing all this to happen? Instead of raising two self-sufficient young men, was I raising two children who wouldn't and couldn't grow up? Was this a consequence of my drinking that I'd never seen until now? Or was I just second-guessing myself, overthinking the situation? I honestly didn't know.

Raising children is not easy. I thought about my own parents. What must they have thought of my drinking? Did they think they'd made their own mistakes when they raised me? If only they'd done this or that differently, would I have turned out normal and not alcoholic? I'd honestly never given much consideration to how my parents felt. But this too was a powerful consequence of my drinking, something I needed to understand. No parents want to see their child fail. How would I have felt if one of my own boys had drank himself into a jail cell, into the emergency room of a hospital, into bankruptcy? What would I have done if I'd seen my own son's life unravelling, making countless trips to the liquor store, shaking and digging through his pockets for change? It just goes to show how selfish the alcoholic is.

Harry and I were on the fourth step, and there were still eight more steps to go. I enjoyed hearing Harry's viewpoints, and I wondered what would be next. Would he start rewriting the steps again? What would he have to say? For the first time in years, I was actually excited about the days ahead.

In the meantime, Amy and I were getting along well. The dust seemed to have settled from the Tijuana fiasco, and so long as I didn't bring it up, Amy stayed in good spirits. The girl's resilience was amazing, and I think part of Amy's ability to put up with all my nonsense had come from her childhood. Unlike my own teetotaler parents, Amy's mom and dad were always big drinkers, and Amy had grown used to the lifestyle. I say she'd grown used to it, but I don't mean to say that she liked it. Unfortunately, no one in her life had ever shown her what life was like without booze. She went straight from her drinking parents to her drinking husband without missing a beat. In this regard, I hadn't done her any favors.

I'd always got along well with Amy's parents; in fact, we all got along famously. Their names were Vern and Lucy. When we'd visit them in Albuquerque, we'd all go out on the town drinking at local restaurants and bars. Vern and Lucy always drove Cadillacs, and I don't mean the midsized Cadillacs they sell today, but the great big tuna boat–sized vehicles they used to manufacture for people of their generation. Amy and I would sit in the giant backseat, while Vern navigated his steel behemoth through city traffic. Lucy told him what to do from the passenger seat, announcing when to turn, when to slow down, and where to stop. It was truly hilarious. Vern never once complained about Lucy's backseat driving; in fact, I think he needed and appreciated it. It was hard for me to imagine this guy ever driving anywhere by himself.

I remember several years after Amy and I were married, we flew to Albuquerque for Lucy's fiftieth birthday. It was a big deal for her, and we went to their favorite Mexican restaurant along with twenty or so of their friends. Vern drove us to the restaurant that night, and he parked in the lot. Everyone was there waiting for us, and Vern had the waiter at the restaurant slide a bunch of the tables alongside each other so we could all sit together as a group.

It was a raucous evening of joking, shouting, eating Mexican food, and drinking margaritas. The restaurant served the margaritas by the pitcher, and it seemed every five minutes Vern was asking the waiter for a new one. I don't think I've ever seen a group of people go through so much booze in a single sitting, and I tried my best to keep up, to do my fair share of the drinking. I remember after the waiter cleared away all our dirty dishes, Vern stood up to make a toast to Lucy. He said, "Here's to my very best pal and the love of my life, happy fiftieth birthday to you, Lucy!" The others all applauded and downed more margaritas.

We must have been at this restaurant for two to three hours. Vern kept tipping the mariachi band with five-dollar bills, so they kept coming by to play more music. Each time they came by, Vern asked if they knew "Moon River," but they said they didn't know what he was talking about. By the time the evening was over, I was feeling pretty drunk. Amy had been drinking along with the others, and she seemed like she was tipsy but having fun. But Vern and Lucy ... these two were plastered. When they stood up from the table, they nearly fell to the floor. They hung on to each other to steady themselves. The group of us staggered out of the restaurant and to the parking lot, and we spent another fifteen minutes saying good-byes and climbing into cars. Amy and I waited in the backseat of the Cadillac, but Vern and Lucy did not come back to the car, and Amy told me to find them. I walked around the parking lot, and I finally found them in the restaurant landscaping, both down on their knees searching for something.

It turned out that Vern had puked in the bushes, and his dentures had shot right out of his mouth. They were looking for his teeth! Lucy finally found them in the gravel next to the bushes, and she handed them over to Vern, who set them back in his mouth. The two of them then stood up and staggered toward the Cadillac. "I think I'll drive," I said, and Vern said that would probably be a good idea. He fumbled in his pocket for his keys, trying to keep his balance, and then handed them over. We left with Vern in the passenger seat and Lucy in the backseat with Amy. Vern was singing "Moon River," and Lucy was falling asleep, her head against Amy's shoulder. Amy was looking out the side window at the passing scenery. I drove about three miles, and then it happened.

My mind must have been on something else, for I was about to run a red light. I was right at the intersection, speeding right into it, with no chance of stopping. An oncoming car was approaching from the side, and he honked his horn and slammed on the brakes. Everything from that point on felt like slow motion. I yanked the steering wheel hard to my left, and the gigantic Cadillac screeched slowly out of control. We spun around and wound up on the opposite side of the road, cars all around us, everyone stopped and dumbfounded that there had been no collision. "Jesus," I said, and I guided the big car back into the proper lane. I stepped on the gas, and we sped away from the scene. "That was close," I said, and Vern just laughed. "No harm, no foul," he said. I looked in the rearview mirror at Amy and her mom. Amy had a glazed expression on her face, and her mom was now awake. "What happened?" she asked, and Amy told her she didn't need to know.

Chapter 11

Guardian Angel

I have always been extraordinarily lucky. My aunt Agnes used to say I had a guardian angel looking over me, which was ridiculous, but I guess it was an apt description.

Before I was a teenager, I was friends with a boy named Eddie Montgomery, and we used to get ourselves into all sorts of mischief. This is the same Eddie Montgomery with whom I would later drink from that mayonnaise jar. Before we were teenagers, we spent our after-school hours and summer days devising crazy and childish schemes and activities. We didn't have much adult supervision, and some of the stuff we did was dangerous.

I remember one day it was Eddie's idea for us to make a crossbow. He'd learned how to do this from one of his older brother's friends, and it required an everyday garden rake and a length of medical tubing. Using a hacksaw, we took the garden rake and sawed off the toothy rake part of the tool so that all that was left was the long wooden handle and two metal prongs. To each prong we attached the medical tubing. We ended up with a giant slingshot of a crossbow that would shoot arrows at a remarkable velocity. We shot arrows into the side of Eddie's wood-shingled house, and we shot them into the oak tree in Eddie's backyard. It wasn't very accurate, but it was a very powerful weapon.

Just joking around that afternoon, Eddie loaded the crossbow with an arrow and pointed it at me. "Surrender, or you will die," he said. He was just kidding, of course, but his finger slipped off the medical tubing and the arrow flew at me. It shot off so fast that neither of us saw it travel through the air, but I felt its feathers brush against the side of my neck. I came within an inch of having that arrow lodged in my young throat, and I can remember the thrill of that feeling to this day, the knowledge that I had escaped such a close call.

I'm not going to lie and say that I was fearless, but I did get a thrill out of cheating death and injury. Like many young people, I felt at times that I was invincible. Tragedies seemed to happen only to other people, not to me. It was just a feeling I had.

I remember one Saturday night when Eddie and I were roaming the streets downtown with nothing to do, several police cars and an ambulance roared past us to the scene of an accident. We ran as fast as we could in their same direction, hoping to see what had happened, and when we came upon the scene, we weren't disappointed.

Someone had run a red light at a high rate of speed and broadsided another car in the intersection. I recognized the car that ran the light. It was my neighbor Ted Banner's Chevy Bel Air, his pride and joy. The front end of the car was completely caved in. The entire windshield had shattered and had popped out of the car, and steam and fluids leaked from the engine compartment ... or what was left of it. A man that was standing there with us said they must have been going seventy or eighty miles per hour. Out in the middle of the street was Ted Banner's head, for he had been decapitated by the windshield during the impact. An officer brought over a blanket from the trunk of his car and placed it over the head.

In the newspaper article the next day, they said Ted had been drinking. Also dying in the accident was his girlfriend, Julie Parks, who was a cheerleader for the high school football team and had been sitting in the passenger seat. The newspaper article said both the kids had died immediately in the wreck. The reporter also editorialized a bit, railing against drunk driving and urging parents to warn their children about its tragic consequences.

You would think this scene would have made a big impression on me, and it did in its own way. It taught me that these sorts of things happened to others, but that it was unlikely they would ever happen to me. I realize now this was errant thinking, but it was honestly the way I felt about it, and I would carry these feelings with me into much of my adult life. Other people would die or get injured while I stayed alive and well.

I'm a smoker. I've smoked cigarettes since I was fifteen years old, and now I'm sixty-two. I currently smoke more cigars than I do cigarettes, but I'm still a smoker. I remember when Eddie Montgomery and I first began to smoke. There was a cigarette vending machine at a coffee shop downtown. The machine was located around a corner, secluded off the entryway of the restaurant. This was the perfect place for us to buy smokes, as adults were unlikely to see us making a purchase. Cigarettes were cheap then, easy for us to afford, and despite the fact we were underage, we used to smoke them all the time. This was many years ago, but they did know then that smoking causes cancer. But this didn't worry me. I knew that cancer was one of those things that happened to other people, remembering, I suppose, that it was Ted Banner's head under that blanket in the middle of the intersection, not mine.

The next time I met Harry was on a Tuesday evening at six o'clock. Harry said not to eat before I came, that he would make us dinner. "Do you like pasta?" Harry asked, and I told him that would be fine. He said he looked forward to feeding me.

I arrived at six sharp, and Harry opened the front door and led me to the dining room table. He was nicely dressed, but he was wearing a frilly cotton apron around his waist that I assumed once belonged to his wife. I took a seat while Harry went into the kitchen. He brought out salads and set them down; then he took a seat, and the two of us began to eat.

"This is good," I said. "What are we going to talk about tonight?"

"We're going to do step five."

"Okay," I said.

"Do you know what step five says?"

"Something about admitting to others that we were wrong?"

"That's close. Step five says that we admitted to God, to ourselves, and to another human being the exact nature of our wrongs."

"Yes," I said. "That sounds familiar."

"How are you going to admit your wrongs to God, when you don't believe in him?"

"I'm not," I said.

"Yes," Harry replied. "We'll forget about God and move on. Can you admit your wrongs to yourself?"

"Yes, I think I can. Didn't I already admit all this in step four?"

"You wrote it down, but you didn't own it."

"What does that mean?" I asked.

"It means there's a difference between writing something down and taking ownership of it. There's quite a big difference, actually.

"When I went to rehab, it was right after Janice and Alice left me to live with Kaleb. I went to get sober, but I think the primary reason I went was my hope that Janice and Alice would see it as a reason why we could all get back together. I had no idea what to expect of rehab. I didn't have a clue what they did there or how they did it, and the whole thing came as a complete surprise. Never in my life had I ever taken part in such an annoying process, going to lectures and group therapy sessions, being harassed by underpaid counselors, being required to share a bedroom with a stranger.

"I was to be trapped in this hellhole for twenty-eight days. I guess the lectures were tolerable, but group therapy was like Chinese water torture. I didn't care for listening to others whine about their lives and their drinking, but I didn't like talking about myself. I had an image of myself as someone who was a good person who had simply, through no fault of his own, become addicted to alcohol. I wanted to learn the secret tricks and techniques for kicking the habit, and that's what I expected to be taught. Instead, I was subjected to this daily routine of talking to these groups about all my private problems. After the third or fourth day, I was ready to leave."

"Did you stay?"

"I stayed for the entire twenty-eight days. I didn't like rehab any more on the last day than I did on the first, but in order to get Janice and Alice back, I thought I needed to complete the full sentence. I sat there and listened to their psychobabble and doublespeak for the entire painful month. I heard the counselors tell me that the reason I drank was because I was born an alcoholic, that it was a genetic disease, and that I was powerless.

"Then they'd have me and the others dig into our pasts to look for the underlying causes of our behavior, which was crazy, no? If we drank because we were born alcoholics, what would our childhoods have to do with it? Why were they wasting time digging into all those old and unpleasant memories? Men would recount traumatic events, sobbing and sniveling over what their parents or siblings did to them, feeling sorry for themselves. The other men in the group would pat them on the back or hug them, telling them everything was going to be okay. I hated seeing grown men cry and behave like this, like emotional women, and I found the whole scene very distasteful."

"Yes, I felt the same way."

"When it was my turn to talk, I tried to tell it like it was, exactly the way I saw it. I told them I was no angel, and I described the troubling events in my life that had led me to rehab. I told them I wanted to quit drinking. That was, after all, why we were all there, to learn to quit drinking. We weren't there to be psychoanalyzed or put through an emotional wringer. I told them about my DUIs and my misdeeds at work, about how my partners had forced me to leave my firm. I told them about the incident with Kaleb, how I'd jumped on him and tried to strangle him, and how my daughter had knocked me in the back of the head with that vase. I was very good at describing events for them, and I don't recall feeling much shame or sorrow. For it was the alcohol that had caused these problems, not me, and if only these idiots at the rehab center would teach me how to stay sober, I could go on with my life and live like a normal human being.

"I remember a counselor there named Bo who challenged me on this. I didn't care for this guy at all. He reminded me of a client I had had early in my career who was charged for soliciting child pornography ... the way he smiled and the way he dressed, and the way he tried to be so friendly. Bo had messy sandy-brown hair that I think he messed up on purpose in front of the restroom mirror each morning. This gave him an air of casualness with his group of patients. And Bo always wore soft, warm-colored sweaters over his collared shirts, with one collar purposefully tucked behind the sweater and the other dangling out, like he was just an ordinary guy not overly concerned with having a professional appearance. He was trying hard to come across as unintimidating. It was all a little too transparent and deliberate for my taste, and I wondered if the others saw what I saw when they looked at this joker.

"In any event, Bo and I had a one-on-one after one of the therapy sessions. We met in a private room, and he told me he'd been watching me and was very concerned about my progress with the program. I asked him for some specifics, and he said only one thing to me: that I needed to own my behavior. I had no idea what he was talking about—owning my behavior. "Of course I own it," I said. "It's my behavior.""

"What did he say?"

"You done with your salad?"

"Pardon me?" I looked down at my empty salad bowl and then back up at Harry. "Yeah, I'm done."

"Good. It's time for dinner. What kind of sauce do you like, marinara or Alfredo?"

"Alfredo would be great."

"Coming right up."

Harry removed the empty salad bowls from the table and took them into his kitchen. He was in there for several minutes preparing the food, and then he returned with our pasta dishes. He set the plates down on the table and took his seat. I tasted the food, and it was delicious.

"This is good," I said.

"Thanks. I'm not much of a cook, but I do know how to make pasta. Where were we?"

"You were talking about Bo the counselor."

"Oh, yes," Harry said. He stuffed a mouthful of pasta into his mouth, chewed and swallowed it, and then began to talk. "So anyway, Bo and I went around and around with this ownership issue, and we got absolutely nowhere. It was like that time you told me when you first met with your aunt Agnes. You asked her how to stop drinking, and she told you not to take the first drink. It made no sense to you. It seemed like you were asking her how to stop drinking, and she was telling you to stop drinking."

"Yes," I said. "That's how it seemed."

"Owning one's behavior is like that. Bob was telling me to take ownership of something I thought I already owned. It didn't make any sense."

"So what exactly did he mean?"

"It took me years to solve this puzzle. An alcoholic does not think clearly at first, and sometimes it takes a long while for certain concepts to make sense. I remember it finally clicked for me one day when I was having lunch with Janice. I think I told you after I got sober, Janice went ahead and married Kaleb, but regardless of this marriage the two of us stayed in touch. Every so often we'd meet for lunch. I still loved her, and I think she still loved me, despite everything that had happened between us.

"Anyway, one day when we were eating lunch, we got to talking about wedding anniversaries. I don't know how we got on the subject, but I made the mistake of bringing up our own silver anniversary years ago, during the days I was still drinking.

"I remember I had just won a big case that afternoon, and I stopped at a bar on the way home to celebrate the victory. I was going to have only a few drinks because I knew Janice was waiting for me at home. We had dinner plans that evening, and we were going to our favorite restaurant. What I didn't know was that Janice had planned a surprise party for our anniversary. All our best friends and relatives had been invited to come over to the house. Our home was filled with people and balloons and confetti, and the event was being catered by the restaurant where we were supposedly going to eat. Everyone showed up at six. Janice figured I'd be home around seven.

"Janice had all the guests park down the street so I wouldn't notice their cars, and she left word at the guard gate to call her when I drove through the entrance so she could get everyone prepared. It was to be a complete surprise, yet time dragged on.

"One drink led to another, and the next thing I knew I was getting hammered with some newly made friends at the bar. I completely forgot about our anniversary. Janice tried to reach me by phone, but she couldn't find me. An hour went by, and then another hour. Janice finally began to send the guests home, and they were worried about me. Some of them said to Janice, 'Maybe something's happened to him. Maybe you should call the police.' Janice thanked them for their concern, took them to the door, and saw them out. She didn't want to believe it, but she knew exactly what had happened.

"It would be only a matter of time before I arrived home, and I'd be in no condition to entertain guests. I did finally show up at the house around midnight. The front door was locked, and it seemed like it took over an hour get the stupid key into the keyhole. I staggered into the house and threw my coat over a chair, flicking on the front room lights. It was a very strange scene, all the balloons and confetti and decorations without any people. 'Oh, no,' I said to myself, suddenly realizing what had happened. Janice appeared from the hallway in her nightgown, having heard me enter the house. God, I was dead drunk, but I wasn't too drunk to recognize I had hurt and embarrassed my wife deeply. I could tell she couldn't decide whether to start crying or throw a lamp at me. 'Janice—' I said, beginning to explain, but she interrupted me. 'I hate you!' she snapped. Tears began to fall from her eyes and down her cheeks. 'Sleep on the sofa, Harry. I don't want you anywhere near me.'"

"You hurt her feelings."

"Oh, did I ever. When we were at lunch, I made the mistake of bringing this story up while we were talking about anniversaries. I guess I thought that after all these years she might have forgiven me, or at least not have such strong feelings about it. But I was wrong. She had the same look on her face as she did that night, and I reached out to touch her hand. 'I'm sorry I brought this up,' I said. 'I'm sorry it ever happened.' She pulled her hand away from me and said, 'Are you? The trouble with you, Harry, is that you think you can make all those years go away by saying you're sorry. I know you can't go back in time and fix things, but sorry just isn't enough. You still blame the booze for everything that occurred between us. You've never admitted it was you who decided to drink. You've never owned up to this.'"

"Wow," I said.

"The key word here is *owned*."

"I think I'm understanding this."

"You need to get it. We can't move on to the next step until you get it." Harry looked down at his pasta. "I've been talking too much. My dinner's going to get cold." Harry started eating his pasta, and I continued eating mine. We were quiet for a while, munching on our food. Then Harry said, "When you decide to take ownership of your behavior—and I mean real ownership—the whole situation becomes very frightening."

"Frightening?"

"Yes, that's exactly the word I want to use."

"Okay."

"Lie down in your bed tonight, and think about it. Think about it while the lights are out and the room is dark and silent, while you have no distractions. Think about all the people you've hurt, all the lives you've put at risk, all the loved ones you've betrayed, and then think about the fact that you've done all this of your own free will. Think about the fact that you and you alone are responsible for it all, that you're not the person you thought you were. It wasn't the booze, or the step one powerlessness, or the symptom of some iffy disease. It was you!

"Do you understand what I'm saying? It was you who went to the liquor store, who parked your car in the parking space, who entered through the storefront door, who dug through his wallet for cash and handed it over to the clerk in exchange for your vodka. It was you who stepped into that bar, parked your rear on a bar stool, and asked the bartender to pour you a drink. You knew full well exactly what you were doing each and every time you did it, and you did it with purpose and intention. If you can truly see this, if you get around your old lies and deceptions, it will frighten you like nothing ever has. I promise you, you will feel fear. The blood will rush from your head. Your limbs will feel weak, and your heart will pick up pace. You will understand just the sort of person you are, without all the phony window dressing, without all the clever disguises, without the smoke and mirrors.

"I implore you to do this tonight as you close your eyes in bed. Then after you've done this, look at your wife sleeping beside you and recall all the things you've done to her. I'm not talking about what the alcohol made you do to her, but what you deliberately did by making your sober choices. Then ask yourself why she's still there at your side and ask yourself if you deserve her. If this doesn't scare you to death, nothing will."

"I think I see what you mean."

"Do it tonight. This is your assignment for step five. If you can do this tonight, successfully, you will have finally admitted to yourself the exact nature of your wrongs."

"What about the third part of the step?"

"About admitting your wrongs to another?"

"Yes," I said.

"Isn't necessary."

"Okay."

"Like I said before, this is some very personal stuff. It is your business, not mine. This is not a church confessional; it's just my dining room. I'm only here to share what I've learned."

Harry and I were now both done with our dinners, and Harry stood up and grabbed the empty plates. "You want some coffee?" he asked.

"That would be great."

Harry took the plates to the kitchen sink and turned on the coffeemaker. I could hear him whistling as he rinsed off the dishes and dirty silverware.

When I returned home that night, Amy was looking through a travel brochure while seated on the family room couch. Miles was upstairs working on his music, and Buster was sleeping on the floor with a slobbery toy in his mouth. I thought of Harry, living in that great big house all alone, and I felt sorry for him. "Are we still going to Costa Rica?" I asked. She was reading the brochure to get prepared for our next summer vacation.

"I would like to go there," she answered.

"Have you talked to the boys?"

"They're both on board."

Our family goes on a summer vacation every year—Amy, Miles, Danny, and I, all four of us. Last year we went to the Canadian Rockies, where we hiked, fished, saw the sights, and ate out at restaurants. Boy, did we ever eat, and according to my bathroom scale, I'd gained seven pounds by the time we got back home. The restaurants there were fun, and the food was good.

While our boys were kind of a pair of slobs, Amy always dressed nicely when we went out on the town. She was fifty-eight years old, approaching sixty, but she looked good for her age. I sometimes wondered what other people saw when they looked at her; did they see the same attractive and vibrant girl I saw, or did they just see another woman approaching her sixties? When I looked at Amy, was I seeing a picture of a woman enhanced by my love and memories of her, or was I seeing her as she appeared? And what did Amy see when she looked at me? I'm not sure I wanted an answer to that question, how Amy saw me. She was loyal to a fault, but did she still see me as the love of her life?

I never drank on our summer vacations. You might think I would have, but I never did. Miles loves to fish, and every time we go on vacation we try to find an opportunity for him to do so. In Canada it was easy, because there were lakes everywhere. Danny hates fishing, so we split up on our fishing days—Amy would take Danny for a hike, and I would take Miles on a fishing trip. I'm not one for fishing myself, but I like going with Miles and seeing him enjoy himself. On the lake where we fished, the guide said there were two kinds of trout to catch, and Miles caught three of one, and one of the other. The guide set me up with a rod and line too, but I caught nothing.

We took the trout back to the restaurant at our resort, and they said they would prepare the fish for us to eat that night at dinner. This had become a sort of vacation ritual for us, to have Miles catch fish during the day and then have the hotel cook them up for dinner. It was a lot of fun. I don't have any crazy stories to report from our trip to Canada, for we just had a very pleasant time. This was nice, the four of us together, enjoying each others' company. It was the way normal people lived.

Amy was still looking at her brochure. "Which hotel is that for?" I asked.

"You have to see this," Amy said. "It's for a resort in southern Costa Rica, in the rain forest. It's the latest thing. They call it sustainable."

"What does that mean?"

"They grow their own food, produce their own electricity ... sort of live off the land."

"Interesting."

"It's right in the heart of the rain forest, and you have to get there by boat. They have monkeys, Lester. There are howling monkeys, and you can hear them all the time."

"Weird," I said.

"They have hiking trails and fishing for Miles. And whales are there in the summer months. I think we should do this. It sounds like a lot of fun."

"I thought we were going to Europe this summer. That's what we said last year."

"I think I'd rather go to Costa Rica."

"Okay," I said. "I'm fine either way." I didn't care where we went, so long as it made everybody happy.

"How'd your dinner go with Harry?"

"It was good."

"Is he a good cook?"

"Well, he can make pasta. And he made a pretty decent salad."

"What did you guys talk about?"

"We're working on step five."

"So what exactly is step five?"

"I'm supposed to admit to the wrongs I've done."

"That could take a while," Amy said.

"Yes," I agreed.

"Do you ever remember me talking about Judy Powell from work?"

"No, not really."

"She's in AA. I thought it was supposed to be anonymous, but Judy talks about it all the time. She talks about it like some people talk about their kids."

"Some people do that."

"She says she's rediscovered Jesus."

"Good for her," I said.

"I'm glad you have a sponsor."

"Can I ask you a question?"

"Sure," Amy said.

"Why have you stayed with me all this time, with all my drinking and all the problems it's caused?"

"I don't know," she said. "For better or for worse, I guess."

She didn't say she loved me, but I knew that was what she meant. At least I hoped that was what she meant. We talked some more about Costa Rica, and we talked briefly about the boys. We watched a show on TV, and when it came time to turn in, we turned off the TV and went to our bedroom.

I lay there next to Amy with the lights off and the covers pulled up to my chest, and I thought of Harry's assignment for me. It was dead quiet, except for the soft sound of Amy's breathing. I was supposed to own my past behavior. When Harry had laid the process out, it made so much sense. What exactly did he say, that I chose to drink, that I'd been deliberately putting alcohol into my system knowing full well the consequences? Was it truly deliberate?

I looked up at the ceiling and recalled the afternoon I ran off to Tijuana. I had been sober for so long, so what was my problem? I thought of everything I went through to get that first drink, finding a bar on the way home and parking my truck in the crowded parking lot. I remember I received a call on my cell phone from a customer, and I held off going into the bar until I was done with the call. I didn't want my customer to hear the background sounds of clinking glasses and jukebox music. When I was done with the call, I noticed that all the spaces in the parking lot were metered. I dug through my pocket for a quarter but couldn't find one. I then rummaged through my car and found a quarter under the front seat. Putting the quarter into the parking meter, I then walked to the entry door of the bar and stepped inside.

I took a seat at the bar and waited several minutes for the bartender to get to me. She was involved in a conversation with one of the other patrons and was in no hurry to take my order. After I asked for my drink, she slid it in front of me. I remember looking at the drink and hesitating, asking myself if this was what I wanted to do. I hesitated, didn't I? I was thinking about it, slowly and rationally. Then I lifted the drink to my lips. "Another one," I said to the bartender, and she poured more booze into my glass. Harry was right, that I did this on purpose. But why? What made me do such a stupid thing?

I did this over and over, didn't I? There was the time several months before Tijuana when I didn't go anywhere at all. I got drunk that afternoon and stayed home from work to watch TV. Miles must have seen me, but I don't remember him. So where was Miles? By the time Amy came home, I was pie-eyed and sprawled out on the family room couch in my underwear. I remember I kept telling her how sorry I was, and she cooked me a steak and brewed some coffee to make me sober. Why did I drink then? There was nothing to celebrate and nothing to feel sad about. I just drank. I had gone to the liquor store and bought a half pint of vodka that afternoon. That was all I'd planned to drink, just enough to get a buzz. But the half pint fired up the alcoholic synapses in my brain, and the next thing I knew I was back at the same liquor store buying a full quart from the same cashier. He must have thought I was crazy.

It wasn't like this was the first time this had ever happened; in fact, it had happened over and over my whole adult life. It had been this way for over forty years—I would take the first drink, and then another, and then another after that. I knew what I was doing! Yes, I knew exactly what would happen. Each time I took a drink, I'd plummet into the same hell with my eyes wide open, knowing where I was headed. Harry was right, that I was doing this on purpose. I was not the victim of some irresistible siren song. Everything that happened to me, and everything I did to others, was the result of intention.

Harry said it was frightening, and he was right. I was terrified to discover the sort of person I was. It was scary to strip away the lies and lie there naked in the darkness. What a horrible person I'd been. What a stupid and selfish jerk I was. This was an amazing revelation, for all those years I'd thought of myself as a pretty good guy who'd been victimized by this baffling and destructive disease. I'd always blamed my problems on the bottle and never on myself. I was so wrong. I wasn't a victim at all! And Harry was right, that it was frightening.

It was like a dream I'd had one morning about an earthquake. I stood and watched our house crumble and fall upon itself, our possessions sliding off shelves, the woodwork twisting and splintering, the light bulbs flashing and exploding, and the floor breaking open and swallowing us into its darkness. I woke up from this dream, and everything turned out okay.

But there was no waking up from this raw insight into my drinking. I may have been born with an inability to process alcohol, but I certainly wasn't born with an inability to say no. Yes, it was deliberate! I looked over at Amy, who was now sound asleep. Did she know all this about me, or had she been buying my excuses and stories? And if she knew all this, why in the world did she stay married to me? Love is a powerful emotion, but like anything else, it has its limitations. I thought back to Agnes and what she had told me years ago about my guardian angel. I didn't believe in angels, but if there was such a thing as a guardian angel, I certainly had one looking out for me.

CHAPTER 12

On a Clear Day

How do I explain this? I woke up the next day feeling wonderful! Amy was already out of bed and in the bathroom getting ready for work, and she had her little TV tuned to her morning news show. I went downstairs to get some coffee and stepped out to the back patio to smoke a morning cigar. It was eight o'clock, and there wasn't a cloud in the sky. The birds were singing melodies in the trees, and as I smoked my cigar I heard a plane pass high overhead, filled with passengers eating peanuts and anticipating the arrival at their destination. As I blew my cigar smoke into the morning air, I told myself it was going to be a glorious day.

They say on a clear day you can see forever, and I now understood. I could in fact see over all the rooftops and trees, into the pallid blue atmosphere, past the faint outline of the moon. I could see into the invisible morning stars and then beyond. For the first time in my life, I could see past everything. I smoked my cigar, drank my coffee, and then returned inside.

I went upstairs, where I showered and shaved and got myself dressed. I hopped down the stairs and found Amy in the kitchen, where I kissed her on the mouth and told her good morning. She said, "Why are you in such a good mood?" and I told her I didn't know, that I just felt so good. But I knew exactly why I was in a good mood, and I needed someone to share this with, someone who would understand. So right after Amy left for work, I picked up the phone and called Harry. Harry answered, and I was so glad to hear the sound of his voice that my own voice cracked when I said hello.

"Is everything okay?" Harry asked.

"Everything is great," I said.

"Have you been drinking?"

"No, not a drop."

"So what can I do for you?"

"I can see, Harry," I said. "I can see everything."

"What do you see?"

"I can see what you've been trying to explain, and I understand what's been going on. It's been up to me all along, and I know I have the power to change my life. There's truly hope. I've made my bed, but I don't have to lie in it. I no longer feel trapped by this notion of powerlessness."

"The truth shall set you free."

I laughed at this. "Yes, exactly. I never knew what that meant, but now I understand."

"And the fear is gone?"

"Last night, I tell you I was terrified. It was just like you said, the overwhelming fear."

"But now it's gone?"

"Yes, it's gone."

Harry said he was glad I called. He said he wanted to meet with me as soon as possible, but that he was going out of town for a week and wouldn't be able to get together with me until he returned. We scheduled our next meeting for the evening following the day Harry was to get back. I asked where he was going, and he said Chicago. He said he'd never been there before, that he was going to explore the town and see the sights. I asked whom he was going with, and he told me he was going alone. It truly seemed a shame that Harry didn't have some friend with whom he could share his experiences. Probably putting my nose where it didn't belong, I brought the matter up. "Isn't there some nice lady who'd like to take the trip with you?"

"No," Harry said.

"Don't you get lonely?"

"Lonely?"

"Do you ever date?" I suddenly realized I was prying, and I said, "Sorry, it's probably none of my business."

"It's okay." Harry laughed. "I guess it's a fair question. You know, I did date women, several years after the divorce was final, when I was getting sober. It was one of the strangest experiences of my life. Since

I no longer went to bars, and since I was out of work, there weren't many places for me to meet available members of the opposite sex. My only social life was at the AA meetings, and I dated several AA women. It was so weird, being around these different women. Have you ever put on someone else's clothes? It was a lot like that, trying on garments that were worn and frayed, made of material that had been in such close proximity to another's body. Think about it, how old clothes have been in regular contact with a previous owner's armpits and hairy arms and sweaty bellies and skinny legs. It's pretty disgusting when you visualize it. I remember when I was drinking, I went to some strip clubs, gawking like an idiot at the undressed women onstage and then having them sit and squirm topless in my lap.

"I remember one girl who was rather lovely, and she sat in my lap and pushed her breasts up toward my face. I wasn't allowed to touch them, but they were right there inches away from my nose. You know what this girl smelled like? Not the perfumed aroma you'd expect from an attractive young girl, but rather the bad breath and body odor of the other male customers at the club on whose laps she'd been sitting. They'd been panting all over her, and she stunk of them. It was stomach-turning, and I had to breathe through my mouth to keep from getting nauseated.

"And that's exactly what I think of wearing another man's clothes. Clothing is a very personal thing, not the sort of item you can readily exchange. Do you understand this? A woman should be all yours, not the former property of some other male, not something that's been worn by another guy. But I went on dating these other AA gals, hoping to meet someone who could replace Janice. I met women with pasts, histories of other lovers and bad relationships and bitter divorces. I was talking with women who were damaged, stained, and cracked, not future partners with whom I would want to spend the rest of my life. I need to tell you about Sarah. Do you want to hear about Sarah?"

"Sure," I said.

"I met Sarah at a Tuesday-night AA meeting. She was about five years younger than I, slim and nicely shaped, with a face that was tolerably attractive. I noticed her when she talked to the group, and she caught my interest. She had just gone through a divorce and said she was three years sober. I introduced myself to her after one of the meetings, telling her that I too was divorced and suggesting we do something together. I told her I would like to get to know her, that I hadn't made many friends since I'd quit drinking. She agreed to have dinner with me, and she gave me her address so I could pick her up.

"I took her out to a nice restaurant here in Newport Beach, and what a story this woman had. I didn't ask her to give me her drunkalog, but she went ahead and gave it to me anyway. I think she thought that because I was an alcoholic, I would be curious about all these details of her drinking life.

"It turned out she had come from Utah. She had lived with her husband in a nice home in Park City, and her husband was a medical doctor who worked at a local hospital. They never did have children, but they had a big Irish setter by the name of Bailey. Her husband kept the dog in the divorce settlement, and Sarah moved out here to California.

"Sarah said she started drinking when she was in her twenties. She discovered that she liked to drink, but it never caused her any real problems. When she was in her thirties, she found herself drinking more and more, but it still didn't interfere with her life. But in her forties something changed, and the alcohol was now making her think and do crazy things.

"She looked in the mirror and saw her aging face, no longer that of a fresh twenty-year-old, no longer that of a vibrant and healthy thirty-year-old, but that of a woman in her forties who drank too much, a face contorted by age and dry martinis. She had bags under her eyes and crow's feet at their corners. She had laugh lines and frown lines, and her teeth were no longer shiny and white like they were when she was younger.

"Her husband, meanwhile, was growing more handsome by the day, distinguished and self-confident, with his thick gray hair and solid jaw. She began to grow jealous, and the more envious she got, the more she drank. And the more she drank, the crazier her life became.

"To get even with her husband and his good looks, she began throwing herself at other men. These were not men of her husband's caliber, but the sort of men who lacked scruples, who even lacked much in the way of looks. She found these men most often in the bars where she drank during the day while her husband was working. There was a neighbor down the street with whom she had a brief affair. There was even a cable TV repairman who acquiesced to her advances. She wasn't particularly shy or choosy, and she was often reckless. The longer this went on, the worse her image in the mirror appeared. Her eyes grew cynical, and her makeup was becoming a mess. She was drunk all the time, even when she applied her morning lipstick and eyeliner. The shakes became a part of her daily reality ... first a few dry martinis, and then the makeup. She was a disaster."

"What did her husband do?"

"Sarah told me the poor guy tried everything. He tried purging the house of all the booze, he tried taking away her checkbook, and he even took away the keys to her car. He eventually made an appointment with a reputable psychiatrist who specialized in addictions, but the man got nowhere with her. It seemed the harder the husband tried, the more she resisted. Then she became convinced that he was having an affair. She accused him of carrying on with one of the nurses at the hospital, and every time he came home late from work, she'd cry and complain as though this imaginary tryst was ruining their lives.

"Finally, one night while he was working late, she drove to the hospital to confront the lovers. She said she didn't find her husband right away, but she did find the nurse. She was at least fifteen years Sarah's junior, pert and very nice-looking. Her name was Rebecca, but everyone called her Becca. Becca was pushing an elderly woman in a wheelchair when Sarah spotted her in the hallway. 'You!' she exclaimed, and she ran right toward the nurse.

"Becca had no idea what was happening. She knew Sarah was the doctor's wife, but she'd never been told about the invented affair. Sarah said she shoved the elderly woman in the wheelchair out of the way, and she grabbed the nurse by the hair with one hand and began socking her in the face with the other. She had so much taken this nurse by surprise, that she did little to defend herself. By the time the other employees were able to pull Sarah off, the nurse's face was swollen and bloodied. 'I really let her have it,' Sarah said to me. Then she laughed as if the whole scene was from a comedy. She said that soon after the incident, her husband filed for a divorce and moved out of the house with the dog."

"I can't blame the guy."

"No, neither can I. So anyway, there I was sitting with this woman who had just poured her heart out to me. She had told me her sordid story, truthfully I think, and very thoroughly. And I asked myself what I was doing there, having dinner with some other man's discarded clothes. If I was to be honest about it, she probably hadn't done anything worse than the things I'd done. We were both alcoholics, I knew. But to pursue any sort of long-term relationship with this woman ... that was an entirely different matter. As Groucho Marx said, 'I'd never want to join a club that had me as one of its members,' and that was the last time Sarah and I ever went out together."

"Surely there are other women?"

"At my age, they're all used clothes."

"So Janice will be the only love of your life?"

"The one and only."

Harry and I chatted briefly about Chicago, and then we ended the call. I got to thinking what would happen if Amy ever did leave me. It would be catastrophic, sorting through all our possessions, dealing with the boys and their questions, and making all the legal maneuvers necessary in a divorce. And what would I do without Amy? She was the one person in this world I cared most about, the one I had picked to live with forever.

I remember before we got married, it was my job to write the vows. I considered myself a pretty good writer and spent hours making sure the words were all just right, but did I take them to heart? I knew that I hadn't. I cared about things that didn't matter, and I ignored things that should have been my first priority. It was bizarre what I was willing to risk just for another opportunity to drink. I was lucky, but it had nothing to do with Agnes and her guardian angel. It was just luck, plain and simple. And ask anyone who's spent any time at a craps table ... they'll tell you luck eventually runs out. That's just the way it is.

I went to an AA meeting two nights later. I still didn't like meetings, but I felt compelled to go. Perhaps it was because Harry was gone, and I just needed to hear people talk. Amy was pleased to see me going, and I was glad that I could make her happy. But when I arrived at the meeting, only a few people showed up, and there were maybe eight of us at the most.

There was an old guy in slacks and a plaid shirt who could barely keep himself awake. He kept nodding off and then coming back to, and I wanted to laugh every time he jerked his head forward and snorted himself awake. There was a young girl in jeans and a T-shirt who might have been very pretty were it not for the piercings and tattoos that marred every square inch of her body. There was one young guy in a three-piece suit who looked like he had come straight from his job, and a housewife was next to him who was wearing a loose cotton dress and sandals. She seemed sad and quiet. There were some other assorted folks, all being typical of those you'd expect to see at any given AA meeting, and there's no need to go into any more detail describing them. But the one person I want to tell you about was a soft-spoken character who identified himself as Alex.

I'd heard Alex talk before at previous meetings. Toward the end of this meeting, Alex raised his hand, and the leader called on him. He said, "Some of you here know a lot about my story, and some of you don't. For those of you who don't know me, you should know I was once like you. I have mellowed over the years, but when I was younger, I would have stepped on my mother's grave for another drink. And when I drank I was incorrigible. I was mean, selfish, and utterly irresponsible. I was spinning like a tornado out of control, harming loved ones, ripping apart relationships, and damaging everything in my path. I was always finding myself in trouble, being arrested and hospitalized more times than I can count.

"My dad used to say I was allergic to alcohol. He said every time I drank, I broke out in handcuffs." Some of the people laughed at this, while others just continued to listen. "So what did I do? I came into these rooms. I admitted I was powerless over alcohol, that my life had become unmanageable. I found myself a sponsor, and we began to work the steps. I wanted what I saw in these rooms, and I was willing to do whatever was necessary to get it. This would take a giant leap of faith, for I was never a great believer in God. But the more I read from the Big Book, and the more I listened to others talk, the clearer my path came to me.

"I would have to dismantle my egotism. It would not be an easy task; for years I'd been trying to do things my way. I'd been beating my head against a wall time and time again. When I began to work the steps with my sponsor, an entirely new world opened up for me. I was suddenly humbled. I was in his caring hands, asking for his guidance and praying for the strength to carry out his will, not mine. I lost my desire to drink in the process. I have not had a drink for twenty-two years. I have a family that I love and that loves me back. I have a great job, and I pay my bills on time. But most importantly, I am happy. And I thank God for this. I thank God that I found these rooms and the twelve steps of AA."

Alex looked up at the clock, and the meeting was almost over. "Okay," he said, "I guess that's all I have to say." When Alex stopped talking, the rest of the group applauded, just as they had for everyone else. I gave the guy a few courteous claps of my own. I felt compelled to raise my hand and offer an opposing opinion, but I kept silent. There was so much I could say, but it just seemed rather pointless. I wasn't going to convince anyone of anything in the few minutes remaining.

When the meeting was over, everyone walked toward the door. As I was about to leave, Alex stepped in front of me. "My name is Alex," he said. He reached for a handshake.

"I'm Lester," I said.

"Haven't seen you at a meeting for a while."

"I haven't been going recently."

"Is everything okay?"

"I'm doing fine," I said.

"Did you ever get a sponsor? I remember the last time you shared at a meeting, you were looking for a sponsor."

"Yes, I found one."

"Who is it? If you don't mind my asking."

"His name is Harry."

"Oh," Alex said knowingly. "Harry the atheist?"

"Yes," I agreed.

"How's that working out for you?"

"We get along well."

"He has his own way of doing things."

"Yes, he does," I agreed, and Alex put his hand on my shoulder in a friendly way.

"Harry's a good man. He just hasn't found God. Give him time, and he'll come around."

"I'm not so sure of that."

"We all believe eventually. It just takes some of us longer than others. Harry will come around, and so will you."

I went home that night, wishing I had never gone to the meeting. Harry called the next evening to see how I was doing. I told him about the AA meeting, and about what Alex had said to me at the end of the gathering. "I know Alex well," Harry said. "He's a nice guy, but he's a pain in the neck."

"AA is a farce, isn't it?"

"Not at all," Harry said.

"But all this talk about God."

"You need to take the good with the bad. Don't throw the baby out with the bathwater, Lester. Make improvements where necessary, but don't shun the entire process. Do you like antique cars?"

"Do I like cars?"

"I mean antique cars."

"I guess so. I mean, they're pretty cool."

"When I was in my thirties, I got interested in antique cars. I bought a few of them for myself, and Janice and I used to drive them around on weekends. For a while it was a lot of fun, but then I began to notice something—that the cars were quite impractical. Many of them were heavy and underpowered. Others guzzled gasoline and polluted the air. When it rained, the roofs and windows leaked like sieves, and the windshield wipers were terrible. The cars didn't handle very well, and even the sports cars drove like trucks. This doesn't mean that the idea of the automobile was a bad one, for cars are a terrific way to get around.

"But like for anything, the automobile has had room for improvement. Engines have been made more efficient, interiors more comfortable, instruments more sophisticated, and structures much safer. Even the cheapest automobiles on the road today are marvels of modern engineering. I look at AA like I look at cars. It's a terrific idea, but like anything, there's always room for improvement. People like Alex are stuck in the past, clinging to words written almost a hundred years ago by men who were new at their calling. Alex is driving around in an antique car."

"I guess that makes sense."

"Don't let Alex and all his God talk bother you. He means well."

"Can I ask you a question?"

"Sure," Harry said.

"This has nothing to do with AA."

"That's okay."

"Not to say that I do believe in God, but where do you think everything came from? I asked Amy the other night if she believed in God, and she said it was hard for her to accept there wasn't some sort of purpose to things. She said it's inconceivable that everything around us just appeared by accident. I didn't say anything, but I kind of agreed with her."

"Listen," Harry said, "there's nothing wrong with wondering about this sort of stuff. And there's also nothing wrong with saying you just don't know. It's funny, but when I tell people I don't believe in God, they always assume I'm an evolutionist. But I honestly don't think science has any more of a lock on things than religion. It's a false dichotomy. I don't mind admitting that I don't know. And I don't believe in people who claim to have all the answers. It's not that I don't like them personally; I just don't believe them. There are too many inconsistencies in their stories. It's a mystery, and I don't mind leaving it at that."

"Do you believe in anything?"

"I do my best, and I try to believe in myself."

"I think I understand."

"I'll tell you about another of my court cases. Do you have time to listen?"

"Yes," I said.

"Years ago I defended a man named Alvin Peavy, who was charged with murdering his wife and her boyfriend. They were shot to death early one morning at the boyfriend's house in his bed, where the two of them were sleeping. There were three bullets in the man and two in the woman. A neighbor named Henry Cox heard the shots, and he put on his robe and stepped outside to see what was going on. He saw Alvin's car speeding away from the scene. It was dark outside, and he couldn't be positive about the car, but it sure seemed like Alvin's car. He'd seen Alvin's car parked in the street before, and he'd seen Alvin sitting in the car stalking his wife. He knew what the car looked like, and he'd noticed a bumper sticker on the rear bumper. He swore he saw the same bumper sticker on the car that drove away after the shots, even though he couldn't say exactly what the bumper sticker said.

"This identification prompted the police to get a search warrant for Alvin's house. Alvin owned a registered revolver that was the same caliber as the rounds found in the victims. They also searched the neighborhood, and while they didn't find the gun in Alvin's house, they did find it in one of the neighbors' garbage cans. They had a motive, a weapon, and a witness. They had two bullet-riddled victims, and they arrested Alvin. At first Alvin insisted on his innocence, and he hired me to defend him."

"What'd you do?" I asked.

"We needed to address the gun first. I asked Alvin where he kept the gun, and he told me he stored it in the top drawer of his nightstand. I asked when he had last seen it, and he said it was months ago when he had cleaned it. Alvin then said his house had recently been burglarized, that he had a police report listing the missing items. The gun was not listed, but it could have been an oversight, since Alvin did not remember checking to see if the gun was gone.

"Then came the ballistics results, that the five shots had been fired from the gun and that the gun was indeed the murder weapon. No fingerprints had been found on the gun. Someone had wiped the gun clean after shooting the victims, and now I felt we were getting somewhere. Why was the gun wiped clean? And why was it stashed in such an obvious hiding place? I then turned my attention to the witness, Henry Cox. How reliable was his testimony? He admitted it was dark outside, and how sure was he that it was Alvin's car?

"I began to believe in Alvin's innocence, or at least the possibility of it. I hired a private investigator to check out Alvin's wife and boyfriend, to see if anyone else might have had a motive to shoot the couple.

"Meanwhile, Alvin was a nervous wreck. He was being held without bail, and his stint in jail was beginning to get to him. He had a seventeen-year-old son who had been living with him at the time of the murders, and he was not handling the situation well. Alvin's sister moved into the house with the boy and tried to keep things in order. She took the kid several times to visit Alvin, but that only seemed to make matters worse. Then after one of these visits something happened that left me bewildered. Alvin called me in with the investigators and said he was ready to sign a confession. I thought we were building a pretty good defense, and it turned out he was guilty all along. He was willing to pay for his crimes."

"What happened to him?"

"They gave him twenty-five to life."

"Wow," I said.

"Then one day while I was working in my front yard, I saw a neighbor's boy get into his dad's car and drive off. I stopped what I was doing. It suddenly hit me that the wrong person was in prison."

"What do you mean?"

"Alvin didn't shoot the couple."

"Who did?" I asked.

"I believed his son did it. He would have had easy access to the gun. He would have wiped his fingerprints from it and stashed it stupidly in the neighbors' trash. Kids are not very good at committing crimes, and it was just the sort of thing a kid would do. As far as the car goes, the boy didn't have a car of his own and would have needed his father's car. He could have waited for his dad to fall asleep, grabbed his keys, and taken the car to the boyfriend's house. He climbed in through the window, shot the couple, and drove back home. He had no way of knowing his father had been stalking his mother, parking in front of the boyfriend's house, catching the attention of the neighbor who said he'd seen the car before. It all made perfect sense.

"And it was no wonder Alvin was so willing to sign a confession, for he didn't want his son convicted of a crime for which Alvin was ultimately responsible. It was Alvin who, by his own ineptitude as a husband, left the door open for this boyfriend to step in and destroy their family. It was Alvin who ranted and raved in front of the boy about the unfairness of what had happened. There was no way Alvin was going to let his son go to prison for something he had caused."

"Did you do anything?"

"I visited Alvin and asked him about it."

"What did he say?"

"He just said they'd convicted the right man. That's all he would say to me. I left it at that. I made a decision, doing what I thought was best, and I left it at that."

"What does this story have to do with what we were talking about?" I asked.

"What would you have done?"

"About Alvin and his son?"

"Yes," Harry said.

"I don't know."

"Some questions just don't have good answers. You just look things over, do your best, and know that's the best that you can do."

"Yes," I said. "I can see that."

"No one has to believe in God."

"No," I agreed.

"And no one has to believe we share ancestors with apes and monkeys."

"No, I guess not."

"It's okay to just say you don't know why we're here, and carry on to the best of your ability."

CHAPTER 13

Men from the Boys

Harry called on the night he returned from Chicago to confirm our next meeting, and we agreed to get together as planned. He told me to read step six and bring my book, that we were going to talk about it. I asked him how he liked Chicago, and he said it was interesting. He said it wasn't the greatest town he'd ever visited, but that he was glad to have finally seen the place.

I started reading the sixth step that night as Harry had instructed, and I truly had to laugh. The opening sentence of the text read, "This is the step that separates the men from the boys." It reminded me of my junior high school physical education teacher and our first day of school. He lined us boys in the gymnasium so that we were facing him, and then he walked in front of us, back and forth, like some sort of crazy drill sergeant. He wore shorts and a polo shirt with a whistle around his neck, and he put his hands behind his back as he walked. "This is seventh-grade physical education," he said. "This is where we separate the men from the boys." It was kind of an ominous thing to announce, this idea of separating the men from the boys. This teacher went on and on to make sure we understood his protocol, that we were to only call him Coach Andrews, and that we were to always suit up in gym shorts, a T-shirt, white socks, and athletic shoes.

Of course also included in the dress code was the jock strap, that mysterious new piece of uncomfortable elastic underclothing that we were to wear beneath our shorts. He lectured us about the importance of the jock strap, how it was essential not only to self-preservation, but also to the continuation of the species. He said anyone caught without a jock strap beneath his gym shorts would be ejected from the class for the day, and marked down as an unexcused absence.

"There will be lots of jock strap checks," he said. "Although from the looks of things here, all most of you are going to need is a peanut shell and a rubber band." The boys laughed at this, most of us nervously, probably all wondering how each of us was going to measure up when it came time to shower.

I wondered what exactly the coach meant by separating the men from the boys. It seemed obvious on its face, but it wasn't. Was Coach Andrews talking about physical development? This seemed like sort of a cruel thing for a teacher to do, making boys who weren't yet in puberty feel lesser than the other more mature kids, making pubic hair, body odor, and low voices the signposts of acceptance. Or was he just referring to physical strength? Again, this seemed to have more to do with physical maturity than it did with something a boy could control. Or maybe it had to do with emotional maturity, the ability to reason and make wise decisions, to modulate feelings, to behave like an adult. I doubt this was what Coach Andrews had in mind, for emotional maturity has very little to do with performing sit-ups or chin-ups, or lifting weights. Anyone who has spent any time with athletes knows that one can easily excel in a sport or physical activity without the slightest modicum of a mature personality.

I have to tell you about a kid in our PE class. His name was Randy Getz. He was overweight with bright red hair and freckles, and while he looked fairly normal in his street clothes, he looked out of sorts in his gym shorts and T-shirt.

Randy was one of those boys in junior high that hung out with a lot of older kids. His brother was five years his senior, and Randy was often with his brother and his buddies. They used to work on their cars in their driveway, and I'd pass their house walking home every afternoon from school. These boys all smoked cigarettes, and they weren't shy about it; they'd keep cigarettes in their front pockets, rolled up in their sleeves, and tucked behind their ears. They spent all their time after school working on their cars with butts dangling from their lips, revving engines and making adjustments under the hoods. In addition to cars, they worked on their Zippo lighters, constantly filling them with lighter fluid and installing new flints, flipping them open and checking them to be sure they were working.

It was only several days into our first year in junior high that Coach Andrews caught Randy behind the gymnasium smoking a cigarette while he was supposed to be playing basketball with the rest of the boys. Coach Andrews brought Randy into the gym, holding him by his ear, and he told all the boys to make a big circle.

The coach dragged Randy into his office and came out with a large wood paddle. The paddle was a good half inch thick and two feet long, and holes had been bored into it to make it more aerodynamic. With the paddle in one hand and Randy's ear still in the other, Coach Andrews broke into the center of the circle. He let go of Randy's ear, and we watched as the coach told Randy to drop his shorts and bend over. Then with this weird sadistic look on his face, Coach Andrews slapped the paddle against Randy's bare behind—not once, not twice, but ten very painful times. I have to say Randy took the punishment like a man, and he didn't cry out once. When the coach was done, Randy stood up straight and hiked his shorts back up to his fat waist.

"Are you done?" Randy asked, and Coach Andrews nodded his head and gave him a queer smile. Then regaining his composure and looking at the rest of us, the coach said, "That's what happens when you get caught smoking on my watch." Randy's face was expressionless. He hadn't put up a fuss or sobbed during the entire paddling; he hadn't even so much as whimpered. The coach blew his whistle, and Randy walked back to the basketball court in his ill-fitting gym clothes, and all of us boys continued with our basketball games.

Was this what people meant by the difference between the men and the boys, the ability to endure pain without crying, the resolve to face such a situation courageously? Did Coach Andrews realize what he'd actually done? He had promoted Randy Getz from funny-looking fat kid to a seventh-grade hero who could take ten raps of the coach's paddle without shedding a tear. I don't think that was Coach Andrews's intention, although if you asked him to justify this paddling, he might have told you he was turning a boy into a man.

This made me laugh now, this macho idea of separating the men from the boys. It made no sense. I can tell you of times when I've seen young boys display all sorts of courage; likewise, there have been times when I've seen grown men behave like spineless sissies.

Randy Getz was one of the bravest kids I'd ever seen during my years in middle school, and I always admired the way he handled himself.

I showed up at Harry's house at eight, and we went to the library. He got right to the point, asking me to open my book to step six. I found the chapter, and Harry asked me to read step six aloud. I said, "We were entirely ready to have God remove all our defects of character."

"What does this mean to you?" Harry asked.

"That the person is prepared to have God remove his flaws. The person, of course, would have to believe in God."

"True," Harry said.

"Are we going to rewrite this step?"

"We'll have to. So how would you rewrite it?"

"I don't know."

"Tell me one of your character defects."

I thought for a moment. "I guess I can be mean and self-centered," I said.

"Can you give me an example?"

I told Harry about something that had happened several years before that I'd just been thinking about on the way to his house. I don't know why it was on my mind, but perhaps the traffic that evening had triggered the memory. I told Harry about the time I was driving my truck one day on the way to a construction site. I was late for a meeting, weaving in and out of traffic, when it happened. An elderly man in an oversized Lincoln Town Car pulled in front of me going about ten miles under the posted speed limit. He was in the left lane, and a large truck was in the right. The two of them were going the same slow speed, and there was no way for me to get around them.

I pulled up close to the rear of the old man's car, tailgating him, hoping to get his attention. I honked my horn several times and flashed my headlights. I could not get the guy to either speed up or pull over, and this went on and on for at least a mile. It was intolerable. Finally, the truck turned right onto another street, and I swung my truck over into the right lane and tried to pass the old man. No sooner had I changed lanes than I had to stop at a red light. The elderly man and I were now stopped at the intersection, beside each other, waiting for the light to change.

I was fuming. I mean, first it was the old man in his slow-moving Town Car, and now it was this cursed red light. I rolled down my window and looked to my left, and the old man was looking right at me. I motioned for him to roll down his passenger window, and he did so. As he did I grabbed a soft drink from my cup holder and heaved it through his open window. The drink hit him in his shoulder, and soda and ice splashed all over his face and clothes. "Next time, pull the hell over," I shouted. Then the light turned green, and I sped away. I looked in my rearview mirror, and I saw that the elderly man wasn't going anywhere. He was probably busy wiping my drink from his face and shirt.

As I told this story to Harry, he cringed. "What if he had been your own grandfather?" he asked.

"I know," I said. "It was a rotten thing to do. I felt bad about it the rest of that day. I still feel bad about it now."

"So you'd call that a defect of character?"

"Yes, I would. I was mean and self-centered."

"Do you think you're the only mean and self-centered person who drives a car?"

"No, of course not."

"There are lots of mean and self-centered people on the roads?" asked Harry.

"Yes, lots of them."

"Are they all alcoholics?"

"Of course not," I said.

"Doesn't everybody have defects of character?"

"Yes, they do."

"Then why is it so important for alcoholics to address these defects? Why not just everyone?"

"I don't know."

"An alcoholic needs to love himself," said Harry.

"I've been told that before."

"You must love yourself to save yourself."

"So how do we write step six?" I asked.

"Step six should say that we're ready to accept responsibility for our character defects."

"That's it?"

"How does it sound?"

"It sounds so easy."

"Are you game?"

Now, I'm not sure why this happened, but I didn't answer Harry's question. Instead, I drifted off into a daydream. It was weird how I did this, suddenly thinking back to a trip my father and I had taken to Las Vegas years before. It was for my twenty-first birthday, and my dad wanted to take me Vegas to celebrate my passage into manhood. "Are you game?" he had asked. Dad had tickets for a Rowan and Martin show, but I don't remember which hotel it was at. Mom dropped us off at the airport, where we boarded the plane and flew.

I have to say it felt strange going to Vegas with my father, for it just wasn't the sort of thing he would ordinarily do. But since I was now legally able to drink and gamble, Dad wanted to do something special to mark the occasion. To be honest, I would rather have been out with my friends, getting drunk and partying all night, but I didn't want to hurt Dad's feelings.

I remember when we arrived at the hotel, we got our room, dropped our luggage, and went down to the casino floor. It was early evening, a couple hours before the show. Dad took me to the cashier, where he purchased a couple rolls of nickels. He handed one roll to me and kept the other for himself. He then took me over to the nickel slots, where we played the machines together, one slow nickel at a time.

So there we were, this sober father-and-son duo, minding our own business and playing the nickel slot machines when a woman approached us. She seemed old to me at the time, but looking back I'd say she was somewhere in her forties. She had platinum-blond hair and was wearing a tight-fitting sequined dress with pearls. She had a lot of cleavage and wore way too much lipstick. She was holding a drink and was obviously drunk. She put her arm around me and said, "Well, aren't you a cute one!" I could tell Dad wasn't sure what to do, and neither was I. She then planted a big wet kiss on my cheek.

A man suddenly showed up and grabbed the woman by the arm. "You've had enough to drink," he said. "We need to go back to the room."

The woman just laughed and said, "You go back to the room. I'm just getting started."

The man pulled the woman's arm off me, and she spun around and slapped his face. "Come on," he said. "Let's go back to the room."

The woman told the man to leave her alone, and then she suddenly turned sideways and vomited all over the floor. What a sight! Here was this woman in her fancy sequined dress and pearls puking all over the casino floor. Dad grabbed me by my forearm and ushered me away from the couple. I could hear them shouting at each other as we walked away. I turned around to look and saw that the woman had fallen down, and she was now seated on the floor, wriggling in her own vomit. The man and several others were trying to get her back on her feet. You would think I would have been repulsed by this scene, as I'm sure my father was, but for some sick reason I thought it was one of the coolest things I'd ever seen.

Looking back, I couldn't tell you a thing about what my dad was wearing or how he looked. I couldn't tell you what sort of shirt he was wearing, what sort of pants he had on, or anything about his shoes. He was just my dad, taking his son out for a night on the town. But I can remember the woman like I saw her yesterday … her sequined dress and pearls, her platinum-blond hair, and her bright red lipstick. Weird, isn't it?

"Lester?" Harry said. "Are you with me?"

"Oh, yes," I lied. I had no idea what he'd been talking about.

"Step six is not nearly as easy as you might think. Did you read the chapter? Do you remember the opening line from the text?" Harry said.

"Actually, I do," I said. "It says this step separates the men from the boys."

"There's a lot of truth to that."

"There is?" I said. It surprised me that Harry liked this line. "So how exactly does it separate the men from the boys?"

"You tell me," Harry said. "What exactly is a man? Right now, you're a sixty-year-old male who works hard for a living. You have a family, pay taxes, and look after your children. You shave and shower every morning, and you drive a truck, vote in elections, and smoke your cigars.

"But what is a man, Lester? Does a man get drunk and drive off to Tijuana, putting himself and his family at risk? Does he deliberately and continually hurt the woman who loves him? Does he set a bad example for his children and intentionally put others in harm's way? Does he throw his soda at a senior citizen just because he has difficulty keeping up with traffic? You seem to be doing a lot of stupid and irresponsible things for a person your age, for a so-called 'man' at the age of sixty. I said you needed to grow up several weeks ago, and I meant what I said. I wasn't just being glib.

"A real man cherishes and takes good care of his wife. He works tirelessly to make himself a good role model for his children. He understands there are consequences for his actions, and he behaves accordingly. He respects others and treats them kindly. He knows the difference between being young at heart and simply being immature. For reasons of legal convenience, our society calls you a man when you reach eighteen, but in reality this milestone means little. I have met boys under eighteen who I'd call men, and I've met men such as yourself who at the age of sixty still behave like boys.

"Do you love yourself, Lester? For a real man loves himself. He admits his defects of character and is committed to making the best effort he can to eliminate them. He knows he will never be perfect, but he makes his best effort. And this effort begins with willingness, and this willingness is the essence of step six. This is what we're trying to do here."

"Okay," I said.

Harry then told me a long and detailed story about how he worked step six fourteen years before, when he was first getting sober. I won't recount it here, because it's kind of boring. Finally, he said, "It's getting late. Let's call it a night."

"That suits me," I replied.

Harry showed me to the door, and I walked to my truck and drove home. It was dark outside, but there were a lot of cars on the streets. When I arrived home, I parked in the garage and stepped into our house. Amy was watching TV with Miles; they were watching an episode of *The Blacklist*, one of Miles's favorite shows. I sat down and watched the ending of the show with them, and then Miles went back upstairs to work on his music. Amy went to the study, and I watched the evening news.

Amy suddenly called me into the study, and I got up off the couch and walked to her. She was looking at some old pictures of Miles on her computer screen. "Look how young he was," she said. It was a photo of a ten-year-old Miles dressed up in his hockey gear and holding a trophy after his team had won a championship. I hadn't seen that game, since I was in rehab at the time. But I remembered Miles brought his trophy to me during family visiting hours. I was so proud of him, and I wished I hadn't missed the game.

When Amy and I went to bed that night, she rolled over and faced me. She said, "So what are you working on with Harry?"

"Why do you ask?"

"I'm just curious."

"We're separating the men from the boys." I didn't say anything else.

"So that's all you're going to tell me?"

"For now, yes," I said.

Amy rolled her eyes and then faced the other way. "So long as you're not drinking," she said, "you guys can do anything you want."

Chapter 14

Home Sweet Home

I was going to be gone for a couple days. There was a lull in my workload, and I decided to travel alone to San Jose to visit my mother and father. This was more than just a friendly visit. My mom and dad were getting along in years, and I wanted to be sure that their lives were in order, that they were taking proper care of themselves. They were in their late eighties, an age when assistance is often required, and while they were fine the last time I checked, I wanted to be sure nothing had changed.

The drive took about six hours, and I arrived at three in the afternoon. I parked my car in their driveway, and the first thing I did was check the landscaping. I'd been paying a gardener to take care of the yard, and from the looks of things he'd been doing his job. The lawn was mowed, and the shrubs were trimmed and healthy. I looked at the house itself, and it was well preserved. I had sent over a housepainter several years before, and his work seemed to be holding up. There were no signs of cracking or peeling. When I rang the doorbell, Mom answered, and she jumped out to the porch to give me a hug. "Lester!" she exclaimed, and she grabbed my hand and pulled me into the house.

"Is he here?" I heard my dad ask from the front room. Mom shut the door behind me. It was like going back in time.

Here are some things you should know about my mom and dad. First, they are inseparable. They've been married for sixty-three years and will remain married until the day they die. I have seen them bicker and fight about many things, but neither has ever brought up the threat of separation or divorce, not even in the heat of their worst arguments. Second, they take good care of themselves. I don't mean just their health. They've taken good care of themselves financially, and except for a few minor expenses like landscape maintenance and house painting, they pay all their bills with their own funds. Third, neither my mom nor dad drinks alcohol. They might have half a glass of wine at a dinner party just to be polite, but they aren't drinkers. No one on my dad's side of the family drinks at all, but my mom's relatives have some history. My grandfather drank a lot, and Mom's older sister, Agnes, as you already know, was an alcoholic. I never saw my grandfather drunk, although I heard he could be pretty cantankerous when he was. He gave up drinking when he was in his sixties and died sober.

I liked visiting my parents. Everything inside their house was the same as it had been for years—the pictures of our family, the vases and knickknacks, the doilies and tablecloths, and the framed Home Sweet Home needlepoint that hung over the kitchen doorway. Seeing all this stuff brought back memories, and most were good. I'd had a happy childhood, and I don't have much to complain about, except for the fact that my father was rather strict. He was a nice man, but he was a little set in his ways. He'd mellowed over the years, and now in his eighties he was far less stubborn. "Don't try to be liked," he used to say to me, imparting his fatherly wisdom. "Try to be respected." Dad tried his best to raise me according to this code.

Not being a drinker, Dad never did understand my alcoholism, and we never talked about it much, only on a few occasions. Mom, on the other hand, was much easier to talk to. When I arrived at my parents' house that afternoon, we had a very pleasant reunion. Neither of my parents knew anything about my run to Tijuana, or about any of my other recent drinking episodes. They knew nothing about Harry. As far as they were concerned, I'd been sober for quite some time.

We went into the kitchen, where Mom brought out a Key lime pie. "You must be starving," she said, and she cut me a big slice. I used to love this pie when I was a kid, but that was fifty years ago, and my tastes have changed. Mom still saw me as a little boy, and she baked a Key lime pie every time I visited. I'd never had the heart to tell her it was no longer my favorite desert. I acted happy and surprised.

"Wow," I said. "You shouldn't have!"

Mom put the slice of pie on a dish and slid it toward me. "You always loved Key lime pie," she said.

"Thanks, Mom," I said, and I dug into the pie with a fork, stuffing a big gob into my mouth.

"How was the drive?" Dad asked.

"It was pretty easy," I said. "I didn't hit very much traffic."

"Is that a new truck out there?" Dad was looking through the window at my truck in the driveway.

"It's the same old truck," I said.

"How many miles you got on it?"

"I'm not sure."

"What kind of mileage are you getting?"

"Not very good," I admitted.

It was interesting how the first thing my father always wanted to talk about when I visited was my truck. It was sort of sad, really, since Dad no longer drove at all. I think he missed being able to operate his own car, thus all the small talk about mileage, traffic, and the odometer reading. Mom and I decided to take Dad's car keys away from him three years ago, when it became clear he was getting to old to drive safely. He was driving slowly, making illegal turns, and pulling dangerously in front of other cars. Driving with him was a terrifying experience, and we felt it was just a matter of time before he caused a horrible accident. Mom and I got together during one of my visits, and we broke the news to him, that we were taking away his car keys and selling his car. At first he was angry, but then he calmed down. I was glad he finally gave in to our request. I say request, but it was a demand. There was no way I was coming home from that visit without having secured his car keys and his promise not to get behind the wheel of a car again.

Mom never seemed to have any problem with her driving, except for the one time she got a speeding ticket and got into a tiff with the officer. She insisted she was driving the speed limit. The officer wouldn't budge, so she went to court, and after a fifteen-minute rant about the rudeness of the young cop and the general deterioration of respect of youth toward their elders, the judge tore up her ticket and told her to go home. She was so proud of herself when she returned that day.

I was glad to see that Mom still looked so good. She was alert and full of life for a woman her age. It seemed like she was going to be one of those women who would outlive her husband by years. Dad had been in and out of the hospital recently for this and that, getting tests and treatments for several ailments. But my ever-healthy mom kept on running around, living life, and taking care of business like a woman half her age. I hoped her health energy was hereditary, and I told this to Amy. Amy said my mom was a freak of nature, not to get my hopes up, and I laughed.

I spent most of my time with Mom while I was growing up. Dad was either working, or busy with chores, or sitting on the sofa and watching sports on TV. I don't remember him with me much, but Mom was constantly taking me to baseball games, where she was the team mom; or to Cub Scout meetings, where she was the den mother; or to the beach with my buddies. We'd all pile into Mom's VW bus, and she'd take us everywhere. She knew all my friends, and all my friends liked her.

This began to change when I started drinking. I didn't want my mom taking us around anymore, especially not to any of our secret drinking hangouts, or picking us up when we were all plastered. I think part of the problem was that I was seeking my independence as teenagers do, and I think my mom was aware of this and gave me my space. But perhaps it was more than that, and perhaps it was too much space. In retrospect, the drinking was becoming a problem, even if I didn't see it as such.

It's funny, but only once during all those years did my mom ever see me drunk. It was a Friday night when Eddie Montgomery and I secured a quart of whiskey and made a pact to drink the entire thing between ourselves. That was a lot of booze for two boys our age. We went to one of our secret spots at the neighborhood park. It was the perfect place for two boys to polish off a bottle of whiskey. God, I remember the stuff tasted awful, but we drank the entire thing, and a half hour later we were crazy drunk. We were staggering along the sidewalk and into the street.

We ended up on our backs on the asphalt, laughing and reveling in our incapacitation. One of the neighbors drove by and saw us sprawled in the road, and she called my mom to tell her what she'd seen. My mom drove her VW bus to the location, and she kneeled over me to see what was wrong. "Lester," she said. I looked at her face but couldn't make it out. I asked her who she was, and she said she was my mother. I started laughing. She then pulled on my arm, trying to get me up.

Somehow my mom was able to get both Eddie and me into the back of her bus, and she drove away. She took Eddie home first and then brought me to our house. The next thing I knew, it was morning. I was lying in my bed with a monster hangover, my head pounding and my mouth tasting like mud. I thought my parents were going to let me have it something awful, and tell me how disappointed they were in what I'd done. But instead, the household was very quiet, almost serene. When I faced my father, he just laughed at me and said I looked like hell. He said my hangover was probably punishment enough for what I'd done. My head was spinning and my mouth was salivating, and I ran to the bathroom to vomit. I could hear Dad laughing from the other room as I puked and flushed the toilet. It was a miserable morning. I was sick for hours, and adding to this misery was the fact that Eddie had puked all over the floor of my mom's bus. My father charged me with the task of cleaning it up.

I finished my slice of pie, and Mom took the empty plate away. Dad was in the bathroom. Mom came over while he was gone and asked me softly, "How's the drinking, Lester? You're still sober, aren't you?" I debated what I should tell her and decided I would say that I was doing fine. It wasn't a lie, since I'd been coming along nicely with Harry. "I'm so glad to hear you're doing well," Mom said, and she squeezed my hand.

The house held a lot of good memories, and it was a shame that someday my parents would pass away and we'd have to sell the place. It was a big part of my life. I remembered how my friends and I would play marbles in the backyard, on the flat dirt between the apple trees. We'd pretend sword-fight with sticks, play catch with mitts and balls, and dig holes that we anticipated would reach all the way to China. I used to collect toy cars, and we'd race them through the flower beds and across the concrete patio. When the Fourth of July came and fireworks were available, we'd set firecrackers off to explode the cars. Mrs. Helmsley next door used to complain to my mom and say the firecrackers were disturbing her dog. We'd stop what we were doing, wait a few hours, and then do it again.

As I grew older, backyard playtime died down, and the opposite sex became interesting. There were several girls my age in the neighborhood, and I spent a lot of time trying to befriend them. I remember one girl named Patty who lived just two houses down. She had straight brown hair and a face that was more interesting than it was pretty, but she seemed interested in me.

One afternoon I convinced Patty to come to our house, or now that I look back, maybe it was she who convinced me. In any event, we wound up sitting together on the family room sofa watching TV. My dad was at work, and Mom was out buying groceries, so we had the house to ourselves. I don't remember what we were watching, because it was not important. What was important was that I had this living, breathing girl seated next to me on the couch, and we were alone. There were no parents and no pesky neighborhood kids running around sticking their noses into our business. It was just the two of us, and I'm not sure who started it, but somehow we kissed. It was not a short peck of a kiss, but a long, warm period of time during which our young lips were pressed together. Our hands remained awkwardly at our sides, but our mouths were touching in this glorious connection. When we stopped, we wiped our mouths with the backs of our hands, and we stared at each other for a moment, wondering if what just happened had actually happened.

After the kiss, Patty hung around and watched TV. Then she just went home. It is one of my most remarkable childhood memories, and it occurred right here in my parents' house, on that very sofa in the family room. The sofa had been reupholstered since then, but it was the same piece of furniture. I never did tell anyone about the kiss, and to the best of my knowledge, Patty kept it to herself as well. The entire next day, all I could think about was Patty's mouth and how strangely exciting it felt pressed against mine. But days turned into weeks, and weeks to months, and the whole affair was forgotten. Patty and I never became boyfriend and girlfriend; she just became a girl down the street, like any other girl.

There were so many good memories in this house. It was fun being a kid here, and it was great being a family of three. I've sometimes wondered what it would have been like to have a brother or a sister, but that never happened. I didn't have to share my parents' affections with another sibling. The doctors told Mom I would be her first and last, and my parents accepted that we would continue to be a small family. We were nothing like the Fitzpatricks across the street. As Catholics they didn't believe in birth control, and like rabbits they couldn't keep from copulating and producing young ones. They had six kids, an assortment of boys and girls, and their property was a constant madhouse of hair-pulling, screaming, and petulant complaining.

The Fitzpatricks' front yard was always littered with broken toys, and I remember they had an ugly old tire swing hanging from a branch of their mulberry tree. These kids were always up to something, and Mrs. Fitzpatrick, with her hair in curlers and wearing one of her many housedresses, was always at her wits' end keeping them in line. She'd always be yelling at them, chasing them, and grabbing their arms and shaking them silly. Once Bobby Fitzpatrick invited me for dinner and a sleep-over, and it was an experience I'll never forget. Bobby was a year older than I was, but we were both about the same height. He shared a room with his younger brother, Tom, and we hung out in the room until dinner, when Mrs. Fitzpatrick called for us. It was crowded at the table, but somehow we all fit.

Mrs. Fitzpatrick served a pot roast, mashed potatoes, and asparagus, and while the pot roast and potatoes tasted great, I had a thing about asparagus. The stuff actually made me physically ill. It was disgusting and had a horrible smell, and I pushed the spears to the side of my plate with my fork. Dinner went fine, and while there was a lot of talking, all the kids behaved themselves. Then, at the Fitzpatrick dinner table, if you were a kid and you were done eating, you had to ask Mr. Fitzpatrick if you could be excused in order to leave. I watched as the other kids did this, and after Bobby asked to be excused I did the same.

Mr. Fitzpatrick looked at my dinner plate and noticed I hadn't touched the asparagus. "Around here we finish our meals," he said. "Eat your asparagus, kid, and then you can go." I looked at him for a moment and realized he was serious. There were five asparagus spears on my plate, and I took a careful bite out of one of them. I could feel my stomach protesting, and I thought I was going to puke right there at their table. I took another bite and had the same reaction. There was no way I was going to be able to eat the rest of these awful vegetables, so while Mr. Fitzpatrick wasn't looking, I grabbed what was left and stuffed it in my jeans pocket. "Can I go now?" I asked, and Mr. Fitzpatrick looked at my empty plate and grumbled out a yes. I hurried out of the room.

I headed to Bobby's bedroom, and when I arrived Bobby was playing with a toy plane. One thing about the Fitzpatrick household was that there were always lots of things to play with, since their parents and grandparents bought them every toy imaginable. "You want to see something cool?" Bobby asked, and I nodded my head, thinking it might be a new toy. Bobby picked up a wooden box from the dresser, opened the lid, and removed a small paper and cellophane item. It was a silver dollar inside a protective holder, and he held it toward me to examine. "My grandfather gave this to my little brother for his birthday last week. They say it's worth twenty bucks. Go ahead—hold it." I reached out my hand and took the dollar from Bobby and gave it a good looking-over. I agreed with Bobby that it was very cool and handed it back to him. He put it back in the wooden box, and the two of us went to the front yard to play. It was the next day that the problem arose.

Mrs. Fitzpatrick came over to our house and told my mother that Bobby's brother was missing his silver dollar, that Bobby had showed it to me, and that they suspected I had taken it. My mom called me to the front door and asked about the silver dollar. I vehemently denied stealing it, and Mrs. Fitzpatrick grew angry. "I'm very disappointed in you, Lester," she said. I was at a loss for words, since I knew that I hadn't taken the dollar. But in the interest of keeping things civil between neighbors, Mom paid the woman the value of the coin. When Mrs. Fitzpatrick left, Mom went all through my bedroom, looking for the stolen item. Finally, she went through the pockets of the jeans I had worn the previous day, and she discovered the mushed asparagus. "What's this?" she asked, holding a green gob of food, and I told her about Mr. Fitzpatrick and the asparagus. "I think you should stay clear of that family from now on," she said, and I agreed.

So where'd the silver dollar go? As best as I could figure, Bobby had nabbed the coin for himself and hid it somewhere in their house. He had invited me over and showed me the dollar just to set me up, and then he had taken it sometime that night or in the morning.

Our street used to be full of children. They'd be playing in the front yards and in the street, riding bicycles, tossing baseballs, and playing tetherball and basketball in driveways. They'd be buying ice cream bars and popsicles from the ice cream truck that would make its jingling rounds in the afternoons. But no longer. Nowadays the street was quiet. The kids had grown up and moved away, and while a couple families with children had moved in, most of the homes were occupied by elderly couples like my parents.

Dad was done using the bathroom, and he took a seat on the sofa. He was sitting in the same spot where I had first kissed that girl, Patty. "Do you remember Oscar and Mittens?" he asked me.

"Of course I do," I replied.

"Now, that was something."

"Yes," I agreed.

Oscar was our dog, an energetic beagle who got along well with cats, and Mittens was our family cat. We named the cat Mittens because she was all black except for the white socks on her feet. This cat used to get into everything. We'd find her sleeping in the cupboards, hiding under beds, and sometimes perched on the tops of tires in the wheel wells of our cars.

One afternoon Dad was working in the crawl space of our house, running some speaker wire for his new stereo. By evening he was done with the work, and he reattached the wood panel to the access opening on the side of the foundation. Later that evening, it was time to feed our two animals. Oscar was there waiting to be fed, but Mittens didn't show up for dinner. We didn't think much of her absence. We figured she was probably outside somewhere, busy doing whatever it is cats did to amuse themselves. But after several days, there was still no sign of Mittens, and we became concerned.

Mom and I made fliers and put them in mailboxes all over the neighborhood, offering a small reward. We searched on foot from house to house, calling her name and hoping she would appear. We went to the local pound, looking through all the cages of found cats, but we found nothing. A week went by, and there was still no sign of Mittens. We were coming to terms with the fact that she was probably gone for good when one morning when Dad was taking the trash out, he noticed Oscar standing in front of the crawl space panel at the side of the house. Oscar was staring, whimpering, and cocking his head. Dad opened the panel and peered under the house, but he saw nothing. Then he kept completely still and put his ear to the opening. He heard the faint crying of a cat. He went and got a flashlight, and shining the light into the crawl space, he saw our cat cowering clear across the crawl space on the opposite side.

We figured the cat must have crept in while Dad was running his speaker wire, and that Dad had unwittingly sealed her in. Dad came to get us and brought us to the crawl space opening. He instructed me to shine the flashlight toward the cat. He then crawled on his belly clear across the space, through all the spider webs and over the dirt, retrieving our missing pet. Oh, what a happy day! My dad was a hero, and we had Mittens back in our life. We took the cat to the vet, just to be sure she was okay after the ordeal, and the vet said she looked fine.

"You saved the day," I said.

"Oscar and I. If it hadn't been for Oscar, I would never have guessed."

"Oscar was a good dog," Mom said.

The three of us then sat in the family room, reminiscing, telling old stories until the sun went down and it was time for dinner. I offered to take them out to a restaurant, and they said that would be fine so long as it wasn't anywhere fancy. I had been hoping to take them somewhere nice, but we agreed on a cheap diner not too far from the house.

Taking my parents out to dinner is a real experience. In their golden years, my parents have developed a serious aversion to spending money, and they have a perpetual fear that they're paying too much for whatever they purchase. Restaurants are no exception, so they don't look at the menu for items they might find tasty; instead, they search for the most reasonable offerings. In their heads they calculate what the ingredients might cost at the grocery store, adding the prices up to see if the charge is reasonable. "I don't mind them making a profit," Dad will always say, "but some of these prices are ridiculous." I used to get annoyed at this, which began when they were in their seventies, but I've come to accept it for what it is, an indication that my parents are old.

My parents are equally fussy over the service at restaurants, and rather than have conversations like normal people, they'll spend the entire evening talking about their servers ... about whether they were well groomed, had a good personality, were polite and helpful, and got the orders right. Their continuous commentary on the poor waiter or waitress who got stuck with our table becomes like some silly *Saturday Night Live* skit. And it is funny, it really is. Sometimes I laugh, and they give me the strangest look, wondering what I think is so funny. "It's nothing," I will say, and I will put on my straight face.

When the meal is over and the server brings out the bill, Dad will pull his calculator from his pocket. He'll borrow Mom's reading glasses and begin punching numbers, calculating the correct tip and totaling the exact amount. I'm completely serious about this. He'll then dig through his wallet and pockets to leave the right amount. When he doesn't have the exact change on hand, he'll ask the others at the table for a penny or nickel or quarter so he can make it right. I have no idea where he picked this habit up. I've been alive for sixty-two years, and I've never seen anyone else do this, not even once.

So anyway, the three of us went to the diner. I tried to keep the conversation moving along to distract my parents from their usual banter about the service. We talked about Giants baseball, my dad's favorite team ... about how they were doing against the Dodgers that week. We talked about Rudy, the guy I had hired to take care of their yard, and Mom and Dad told me what a nice guy and hard worker he was. I told them that Danny was going back to college to get a degree in computer programming, and Dad said, "Well, that's terrific. It's about time. Do you remember when you wanted to be a writer?"

"Yes, I do."

"You did so well in that creative writing class," Mom said. "That teacher liked you."

"Bah," my Dad scoffed.

"She said you had a lot of talent."

"There's nothing wrong with being a building contractor," Dad said.

"Do you ever write in your spare time?" Mom asked.

"No," I said.

"If you wanted to be a writer, you would have been writing in your spare time," Dad said. "Lots of writers started in their spare time."

"That's what Erma Bombeck did," Mom said.

"This club sandwich is a little dry," Dad said, and he looked for our waiter. He caught the guy's eye, and he came to our table. "My sandwich is a little on the dry side. Can you bring me some mayonnaise?"

"Sure," the waiter said.

"They have pretty good service here," Mom said.

"Not bad," Dad agreed, waiting for his mayonnaise and taking a sip from his iced tea.

"Why don't you try writing in your spare time?" Mom asked.

"I don't know," I said. Then I turned to my dad and said, "I'm curious—did you have any dreams when you were young?"

"Oh, sure I did." The waiter returned with the mayonnaise, and Dad spread it on his sandwich and then continued talking. "I was going to be a famous baseball player. I was going to move to New York and play for the Yankees. I was going to be a center fielder and hit over three hundred every season, and everyone would be climbing over each other for my autograph. I was a good ballplayer in high school, and my coach told me I was a natural. I could knock the skin off the ball every time I came to bat, and there wasn't a fly you could hit to center field that I couldn't snag." Dad took a bite of his sandwich and chewed on it, now staring beyond me toward the restaurant windows.

"So what happened?" I asked.

"What happened to what?" Dad said.

"What happened to your dream?"

"I grew up."

"That's it?"

"That's all there was to it."

"Do you regret not trying to be a ballplayer?"

"Who says I even would have made a team, let alone the Yankees? It was a silly dream."

"How about you, Mom?" I said, turning to her. "Did you have dreams when you were young?"

"I don't know," she said.

"Come on, you must have wanted to do something."

"For as far back as I can remember, I just wanted to be a mom. I wanted to get married and have a family, like I do now. I guess I pictured myself having more kids, but that wasn't possible. You've been quite enough for me, Lester. You've been a handful."

It was weird that we'd never talked about this sort of stuff before. I had no idea Dad had ever wanted to be a baseball player, and it felt good to learn a little more about him. When everyone had finished eating, the waiter came by and picked up our dishes. When the waiter brought the bill, he put it at the center of the table. I began to reach for it, but Dad grabbed it first. "This is on us," he said. I told Dad he didn't have to pay, but he insisted. He then procured his calculator and set it beside the bill. He borrowed Mom's reading glasses and went to work. "Wow," he said, "I just can't believe what it costs to eat out."

I told him again that I'd pay for dinner if it was too much, but he said no, that he wanted to take care of it. Poking at the buttons on his calculator, he added in the tip, and he removed the paper money from his wallet. He then rummaged through his pocket, feeling for loose change. He dropped a handful of coins on the table, and one by one he separated them as needed. "Looks like I'm a couple cents short," he said, and he looked up at Mom and me, still wearing the woman's reading glasses. He asked, "Does anyone have a couple pennies?"

On the way home we drove past the neighborhood park, the same park where Eddie Montgomery and I had polished off that quart of whiskey. I wondered what Eddie was up to after all these years, and I regretted that we hadn't stayed in touch. We used to do so much together. I asked my parents, "Have either of you heard anything about Eddie Montgomery?"

"I have," Mom said. "I ran into his mother at the grocery store last year."

"Why didn't you tell me?"

"I don't know," Mom said. "I gave Emma your phone number and told her to have Eddie call you. I just assumed he called you."

"No, he never called."

"Emma says he's an architect."

"Eddie is an architect?" I said.

"He's working for a firm in downtown San Francisco."

"I'll be darned."

"She says he's doing quite well."

"That's good to hear," I said. Of course, I knew all mothers lied about their sons. When they bump into old acquaintances, they're hardly going to carry on about how their son is in rehab or in jail, how his life is a complete disaster, how he's in the middle of a divorce, or how he's just lost his job for the third time. I wondered how Eddie was doing, and why he hadn't called me. Was he embarrassed about something? Or was he just disinterested? Or maybe he just didn't think it was wise to stoke up an old friendship like ours. It can be weird digging like that into your past, since you never know what you're getting yourself into. I suppose sometimes it's better to leave things as they are.

"What did you tell Emma about me?" I asked.

"I told her you were a successful building contractor in Southern California, and still happily married to Amy with two darling children. What do you think I told her?"

"I was just curious," I said.

CHAPTER 15

Lights, Camera, Action

When I met with Harry again, it was shortly after I'd returned from visiting my parents. We were sitting in his family room, and the TV was tuned to a Lakers game with the sound turned off. "So how'd your visit go?" Harry asked.

"It went pretty well."

"Do you get along with your parents?"

"Yes, I'd say I do."

"What do they think of your drinking?"

"I don't think my dad understands it. We don't talk about it much."

"How about your mom?"

"She's been around it with her family, so I can probably talk to her. But I still don't confide in her much."

"She's Agnes's sister, right?"

"Yes," I said. "Do you think I should be talking more to my parents about my alcoholism?"

"No, it's not necessary. It's not even necessary to waste Amy's time with it."

"Why not?"

"Because you have me, Lester. That's the beauty of AA—you have a sponsor to talk to who understands and knows what you need to get better."

"You're probably right."

"Do you remember much about your childhood?"

"Actually, I think I do."

"Did you ever play a game called Machine Gun?"

"Not that I remember."

"When we were kids, we played this game on our front lawns, and it would require five or six children. We called it Machine Gun. Everyone would line up at the bottom of the lawn, and at the top there would be one kid with an imaginary machine gun. It would be like a movie. The kid with the imaginary gun would yell, 'Lights, camera, action,' and the kids at the bottom of the lawn would all run toward him, feigning an attack. The kid at the top would spray them all with pretend bullets, and they'd tumble and fall and flip over, trying to outdo each other with the best stunt. Then the kid with the machine gun would choose the best as the winner, and that kid would get to be the next gunner. We'd play this game for hours, and it never got dull. Every time the shooter yelled, 'Lights, camera, action,' my heart would race."

"Sounds like fun."

"You probably had your own games when you were a kid that bring back memories."

"Yes, of course."

"We're about to do step seven. Do you think you're ready?"

"I think so."

"Step seven states that we humbly asked God to remove our shortcomings."

"Yes, I remember that."

"That's not exactly what we're going to do. We're going to drop the God business."

"Yes," I said.

"So what do we do?" asked Harry.

"I don't know."

"Let's go back to our game of chess. Do you remember when we talked about chess?"

"Of course," I said.

"So what exactly is chess, besides being a game and a microcosm of life? It's a series of choices we make in an effort to produce a winning outcome. Lester, the key word here is *choices*. Every time your opponent moves a chess piece, you have choices to make, depending on how you're planning to win the game. You look at all the possible board moves and calculate their outcomes, trying to predict what will happen with each. When you play, you don't make moves that will deliberately jeopardize your king, do you?"

"No, of course not."

"Or allow easy capture of your queen? Or of any of your other pieces, for that matter? You use your head and make the best choices."

"Right," I said.

"You try to choose wisely. Of course, if you're a novice player and you make some foolish moves, people will understand that you're new to the game and just need some more time and experience. But if you're a sixty-year-old man who's been playing the game for years, you would expect more from him, wouldn't you? You wouldn't expect novice moves?"

"No, and I see what you're getting at."

"So why are you still choosing foolishly? What is it inside of you that motivates you to lose?"

"I don't know."

"We've already answered this question."

"We have?"

"It's that notion of powerlessness. It's the belief that for some mysterious reason you're incapable of making good choices, that a loss is inevitable."

"So then I'm told to reach out to God."

"Exactly. But just for the heck of it, let's say you did believe in God. Isn't reaching out to him a slap in his face? Isn't it an insult of the worst kind? It doesn't show any reverence or respect for your maker at all; in fact, it's quite the opposite. You're saying that God didn't give you the means to run your own life. You're saying that his handiwork is flawed, that God himself needs to be placed in the driver's seat to steer and operate his defective product. Are we incapable of moving in the right direction ourselves, without his help? I maintain that asking for God's assistance is an affront rather than a proper act of faith. Of course, since you and I are not believers, this point isn't even of importance. What is important is learning how to make the right choices."

"Yes, I understand that."

"And you understand you're not powerless?"

"Yes," I said.

"Then you're ready for our version of step seven."

"And what exactly is it?"

"Back when I was in my thirties, I had a client named Harvey Blackstone. We were about the same age, except Harvey had been arrested and charged with burglary. I told Harvey how much I'd charge to defend him, and he brought me the full amount in cash the same day. I never did ask where he got so much cash. He supposedly had a small private investigation company, but that wouldn't have accounted for his easy access to the money. But it didn't matter. I put on a great defense for the guy, and I got the DA to completely drop the charges based on some errors the police had made processing the arrest. Harvey thanked me for my services and went on with his life.

"I didn't hear from Harvey for years, at which time he was back in jail. He'd been arrested for another burglary and needed my services. I got him released on bond, and again there was no problem with his paying my fee in cash. I went to work on his case. Unfortunately for Harvey, this time there were no easy technicality angles to work, and the case would have to go to trial. I looked over the evidence, and the police had a lot going for them. They'd recently raided a fence named Andy Goldberg who owned a pawnshop in Santa Ana, and they found Harvey's name and phone number in his Rolodex. That was important. They also found Harvey's fingerprints on a couple of Andy's stolen watches. They then got a search warrant for Harvey's house, and they found all sorts of burglary equipment laid out in his garage on the workbench. Like I said, they had a pretty good case."

"So what'd you do?"

"Well, first we addressed the Rolodex. The fact was that Harvey had his private investigation business. We would explain to the jurors that Andy had used Harvey to check some sellers out, that Andy was one of Harvey's legitimate clients, so it made sense he would have his name and number in his Rolodex. Second came the stolen watches. I would have Harvey explain that he did indeed look at the watches and try them on, but only for the purpose of purchasing them from Andy's pawnshop during one of his visits there. It wasn't illegal to try on a couple watches, and he had no idea they'd been stolen.

"Third were all the burglary tools they had found in Harvey's garage. We would readily admit that these belonged to Harvey, that they were the tools of his trade—as a private investigator he sometimes had to gain access to locked rooms and buildings to look for evidence. We said if the police were aware of any instances of illegal breaking and entering, they should charge him for those specific crimes, and not for the burglary in question. The trial went into deliberation. Harvey was found innocent that same day, and he walked out a free man."

"Do you think he was guilty?"

"Of course he was. It was genius, really, setting up this private investigation business as a front. He could channel some of his income through it, explain away a lot of his behavior, and pay taxes like a regular law-abiding citizen."

"And you were okay with that?"

"I did my job," Harry said. Then he looked at the Laker game on the TV and complained, "Did you see that? These refs are getting out of control. A player sneezes or looks sideways, and they call a foul on him. Pretty soon all we're going to be watching is players making free throws. How boring will that be? Do you watch much basketball?"

"Just once in a while."

"It's ridiculous," Harry said.

"So what ever happened to Harvey Blackstone?" I asked, trying to get back on subject.

"Harvey called me again years later. He'd been arrested again, but this time I couldn't help. I'd been booted out of my firm, and I was no longer practicing law. Instead, I was going to AA meetings and trying to get sober. I talked to Harvey a long time on the phone, and he said they had him this time, that they'd finally caught him in the act. Despite what he did for a living, I always kind of liked the guy and now felt he needed someone to talk to. I didn't mind doing that for him. And after all, considering the things I'd done over the past few years, I was hardly one to be looking down my nose at him. And the more he talked, the more I felt like I could relate.

"I asked him why he chose to do what he did for a living, knowing what the eventual consequences would be, and he said he felt he couldn't help it, that the lifestyle had just pulled him in. He thrived on the risk and excitement, and he reveled in the thrill of getting away with something. Of course, now there would be consequences. He was only fifty-seven, and he was most likely going to prison. There was something oddly self-destructive in Harvey's behavior, and he suddenly reminded me of myself. I'd been no different."

"So what's the answer?"

"To what?" Harry asked. His head was turned, and he was watching the TV again.

"How would you rewrite step seven?"

Harry turned and looked at me. "It's all about making the right choices. Fate is an idea, not a reality. Harvey made some bad choices. I've made my bad choices, and so have you. But things can change."

"How?" I asked.

"By realizing you're not powerless. Believing that you're powerless is suicide, and telling others they're powerless can be the worst thing you've ever done to them. People need to believe in themselves, no matter what their history tells them. Miracles can happen—not silly miracles like parting seas or turning water into wine, but real miracles, like men making something of themselves. Ask any successful man if his journey to the top has been without obstacles, and you will likely get a whole litany of troubles he had to overcome. Life requires hard work and perseverance. It requires that we believe in ourselves and our abilities."

"So I'm asking you again, how would you rewrite step seven?

"I would say we stopped making bad choices and once and for all took responsibility for ourselves."

"I can try to do that."

"I'll make a suggestion to you."

"Okay," said.

"Every morning when you get up, go to the bathroom mirror and look yourself in the eye. Say to yourself, 'Lights, camera, action!'"

"What's that mean?"

"It means the film is rolling."

"And?"

"That each new day is an opportunity. Years ago there was a very popular saying, 'Today is the first day of the rest of your life.' If you don't like the film analogy, tell yourself that."

"Okay."

"Then for the rest of the day, look for your choices. There will be tons of them—what to have for breakfast, how to dress for work, whether to stop for gas or wait until the gauge on the dashboard is lower. I tell you, I'm barely scratching the surface. Each day is a whole new universe of different choices. If you begin looking for them, you'll see what I mean."

"I can see that."

"Choices are everything."

"Yes," I said.

"And good choices make for a good life."

"What if it isn't clear which are good?"

"Like I've said before, you just do your best. Nobody expects you to be perfect, and you shouldn't expect that of yourself. But bonehead choices—like deciding to take a drink—are strictly verboten."

Harry turned to watch his basketball game again, and I could see he was getting interested in the outcome. The score was close, and less than four minutes were left. I decided to give Harry a break, and I said, "I've got to get going. I promised Amy I'd be home in time to watch a TV show with her."

"Fine," Harry said. He was still watching the game. "I'll give you a call tomorrow."

"I'll see my way out."

"Thanks," Harry said, and he turned up the TV volume. He was fully engrossed in the game, and I left Harry's house. I hopped in my car and drove.

On the way home I thought about everything Harry had said. He was right that I needed to take responsibility for myself. I liked all this talk about choices, and the idea of not being powerless still intrigued me. I'd been to three different rehabs, months of group therapy, and countless AA meetings, and never had I heard sobriety put to me in such inspiring terms.

I remembered Tijuana. I tried to recount what had gone through my head that afternoon. I had had choices to make, and I had chosen poorly. Yes, it was all about choices.

When I arrived home, Amy was reading a novel on the sofa, and almost all the lights were off except for her reading light. I could hear

Miles upstairs in his bedroom working on his music. "How'd it go?" Amy asked.

"Really well," I replied.

"I made some corn bread."

"That sounds great."

"It's on the counter, and there's butter in the refrigerator."

"Thanks," I said. I went to the kitchen, cut a cube of bread, and stuck it in the microwave. I then applied a thick slice of butter and stuffed the treat into my mouth. With my mouthful, I said, "This is very good."

"I made it for Miles and his friends, so don't eat it all."

"Does Miles have friends over?"

"They went home a half hour ago."

"What are you reading?"

"It's the story of the Donner Party. It's not a new book, but it's very interesting. It's amazing what people went through just to get to California. Now all you have to do is hop on a plane, buy a bus ticket, or drive a car."

"Yes," I agreed.

"You should read this book. I think you'd like it. So how's your friend Harry?"

"He's doing good. Going to see him was one of my good choices. I have made some good choices, haven't I?"

"Of course you have. You chose me as your wife, didn't you?" I laughed at this.

"Yes, of course," I said.

"Well, there you have it."

"Do you think I'm powerless?"

Amy thought about this for a moment. "Powerless over what?" she asked.

"Powerless over alcohol."

"It certainly seems so." Amy stuck her nose back in her book, and I decided not to argue about it.

The next day I woke up in a fog. I was half-asleep and half-awake, and the alarm clock had pulled me out of a strange dream. I tried to recall the details of the dream, but I couldn't do it. I climbed out of bed and went into the bathroom. Amy was downstairs, probably having her coffee and cereal or feeding Buster, or maybe reading the morning paper. She's been an early riser for as long as I've known her.

In the bathroom, I stared at myself in the mirror, looking eye-to-eye with my image, and I said the words aloud just as Harry had suggested: "Lights, camera, action." I told myself the film was rolling. I told myself that today was the first day of the rest of my life.

Then I began to make my choices, just like Harry had said I would. My mouth tasted awful, so I chose to brush my teeth. I didn't feel like showering yet, so I chose to put on some sweats and a T-shirt and went downstairs. I didn't see Amy, and I figured she was in the study sorting through work-related e-mails. I chose to make myself a cup of coffee and grab a cigar, and to head out to the backyard patio. It was a good choice, for it was a beautiful morning—just the right temperature—and the cigar and coffee tasted good together. I thought about all the choices I would have to make that day. Now, if you don't want to hear the details of my entire day, you can skip ahead to the next chapter. You may or may not find this tedious.

To continue, when the cigar was done and my cup was empty, I chose to go back upstairs and shower and shave and dress. I chose a pair of jeans and a gray LA Kings T-shirt. I chose the T-shirt because it was comfortable and because I was an LA Kings fan. My company was building a project for a dentist in Huntington Beach. It was a complicated project, and we'd run into some problems recently. Most of the problems had been resolved, but I still had some concerns, so I chose to go visit the project first thing this morning. Work traffic would be heavy, so I chose to take surface streets to the site.

I then came upon another choice. It was similar to the situation I had faced with the elderly man in his Town Car. This time it was a middle-aged Asian woman in an old Toyota who pulled in front of me and forced me to slow down.

I chose to wait patiently behind the woman until she turned left and got out of my way. When I arrived at the job site, I chose to park in the neighboring street since the parking on our street was congested with workers' trucks and cars. I walked to the building that housed our project, and before I could do anything I was accosted by Sean Spears. I can tell you a few things about Sean—that he is an excellent plumber and that his prices are very reasonable, and his low prices are the reason I hire him. But he has a volatile personality that can be very difficult to handle, and this morning he was ranting about the parking situation, claiming that the framers had parked in his space. By his space he meant the parking spot located directly in front of our project. He claimed he needed this spot because he required constant access to his truck for tools and other supplies.

"All the framers need is their saws and tool belts," Sean complained. "They don't need to visit their truck steadily like I do." I asked him if he'd asked the framers to change spots with him, and he told me he had and that they had told him to go climb a tree. He told me that as the general contractor, it was my responsibility to ensure he got his parking space. The truth was, his truck was only a few cars down the street, and he had to walk only an extra thirty or so feet. Jeez, what a pain in the neck this guy was. His face was bright red, and his veins were throbbing at his forehead, and he was demanding action. I had a choice to make, to either tell Sean nicely to grow up or tell the framers to move their truck.

The framers were a pair of friendly, easygoing Mexican men, and both of them spoke good English. I knew they were keeping their truck in Sean's parking spot just to irritate him and amuse themselves at his reaction. I don't think they cared one way or the other where they parked. I had a choice to make, and I chose to approach the framers and ask them to change spaces with Sean. I asked them to please do this for me, that I would appreciate their help. They moved their truck, no problem, and Sean got his precious parking space. Sean would surely get angry about something else later in the day, but for now he was calmed.

I had made a choice, the best choice I could come up with. This wasn't the only choice I had to make at the job site that day. I won't list every detail of the other choices I had to make; let's just say I was busy for the next three hours putting out fires and telling people what to do.

When I returned to the office, the first thing I chose to do was to open the day's mail. There was a letter from my old college, and I chose to open it first. It was a letter asking me to donate money. I had received several of these requests over the past year, and I found them aggravating. Going to college was like raising children; they always had their hands out for cash. When Danny called from

Laguna Beach, he'd say hi and how's it going and engage in small talk; then he'd always get around to asking for money. When Miles came downstairs from his bedroom, he'd always check out the show we were watching on TV, pretend to be interested for a minute or so, and then get around to asking for money. It seemed my college was no different. They'd send these letters to me describing some program or accomplishment at the school, and then they'd turn the announcement into a request for a donation.

I don't think in all the years since I've graduated, I've received a single letter from them just saying hi and asking how things are going. So I made a decision that afternoon to write the school back, to point out the childish nature of their behavior. It wasn't a nasty letter; in fact, I thought it was quite funny. I chose to make the letter humorous, and I was truly curious to see how they'd respond. It was a good choice, since it made me laugh. Sometimes we just need to make ourselves laugh. After putting the letter in an envelope and affixing the proper postage, I turned to other tasks. I had a whole list of items that needed to get done.

A construction proposal for an extensive remodel and room addition in Newport Beach needed my attention, and I'd been putting it off for the past week. I chose to take care of this, and I opened up the plans on my office table. I went to work with my architect's scale and calculator, choosing prices to assign each trade based on my experience building similar projects. I was making all sorts of choices now—measuring, counting, and calculating—making one decision after the other. I was interrupted by the phone several times ... people calling me and asking me to make more choices. I took care of my responsibilities like an adult, and I worked on the estimate until six o'clock. I wasn't quite done, but I chose to go home rather than finish, for I was hungry, tired, and ready to relax.

When I arrived home, Amy had dinner ready. It always amazed me how she was able to work a full-time job, do her chores, and still have time to prepare dinner. We were waiting at the table for Miles to come downstairs. He was in the middle of recording a song, and he told Amy he'd be down in a minute. Amy had prepared pork chops and rice and asparagus. You might wonder about the asparagus. As an adult I'd learned to like the vegetable, and it no longer made me queasy to see it on my plate. In fact, I often chose it to go with my meals, asking Amy to cook it.

While we were waiting for Miles, I told Amy the story about the Fitzpatricks and the asparagus spears. Miles finally showed up, and the three of us began to eat. I asked Miles how his music was coming along, and he said fine. And that was all he said. Like any nineteen-year-old, he had to be pumped for you to get much information.

Amy mentioned that she'd been talking to one of Miles's friends and that the boy had got a job. He was now working at the local supermarket, bagging groceries and fetching shopping carts from the parking lot. It occurred to me this would be a good time to talk to Miles about getting his own job, but what would he do? Bag groceries? It seemed like such a waste of time. I thought about it and chose not to bring the subject up, but this was probably a bad choice. The boy needed to get a job, and I wasn't doing him any favors by letting the subject slide. Harry said I shouldn't expect myself to be perfect, but I wasn't happy with the choice. So while I chose to ignore the matter this evening, I decided I would definitely bring it up to Miles the next day. This, I thought, was a much improved choice, and it made me feel better about myself.

The pork, rice, and asparagus were delicious, and for the time being everyone seemed happy. I chose to bring up my visit to my parents' house, and Miles seemed interested. He said next time I went, he would like to come along for the ride, and this surprised me. After the meal was over, I chose to help Amy wash and put away the dishes. That was a good choice, and Amy appreciated it. Harry called, and I chose to meet with him in a couple days. I always looked forward to meeting with Harry, so yes, that was another good choice. Amy and I then chose what to watch on TV, chose when to change the channel, chose when to go to bed, and chose what time to set our alarms for the morning. The day had been full of choices, and I thought I'd done a decent job.

When we went to bed, the action had ended, the lights were off, and the film had stopped rolling. I leaned over and kissed Amy on the neck and told her I loved her. Then I pulled the covers up to my chest and closed my eyes. It felt like the perfect ending to an imperfect, yet perfect, day of choices.

CHAPTER 16

Winning the War

The next day I soared through my routine again. I looked at myself in the mirror that morning and said Harry's magic words. I went through the day sorting through good and bad choices and patting myself on the back for making wise decisions. Then came dinnertime with my family, and I knew I'd promised myself last night to bring up the subject of Miles getting a job. That was my choice, wasn't it? And procrastination never makes people feel good about themselves; I knew it from experience. I was acting like an adult father when I said, "Miles, there's something we need to talk about."

"What is it?" Miles asked.

"We need you to get a job."

"Why?"

"Because you're nineteen. Because you're not going to school. You need to either go to college or get a job."

"What about my music?"

"There'll be plenty of time for your music. You could get a part-time job and still work on your music. Even a part-time job would be acceptable."

"A part-time job would be fine," Amy said.

"Don't you want to earn your own money?" I asked.

"I don't need money," Miles said.

"Only because you're living off us," I said.

"Well, I don't need to live off you."

"Then how will you survive?"

"I don't know."

"What's so bad about getting a job?" Amy asked.

"Yes," I agreed. "Why do you have such a problem with doing that?"

"Because you told me I could work on my music. It was your idea, remember? You told me to follow my dream. You said you'd back me up."

"I still want you to follow your dream, Miles, but I also want you to get a job."

"I think you're just embarrassed."

"Embarrassed?" I said.

Miles is a smart kid, and he knows how to push my buttons. And when you corner him, he doesn't cower. He fights right back, and he said, "Your friends are probably telling you how great their kids are doing, starting their careers and working at their jobs. Then they ask you how I'm doing, and all you can say is that I'm up in my rent-free bedroom working on music and eating your food. It's obvious to me that you just want to be able to tell your friends that your son is working ... you know, so you won't be embarrassed."

"It's more than that, Miles."

"Well, what is it then?"

"I want you to learn to be self-sufficient. I want you to grow and reap the rewards of working a job. It will help you to grow."

"I don't see how bagging groceries or packing burgers into bags will help me to grow."

"Everyone has to start somewhere," Amy said.

"Your mother is right."

This went on for about twenty minutes, and there's no need to recount it all. Let's just say it was very frustrating. The long and the short of it was that Miles would think it over and consider our request. When dinner was over, Miles went back upstairs to work on his music, and I chose to help Amy again with the cleanup. I then left for Harry's house, as our meeting was scheduled for eight.

"Good evening, Lester," he said after opening the front door.

"How's it going?" I said.

"Everything is just peachy."

I laughed at this and entered the house. Harry closed the front door, and we stepped into the library and took our seats in the leather chairs.

"I think I've created a monster," I said.

"How so?" Harry asked.

"It's my son Miles. He thinks he doesn't have to get a job."

"Did you ask him to get one?"

"Yes, tonight at dinner. Amy and I both made our wishes pretty clear."

"So what exactly did he say?"

"We went around with him on the subject for a good twenty minutes."

"Did he flat out say no?"

"No, he said he'd think about it."

"Well, that's a start."

"Do you know what he said to me? He said the only reason I wanted him to get a job was because of my friends, that I was embarrassed that he was out of school, living at home, and still unemployed."

"So, are you embarrassed?"

"A little, I suppose."

"Give the kid some time, and he'll come around."

"Are you sure?"

"Unless he's a total jerk, which I doubt that he is, he'll come around eventually."

"I hope so."

"Be a role model. When he sees you behaving like an adult, he may want to grow up himself."

I got the message and continued, "Well, I'm trying to act like an adult, and I certainly don't feel like drinking now. But I have a question for you. What if I do get the urge? Every recovering alcoholic experiences the urge to drink. Sometimes it can be more powerful than common sense."

"More powerful than common sense?"

"Yes," I said.

"More powerful than your love for your wife?"

"Maybe."

"More powerful than the love you have for your sons?"

"I don't know."

"This always amazes me, the power alcoholics attribute to their urges. It isn't childish to have urges; but it is childish to act on them when you know they'll have negative consequences."

"Do you still have urges?"

"Of course I do," Harry answered.

"What do you do?"

"Several years ago I went to a play. It wasn't a big production in LA, but rather at a small local venue here in Orange County. I don't remember the name of the play; in fact, I don't even remember the plot. All I remember is that the actors were drinking onstage and bantering with each other the way drunks do. I'm sure it wasn't real whiskey in their glasses, and that they were just acting. But they were very good at what they were doing, and the scene got under my skin, bringing back memories of my own drinking. I wanted so much to be up on the stage with them, gulping whiskey from my own tumbler and adding my own stupid and inebriated dialog and phony laughter. I'd been sober for years, and I couldn't believe this was happening to me. The urge to go back to my drinking days felt overwhelming, and I stood up in the middle of the play and left. I got in my car and drove home, and I have to admit that this urge frightened me.

"It didn't frighten me to know that I felt the urge, but it frightened me to know I could act upon it so readily. I lived alone, and there was no one who could stop me from making a trip to the store that evening for a quart of Scotch. I was an adult, wasn't I? I could do anything I wanted, and I had a choice to make. I thought to myself, *Yes, I am an adult.*

"Being an adult doesn't just mean you can do anything you want; it means doing what is right. It means acting responsibly and taking good care of yourself. It means making adult-sized chess moves. So I talked myself out of the urge. Those who say the urge of an alcoholic to drink is stronger than the power of free will are wrong. They overstate its strength, and they underestimate the ability of the alcoholic to say no. The urge to drink is not some amazing and impervious force of the universe; it is just one of many urges human beings have to contend with. It can be a beast, but it's a manageable beast."

"The way you explain it makes sense."

"It's not just the way I explain it; it's the way it is. Alcoholics have a tendency to exaggerate the severity of their predicament."

"What about all the alcoholics who've tried to talk themselves down from the urge and failed? Doesn't this happen all the time?"

"What about all the marriages that end in divorce? Would you say marriage is a bad thing just because so many people botched their relationships? There is always going to be a percentage of failures in any endeavor. The fact is that the AA God solution doesn't have such a great a track record either. Lots of alcoholics try to hand the reigns over to God fail miserably and turn right back to alcohol. Society is chock-full of these failures. I'm not providing you with a guaranteed alternative to the God approach. I'm only telling you what's worked for me."

"Okay," I said.

"If you're worried about it, the next time you have the urge to drink, ask yourself if you want to wind up in a jail or hospital, ask yourself if you want to hurt Amy again, and ask yourself if that's the sort of example you want to set for your sons. Ask yourself very seriously, and listen to yourself. Then ask yourself about all the yets, about the things that have yet to happen. You haven't lost your wife or children, wound up in bankruptcy court again, killed anyone in a car accident, or committed suicide. If these looming consequences aren't enough to keep you from drinking, then you probably deserve whatever you get. For in your heart of hearts, you knew better."

"You're right about that."

"This is why you have to love yourself, Lester. We've talked about this before, and we'll probably keep talking about it. If you want to punish yourself and fail, there isn't much anyone can do."

"I don't want to fail."

"Well, that's a good thing."

"But I'm not sure I'd say I love myself."

"We'll get to that later. Let's talk about failing. That's what I'd like to talk to you about this evening."

"Okay," I said.

"What is failure to you?"

I thought about this a moment and then said, "It's when you don't meet a goal."

"That's a good definition. We can definitely work with that. What is your goal?"

"I guess I have a lot of them."

"But what is your goal in working with me as your sponsor?"

"To stop drinking."

"To stop drinking forever?"

"Yes, forever. I don't want to drink."

"This is very important."

"Why?" I asked.

"I don't think most alcoholics want to stop drinking. I wouldn't classify them as failures. You have to be reaching for a goal to fail, and these people don't have goals. Many of them come to AA when the heat is on, when the law is on their case, or when their wives are making ultimatums, but they don't really want to stop drinking. Then AA can't do a thing for them. You truly have to want to stop. Making the choice to quit means everything."

"I can see that."

"So then what do we do with all the true failures who think like you and me? Do you understand who I'm talking about? Courthouses, jails, hospital beds, and cemeteries are filled with them ... people who genuinely wanted to stop drinking who couldn't find their way. They were told to go to AA meetings, to work the steps, to get a sponsor, to turn their lives over to a supernatural power and ask for divine guidance. What becomes of people for whom this nonsense doesn't work? What happens to honest and intelligent human beings who know better than to think some omnipotent and mysterious force is going to drop everything and save them from their woes? AA leaves an awful lot of good people unattended. I think to leave them by the wayside is a scandal, a great failure in and of itself. AA is a terrific concept, one drunk helping another, but it needs to be more inclusive. Those who don't believe in God, and even those who are just skeptical, deserve a fighting chance."

"Yes, I agree."

"Pope Francis said in so many words that those who do good works, even atheists, will go to heaven. Many devout Catholics argue this interpretation of his words, but the fact is, at the very least, his intentions were muddled enough so that the interpretation could be made. I like this pope, not because he thinks there may be room in his pretend heaven for us atheists, but because he's acknowledging that some very good people don't believe in God. This whole notion that you are a better person because you believe in this crazy mythology is preposterous on its face. I know God-fearing men and women whom I wouldn't trust to wash my socks. I also know atheists I would trust with my life. If the goal of AA is to help every alcoholic who suffers, it is tripping over its own feet with this God issue, and it should be reevaluating the way it's doing business. It's a failure by any stretch of the imagination."

"Yes, it is."

"And your own failure to stop drinking? How do you account for that?"

"I don't know."

"How many years have you been going to AA meetings?"

"Off and on since I was about twenty-eight, which would make it about thirty-two years."

"Have you turned your shortcomings over to God?"

"No," I said.

"Have you sought his will and the strength to carry it out?"

"No, I haven't."

"After thirty-two years, you've failed at both of these things?"

"I wouldn't say I've failed."

"What would you say?"

"I never had any desire to believe in God, so these were not goals I failed to reach."

"But you failed to stop drinking?"

"Yes, you can say that."

"Is failure acceptable?"

"It shouldn't be."

"What do they call it when you take a drink after having been sober for a period of time?"

"They call it a relapse."

"It isn't a relapse, is it? It's just another failure. It's not the end of the world, but it is a failure."

"Why is that distinction important?"

"Because although relapse is a nice euphemism, it implies we have a disease, and a disease implies that it must be treated by a doctor. And the only treatment being offered by doctors is for one to crack open the pages of the Big Book, attend meetings, and pray to a benevolent higher power. It's ludicrous, isn't it? If it wasn't such a serious problem, it would be hilarious."

"I see what you mean."

"Sometimes I feel like I'm beating a dead horse."

"No, keep going."

"We were talking about failure."

"Yes," I said.

"Is failure inevitable?" I thought about this a moment, and not knowing what Harry was driving at, I said I didn't know. Harry then said, "Failure is as right as rain."

"Failure is good?"

"Our lives are made of failures, one painful failure after the other. It's how we learn. It's how we ultimately reach our goals, learning what works and what doesn't work, and applying this knowledge successfully. All those inconveniences, bumps in the road, setbacks we suffer … they all prove we're getting somewhere. Only people who have no goals can honestly say they've had no failures. The rest of us fail and learn, learn and fail, and fail and win. It's just what life is, Lester. We lose many battles, but we try to win the war."

Harry then decided to change the subject. Now he wanted to complain about profanity at AA meetings. I have no idea why this subject was on his mind, but he said over the years he'd noticed more and more profanity being used by people at meetings, and it bothered him. "It isn't just AA meetings," Harry said. "You see it more and more in modern literature, movies, music, and on television. I've never seen such a need to cuss in all my life, and I wonder what exactly the point is. It doesn't enhance our discourse or emphasize points or make our language any more colorful; it's just annoying and unnecessary. While I was not against it when I was younger, I've come to believe it shows the general degradation of our society. It's become ugly and pervasive. It's become the status quo. Are you familiar with Lenny Bruce?"

"I've heard of him."

"I used to be a huge fan of his when I was in college. His kind are largely to blame for this."

"He was a comedian, right?"

"Yes, he was a very talented guy. He found most of his success in the early sixties. But for some reason, Lenny went from a budding young comic to a foul-mouthed commentator on life. He spent much of his time sloshing around in the gutter to prove a point. Over and over again he was arrested by the police for obscenity in his comedy routines, and he spent years fighting for his free-speech rights in the courts. But what was the point of it all? Was it just so he could swear? He was such a funny and insightful guy that the cuss words weren't necessary. I guess at the time his free-speech efforts were essential to loosening up a very uptight society, but now I think it's all gone overboard. It's actually become commercialized, and I think Lenny would be turning in his grave.

"I don't like hearing cuss words and offensive jokes everywhere I go. Am I alone in this? Am I the only person who cringes when I hear profanity in public? Or during a TV show or movie? Or in a popular song? And it isn't just the cussing. It's the violence and pornography and ambivalence when it comes to alcohol and drug abuse. It seems to me that these are all signs of social decay, and it makes me uncomfortable.

"I firmly believe in free speech, but I also believe citizens have a moral obligation to exercise it prudently. I remember seeing a black-and-white police photo of Lenny Bruce taken after he died; he was sprawled naked and bloated on the floor of his Hollywood Hills home, a syringe nearby. It was as though his foray into profanity got the best of him. He was so bright and clever; he shouldn't have died like this. I'm not saying he died because he said bad words, but I am saying it's indicative of a way of life that scoffed at the notion of decency. The death was ruled as acute morphine poisoning brought on by an accidental overdose."

"Did you ever take drugs?"

"Never," Harry said. "I'm just a drinker. How about you?"

"We took some illegal drugs in high school. But alcohol was my primary means of getting high. I felt that it was legal and therefore okay."

"If only you had known."

"Yes, if only I'd known."

"Do you suppose Lenny Bruce ever went to an AA meeting?" Harry asked.

"I have no way of knowing."

"Do you want to know what he said about religion? I remember the first time I heard this line, I had a good laugh. He said, 'Everyday people are straying away from church, and going back to God.'"

"Yes," I said. "That's a good line."

"It was such a waste of talent. He died when he was only forty."

As I was driving home, I tried to light a cigarette, but my lighter was out of fluid. I stopped at a liquor store to buy a new one. It was weird stepping into a liquor store, all those bottles of booze on the shelves, and I felt like I was under water, holding my breath until I got out. The clerk at the cash register was a guy in his fifties, his face swollen from drinking and his cheeks covered with spidery veins. His blue eyes were glazed, dulling much of their color, and his hair was oily and carelessly combed. I grabbed a lighter from the display stand, setting it on the counter, and the man scanned the price. I handed him the money. He tried to get me change out of the cash register, but he dropped several coins on the floor and bent over awkwardly to pick them up. He was having trouble with a dime, it being too thin for his thick fingers to pinch. He finally said to heck with it, standing up and taking a second dime from the cash drawer. "Here you go," he said, handing me my change. I said thanks, and then I stared at him, at his pale blue eyes and alcoholic complexion, and I wondered what this poor fellow's story was.

What had this guy looked like when he was younger? Was he once full of life and handsome the way so many young men are? Did he have plans and dreams? Was there a special girl in his life? It's hard to believe when he was younger that he would have imagined himself looking as he now did, worn-out and half-drunk, working the night shift at some neighborhood liquor store. "Can I get you anything else?" he said, noticing that I was still staring at him. I said no, thanks, that I just needed the lighter. Then I walked out of the store. It made me sort of sad, seeing this guy, the Big Book step twelve alcoholic who was still suffering. It also made me feel glad that

I had made the choice to give booze up. I hopped in my truck and lit a cigarette, rolled down the window, and turned on the radio. I was looking forward to seeing Amy and Miles when I got home.

When I arrived, two cars belonging to Miles's friends were in the driveway. I recognized both of them, and they were parked to the side so that I was able to pull my truck into the garage. When I entered the house, I found Amy and the boys in the kitchen, baking frozen pizzas and talking and laughing. "What's new?" I said.

"Jeff got a job today," Amy replied. Jeff was one of Miles's friends. Miles groaned.

"What are you going to be doing?" I asked Jeff.

"I'm working as a laborer for a construction guy in Fullerton."

"Are his jobs in Fullerton?"

"No, they're all over the place. Just his office is in Fullerton."

"You hear that, Miles?" I said.

Miles groaned again.

Miles's other friend, Christian, was checking on the pizzas in the oven. "I think they're almost ready."

"I'll get you some plates," Amy said.

"Don't we have any milk?" Miles asked, looking into the refrigerator.

"I'll go to the store tomorrow," Amy said. "I can't keep up with you guys."

CHAPTER 17

Harm's Way

The next time I met Harry, we got together in his backyard on a Saturday afternoon, sitting on a couple patio chairs next to a glass table. Harry's backyard was nothing like ours. Every piece of Harry's patio furniture was clean and properly arranged. Every shrub and flowering plant was in its proper place, and the lawn was lush and recently mowed. There was a nice little stone fountain at the far end of the yard that trickled water continuously and gave the backyard a pleasant vibe.

I have to say our backyard at home was a disaster by comparison. There was no pleasant trickling of water from a fountain in our backyard; what you usually heard was the neighbors' TVs or barking dogs. Our lawn was a balding mess and hadn't been mowed in months. There were five or six potted plants, most of which looked diseased or dead. It had been on my list to replace these plants, but I just never got around to it. We had an ugly twenty-year-old black BBQ and propane tank that we used in the summer months, and there was a rusty old swing set that hadn't been used by anyone for years. If I ever invited people to our house, our backyard would be the last place I'd take them.

"You have such a nice yard," I said to Harry.

"Thanks," he said.

"What are we going to talk about today?"

"Harm," Harry said. "We're going to do step eight. But first let me tell you a little story about a man we'll call Fred. You'll need to get comfortable, because this is going to take a while. Let's say, for the sake of this story, that it was a normal Monday morning. The sun was out, the birds were singing, and there wasn't a cloud in the sky.

This fellow Fred stepped out of his house all dressed up for work, and he was about to hop into his car when the police showed up in his driveway and arrested him. They put him in handcuffs and led him to the backseat of their patrol car. Fred was astonished and asked why he was being arrested, and the cop said he was being charged with a murder. 'Whom exactly do you think I murdered?' Fred asked, and the cops said it was some woman across town named Abby Chandler. 'Never even heard of her,' Fred complained, but the cop told Fred to save his story for the detectives.

"When they finally arrived at the station, Fred was walked into the building and booked; then he was led to a bleak little interrogation room. He sat on a metal chair in front of a table and waited nervously for the detectives to show up. When they arrived, he demanded an explanation. He said, 'I don't even know anyone named Abby Chandler. Why in the world would I have killed her?' One of the detectives took a seat across from Fred, while the other remained standing. For a moment they just stared at Fred, sizing him up, and then the seated detective began to speak. He slid a photograph of an attractive young woman toward Fred across the table. 'Do you recognize her?' the detective asked, and Fred shook his head no. The detective told Fred the photo was of Abby Chandler, the victim of the crime. 'You're being charged with her death,' the detective said, and Fred said he'd never seen the woman in his life. 'Did you or did you not take your wife out to dinner last Saturday night at Alfredo's Bistro?' Fred was now curious, because he had in fact taken his wife out to the restaurant, and he told the detective he'd been there.

"The detective removed a small notepad from his pocket and flipped through the pages; then he read from it. 'You ordered a Caesar's salad, the rack of lamb, and a Diet Coke. Your wife also ordered a salad, the salmon, and a glass of wine. Do I have the order correct?'

"Fred said, 'That sounds right.' Then the detective brought out a small piece of paper and flattened it on the table. It was the merchant's copy of the credit card receipt for the dinner. The detective pointed to the receipt and asked Fred to read the amount of the tip he wrote down for the waiter. 'I didn't leave him a tip,' Fred explained. 'The service was awful. It took an hour to get our salads, and another half hour to get our dinners. The lettuce was wilted, and our dinners were cold by the time we got them. The people seated next to us, who arrived fifteen minutes after us, were getting their entrees before we even got our salads. We tried to find the waiter for an explanation, but he was always busy waiting other tables or in the kitchen. Then he brought us the final bill.

"'I gave the waiter my credit card, and he ran it through their system. He then gave me this receipt to sign, and yes, I signed it without leaving a tip. I was not happy with the service, and when I get bad service at any restaurant, I don't leave a tip. When we got up to leave, the waiter grabbed the receipt and looked at it. Then seeing that I'd left him nothing, he cursed at me, not softly or discreetly, but very loudly so that everyone in the restaurant could hear. So tell me, why do you have this receipt?' The detective told Fred it was evidence. 'Evidence of what?' Fred asked. 'That I didn't leave a tip?' The two detectives looked at each other as though trying to decide who should speak next.

"The seated detective continued and said, 'Were you aware that the restaurant was shorthanded that night, that there were only two waiters trying to do the work of four? The kitchen was equally shorthanded and having difficulty processing the orders. In case you're curious, your waiter's name was Earl Bellamy. Waiters don't exactly make doctor's wages, you know, and Earl was planning for his tips that evening to cover a shortage due on his past-due electric bill.

"'They were scheduled to shut off Earl's power the next day. Earl lived with his wife and six-month-old son, and they were counting on taking a cash payment to the power company first thing the next morning. Earl was doing his best to handle all the extra tables that night, and you weren't the only patron to stiff Earl out of a tip. Two others had been just as unhappy with the service, and they also left Earl nothing. But you were the last straw. When he cussed you out while you were leaving, the restaurant owner heard the ruckus and fired Earl. Now not only would Earl be unable to keep his power on, but he was now also out of a job with a wife and six-month-old child to take care of. He was in an awful state.' The seated detective stopped talking, and the two detectives just stared at Fred."

"So what happened?" I asked.

"That's exactly what Fred wanted to know. The seated detective continued talking. He told Fred that Earl, now despondent over losing his job and not having enough money to keep the electricity on, stopped at a liquor store on the way home and bought a bottle of rum. He sat in his car drinking, trying to decide what he was going to do about his situation. He was also trying to work up the nerve to tell his wife what had happened, but rather than work up the nerve, he found himself getting drunk. He decided to get rid of the bottle, and he stepped out of his car to put the half-empty bottle in a nearby trash can. He was parked along a busy street, and as he tried to walk around his car, he stumbled and fell into the roadway. A motorist, seeing Fred on the asphalt, swerved to avoid hitting him and sideswiped an adjacent car. That car slammed on its brakes, and the car behind plowed into his rear end. Fred, seeing what he'd caused, ran from the scene.

"Now we had three motorists standing in the street, all arguing over what had happened. The first driver, a young woman named Cindy Dean, was being blamed by the other two drivers for having caused the pileup. Fred was gone, and they didn't believe her story about his being in the street. 'She was probably talking on her cell phone,' one driver said, and the other nodded his head. The police arrived soon after the accident, and they tried to sort things out. Cindy was allowed to call her husband to tell him what had happened, and her husband said he was on his way. The husband called a neighbor, Mrs. Bradford, to come watch his own three-month-old baby while he was out of the house, and she agreed. She came to the house and made herself at home, turning on the TV to continue with the show she'd been watching at her own home.

"Not long after Mrs. Bradford arrived to do the babysitting, her own husband, Howard, was trying desperately to reach her on the phone. Since she was at the neighbors' house babysitting, she didn't hear the phone ringing at her own home. Howard tried again and again to reach his wife, but there was no answer. Howard was in serious trouble. He was the manager of a jewelry store downtown, and it was now about eleven at night. The store had been closed, but he was still there with his assistant, Abby Chandler. They had been taking inventory and putting the more valuable jewelry pieces and cash in the store safe. It was a new safe with a new combination, and since Howard often had trouble remembering numbers, he had written the combination down on a piece of paper, which he kept safely at home. If he ever had difficulty remembering the combination, all he had to do was call his wife, and she could give it to him over the phone.

"Fred interrupted the detective, and said to him, 'Did you say Abby Chandler was Howard's assistant? Isn't she the woman you're claiming I killed?' The detective nodded his head and then went on. He said that two robbers broke into the jewelry store. They took Howard and Abby by complete surprise. One of the robbers grabbed Abby, and with one arm around her neck, and the other holding a gun against her head, he demanded that Howard open the safe, which he had just closed. The robber said to open the safe or he'd shoot Abby for sure. Howard hesitated, and the other robber stepped forward and slugged Howard in the ear, knocking him to the floor. They were letting Howard know that they were serious, that there was absolutely no way they were leaving the jewelry store until Howard opened the safe.

"Howard told the robbers that he'd open the safe, but with the ringing in his punched ear, and with the imminent threat of the gun still pressed against Abby's temple, he got flustered and could not recall the combination. He told the robbers his problem and said he could call his wife to get it. He said he did it often, and she wouldn't suspect a thing, and they let him pick up the phone to make the call. All this time Howard's wife was still babysitting Cindy Dean's kid at her house, and when Howard called, she didn't hear it. He let it ring and ring, and then he called again. He did this three or four times. He told the robbers he was getting no answer, that he had no idea why his wife wouldn't pick up. The guy with the gun grew impatient. He began poking the side of Abby's head with the tip of the gun barrel. The situation was getting out of control.

"Then by accident, the robber's gun went off. Abby's head jerked sideways, and she fell to the floor; the gun was dropped near the robber's feet. Howard lunged for the gun, and the two robbers panicked and ran. He shot at them, but he'd never fired a gun before and his aim was terrible. Bullets were flying everywhere, hitting the walls and ceiling and storefront glass, and the robbers got away.

Abby's body was curled up on the floor, oozing blood. They said she died instantly."

"So Fred didn't kill the girl," I said.

"Quite the contrary," Harry said. "Follow along with the detectives' train of thought. The detectives had made a case with both physical evidence and several eyewitnesses. Here's what they had to say—had Fred not deliberately withheld Earl Bellamy's tip that night at the restaurant, Earl would not have lost his temper and been fired. Had Earl not been fired, he would not have stopped on the way home and drank, and had he not been drinking, he wouldn't have stumbled and fallen into the road and caused the car accident. And had there not been a car accident, Cindy Dean would not have called on her husband, and her husband wouldn't have called Mrs. Bradford to come over to babysit. And had Mrs. Bradford been home rather than watching the Deans' baby, she would have been able to answer the phone when Howard Bradford first called, and Howard would've been able to open the safe for the robbers. Abby Chandler would not have been shot in the head, since Howard would have been able to open the safe. The detective said to Fred, 'You may as well have pulled the trigger yourself.'"

"That story is hard to believe," I said. "And even if it were true, Fred would never have been arrested."

"Yes, I just made it up," Harry said. "But I made it up to prove a point."

"Which is?"

"Everything we do in life, every step we make, every smile we give, every word we say, is connected to the well-being of others. No one is an island."

"Okay."

"Have you heard of the butterfly effect?"

"No, I haven't."

"It's a scientific model that says a small, seemingly insignificant event can lead directly to the occurrence of a much larger event. They ask if the flap of a butterfly's wings in Brazil can set off a tornado in Texas. And so now I ask you, in the very same vein, if a man who stiffs a waiter for his tip can cause the killing of an innocent woman in another part of town. My story about Fred is surely fiction, but

I believe this sort of thing happens all the time. It's not something you should necessarily worry about, but it is something you should keep in mind when you're working on your eighth step—people can be affected adversely by nearly everything you do. Does this make sense to you?"

"Sort of."

"Do you know what step eight is?"

"Something about listing people we've hurt."

"That's pretty close. What it actually says is that we made a list of all persons we had harmed and became willing to make amends to them all."

"Yes," I said.

"Do you have any idea how many people you've harmed in your life?"

"Probably not."

"It's an impossible task, listing all these people. There is no way of knowing who they all are. Many of them may be obvious, but many you may have harmed obliquely, by doing something completely innocuous, or even by having tried to help someone. Or you may have harmed them the way Fred killed Abby Chandler. There's just no way on earth to pin this list down, unless you're God, who sees all and knows all. Are you God?"

"Of course not."

"Then we need to rewrite this step. How would you suggest we do this?"

"I don't know," I said.

"How about this? How about we say that we made a list of some obvious people we harmed as a direct result of our drinking?"

"That's it?"

"Yes, that's it."

"I guess I can live with that."

"You make a list of your most obvious victims. It's pretty basic stuff. We're not going to do anything with the list, not even make the amends they have planned for you in step nine, so it doesn't have to be comprehensive. We're only trying to prove a point."

"I'm not going to make amends?"

"No," Harry said.

"I thought this was an essential part of the program, making amends."

"Don't worry about that now. You're talking about step nine, and we're still working on eight. Just concern yourself with making the list."

"Okay."

"Are you ready?"

"You want me to do this now?"

"I'll get you a pen and paper." Harry stood up and walked into the house, and he returned with a pen and a single sheet of paper. He set the items down on the glass table and told me to call for him when I was done.

"Only one sheet of paper?"

"It's all you'll need."

"Fine," I said, and I went to work. I decided to start with family. I began with the most obvious victim, Amy. Wow, there were so many things about Amy I could write about, all the different ways I'd harmed her by my drinking. It would take a full ream of paper to write them all down. Then there were the boys, Miles and Danny, and also my parents and probably Amy's parents.

There was of course Agnes, to whom I caused harm over and over again while she struggled to get me sober. I drove that poor woman crazy. All she wanted to do was help me, and I fought her every step of the way. When she took me to AA meetings, I'd show up drunk and embarrass her in front of her AA friends. I'd wake up in strange towns and call her to come get me. I had her driving all over Southern California and Nevada for months, chasing me down and bringing me home. Every time I drank, I'd expect her to calm down Amy, who was struggling to understand just what the heck was happening to her life. I was belligerent and unappreciative.

I remember one night I drove drunk to Agnes's house in Long Beach to yell at her and ask her why I was still drinking. I ended up spending the night there on the couch because Agnes was too tired to drive me home, and because Amy didn't want to come get me. I got up that night for some water, and I stumbled and fell in the kitchen. As I fell I reached out and grabbed a shelf full of glass and porcelain mementos, and they all came crashing down. I broke things Agnes had held onto since she was a little girl, irreplaceable stuff that had survived many years. I remember Agnes sweeping the pieces up in a dustpan the next morning. It was a pitiful sight, and I apologized profusely, but Agnes told me not to worry about it. It has always bothered me tremendously that I never made it to see her in the hospital on the day that she died. Sure, I was headed there, but of course I never made it. I never got to say good-bye or even thank you. I never told her I loved her. She just passed away, and I never saw her again.

I realized this list was going to take forever if I stopped to think much about the people I had hurt, but it became impossible to write down some of the names without triggering a ton of memories and stopping to think about them. The list was very slow going, but I trudged ahead. Harry interrupted me when I was on my sixteenth name. "How's it coming?" he asked.

"I'm on number sixteen," I replied.

"That's it?"

"It's taking some time."

"You've been at it for over an hour now."

"I have?"

Harry picked up the sheet of paper and then then took the pen out of my hand. "This is fine," he said.

"You think so?"

"Did it bring back some memories?"

"Yes, quite a few. It makes me feel bad knowing what I've done to some of these people, especially those I love. I haven't exactly been the greatest guy."

"But are you still drinking?"

"No, of course not."

"Then don't worry about them. They'll be fine."

I asked Harry what to do with the list, and he said he would throw it away for me. That was the end of our meeting.

I left Harry's house and drove home thinking about some of the names on the list. Some of them I hadn't thought about for years. It was still sunny and warm outside, and there were several good hours left in the day. I decided to stop at the roller hockey rink on the way home, to sit and watch the kids play. Both my boys used to play roller hockey when they were younger, and I'd spent countless hours at this rink watching their teams compete. Those were such good times, and the boys and I were very close, spending hours in the truck together, talking and listening to music, and stopping at restaurants on the way home for dinner. I found a parking place and walked to the busy rink. Parents were all cheering, yelling, and socializing while their kids swatted pucks, pushing and shoving each other.

I loved the click-clack of hockey sticks and the continuous rush of busy in-line skates. I found a seat high in the bleachers and sat down next to a young couple whose son was playing in the game. It was easy to tell which kid was theirs, because every time the boy got possession of the puck, they'd stand up and start shouting instructions. Watching these people was so nostalgic. There was the perpetually miffed father seated at the bottom of the bleachers who spent the entire game shouting insults at the refs, telling them they didn't know what they were doing, telling them they were either missing calls or just plain hallucinating. There was also the mother who stood off to the side of the bleachers, her hands and face against the protective glass, who would let out an earsplitting shriek every time her team shot on the opposing goalie, like someone was jabbing bamboo under her fingernails. Then there was a group of three or four teenage girls off to the other side who were debating over which boy out on the floor was the cutest. And of course there were the rug rats, the younger siblings of the players, who were running around the bleachers, chasing each other, playing tag, and having no idea what was happening in the actual game.

Things hadn't changed a bit since I used to come here with my own boys, and I had to laugh. The only thing different now was that my sons weren't involved in any way, so I didn't care which side won. I cheered when one team scored a goal, and I cheered when the other scored as well. These people probably thought I was crazy, but I stayed there a couple hours. When the last game was over, I got up and walked back to my truck.

On the way home I recalled that I had not always been sober when I went to the games. Often I would drop the boys off and make a run to the liquor store down the street, where I'd buy a half pint of vodka, drink it quickly in the truck, and then return. A half pint was just enough to get me high without being drunk, and I remember those were some of my favorite games. I'd stand by myself at the glass, in my own world, and watch my sons play their hearts out, trying to win. If one of the parents approached me, I'd keep my distance while they talked so they couldn't smell the vodka on my breath. I'd then say a few polite words to get rid of them and get back to watching the game. There was one time when this didn't quite work out so well. I drank a full pint instead of a half pint, thinking stupidly it would make the game twice as fun, but when I arrived at the game, my alcoholic synapses were firing.

I didn't watch the game at all; instead, I looked for the father of one of Miles's friends who lived near our house. I couldn't stand this guy, but I enlisted his help. I told him I had an emergency at one of my construction jobs, and I asked him if he could please take Miles home to our house after the game. He said not to worry about it, that he'd take care of everything. Then I went to my truck and drove down the street. I filled the truck with gas and stopped at the liquor store again, where I bought a fresh quart of vodka. I then drove to the bank, where I withdrew several thousand dollars cash from my checking account, and I was off to the races, off to Las Vegas.

I have no way of explaining this behavior except to say this is the sort of thing I often do when I'm drinking, running away. When I arrived in Vegas four hours later, I had finished most of the vodka and was terribly drunk. Believe me, in the condition I was in, it was no easy task steering my truck through the busy Vegas streets, dodging cars and pedestrians, and finding a place to park. I staggered from casino to casino … searching for what? I still don't know what I was doing there. I never did call Amy to tell her where I was, and I didn't return home for three days. When I arrived at home, I was exhausted and embarrassed, and I hadn't changed my clothes or showered the entire time I was gone. I undressed and plopped my bad-smelling body in our bed, sleeping off days of alcoholic drinking.

To this day I can't remember what I did during that three-day absence. I remember only the smallest bits and pieces—hanging around at a bar, talking to several prostitutes, laughing, and telling jokes and lies. I remember gambling a little at a couple craps tables, but I don't recall winning anything, not a single bet. I remember once feeling a little sick, and I went to a nice restaurant to sober up. I got a table to myself, and I must have been quite a sight, this drunken slob eating all alone in his booth. My head was spinning, and my words were slurred. The waiter was having a difficult time understanding me, but he finally got the order straight. But for three full days? How did I spend all that time, and what exactly did I do during all those hours? I have no idea.

They say all roads lead to Rome, but for me all roads lead to my drinking. I can't even enjoy an afternoon of watching roller hockey without some disturbing drinking memory coming up. It is so ingrained in my life that it has become a part of everything I am, usually in a big and embarrassing way.

When I made that list for Harry this afternoon, Amy was at the top of the page, as she should have been. In fact, when Harry gave me the pen and paper and asked for a short list, I should've just written Amy's name on it and told him I was done. I'd put her in harm's way for forty-three years. It was amazing she was still with me, waiting at home for me now, probably wondering what Harry and I had talked about. Would I tell her about the list I made for Harry? Would I tell her about the time I just spent at the hockey rink?

I know Amy loves me, but I don't know how much she wants to know about me these days. Does that make any sense? When you harm a person as much as I've harmed Amy, intimacy—and I mean real intimacy—does not come the same way as it comes for young lovers. There are a lot of things neither person wants to talk about.

When I got home, Amy said she had purchased steaks and a bag of potatoes, and she wanted me to light the BBQ for the steaks. She would bake the potatoes in the oven. We were having several of Miles's friends over for dinner, three of them to be exact, and Amy was looking forward to entertaining her boys. I went to the backyard to light the BBQ, and I stood there and stared at everything … the balding grass, the dead plants, and the rusty old swing set. Amy came out to see what I was doing. "What are you looking at?" she asked.

"Our backyard," I said.

"What's wrong with it?"

"I think we ought to fix it up. We don't even use it, the way it is."

"I think that's a great idea."

CHAPTER 18

Here and Now

The next day I called a landscape architect friend of mine named Chester Davies. I first met Chester several years ago at one of my projects on which he was the designer. Chester did lots of small projects for people, and I thought he would be perfect for what I had in mind. Chester came over to the house on the following Monday afternoon, and I took him through the house, through the sliding patio doors, and to our pitiful backyard. "This is it," I said, and I explained what I had in mind. There was no way I'd be able to afford a nice backyard like Harry's, but with some creativity and hard work, we would certainly be able to come up with something a lot better than what we had. Chester walked around the yard for a while, looking at it from different angles, peering over the fences to see what the neighbors had done with their yards. "Do you think you can do something?" I asked.

"It depends on how much money you spend."

"I'll do most of the work myself."

"That will help. Yes, I think I can come up with something you'll like."

"That's terrific," I said. We then agreed on a price for his work and shook hands to close the deal. Chester said he would have something on paper for me in a week, and I made a mental note to call him. He then took measurements and scribbled some information in his notebook and left.

When Amy returned home from work that evening, I told her about my meeting with Chester, and she seemed surprised. "I didn't think you'd actually go out and hire an architect," she said.

"I want it done right."

"Can we afford this?"

"I'll do the work myself," I said.

"Are you sure you'll know what you're doing?"

"I'm a contractor. I do this sort of stuff for a living."

"But you use employees and subcontractors. You don't do any of the work yourself. I can't even picture you doing the work with your own hands. Do you have any tools?"

"I have some in the garage. I'll buy what I don't have."

"This will be amusing, Lester."

"It will be fun."

"I guess anything will be an improvement over what we have now. It's been so neglected for so long. But I have a question for you. Why the sudden interest in fixing up the backyard?"

"It just seemed like it ought to be done."

"But why now?"

"Because there's no time like the present. You know, lights, camera, action."

"What does that mean?"

"It's something Harry says."

Amy didn't ask any more questions, and she went in the house to prepare dinner. She seemed a little skeptical, but I knew she would have a change of heart once she saw the improvements being made.

My next meeting with Harry was scheduled for Wednesday evening. He told me in advance that we were going to work on step nine. He said once I got step nine under my belt, that it would be pretty easy going for the rest of the race. I opened up my Big Book at home and read the ninth step in advance of our meeting. The book said, once we had listed all the people we had harmed, that we were to make direct amends to them wherever possible. I was curious what Harry would do with this step, since he'd said already during step eight that he would not have me make amends. Clearly, Harry planned to rewrite this step, but I wondered why. It made sense to make amends to the people we'd harmed, not only as a way of clearing our conscience, but also because it was the right thing to do.

I thought that when you wrong someone, you should make amends. You should certainly try to make things right; I'd been taught this ever since I was a small boy. When I did something wrong to another kid, I was required to say I was sorry. When I damaged someone's property, I was expected to pay for the loss out of my allowance, or by working it off doing yard work or cleaning cars. This is how I was raised and how I tried to raise my boys.

Harry and I met in his library, seated as usual on the leather chairs, and Harry began the discussion recounting one of his old court cases. This particular trial concerned a man named Raymond Booth, a forty-two-year-old real estate developer who had been accused of murdering his wife, a lovely young woman by the name of Maria. Ray and Maria had two children, boys aged four and six, and they lived in a home in the hills of Laguna Beach. Maria was ten years younger than Ray, and the two were married when Maria was twenty-four. She adored her husband and looked forward to starting a family with him.

But as the years went by, Maria discovered that her husband was not as faithful as she'd hoped, and she caught him in affairs several times. Each time she caught him, he'd swear it would never happen again. Then Maria would notice the signs just as before … the suspicious late evenings at the office, the mysterious out-of-town business trips, and Ray's lackluster performance in bed.

By the fourth affair, Maria had had enough. It was a terribly difficult decision for her, but she told Ray she was leaving him and taking the boys with her. She told him nothing could change her mind. According to neighbors, the couple had a horrible fight the night of the shooting, and several neighbors said they could hear them shouting for hours. It was at around eleven o'clock that the shots rang out, and within minutes the police were parked in the driveway. It wasn't one of the neighbors who had called the police; in fact, it was Ray himself. He told the 911 operator he'd just shot his wife, that she was no longer breathing.

Fortunately for Harry, Ray had a good deal of money to burn on his defense, but unfortunately for Ray, there wasn't a whole lot Harry could do. Ray had confessed to the police the night of the shooting. Furthermore, the weapon belonged to him, there were powder burns on his right hand, and his fingerprints were all over the gun. "It was going to be a tough case," Harry said.

"What'd you do?"

"I did what any good trial lawyer would do. I blamed the shooting on Maria."

"You what?"

Harry explained that nowhere in Ray's signed confession was there any clear statement that would contradict the idea that it had been Maria who was having the extramarital affair. Ray had simply confessed to shooting her because she was moving out with the kids. He never actually said why she was moving. Harry concocted a story that she was leaving Ray to move in with a secret lover, a lover who was now keeping quiet about the affair to protect Maria's honor and also to keep from getting involved in the messy court case. Harry told the jury they would probably never know who this man was. "I had them thinking about it," Harry said. "Ray just sat solemnly beside me, playing the part of the victim." Since he had shot Maria, Harry said there was no way Ray would ever get off without some kind of prison time, but that the story about her lover would certainly lessen the charge and severity of the sentence.

"So what was the verdict?"

"After over a week of deliberation, he was found guilty of manslaughter. Maria's father was furious. When they read the verdict, he was complaining and shouting and disrupting the courtroom, and the judge was banging his gavel. Finally, the prosecuting attorney was able to calm the old man down. When it came time for sentencing, the judge allowed Ray to address the court and the victim's father, and Ray took the opportunity to apologize. I didn't think this guy had it in him to deliver such an eloquent and powerful speech. He spoke for fifteen minutes about his life with Maria, about how they first met, about their wonderful vacations together, about what family life meant to him and how he loved his two beautiful sons, and finally about how much he regretted what he'd done. Then he sat down, and he began to sob. I swear there wasn't a dry eye in the courtroom, with the exception of Maria's father. He stood up and shook his fist at Ray and shouted, 'I hope you rot in hell!'"

"And this has what to do with step nine?"

"Don't you see? It has everything to do with it."

"You need to explain."

"What's done is done," Harry said.

"That's it?"

"Do you remember when you were a child, how if you wronged some other kid, your parents would make you apologize? You'd have to swallow your pride and say you were sorry, perhaps even shake hands with the other kid to put the matter to rest?"

"Yes, of course, I remember that."

"It was a lousy lesson."

"It was?"

"It doesn't work that way in the real world with adults. When you wrong another adult, an apology is pointless. It would be like kissing someone's wound to make it better. How silly would it be for a grown-up doctor to kiss your injury to heal it?"

"I see what you mean."

"There was nothing Ray could ever do to make amends for his crime. Even if Ray had been given life in prison, or a lethal injection, Maria's father wouldn't have found satisfaction. In order to make her father happy, Ray would need to travel back in time to undo the killing, but time travel isn't something we've learned to do. We can do many amazing things in this world, but going back in time to fix our screwups isn't one of them. We have to live with our mistakes, and the people we have harmed have to live with them too."

"I understand that," I said.

"Let's put the shoe on the other foot. Has anyone harmed you recently?"

I thought about this for a moment and then said, "I can't think of anything happening recently."

"How about at work?"

"My customers have been pretty good, but there was an incident with one of my workers last fall."

"What happened?"

"I sent him to do some repair on a customer's roof where he had to replace a termite-infested fascia board. While he was up on the roof, he stepped on a main roof drain and cracked the pipe. He knew about the damage, yet he didn't tell me. When the first rain came, the drain leaked like Niagara Falls, and rainwater began pouring from the ceiling all over my customer's study, splashing all over his desk and files, soaking his computer, and drenching his hardwood floors, causing them to buckle. It created thousands of dollars in damage.

"The customer called me in the middle of the night during this rainstorm, and I drove over to his house with several buckets and a stack of towels hoping to contain the situation, but the water was literally everywhere. No matter what I did, I was unable to prevent what was happening. I was furious at my worker, for not only did I have to clean up and pay for the damage, but I also had to pay a plumber and a roofer to come out and fix the broken drain and patch the roof.

"The entire disaster cost me a small fortune, and my customer was irate that I had not kept a better watch on his project and my worker. This customer was very hard to please, and he hadn't been very impressed with us prior to the roof leak. The leak confirmed what he thought of me and my company. He called me a buffoon. It was a bad situation all the way around."

"What'd you do to the worker?"

"I fired him. It wasn't the first time he'd done something stupid, and this was the last straw."

"What's he doing now?"

"He got a job with another contractor."

"Tell me how you'd feel if one day he showed up on your doorstep and said he was sorry for what had happened; would you accept his apology?" said Harry.

"I don't know."

"Would his apology make you feel better?"

"No, I doubt it."

"Would you still be angry at him?"

"Maybe."

"What if he offered to pay all your damages?"

"That would never happen," I replied, laughing.

"Tell me about your trip to Tijuana. When you got back from Mexico, did you apologize to Amy?"

"Of course."

"How do you think she felt about your apology?"

"She was livid, and I doubt my apology meant too much to her. She was terribly frustrated. And I think she felt defeated, like there was nothing we'd ever be able to do to stop me from drinking again. Surely she didn't want me groveling at her feet over how sorry I was; she just wanted me to stop."

"If you apologized to her again tonight, do you think it would help?"

"I know it wouldn't."

"Apologies are pointless, aren't they? And so are amends. Adults need to understand they just have to live with harm caused by the misbehavior of others. It's a tough fact of life, but people need to understand this. By the same token, people who have caused harm have to live with the fact that they can't do anything to make things right. There's no way they can go back in history and change the course of events. We all live in the present, in the here and now. What's done is done, and trying to make amends for something that happened in the past is a waste of time."

"So how would you state the ninth step?"

"I would say that we let bygones be bygones and chose to concern ourselves with the here and now."

"Can this be done?"

"I know of no one capable of living like this perfectly. Human beings have a powerful attraction to the past. They dwell on it and stew in it and revel in it like a dog rolling around in a bad smell. But I promise, the more thoroughly you work this step, the better off you'll be. It's one day at a time, Lester. Of all the slogans to come out of AA, this is one of the best— to face life one day at a time. You need to live in the present, and slowly but surely, you'll build a life you can be proud of by virtue of your own responsible acts."

"And the people I've harmed?"

"Let them work it out themselves. They don't need any of your meddling."

As I drove home from Harry's that evening, I thought about everything Harry had said about making amends. It was a completely different way of looking at things than I'd been accustomed to. Harry probably was right that he was an excellent attorney, for he was very good at putting together a cogent and convincing argument.

As I drove, I remembered an incident from my childhood when my father forced me to apologize to another boy named Joey Miller.

The neighbors across the street had a rock garden in their front yard. None of the other neighbors liked it much, since it was kind of out of place among the other green front lawns, hedges, and many flower beds. But we kids loved the rock garden, for in the yard was a section of white quartz stones that were the perfect size for picking up and throwing.

Although all of us were told by our parents to avoid the rock garden, one summer afternoon we decided to have a rock fight. It wasn't as though we all got together and made the decision; it just sort of happened. One stone was tossed, then another, and then a bunch of them. It was a free-for-all, and none of us had very good throwing arms, so no one was actually being hit.

But then, as luck would have it, I threw one of the quartz rocks with all my might and it hit Joey Miller square in the face. He shrieked at first, and then he started crying, holding his hand over his nose. It didn't take long for the blood to appear from behind his fingers, and there was a lot of it. The blood was running down over Joey's lips and dripping off his chin and onto his T-shirt. He ran crying to his house, his hand still covering his nose. The rest of us stopped what we were doing and moved away from the rock garden, looking for something else to do. Soon after, Joey's father come storming out of their house holding Joey by the hand, and the two of them walked down the sidewalk. They stopped when they reached my house, and they marched right up to the front door.

Joey's dad pressed the doorbell, and my father answered. They talked for a minute or so and then examined the big white bandage on Joey's nose. My dad stepped to the porch and called for me to come home. I knew I was in trouble, having been told previously by my parents to avoid the rock garden, and having known better than to throw rocks at others. "Did you do this?" my father asked, and I nodded my head. Dad then said, "I want you to apologize." I said I was sorry to Joey, and Dad then told me to get in the house. I was lucky not to get a spanking, but I was told to stay in my room for the rest of the day. It didn't seem fair, as all of us kids had been throwing rocks. Mine just happened to hit Joey Miller in the nose.

When I got home from my meeting with Harry, it was close to eleven, and Amy was not downstairs. I found her up in our bedroom packing her suitcase, and I asked her what she was doing.

While I was gone, she had received a call from her mother, telling her that her dad was in the hospital for a massive heart attack he had suffered that evening. Amy had already been on the Internet purchasing plane tickets to Albuquerque for the next morning. No night flights were available. She said she had talked with the doctor at the hospital, and that things did not look good for Vern; he was in an ICU, and they were doing their best to keep him alive. All four of us were scheduled to board the plane early in the morning, and Miles had already packed his bag. Danny was on his way to the house and would be home any minute.

When we arrived in Albuquerque, we rented a car and drove straight to the hospital. We asked the nurse where we could find Vern's bed. We were informed that Vern had just passed away a couple hours before, and that his body had been transferred to the morgue. Amy started crying, and I put my arms around her to comfort her. Lucy then appeared in the hallway, her eyes red and swollen. I let go of Amy, and she ran to her mother to embrace her while the boys and I stood there watching. After several minutes of talking, we decided to go to Vern and Lucy's house. Danny would take his grandma in her Cadillac, and the rest of us would go in the rental car. We arrived at the house late in the morning. "We need to arrange things," Lucy said. "We need to get all this done while the four of you are here."

Lucy poured herself a stiff drink from the wet bar and got down to business. She said, "Vern and I already talked about our wishes. We knew this day was coming for each of us, and we decided neither of us wanted a fancy funeral or big memorial service. We both wanted to be cremated and disposed of as quickly as possible. Vern wanted his ashes to be spread in a special spot in the desert where we used to hike when we first moved here. I can take you to the spot. It's only about a half hour from here. He then wanted all of us to go out to dinner at a nice restaurant and celebrate his life, not bawl and grieve and act like fools. 'Try real hard to think of some nice things to say about me,' he said, kidding of course. I told him it would be easy."

Lucy began crying again, and Amy took her drink from her hand and gave her another hug.

The four of us stayed with Lucy for the next few days. When it came time to spread Vern's ashes, we all piled into Lucy's Cadillac and drove to the special spot in the desert, where Lucy let them loose. That evening we drove to Vern's favorite restaurant and took our seats in a large comfortable booth. The waiter recognized Lucy and asked her where Vern was this evening, and Lucy explained he had just passed away. "I'm so sorry," the man said. Lucy smiled at him as her eyes welled up with tears, and she then said, "We're here to celebrate Vern's life, not feel sorry for ourselves. I think each of us should tell a favorite story about Vern. So who wants to start?"

Miles immediately raised his hand like he was in a school classroom. "I'll start," he said. Lucy smiled and told Miles to go ahead, and Miles began his story.

Miles said to his grandmother, "I remember when I was visiting here by myself, when I was in sixth grade. Mom and Dad didn't come because of their work, and Danny was busy setting up his art studio in Laguna. It was just me and you guys for three whole days. Do you remember that visit, Grandma? You and Grandpa took me out to eat. I had a hamburger and fries, and I remember the hamburger had all kinds of lettuce and onions and tomato, which I scraped off, but the fries were great. I remember eating my fries with lots of catsup. Grandpa kept ordering cocktails, and he was in a good mood. He was telling jokes and kidding around and talking to everyone in the restaurant. When we left, Grandpa was too dizzy, so you drove. About halfway home, we were pulled over by the cops, and they made you get out of the car to do a test.

"I was only twelve, and I didn't know what was going on, but I watched as you tried to follow instructions. Then I watched as one of the cops put handcuffs on you. Suddenly Grandpa swung his door open and got out of the car. 'What the hell do you think you're doing?' Grandpa yelled at the cops, and before either officer could answer him, he took a swing at one of them. The punch would've knocked the cop clean over, except he missed by a mile and fell to the street. Grandpa landed on his face, and there was now a big cut on his cheek where he'd hit the asphalt. Then the cops got a call on their car radio, and one of them ran to answer it. 'We've got to go,' he said, and the other cop quickly removed the cuffs from you. 'It's your lucky night,' he said, and they hopped into their patrol car and sped away."

"I remember that night," Lucy said.

"I'd never seen anyone throw a punch at a cop before. Even if he did miss, it was so cool."

"Why didn't I ever hear about this?" Amy asked.

"The next day Grandpa gave me twenty bucks for me to promise not to tell."

"That was Vern," Lucy said. "He was such a handful."

"I can't believe I let Miles visit with you guys unsupervised."

Lucy then said to Miles, "We had some good times together, didn't we?"

"I loved my grandpa," Miles said.

"Any other stories?" Lucy asked. "How about you, Danny? Are there any good stories you'd like to share?"

Danny gave it a little thought and then said, "My favorite story is the one he used to tell about high school, about how he and his friend put Betsy Fisher's bicycle up in the top of a pine tree. Grandpa said Betsy Fisher was the smartest kid in school, and she always parked her bicycle in the rack near the pine trees. One afternoon Grandpa and his friend saw her bike there by itself, a couple hours after school had let out. They figured she was still studying in the library, and they had the great idea to climb one of the trees and hoist the bike up in it to teach Betsy a lesson for trying so hard in school. Just as they were about to the top, the dean walked by below, and hearing a branch break under Grandpa's foot, he looked up at the boys in the tree.

"The dean asked what they were doing up there with Betsy Fisher's bike, and Grandpa said they'd seen the bike in the tree and were bringing it down, that someone must have carried it up as some sort of prank. The dean fell for Grandpa's story, and he was so impressed with the boys' act of goodwill that he called Betsy's dad and told him what they had done. Mr. Fisher owned the ice cream parlor about a half mile from the school, and to repay the boys he promised them each a free bowl of ice cream. He told Grandpa and his friend to come to the store that evening to claim their prize.

"Mr. Fisher was friends with a reporter from the local paper, and he had the reporter come to the store as well. The reporter agreed that the story about the boys would make a great human interest item in the paper, and he took a picture of Grandpa, his friend, and Betsy Fisher eating ice cream together. The picture made the second page of the paper, and there was a short article about the good deed Grandpa and his friend had done. Grandpa showed me the newspaper with the photo."

"I've seen that stupid picture," Amy said.

"He was such a rascal." Lucy laughed.

"I'll tell you my favorite story about Dad," Amy said.

"Although it isn't really a story. It's just something he did. This was before you boys were born, when your dad and I were having to file bankruptcy. This was when Lester was first trying to stop drinking and everyone and their brother were after us for money. It was horrible, and I thought we'd never get through it. Dad called one day and said he sent a Federal Express package addressed to me, and to be sure to look for it. I asked what was in it, and he wouldn't say. When I got the package, I opened it, and there was a letter from Dad and an envelope full of hundred-dollar bills. I read the letter, and Dad said he was sending me five thousand dollars to help me through our rough times. He said not to tell anyone he'd sent it, that it was just between us. He said the money was a gift and not a loan, and that I didn't have to worry about paying him back, not ever. In the letter he said he loved me."

"I had no idea," I said.

"I didn't know about it either," Lucy added.

"I always wondered how we were able to pay some of those bills," I said.

"Your father did love you," Lucy said to Amy. "He thought the world of you, and he was very worried when you and Lester were going through your problems."

The boys had nothing to say about this story. All these events occurred before they were born, and Amy and I seldom talked to them about those years. As far as they were concerned, it was ancient history.

Now it was Lucy's turn. She said, "My favorite story about Vern was the day he proposed to me. I can remember like it was yesterday.

We were living in California, and Vern took me to the beach. I remember sitting on our towels, drinking beer and soaking up the sun. We didn't have a cooler, so Vern used to dig a deep hole in the sand and drop our beers in it to keep them cool. We'd just come out of the water and were drying off when Vern suddenly placed his towel on the sand and dropped to his knee. He removed the engagement ring from his swimming trunks pocket and held it toward me. 'Lucy,' he said, 'will you marry me?' I was in shock. We'd never even discussed marriage, and the proposal came as a complete surprise. But I said, 'Yes, Vern, of course I will.' Vern then put the ring on my finger, stood up, and hugged me. He then put two fingers in his mouth and whistled.

"The next thing I knew, all our friends were coming over to us; they'd been hiding not far away, lying down on the sand so I couldn't see them. There must have been fifteen to twenty kids there. They brought a cooler full of beer, and Tommy Albright brought his ukulele. We drank and sang popular songs and celebrated the engagement for the rest of the afternoon. Even though I came home with a terrible sunburn, it was one of the happiest days of my life."

Lucy caught the attention of the waiter, and he came to our table. She ordered a double Scotch, and Amy ordered a glass of wine. I ordered a coffee, and the boys ordered Cokes. The waiter asked if we were ready to order dinner, and we told him we needed a few more minutes.

"How about you, Lester," Lucy said. "Do you have a favorite story?"

"I don't know," I said. I hated being put on the spot like this. I'm not a very spontaneous person, and if I'd known we were going to share stories about Vern, I would've taken the time in advance to come up with a good one. Instead I told the story about Vern puking up his dentures, and I said, "I'd never seen anyone do that before, not in my entire life."

"I remember that night," Lucy said. "We had a lot of fun. Poor Vern and those awful dentures."

We spent the rest of the evening telling more stories and eating dinner. Lucy had three more doubles, but you would never have known it. It was just the way Vern would've wanted it, his family all getting together and having a good time, talking and laughing and telling stories about his life.

When we returned to California, I called Harry to set up our next meeting. He asked me how everything had gone, and I told him what had happened. You know, I was sorry that Vern had passed, but I was pleased with the way things had gone. It wasn't as bad as I thought it would be.

CHAPTER 19

Captain's Log

Harry did love talking about his court cases. Despite his apparent distaste for what he did for a living, he still had a fascination with criminal trials. The next time we met, he began our conversation by telling me about a nineteen-year-old client named Joel Bennett who was charged with the murder of a twenty-eight-year-old woman named April Sanders. Harry said Joel had been drinking heavily at a party, and he had climbed into his car to leave despite attempts to stop him. "He shouldn't have been driving at all," one of his friends said at trial. "He was so drunk he could barely walk, let alone drive a car."

Joel did climb into his car and drove about five hundred feet before sideswiping a parked vehicle. He swerved to the other side of the street and hit yet another parked car. Rather than stop to assess the damage, he sped down the street, skidding around a turn and accelerating into oncoming traffic. He plowed head-on into April's car, killing her instantly. The police estimated he was going about seventy miles per hour at the time of impact. April was driving a small older sports car with no seat belt and no air bags, and her car was demolished.

Harry said the police took lots of photos of the gruesome wreck, and the DA used them at trial to sway the jury. No one could understand why Joel did what he did, bouncing off the cars and accelerating into April. It was maniacal, and when asked about it, Joel said he completely blacked out, that he couldn't remember either leaving the party or driving the car. The only thing he remembered was lying in the back of the ambulance, strapped to a gurney with a paramedic at his side. He sustained a severely sprained wrist and some ugly fascial contusions from his air bag, but that was all. After being examined at the hospital, he was taken to jail to be booked and detained.

"How did you defend him?" I asked.

"This was about twenty-four years ago. I wasn't drinking back then, so I had little firsthand knowledge of alcoholism. The only things I knew about excessive drinking had been my experiences with my father, and Dad certainly never went out and killed anyone. But from the little I knew, I convinced myself the boy was an alcoholic, so I went to the experts. I called upon several psychiatrists I found in the phone book who specialized in helping people with drinking problems. They all had the same thing to say, that Joel wasn't in charge of his faculties when he caused the accident. They explained that alcoholics were powerless over alcohol, and that for the alcoholic, the ingestion of alcohol could result in the most immoral behavior from even the most moral person. This is what I wanted to hear, that Joel couldn't be held accountable for his actions when drinking, so I decided to defend Joel by labeling him as an alcoholic and bringing in expert testimony to prove my case. I would say he wasn't himself when he killed April, that he was someone else, someone evil and irresponsible—a Mr. Hyde, if you will."

"Did this work?"

"I was certainly not the first attorney to think of providing this kind of defense, but I had a big problem. Joel's dad, who was paying my fee, was not at all happy about the idea of having his son labeled an alcoholic. The case was being followed by the local paper, and it even got some time on the evening news, and Joel's father didn't want the world thinking his son was a drunk. He said his boy was just having fun with a group of friends, and that he got carried away and made an error in judgment. The consequences were horrific, but he said if they put every teenager in jail who made a bad decision while drinking, our jails would be bursting at the seams. 'It's simple,' he said to me. 'You defend Joel as a good young man who, like so many of us did when we were young, drank too much and made a bad choice.' Joel's dad felt this defense would resonate with the jury, twelve men and women who had also been nineteen at some time in their lives, who must have known what it was like to be a teenager. With this defense, the stigma of labeling Joel as an alcoholic would be avoided, and he would still have as good a chance as any of getting a lenient decision in the courtroom. Since Joel's father was footing the bill, I went along with his plan and did as I was told."

"So what happened?"

"The trial lasted a couple weeks. We didn't debate the facts of the accident, but we brought in witnesses to testify regarding Joel's character. We wanted to show the jury that Joel was basically a good kid. The prosecution brought in several other young people who described other times when Joel got a little crazy while drinking, but I cross-examined and asked if Joel was the only kid they knew who did this, and of course they had to say no. The fact was, I told the jury, that many boys Joel's age misbehaved under the influence of alcohol. It was a rite of passage, this drinking thing, and I said as much in my summation, which I believed was a pretty darn good speech. I saw several jurors nodding their heads when I made my points, and I felt Joel had a fair chance of avoiding a lot of prison time. When I was done, I looked over at Joel's dad, and he seemed satisfied with what I'd done, giving me a thumbs-up. Then the jury deliberated."

"What was the verdict?"

"They found Joel guilty of vehicular manslaughter."

"Wow," I said.

"His father was not at all happy, but I have to tell you that Joel paid me a visit years after he was released from prison. He was no longer a teenager, but now a fully grown man in his thirties. I was in my second year trying to get sober when Joel visited. Coincidentally, Joel was also working the AA program, and he'd come to make amends. I didn't understand what he had to make amends for, but he explained that for years following his conviction he had blamed me for his prison time. He'd finally come to realize that these consequences were not my fault, and he wanted to be sure I understood this. I told him I appreciated his visit, though it wasn't necessary, and then I asked how his dad was doing. Joel said his dad still didn't understand the whole alcoholism and AA thing, and he blamed Joel's drinking on the time he spent in prison.

"It's curious how adamant his dad was about not labeling Joel as alcoholic, yet now Joel had willingly done it on his own. I told him that I too was in AA, and he couldn't believe it. 'You always seemed

like you had things so together,' he said. 'I would never have guessed.'
Of course, Joel had only seen me when I wasn't drinking. He didn't
know me when my own Mr. Hyde was running amok."

"How's Joel doing now?"

"I have no idea."

"Have you ever tried to contact him?"

"In my line of work, it's wise to keep a distance from past clients."

"I see."

"Are you a *Star Trek* fan?" Harry asked.

"Yes," I said. "I loved that show."

"Do you remember the episode when there was a malfunction
in the transporter, and two Kirks were beamed aboard the ship, one
good and one evil?"

"I remember that."

"The good Kirk was indecisive and docile to a flaw, while the
bad Kirk was aggressive and mean-spirited. The good Kirk spent his
time hanging around with Spock and the others, while the bad Kirk
roamed about the ship causing all sorts of trouble, drinking alcohol
and accosting women. Don't you find it interesting that one of the
first things the evil Kirk did was to drink?"

"I never thought of that."

"The writers must have had some experience with alcoholics."

"Yes," I said.

Harry sat quiet for a moment and then asked, "How are you doing
with step nine?"

"What do you mean?"

"Are you practicing it?"

"I suppose so."

"Can you give me an example?"

"Yes," I said. "I think I can. When we all went out to dinner in
Albuquerque after tossing Vern's ashes, Lucy asked me to recall a
story about my father-in-law. It took me by surprise, and I didn't
have any good story in mind. I told about a time Vern got so drunk
that he puked up his dentures in a restaurant parking lot, and as
soon as I told the story I realized it probably wasn't the greatest tale
to recount. Who wants to be remembered by a story like that? Lucy
was polite and she laughed, but I could have done a better job for her.

Ordinarily, I would've been bothered by my bad judgment and stewed over it for days, worrying about what Lucy thought of me, about what Amy thought, and about how dumb I'd been. But I told myself to let bygones be bygones and to live in the here and now, and that's what I did. I paid attention to what I was doing presently, and the balance of the day went well. And I didn't make any more careless mistakes for the rest of our trip."

"That's good," Harry said. "So do you think you're ready for step ten?"

"I guess so."

"Do you know what step ten is?"

"Vaguely."

"Step ten says we continue to take personal inventory, and when we are wrong promptly admit it."

"Yes, now I remember."

"What do you think of the way this step has been written?"

"I don't see a problem with it."

"Neither do I," Harry said. "We'll leave this one exactly as it is. The point of this step is to be on a constant watch for mistakes and miscues. We need to be aware of what we're doing, just as you were aware of the inappropriate story you told about Vern. We don't need to beat ourselves up over errors; we just need to be aware. It's important that we know what we're doing every step of the way. It keeps us from being lazy.

"Left to our own devices, we let things slide. We let our self-awareness slide, and when we let our self-awareness slide, we let our behavior slide. And when we let our behavior slide, we slip right into our drinking mode. We need to force ourselves to stay on top of things, to be keenly aware of what we're doing and how our actions affect ourselves and others. Being sober doesn't just mean abstaining from alcohol; it means becoming better people, people who are conscious of their actions and strive to do the right things. You will hear in AA that there are lots of people who quit drinking, but that there are only a few who are actually sober. And sobriety means longevity, and isn't this what you're seeking from me?"

"Yes, of course."

"And being aware of yourself means loving yourself. Yes, we're back to that subject again. If you don't learn to love yourself, you won't care enough to pay attention. Would you say you love yourself?"

"I'm not sure what it means."

"I can tell you what it doesn't mean. It doesn't mean spending hours in front of the mirror, admiring your face, combing your hair, and whitening your teeth. It doesn't mean shoving yourself ahead of others, pushing them out of the way in lines, throwing them under the bus because you think you're more important. What it means is quite different.

"I read a story in the paper the other day about a home that caught fire in Santa Ana. By the time the firefighters arrived, the house was engulfed in flames. In the street, being contained by police and paramedics, were the mother, father, and one of the two children. The other six-year-old child was missing, and the parents were beside themselves.

"One of the firemen, unable to live with the idea of the child burning to death in the house, ran in through the front door and up the burning stairs. He found the girl huddled in a corner of her bedroom, sobbing and coughing up black soot. He ran and picked up the girl; then he hurried down the burning stairs and out the front door to safety. He quickly gave the girl to the waiting paramedics. His superior chastised him for risking his life, but that soon gave way to praise from everyone who learned of the incident. He was interviewed on TV with the family of the girl, and he was shown bringing flowers to her in her hospital room. He was hailed as a hero, but that's not why he did what he did. He wasn't looking for adulation; he rescued the girl because he loved himself."

"That doesn't make sense."

"Do you remember the story I told you about Alvin Peavy, my client who was charged and convicted for murdering his wife and her boyfriend? It was a murder that I said I believed was committed by his son?"

"Yes," I said.

"I believe Alvin let the court convict him so that his son would not be charged. Alvin sacrificed his freedom for his son, but it wasn't just a father's love; it primarily had to do with Alvin's love for himself. He would never have gone to prison like that if he hadn't loved himself."

"I still don't understand."

"When you love yourself, it means you're able to live with yourself. Would you agree?"

"I suppose so."

"You wouldn't want to live the rest of your life with someone you didn't love, would you?"

"No," I said.

"Both the firefighter and Alvin did what they had to do in order to live with themselves, not just in the moment, but for the rest of their lives. They had to do what they thought was right, all negative consequences be damned. They loved themselves, and they acted accordingly. Can you see this now?"

"Yes, I think I can."

"Do you want to be able to live with yourself?"

"Yes, of course."

"Then you need to learn to love yourself."

"It sounds so simple."

"It is simple, but it's a concept most alcoholics have a very difficult time understanding."

I went home from Harry's house that evening having learned something new. I'd heard people tell me to love myself before, but I'd never had it explained in quite this way. It actually made some sense.

The next day I woke up energized and looking for something to do. Amy had already gone to work. I was up-to-date with all my paperwork, and my construction jobs didn't require my presence. I made myself a cup of coffee and stepped to my office. I was running low on cigars, so I placed my order over the Internet using a credit card I kept in my wallet. I then decided to start work on our backyard. I hadn't received any plans from Chester yet, but I could begin by taking down the old swing set. I decided to take the thing apart, load it into my truck, and take it to the dump. It was a simple job, and I should have been able to accomplish the task in a few hours. I found a couple old crescent wrenches in the garage and grabbed a ladder. I took the tools to the backyard and set the ladder up against the swing set, where I positioned myself to unscrew the rusty bolts and take the structure apart.

I immediately ran into a problem, since the rusty bolts wouldn't budge. I decided to make a trip to Home Depot to buy some antirust product, and I brought the stuff back home. I squirted the liquid all over the rusty bolts, and let it set in for a few minutes. I then went back to work with the wrenches, but still the bolts wouldn't twist. So I decided what I needed was a power grinder, and I knew they also sold them at Home Depot. I got in my truck and drove back to Home Depot to purchase the tool. It was now midmorning. When I arrived home, I went to work with the grinder, cutting all the rusty bolts. As luck would have it, when I removed the final bolts the entire swing set collapsed, and I fell off the ladder and cut my arm reaching for one of the rusty struts to break my fall. I went into the house looked for something to bandage the bloody wound, but I couldn't find anything.

Not wanting the injury to get infected, I ran some water on it and cleaned it with soap. I then tried to recall the last time I'd had a tetanus shot, and I figured it was many years ago. It was now close to noon, and I was on my way to the local walk-in clinic to get a proper dressing for the wound and a shot. When I arrived at the clinic, four people were ahead of me, sitting on chairs and waiting for their names to be called by the receptionist. One was an elderly fellow with a bandage on his cheek, and another was a middle-aged woman with an elastic bandage around her knee. The other two were a mother and son duo, and the contagious boy kept coughing and sniffing such that I assumed he was there to be treated for a cold or the flu. I spent at least an hour waiting to see the doctor, and when my turn came up, I was led to an examination room and told to take a seat.

Although I was told that the doctor would be right with me, it took another forty minutes for the doctor to finally enter the room. The doctor washed out the wound again and wrapped my arm with a big gauze bandage. He then had his nurse come in and give me the tetanus shot. After paying my bill, I was back on my way.

It was late afternoon by the time I finally arrived home to load the dismantled swing set into my truck. I had a quick cup of coffee to perk me up and then drove off. The dump is not far from our house, but that's during the middle part of the day when traffic is good. By the time I got on the road, everyone was leaving from work and clogging the streets something awful. When I arrived, the surly guy at the booth looked toward the back of my truck and told me the amount due, but when I reached to my back pocket for my wallet, I discovered it wasn't there.

I figured I must have left the wallet on my desk when I was ordering my cigars that morning, so I turned around and made my way back home. I would be lucky to make it back to the dump with my wallet before it closed. But I hurried and did make it back in time. I paid my fee, drove to the dumping area, and unloaded the swing set.

By the time I returned home, it was dark and Amy's car was in the driveway. I pulled up alongside it and stepped into the house. Amy was in the kitchen preparing dinner, and I moved past her carefully so she wouldn't see my bandage. I then stepped out through the patio door to the backyard, and I stood with my hands on my hips, surveying the spot where the swing set once stood. It was now just a patch of damaged grass, and I said proudly, "Captain's log, phase one complete."

"Phase one of what?" Amy asked. She was standing in the doorway looking at me.

"Don't you notice anything different?"

"The swing set is gone."

"It was so simple. I took the thing apart and drove it to the dump."

"What's that on your arm?" I raised my arm, admitting to the big gauze bandage. Amy said, "I thought you said it was simple."

"I told you it was simple," I said. "I didn't say it was easy."

CHAPTER 20

The Brass Ring

As I've said, Amy and I have been together since high school. We first met when she was fifteen and I was seventeen. At the time Amy's parents were still living in California, and they didn't actually move to Albuquerque until Amy's senior year. I remember when I first met Amy's dad, he worked as a manager for a furniture manufacturing company in Santa Clara. The company decided to move to Albuquerque when Amy was seventeen, and Vern decided to move with them. Vern and Lucy moved to New Mexico, leaving Amy to live with Vern's sister so she wouldn't have to change schools.

But I remember the years when Amy was still living with her parents. They had a great big house in a nice neighborhood, and a gigantic yard stuffed with trees and shrubs. I used to drive over to Amy's house every day after school, where Vern had set up a kid's room just for Amy and us friends. There was a sofa, a couple chairs, a stereo, and a TV, and we'd hang out in the room for hours, listening to music and watching dumb shows on the TV. They also had a pool, and Amy would invite all of us over during summer days to hang out in the sun and go swimming. Amy's house was a great place to be.

I first talked to Amy at a high school party on a Saturday night. I had seen her before at school, but our paths had never crossed and we didn't know each other. I found her sitting on the bottom step of a staircase inside the house with a can of beer in her hand and a finger over one eye. I sat down next to her and asked why the finger, and she said she'd been drinking a little too much beer, that keeping one eye closed stopped her from seeing double. She didn't seem drunk; in fact, she seemed quite sober, except for the finger over her eye. We made some small talk, and then I asked her if she wanted to go outside for some fresh air. She agreed, and taking her by the hand I walked her through the crowd of rowdy teenagers out to the backyard.

It was a clear night, and I looked up at the sky with her; there was no moon, but there were billions of twinkling stars. She set her beer down on a patio table and without warning she just fell into my arms. The warmth of her body felt nice in the chilly night air, and she was wearing a perfume that nearly made me swoon. I put my arms around her and kissed her on the mouth, and that was the start of a love affair that would last until today, for over forty years. Okay, I'll admit that she was probably a little drunk that night, but I'd like to think it was love at first sight.

I have to tell you about our adventure in the Santa Cruz Mountains. Amy and I had been going together for about six months, and usually we spent the weekends partying with friends. But one Saturday night we decided to drive up into the mountains to a remote place I knew of where we could park my car and look at the city lights. We brought a six-pack of beer, a stick of salami, and a loaf of French bread. I maneuvered the car so that it was facing the view and turned off the engine and headlights, but I left the radio on so we could listen to music. We arrived there at dusk, and the city lights were spectacular. I had the radio tuned to an oldies station, and we listened to tunes from the fifties, eating our French bread and salami, and drinking our cold beers.

We talked about everything in the world … about other kids at school, about our parents, about our favorite things to do. Amy didn't have to be home until midnight, so we had plenty of time. I remember thinking how lucky I was to have this lovely young girl in my life, and I knew all my friends were jealous. As the hour grew later, and we were done eating and drinking, we turned our attention to each other, kissing and touching, embracing, doing the things young lovers do in a car at night.

It was a little after eleven when I decided we should probably head back home, to be sure I got Amy back to her parents' house by twelve. I had established a reputation with Vern and Lucy for bringing their daughter home before curfew, and I didn't want to break this trust. We put the empty beer cans in a paper bag and put them in the trunk. Amy then put the leftover salami and bread on the backseat, and brushed crumbs from her lap. I turned the key in the car ignition, and nothing happened. We both turned to look at each other. We had run the battery down by listening to the radio for the past several hours, and the battery was dead.

I felt a weird knot in my stomach. I knew we were miles away from anything. This was before cell phones, and Amy asked what we were going to do. We needed to call for help, so we decided to start walking. I locked up the car, and we made our way down the road. It was pitch-black, and there weren't any streetlights, so we walked blindly in the darkness along the edge of the narrow mountain road. At this time of night there was no one driving that we could flag down and ask for a lift. We were by ourselves in the mountains, and Amy was getting nervous. "What if someone attacks us?" she asked, and I played the role that was expected of me and told her not to worry. But I was a little nervous myself. It was creepy being alone late at night in the darkness in this unfamiliar place.

After over an hour of walking and nearly giving up hope, we came across a house. It had a long, dark driveway, and the house lights were off. I figured the people must be sleeping, but we stepped to the porch and I knocked on the door. We waited hoping someone would answer. I knocked again. "I'm coming, I'm coming," a perturbed voice said from inside, and suddenly the door flew open. "What the hell do you want?" the man said. He was an elderly man dressed in pajamas, and he had a head full of fuzzy gray hair and a pair of angry blue eyes. He was aiming a shotgun right at my chest. "Well, speak up," he said.

"I'm sorry to bother you," I said. "Our battery ran down, and we can't get our car to start. We were wondering if we could use your phone."

The man stared for a moment, sizing us up, and then he lowered his shotgun. "I guess it won't do any harm," he said, and he motioned for us to enter his house.

"Who's there?" a woman's voice asked. It was the man's wife, speaking from the hallway.

"A couple kids. Their battery ran out of juice, and they need to use our phone. Go back to bed."

"We appreciate this," I said.

"It's not a problem."

"I just need to call my dad."

"Help yourself," the man said, and he pointed to the phone on the wall. I picked up the receiver and dialed the number to my home. My dad answered, and when he heard it was me, he asked what was wrong. I told him what had happened and asked him if he could come start up my car. I knew he had a set of jumper cables in the garage.

"For crying out loud," Dad said. "Where exactly are you?" I got the address from the old man and told it to my dad. "I'll be up there as soon as I can. That is, if I don't get lost. I can't believe you and Amy are in the mountains. I thought you were going to a party."

"We changed our plans."

We hadn't actually changed our plans. We intended to drive up to the mountains all along, but I didn't want to tell my parents I was parking my car with Amy to neck at some lovers' lookout. It just didn't seem like the kind of thing one said to one's parents.

We waited inside the house, and the man's wife got dressed and came out to meet us. She was very nice, and she served us milk and cookies at the kitchen table while the man took a seat in the front room, watching TV and waiting for us to leave. We talked to the man's wife at the table, and she told us all about what life had been like when she was our age. This woman was a real talker. There was no end to her memories, and I was convinced she could have kept at this for days.

After an hour had passed, I grew worried about my father. He should have shown up. I asked the woman if I could use the phone again, and she said yes, so I called my house. This time my mom answered the phone, and I told her Dad hadn't arrived. "He left an hour ago," she said. "He should've been there by now. Maybe he got lost." I asked my mom if she could come get us, that it was after one in the morning, and we needed to get out of this couple's house. She agreed, and I gave her the address. She said it would take her about thirty minutes, that she would leave as soon as she found the street on her road map.

So we continued to wait, sure that either my mom or my dad would show up soon. The old man fell asleep in front of the TV, and I could now hear him snoring. His wife told us not to worry about waking him, that he could sleep through anything. She then continued to talk to us about her life as a teenager, how she was raised on a farm and how she fed the chickens and milked the cows. Believe it or not, this went on for another hour, and there still was absolutely no sign of my parents. It was now after two.

What we didn't know was that on his way to the house, my dad had run over a rock and punctured one of his front tires. He opened the trunk and discovered that the spare tire was also flat, so he began to walk, looking for a house with a phone, just as we had. He was not having much luck, while meanwhile Mom was driving around in the completely wrong neighborhood, lost in the darkness and unable to find our street. Mom never was too good at reading maps, and my having her come to get us in the middle of the night like this was probably a big mistake.

"Can we use your phone again?" Amy asked, and the woman said yes. Amy then called her parents, who were now wondering where the heck she was. They were so relieved to hear her voice that they didn't get mad. They asked Amy what was going on, and Amy said, "We're stuck up in the mountains with a dead battery. We're at this house waiting for Lester's parents, but they never showed up. Can you come get us?" Amy then gave Vern the address, he and Lucy hopped in their Cadillac, and now three parties were out searching for us.

About thirty minutes later a cop happened to drive by my dad, who was still walking, and he pulled over to see where my dad was going. Dad explained the situation, and the officer told my dad to climb in his patrol car. Then he drove Dad to the couple's house, where they parked in the driveway. The cop walked with Dad to the door, and the old man's wife, who had seen them arrive from the kitchen window, let them both in. She left the front door wide open, expecting all of us to leave shortly, but just a couple minutes later, Mom finally arrived at the house and parked behind the police car. She ran to the open front door and into the house, thinking something horrible had happened—otherwise, why would a police car be in the driveway? Dad calmed her down and explained what was going on.

We were all now standing in the kitchen with the old man's wife, when Vern and Lucy arrived in their big car. Vern parked behind Mom, and they too ran to the house, just like my mom had. Amy met them on the porch and quickly explained things. She brought them into the kitchen with the rest of us. What a sight! We now had the old man's wife, me and Amy, my mom and dad, the police officer, and Vern and Lucy all standing in this poor woman's kitchen at three in the morning. We were talking and laughing, and we must have woke the old guy up with all our loud voices, for he came stumbling to the kitchen door still dressed in his pajamas. "What in the hell?" he said, rubbing his eyes.

If you were to ask me to honestly tell you whether I enjoyed being a teenager, I would have to answer that I don't know. I don't recall being all that happy, but I have a lot of good memories. Most of my memories revolve around drinking, which I did mostly on weekends. It's amazing how even at that age, alcohol played such a dominant role in my life. I remember we used to go to the roller rink downtown and skate drunk and crazy through all the other kids, falling down, running into each other, and laughing. We used to drink and go to the bowling alley, rolling our bowling balls like maniacs, smashing them into the pin setting machinery. Sometimes we would just hang out and talk at the neighborhood park, drinking beers or passing around a bottle of hard liquor, telling jokes and acting stupid until we had to go home.

I remember one Friday night at Amy's house when Vern and Lucy were out for the evening, my friends and I pooled our cash for a beer purchase. The guys left the girls at Amy's and drove off to the local liquor store. We stood in front of the store asking people to buy us our beer. Two rough-looking guys in their early twenties agreed to do the task, and we handed them our wad of money. They went inside and purchased a couple quarts of whiskey, and then they walked out the door and showed us what they had bought. "Thanks for the whiskey, boys," one of them said, and they both had a good laugh.

They got in their car and backed out to leave, and we ran to our own car and followed them. They took us on a wild-goose chase all over town, and finally pulled into a vacant lot in a dimly lighted neighborhood. They stopped in the middle of the lot and let the dust settle around their car. "They want to fight us," one of my friends said. And another said, "There's no way I'm fighting those guys." We all agreed they were bigger than us, and probably meaner than us, and that they would easily pound us black and blue. We pretended to drive away but hid around a corner, and when they left the vacant lot, we followed their car. They pulled into a driveway, where we watched them walk into their house. We now knew where they lived.

"What do we do now?" one of my friends asked, and we decided that we would all dig deep and come up with some more money and go back to the liquor store. We eventually were able to find someone to purchase our beer, and we took it to Amy's house, where the girls were waiting. "What took so long?" Amy asked, and I told her the story. We cracked open our beers and talked about the two guys who'd just ripped us off, and the more we talked, the more we wanted revenge, and the more we drank, the braver we got. Finally, we all decided to teach them a lesson, teach them not to mess with kids like us. We went into Vern and Lucy's garage and found what we were looking for: a tire iron, a couple hammers, and a large, heavy pipe wrench.

Amy tried to talk us out of it, but we drove to the guys' house. We skidded to a stop in front of their driveway and jumped out of our car. The windows of their car were rolled down, so we began by peeing all over their front seats and dashboard. Then one of my friends said, "Ready?" Another said, "Now!" And in a fury, we attacked the car. We snapped off the antenna and side mirror, broke out the headlights and taillights, smashed the front and back windows, and put several large dents in the hood and fenders. In just a matter of seconds we had all but demolished the car.

We piled back into our car and sped to Amy's, our hearts beating hard. We spent the rest of the night listening to music and bragging about what we'd done, laughing at the thought of those two jerks coming out to the driveway the next morning, hungover and seeing their ruined car. It still makes me smile to this day. I can't even imagine how angry they must have been.

I didn't always drink just on weekends. Sometimes I drank during the school week. Sometimes I would hide booze in my locker and sneak it into the restroom during lunch break. I'd drink the stuff privately in one of the toilet stalls, and then I would bury the empty bottle in the trash container when no one was looking. It was kind of a thrill, being high while everyone else at the school was sober.

This caused me a problem only once that I remember, and that was in Mr. McClusky's civics class. First, let me describe Mr. McClusky. He was an unassuming fellow with short black hair and a very neatly trimmed beard. He always wore a suit and tie to class, not the sort of suit and tie you'd expect a teacher to wear, but the sort you'd expect a businessman to wear to a board meeting. He had a black leather briefcase in which he kept his papers and pens.

I remember I felt a little sorry for Mr. McClusky. It was bad enough that he had to teach civics, probably the most boring subject at school, but on top of that he was a most boring teacher, sadly incapable of igniting his lectures with the slightest bit of life. I think deep down he wanted to be popular and interesting, but he wasn't. I remember he'd go on and on about the ins and outs of our government, scribbling charts and terms and titles on the blackboard, expecting us to fervently take notes. But no one in class was interested.

One day I came to his class half-drunk. I was sitting restlessly in my seat and listening to him tell us about George Washington and that stupid fable of the cherry tree, like none of us had ever heard it before. He was interrupted by a knock on the door. It was one of the school secretaries, and she needed to talk to him in the hall. "I'll be just a minute," he said to the class, and the two of them stepped out of the room.

Everyone began talking, and to liven things up I walked to the blackboard and picked up a piece of chalk. The kids were now watching me as I drew a stick figure with a beard on its face, representing Mr. McClusky. I then wrote in quotations something to the effect of, "Hi, I'm Mr. McClusky. Welcome to the most boring class in school, taught by the most boring teacher in the universe. Glad I could be of service." Well, this isn't exactly what I wrote. The lines I wrote on the board contained a number of obscenities. I took my seat, and Mr. McClusky stepped back into the room. He saw my stick figure and obscene addendum to his notes on the blackboard, and the whole class turned quiet. "Who did this?" he asked.

I didn't fess up right away, but everyone in the class was now looking at me, and it was obvious I was the culprit. "Lester," he said, "are you responsible for this?" I tried to think of what to say. I was trying to be funny when I replied, "I cannot tell a lie, sir. It was I who chopped down the cherry tree."

I was taken to the principal's office, where Mr. McClusky told the principal what I'd done. Mr. McClusky then went back to class, and I waited. By the time I finally met with the principal, most of the effects of the alcohol had worn off, and I was no longer feeling so chipper. I was sternly reprimanded for what I'd done and given a choice; either I could apologize to Mr. McClusky after school, or I could take a three-day suspension. It wasn't much of a choice, and when school was dismissed that day, I went directly to Mr. McClusky's classroom. He was putting some papers into his leather briefcase, but he stopped what he was doing when I walked into the room. He asked, "What can I do for you, Lester?" I told him I was there to apologize. It's funny, but he wasn't at all angry. He then asked me quite seriously if I disliked him, and I said no. Now I felt sort of bad. He said I had always seemed like a good kid, and he asked why I'd written on his chalkboard that afternoon. And all I could say was, "I don't know. It was a stupid thing to do."

The next time I met with Harry, I brought up the story of Mr. McClusky's civics class. When I recited to Harry the uncensored version of what I had written on the board, he laughed loudly and said, "You actually wrote that on your teacher's chalkboard?" I nodded my head, and he laughed again. I told Harry I thought I had hurt Mr. McClusky's feelings more than I had made him mad, and Harry said I was probably right.

I was curious what Harry's own high school years had been like, so I asked him. He said the worst thing he ever did in high school was to put a sleeping Teddy Reardon's hand in a pan of warm water at the boy's house when Harry was spending the night. Teddy Reardon was one of Harry's friends. Harry said, "He wet himself and complained to his mother, and she drove me back to my dad's house in the middle of the night. She was all up in arms, and she woke up my dad by ringing the doorbell. He was half-drunk when he answered the door, but he listened and then apologized to the woman. He then told her I would be punished. When the woman left, Dad just told me to go to sleep. He then stumbled into his room and plopped down on the bed, and that was the last I ever heard of it."

"I wish I had a dad like that," I said.

"No, you don't."

"No, I suppose you're right."

"Listen, I loved my dad, but I hated his drinking with a passion. I swore to myself that I'd never touch the stuff as long as I lived. I chose my friends according to this credo. None of my high school buddies drank at all, and we were not an exciting group of teenagers by any stretch of the imagination. We went to school every day, behaved ourselves, and studied when we got home. I didn't even have a girlfriend until Janice, and that wasn't until college. All I wanted to do in high school was to prepare myself for college, and all I wanted to do in college was to prepare myself to live a promising and successful life.

"I didn't know when I was a teenager that I would grow up to be a criminal defense attorney, but I knew for sure that I wasn't going to be a steelworker like my old man. I knew I wasn't going to work my fingers to the bone earning an average paycheck, driving an average car, living in an average house. I wasn't going to drown my mediocrity every night in whiskey, only to get up the next day and do the very same thing. I would make something of myself. I would reach for the brass ring. I wouldn't just be my father's son."

"And you did well for yourself."

"Did I?"

"I think you did."

"My wife left me. My daughter won't talk to me. I was booted out of the business I started. I've never even met my grandchildren. All that hardly qualifies me as a success."

"But you're not poor," I said.

"No, I'm not poor."

"And you're helping people. You're helping me."

"Am I?"

"I think you are."

"I'm glad to hear you say that, Lester."

"That's a good thing, isn't it?"

Harry smiled and then asked, "Do you remember when you first met Amy?"

"Yes," I said. "Of course I do."

"I still remember the first day I met Janice. I actually had noticed her weeks before. The first time I saw her, she was sitting several seats away from me in my psychology class. It was cold that day, and she was wearing a heavy green sweater that brought out the color of her Irish eyes. She had auburn hair, straight and most perfectly brushed. She was sitting next to one of her girlfriends, talking before class, and every so often she'd laugh and show off her perfect white teeth. She had soft red lips and a clear pink complexion like a goddess. I tell you, Lester, I'd never seen a more beautiful creature in all my life. I was awestruck, and for the first time in my young life I knew what it was like to yearn for a specific girl."

"I know that feeling," I said.

"I had no experience. I had no idea what to do. It was most troubling to have all this desire burning inside of me with no clue as to how to get myself into her life. So I followed her."

"You followed her?"

"That day when our psychology class let out, I followed her to the cafeteria, where she had lunch with her girlfriend. I grabbed some lunch for myself, even though I seldom eat lunch, and sat several tables away from the girls. When they were done, they carried their trays to the counter, and I followed them to the exit. They hugged and split up, and I followed Janice to the library, where she found an open desk. She opened a book and proceeded to read and take notes on a pad of paper.

I pretended to be looking for my own book, took one from the shelf, and then found a desk nearby, where I acted like I was reading as well. I did this for a couple hours, until Janice stood up and went to her next class. It was a class on art history held in a large auditorium, and I took a seat several rows behind her where I could stare at the back of her head for an hour. I followed Janice like this for the rest of the day, until it was dark and she finally wound up at her dorm."

"You were stalking her."

"Yes, I guess I was. This went on for a couple weeks until I decided it was time to come up with a plan. It was so frustrating, not knowing what to do."

"So what was your plan?"

"Well, the first idea I came up with was to compose a love letter. I would tell her about the first time I saw her in our psychology class, about all the times I'd followed her, about how I longed to get to know the lovely girl with bright green eyes and straight auburn hair. I would tell her she was all I could think about, morning, noon, and night, that if she would just give me a chance, just the smallest chance, that I was sure I'd find a place in her heart. I thought I might slip a letter like this into her purse when she wasn't looking and then introduce myself to her the next day. Then I thought to myself that this was sort of creepy, to be getting all mushy with a girl I didn't even know. So I nixed this idea."

"So what'd you do?"

"Well, my second idea wasn't much better. I thought I might keep running into her by accident. Of course, it wouldn't be by accident, but I would see to it that she thought it was. I knew her schedule from having followed her around for so many days, and I could put myself in the right situations. For example, I could sit next to her in psychology class and ask if I could borrow a pen. Or I could bump into her in the cafeteria and pretend to drop my tray. Or I could go after the same desk in the library and then say, 'Oh, excuse me, were you going to sit here?' Eventually, after all these coincidental meetings, I would comment on how we kept running into each other and introduce myself. But this too seemed a little on the creepy side, having me popping into her life over and over. So I nixed this idea as well."

"Yes," I said. "Being constantly in her face might have scared her off."

"Ultimately, I decided that the best way to go about this was to just bite the bullet and ask her out. I would walk right up to her and say, 'My name is Harry, and I'd like to get to know you.' Then I'd ask her to dinner or a movie and see what she said. It was a little blunt, but I couldn't think of any other way.

"It took me a week to muster up the courage. I waited until she was done having lunch with her friend at the cafeteria, waited until they parted ways. Then I walked right up to her and said, 'You don't know me, but my name is Harry. I was wondering if we could have dinner together.' You should have seen the look on her face! She had no idea who I was, and here I was asking her for a date. I think she just wanted to disappear, but she stood there and kindly said, 'I don't even know who you are.' 'Okay,' I said, and I turned and walked away. Actually, ran is more like it. Yes, I turned and ran to my dorm room, where I threw myself on my bed and cried like an idiot, hurt and humiliated. I had made a complete fool of myself in front of the girl I adored."

"So what happened?"

"The next time I saw her in our psychology class, she was sitting with her girlfriend again. She noticed me sitting in the back of the room, and after saying something to her friend, she stood up and walked toward me. My mouth turned dry, and perspiration began to roll down my sides. She sat down beside me and put her hand atop mine. She said, 'I'd like to have dinner with you, Harry.' I said, 'You would?' And she said, 'Where exactly do you want to go?'"

"Wow," I said.

"We decided on a popular pizza joint downtown, and I met her there that night. I asked her what kind of pizza she wanted, and she said everything except anchovies. I told her that was just the way I would have ordered it for myself. We spent a couple hours talking and eating. When we were done, I walked her back to her dorm, and after an awkward good-bye, I summoned up the nerve to kiss her good-night. I was so vulnerable then, but sometimes good things come to us when we're vulnerable."

"Yes," I said.

"Right now, you're vulnerable."

"I am?"

"And some good things are coming your way ... so long as you're willing to work for them. You've got to work hard for them, Lester."

CHAPTER 21

Oxygen

I've been a building contractor for over thirty years, and I can tell you that the worst thing about residential jobs is the involvement of women. I don't mean to sound sexist, but this is a real fact of life. If left up to husbands, these jobs would be so much easier, but throw a wife into the mix, and you've immediately got a challenge on your hands.

This is why when I got our backyard plans from Chester, I kept them to myself. I told Amy they were done, but I wouldn't let her see them. I wanted to do this job by myself, since it was after all my idea to fix up the yard. Despite a few improvements I'd tried to make, it had been a mess for as long as we'd lived in the house, and Amy had never complained about it, not once. I asked her to please have faith in my abilities. "Let me surprise you," I said. "You have to agree that no matter what I do, it can only look better." She wasn't too happy about this idea at first, but eventually she acquiesced. It would be my project.

So, score one for the guy with the gauze bandage on his arm. I began by digging. According to Chester's plan, I had to dig out all the old plants and trees. There weren't a lot of them, but there were enough to keep me busy for a while. I still had other projects going with my business, so I would have to juggle my time. I decided to work my regular jobs during the mornings, and then I would switch my attention to the backyard during the afternoons and evenings. I began with the bougainvillea shrubs against the far fence. I had planted these years ago, hoping they would climb all over the fence and flower bright red, orange, and purple. They never did take and had always been a ratty and jumbled eyesore, always full of dead leaves and spiderwebs. I would be glad to see these go, and I began by snipping them to bits with a pair of gardening shears I found in the garage, piling the thorny branches in a big heap.

I then went to work digging up what was left of the plants with a shovel, turning the soil, and chopping at the roots and pulling them out. It was miserable work, and I was sweating something awful, with little flies buzzing in and out of my ears and eyes. My hair was sticking to my forehead, and my shirt was sticking to my back. Dirt was now getting into my socks and shoes. But I kept at it for several hours, up until blisters started appearing on the palms of my hands, painful little pus-filled blisters.

I decided to call it a day and took a shower. After cleaning up, I returned to the yard and smoked a cigar, looking at what I had done. When Amy came home, she found me still sitting in the yard and staring, and she said, "Oh, wow, look at what a mess you've made." Bougainvillea branches and roots, and piles of dirt were everywhere; it looked like an army of giant gophers had had a field day with our backyard.

"It's a lot of work," I said.

"Are you sure you don't want to hire some help?"

"We can't afford it."

I was picking the skin on one of my blisters, and Amy said, "Look at your hands!"

"Yeah, I've got some blisters," I admitted.

"Didn't you wear gloves?"

"No, I'll pick some up tomorrow morning. I also need a better shovel, and a pickaxe would help."

"I guess it's your project," she said, and she was right. It was my project.

I met with Harry a couple weeks later on a Tuesday evening, and I told him about my backyard job, describing the progress I'd made and showing him some pictures I'd taken with my cell phone. I also showed him what was left of the blisters on my hands, and he suggested I wear gloves. I told him I'd already bought a pair, that the blisters were just from the first day. Harry then asked how I was doing in general, and I told him I was doing fine.

"You feel like we're getting somewhere?" Harry asked.

"Oh, yes," I replied.

"You won't always feel so good. Sometimes you'll just have to tough it out."

"Okay."

"So," he said, changing the subject, "you'll never guess who came to visit me three days ago."

"Who?" I asked.

"Alice and the grandchildren."

"You're kidding me."

"They were here in California, visiting with Janice and Kaleb. Janice talked Alice into seeing me with the grandkids, and she brought them over. I couldn't believe it."

"Wow," I said.

"You know, I've always been quite a talker. I made my living by talking. When I was sober I talked, and when I was drunk I talked even more. I've never been at a loss for words, but when Alice and the grandkids stepped into the house, I was speechless."

"What were they like?"

"They looked just like the photographs Janice had shared with me, except now they were right here in the flesh, with real human hair and skin and arms and hands, wearing real clothes and shoes. It literally made my heart skip a beat to see them in person. If only they'd known for how many years I'd longed for this moment, and now here they were, standing in the foyer of my house.

"I'm not the hugging kind, but I wanted to reach out and hug each of them so tight. Instead, we just stood there staring at each other, not quite sure what to do. I invited them into the front room, where we all sat down on the sofas. 'Is he my grandpa?' Robbie asked. He was pointing right at me. Alice affirmed that I was indeed his grandpa, and Robbie then asked if I lived in this great big house all by myself. Alice confirmed this as well, and she explained that she used to live here when she was a girl. Then we all sat quietly for what seemed like a full minute. It was kind of awkward. You know, it was funny how after sixteen years, we would be so tongue-tied.

"Surely there were hundreds of things we could've talked about— what we'd been doing, places we'd gone, and friends we'd made. But we all sat on my sofas, with nothing to say. Janice finally broke the silence and said, 'We stopped at that new shopping center by the freeway for lunch. They have a nice café there.' I said that I'd noticed the place and had been meaning to try it out. 'They make a great Cobb salad,' Alice said. 'It's impossible to find a good Cobb salad where we live in Vermont.' So there we were, the five of us, talking about Cobb salads and a new shopping center. It would have been hilarious if it weren't so pathetic. But I would take what I could get.

"We then made some more insipid small talk, and the doorbell suddenly rang. It was a man I've been sponsoring with AA. I say man, but I mean kid. This boy is in his twenties, and he's been having a terrible time staying sober, even though I believe he wants to stop drinking. His name is David, and he's been working with me for nearly a year. He showed up right in the middle of our family get-together, drunk and crying and complaining about some fight he had had with his girlfriend. 'This is not a good time,' I said. Really, his timing couldn't have been worse. But he said, 'I need to talk to you now. It can't wait.' Not only was David demanding to talk to me on the spot, but he was so obviously drunk that I couldn't very well just send him away. In his condition, even if I could convince him to go, I would have had to give him a ride.

"It was a frustrating turn of events. 'We should leave,' Janice said. She was now standing with Alice and the kids just a few feet away, and I told her she was probably right. David bolted past us and to the library, where he sat and waited for me to join him. 'I guess I'll see you all later,' I said. Everyone said good-bye, and I held the door open so they could leave. Before they got too far down the path, I said, 'Alice?' and she turned around. It took a lot of courage, but I asked if I could call her. She thought about it for a moment and said, 'You can call me when I get back to Vermont. Mom has my number.' I said thanks and then watched them walk away."

"So she'll talk to you?" I asked.

"It sounds like it," Harry said.

"You haven't called her yet?"

"Not yet, but I will."

"That's great, isn't it?"

"Yes, it is."

"I guess it's like they say, that good things come to those who wait."

"And that patience is a virtue. And that time heals all wounds."

"Yes," I said.

"What do you suppose we should talk about when I call her?"

"I don't know."

"I thought I might bring up some happier times from our past, from those times when I wasn't drinking. She was such a lovely little girl, with golden blond hair and big brown eyes, and a smile that would melt your heart. And she was so smart, always bringing home good grades from school. Her teachers loved her, and they would go out of their way to tell us so. I remember on the last day of school when she was in fourth grade, her teacher sent her home with a note in a sealed envelope. Janice opened the letter and read it, and then she handed it off to me so that I could read it too. The teacher just wanted to tell us what a joy it was having Alice in her class, that she was one of the brightest and most well-behaved children she had ever had. That was my Alice."

"What does she do now?" I asked.

"She's a housewife. I guess these days they call it being a stay-at-home mom."

"What does her husband do?"

"George is an architect. He owns his own firm, and I think they have around twenty employees. He's been very successful, according to Janice. I've never met him, but I hear from Janice that he's a very nice man. He doesn't drink, which I guess is a good thing. And Alice doesn't drink either, probably because of what she went through with me.

"I wonder if Alice remembers the report we did together for her fifth-grade class about the justice system. We worked on an oral report that Alice had to present to class about being presumed innocent until proven guilty … about how every person charged with a crime in this country deserved a fair trial and the best defense possible … that this was a hallmark of our legal system. She asked me for examples from my own experience, and I made up some stories about how I'd defended innocent people and kept them from being unjustly incarcerated. I didn't tell her the true nature of my business, which was primarily keeping guilty criminals from paying for their crimes. I felt she was too young to hear this sort of honesty coming from her own father. She would grow up and lose her innocence soon enough."

"Did she ever have aspirations to be something other than a stay-at-home mom?"

"I remember for a while in elementary school she wanted to become an attorney like me. She also wanted to be a doctor. She had the brains to become either, but I'm not sure what happened—by the time she was in high school, I was drinking a lot and no longer paying attention. Perhaps when I call her, I'll bring up Snowball."

"Who's Snowball?"

"That was the name of Alice's first kitten. I think Alice was around eight years old when she told Janice and me that she wanted to get a cat. We'd never had a pet in the house before, so this was kind of a big step. We told Alice she'd have to be responsible for taking care of the animal, feeding it on time and changing its litter box. She promised to do all of this on her own, and one Saturday afternoon the three of us piled in the car and drove to the pet store. I remember they had five or six kittens for sale, and we told Alice to pick one out. She immediately gravitated to this little pure-white kitten, and she said she was going to name her Snowball. We purchased the cat and brought her home in a cardboard box. Alice was infatuated with this animal, playing with it, having us buy all kinds of silly cat toys, and sleeping with it in her bed at night. For the next couple weeks, anywhere you'd find Alice, you'd find her with Snowball.

"People are sometimes surprised when I say this, but we have coyotes in Newport; I've seen them several times in neighbors' yards, even roaming our streets in the early morning hours. One morning while I was getting ready for work, I heard Alice screaming for me. I ran out of the house and found her in the front yard. Snowball was standing on the lawn with two mangy coyotes. One of them was in front of Snowball, keeping her attention, while the other crept up behind the cat, getting ready to strike.

"Before I could do anything, the coyote from behind lunged and grabbed Snowball with its teeth, shaking it about like a rag doll. The cat let out this awful sound and then fell limp and quiet in the coyote's jaws. 'Daddy, do something!' Alice screamed, but there was nothing I could do. Snowball was history. I yelled at the coyotes, but they just ran off with the cat. Meanwhile, Alice was bawling and beating her fists on my leg. 'Why didn't you stop them?' she sobbed. I brought Alice into the house. She was beside herself with grief and horror. It was the kind of thing a little girl shouldn't have seen, but what was done was done. When she stopped crying, I told her I was so sorry about Snowball, and I told her that sometimes bad things happen in life. I didn't have any consoling explanation for the gruesome event, just that life could sometimes be sad and ugly."

"How'd she take it?"

"She was quiet and morose for several days. Then we took her to the pet store and bought her a new cat. We were careful to keep this new cat indoors, and the animal lived a long and healthy life."

"Why would you bring this story up to her?"

"To remind her that sometimes bad things happen, but that it isn't the end of the world."

"How old is Alice now?"

"She's thirty-three."

"Don't you think she's a little old to be getting life lessons from you?"

"You're probably right."

"Why don't you try talking about your grandkids? People love talking about their kids. There's probably plenty she could tell you."

"That's a good idea."

It felt good to give Harry some good advice. It was good to know he wasn't perfect and that I could help him in some way. Up until this time in our relationship, it had been a one-way street, with him giving me the advice and me just listening. I was, after all, a sixty-year-old man, and despite all my flaws, I had still learned a thing or two about people and relationships.

Three days after this meeting with Harry, I received an afternoon phone call from my son Danny that would shake my world. He told me he had something important to say, and so I sat down and listened quietly. "Dad—" he said, and then he broke down and started crying.

"What is it?" I asked. It's funny what goes through your mind at a time like this, wondering what your son is about to say. The first thing that popped into my mind was that Danny was gay and he was coming out of the closet. Danny was twenty-seven years old, and he had never had a girlfriend that I could remember. He and his friends hung out with girls, but he'd never become attached to one in particular. Was he truly gay? And how would I handle this? When I was younger, I thought gays were ridiculous, if not revolting, but as a grown man I'd become much more tolerant. I could remember times when Danny was younger, when I'd make comments about gays that weren't exactly complimentary. So did he remember those comments? Is that why he was now crying, thinking that I would be devastated by the news? "What is it?" I asked again.

"Dad," Danny said, "I think I'm an alcoholic."

"A what?" I asked.

"An alcoholic, like you," he said. He was done crying and was waiting for my reaction. I was shocked.

"Okay," I said. "We need to talk in person. We shouldn't be doing this over the phone. Where are you now?"

"I'm at my studio."

"It'll take me twenty minutes to get there."

Wow, was this true? How had Amy and I missed something as important as this? Were we both so involved in our own lives and problems that we hadn't seen what was going on with our own son? It was the last thing I would have wanted for Danny, yet there I was, speeding in my truck toward Danny's house, listening to music on the radio, yet not listening at all. When I arrived, he was drunk and there was a half-empty bottle of rum sitting on his kitchen counter. I poured the rum down the sink and sat down so he could explain.

It was bizarre, listening to Danny's story. He had hid his drinking so well over the past several years that I had had no idea what was going on. It was like watching one of those aliens in that movie *The Body Snatchers*, emerging from a pod as an exact replica of Danny, yet a completely different person, a person I had no idea even existed. The old Danny just turned to dust. Have you seen that movie? This is the best way I can describe my afternoon with him.

When he was done talking, I took him home with me and put him to bed in our guest room to sleep off the rum. I then called Amy. Her reaction to the news surprised me, since she did not start crying, or shouting, or exhibiting any other strong outward emotions; instead, she took the information in with a calm resolve. "We need to get him into rehab," she said. Two days later we admitted Danny to a facility in Riverside, and he was to stay there for thirty days.

So now the shoe was on the other foot, and I was beginning to see what it felt like to worry about a loved one with a drinking problem. I wasn't worried about Danny so long as he was safe in the facility, but I began to worry about his future once he got out. There were so many disconcerting questions up in the air. Would he stay sober once released, or would this be one of those battles with the bottle that lasted months, or even years? Would this obsession to drink hound him until he was sixty years old, as it did me? What kind of trouble would he get himself into in the meantime? Whom would he hurt in the process, and how would he harm himself? And, of course, there was the most troubling question of all—was the entire situation all my fault? Was Danny just following in my footsteps? Had I passed down the defective genes? Was it like they say, that the apple doesn't fall far from the tree? And, seriously, what kind of lousy role model had I been for my own beloved son?

I thought back. You know, while most days I look back on are just a blur, a forgettable haze of times gone by, there are some special days I can remember with astonishing clarity. The day I learned Amy was pregnant with Danny was one of those special days. I can remember the weather, where we were, and exactly what Amy was wearing.

It was the middle of September, the Santa Ana winds were gusting, and I had just come home from work to find Amy waiting for me at the front door. She was dressed in a yellow shirt, white shorts, and sandals. She had a terrific smile on her face, and she was hiding something behind her back. "Why the big smile?" I asked, and she showed me what she was hiding. It was a small stuffed bear with pure white polyester fur and a red ribbon around its neck. "What's this for?" I asked, and she said, "Can't you guess?" I had no idea what she was up to, and I asked her to fill me in. "I'm pregnant!" she said. Wow, my jaw must have hit the floor. This was one of the happiest moments of my life, learning that we were going to have a child, that we were finally going to become a family.

The nine months that followed were absolutely crazy, and we did all the things young expectant couples do. We bought a stroller, car seat, crib, changing table, and wild bouncy seat contraption. We baby-proofed the entire house, stowing away all our breakable items, installing special latches on the cabinets, taping tennis balls to the sharp corners of our glass coffee table, and plugging unused electrical sockets. Amy went to two baby showers, one held by her girlfriends at work and the other put on by Agnes at her little house in Long Beach. Lucy and my mom flew out, making it to both showers, and by the time the showers were over, we had a whole roomful of rattles, books, teething rings, baby clothes, bibs, formula bottles, and assorted toys.

The closer we came to the scheduled delivery date, the more intense Amy became. She bought several books on raising infants and toddlers, and she studied them every night like she was cramming for an important college exam. She took all sorts of notes, highlighting important sentences and paragraphs, and sticking yellow Post-it notes to the pages. I remember when went to the hospital together for an ultrasound. They jellied up Amy's pregnant belly and ran their transducer over it, showing us an image of Danny sleeping soundly in her womb. They printed out a black-and-white photo that we framed and set on our fireplace mantel along with our other family pictures.

Finally, as the delivery date grew even nearer, we went to those silly Lamaze classes, where a gray-haired female sixties throwback taught us all about breathing, massaging, and meditating as a means through which Amy could naturally withstand the pain. Amy did take these classes seriously, but the lessons all went out the window when the moment of truth arrived. "To hell with all this breathing nonsense," Amy said. "Just do the epidural, and give me some drugs!" I'd never seen Amy in so much discomfort.

Then it was push, and push harder, and push again and again, and out came Danny, a little purple eggplant of a baby covered with slippery blood and slime. They cut the umbilical cord and washed him off and bundled him in a little cotton blanket, handing him off like a football to Amy. There he was, our little baby boy, so perfect and completely innocent, unmarred by the world. He was all ours to teach and guide and love. And now, in the blink of any eye, I was sixty, and he was a twenty-seven-year-old alcoholic.

Several days after we dropped Danny off at rehab, I met with Harry at his house. We were in the library when I told him all about Danny and his secret drinking life, about how he fessed up to me over the phone on that fateful afternoon, and about how guilty I felt over Danny's unsettling predicament. Harry told me it was now more important than ever that I get my own house in order. "It's like they tell you in airplanes," he said.

"And what is that?"

"They say when the oxygen masks drop, to put yours on first before helping your children with theirs."

CHAPTER 22

Family Week

Harry and I were still in the library, talking. "Do you think Danny's drinking is my fault?" I asked.

"Does it matter one way or the other?"

"It matters to me."

"This would be a good time for you to recall our ninth step."

"I forget what we said."

"We decided to let bygones be bygones, to choose to concern ourselves with the here and now."

I thought about this for a moment. "That's easier said than done."

"Everything in life is easier said than done."

"I guess that's true."

"So how's your backyard coming?" Harry asked, seeming to change the subject.

"It was coming along fine, but I stopped working on it after learning about Danny."

"Why?" Harry asked.

"I don't know. I guess I've been distracted."

"It's important that you keep up with your work. You need to keep up with your plans and responsibilities as though nothing has happened."

"Okay."

"You'll feel better about yourself. Have we talked about being tough?"

"I don't think so."

"You've got to be tough. You don't hear people talk about toughness at AA meetings, and it isn't specifically mentioned in the

Big Book, but toughness is essential. Do you know what I mean by toughness? How would you define it?"

I thought for a moment and then said, "I would say it's when something is able to withstand destructive forces."

"Yes," Harry said. "That's exactly what I mean. So, are you tough, Lester?"

"I don't know."

"I'll tell you about a client of mine named Vince Ackerman. I would describe Vince as a tough man. He was a mild-mannered high school science teacher here in Orange County, and he'd been teaching at the same school for over sixteen years. He was an excellent instructor, and he was popular with his students. He had a real knack for making science topics interesting to teenagers, and he had a charming personality. Life was good for Vince; he wasn't exactly getting rich, but he truly enjoyed what he did for a living. Enter Judy Campbell, an attractive seventeen-year-old senior and member of the football cheerleading squad. Judy took chemistry under a different teacher when she was a junior, and unfortunately she failed the class. As a senior she took the class over again, but this time with Vince; she needed to pass his class in order to get her diploma.

"I told you Judy was attractive, but she was actually much more than that. She was the perfect girl next door, a lovely young thing with the sort of wholesome countenance and demeanor that made you want to believe everything that spilled from her lips. When I saw and heard her for myself, even I had a hard time believing the girl could tell a lie, and when I read the accusation she'd made against Vince, I knew he was in serious trouble.

"According to Judy, she was having difficulty with Vince's class, and he asked her to see him after school. She thought he was going to propose some sort of tutoring arrangement, but instead she said he made sexual advances to her, telling her if she acquiesced, he would raise her grades so that she would pass. Judy said he then told her to stand close to him, and dumbly she obliged, giving him the opportunity to slip his right hand up her skirt and underneath her panties, groping her pubic area. She said at first she just stood there, not sure what to do, but then she turned and ran out of the room.

"When she came home that afternoon, she told her mother what had happened, and her mother threw a fit. Of course, none of this had actually taken place, but her mom believed every word of the story. In Judy's devious yet naïve mind, this was the perfect way to get out of the chemistry class and still get her much-needed diploma; surely the school wouldn't require her to complete the course given what she had gone through with Vince.

"When Judy's parents brought their daughter's alarming experience to the principal, Vince was immediately called into a meeting and told the parents were taking the matter to the police. The principal had no choice but to suspend Vince from his duties until all had been resolved. That was when Vince called me. He told me he was entirely innocent, that Judy had made the story up, and that he saw no reason why he couldn't continue teaching. He did not want to be suspended, or even mildly reprimanded, and he asked me to argue his case with the school.

"After a lot of posturing between myself, the school's attorney, and the girl's attorney, the principal finally decided to let Vince continue teaching until the matter was resolved in court. Vince returned to his class, and all hell broke loose. The paper ran an article on the story and published a picture of Vince's face. Some parents protested by barging into the principal's office and demanding Vince be fired, and several of his students refused to attend his class. It was an ugly scene, but like I said, Vince was tough; he held his ground and continued to work despite it all.

"This went on for six or seven months. He told me, 'If the world stopped for every wrench that fell in the works, nothing would ever get done. I'm a teacher, and I need to teach.' At first I thought he was a little crazy, taking the situation on the way he did, but then the more I thought about it, the more sense it made. For doesn't life always present us with challenges? It's the one thing you can be sure of, that you will be tested. Vince was right—despite everything, he needed to keep teaching—and I admired Vince's wisdom and fortitude."

"So what happened to him?" I asked.

"Actually, we got lucky. While we were preparing to go to trial, Judy started dating a boy name Chad Baker, who was a wide receiver on the high school football team. Chad and Judy went out one night to a party, where they drank beer and smoked marijuana. After the party on their way home, an intoxicated Judy bragged to Chad about what she'd done, telling him about Vince and the false charges she'd made in order to get out of chemistry class. Chad was an interesting boy, for at first he kept this information to himself, not planning to tell anyone and not wanting to sabotage his relationship with Judy. But then seeing that the trial was about to take place and suddenly realizing the severity of the situation, he told his parents exactly what Judy had told him. Chad's father went to the principal, telling him his son's story, and the principal called the district attorney.

"Well, one thing led to another, and after a long interrogation, Judy finally recanted her story. The charges were dropped, and Vince was let off the hook. The paper printed a small article on the matter, buried in the back pages of the local section next to the obituaries. A few of the parents wrote letters to Vince, apologizing for not believing in him, but most of the parents were just quiet about the matter, going on with their lives as though nothing had happened."

"Wow," I said.

"Vince was tough."

"Yes, he was."

"You need to be tough like Vince. Danny's problems with alcohol will come and go, but life needs to keep moving forward."

"I can see that."

"You will be tested over and over again."

"Yes," I said.

"And Danny's alcoholism could be the best thing that ever happened to you."

"How so?"

"This thing with Danny could be very good. Many people see alcoholism as a hopeless and disgraceful predicament, but it can be a great builder of men. You just need to have the right attitude. That's another thing you won't find mentioned in the Big Book—attitude."

"Attitude?"

"A person without the right attitude is like a tree without its trunk."

"Do I have the right attitude?"

"I don't know. Do you?" Harry asked.

"I don't want Danny to drink."

"That's a good start."

"So what else is there?" I asked.

"Do you believe in yourself? Do you see this as an opportunity rather than as an obstacle?"

"I'm honestly not sure."

"When you can answer yes, you'll have the right attitude."

It was three weeks into Danny's stay at rehab that the facility put on Family Week. Amy and I decided to go without Miles, since he didn't express an interest. He could have come if he wanted, but he opted out. I've been through three of these events before during my own rehabs, and they're all about the same. The facility invites the parents, spouses, partners, siblings, children, and close friends of the loved one for a program through which an attempt is made to work on relationships as they've been affected by the loved one's addiction. I might be oversimplifying the process, but you get the general idea. Although they called it Family Week at Danny's rehab, it was only three days and not a full week. The first day involved our sitting through some lectures by doctors and therapists. The second day involved group sessions without the loved one, and the last day was a long group session where everyone was included.

This was the first time I would attend a family program on the family side of the equation, and not as the alcoholic getting treatment. It was so strange, sitting there as one of the affected family members when I had only about eight months of sobriety myself. I felt like a peeping Tom, but I played my role well. I sat patiently through the first day of lectures, quite honestly hearing nothing I hadn't already heard many times before. I then sat through the therapy sessions on the second day, playing the part of the affected dad whose son was an alcoholic in need of help. It was so odd, being with these people and listening to their different stories, pretending to be one of them. Or was I one of them? It wasn't exactly clear to me.

I should tell you more about the second day. It was pretty interesting. The stories you hear in these sessions are all different, yet they're all the same. There was one couple, about the same age as Amy and I, whose twenty-one-year-old son was addicted to methamphetamine. The father was quiet and stoic, so the mom did all the talking. Her eyes would get wet while she was telling their story, and occasionally tears would fall down her cheeks and run into her mouth. One of the therapists handed her a box of tissues to keep her face dry.

She explained to the group that this was their son's fourth rehab, that he'd been struggling with his addiction for the past three years. They were hoping this fourth treatment would do the trick. They described their son as a wonderful boy, loaded with talent and bursting with personality, yet the things they said this kid did were awful— stealing jewelry from his mom and credit cards from the dad's wallet, forging checks on their bank account, and even borrowing thousands of dollars from the grandmother, who had no idea what was going on.

He'd been kicked out of two colleges, evicted from three apartments, and arrested six times on narcotics and shoplifting charges. He sounded like a terrible person, yet this mother's love for him was steadfast. If only they could get him to stop using drugs, she said, everything would go back to normal, back to the way it once was, and everyone would see what a terrific young man they had raised. I couldn't wait to see this kid in person. He sounded like a real piece of work.

Right next to this couple was a man's wife who I figured to be in her thirties, who came to family week by herself. Her name was Mary, and her husband was an alcoholic. She was nicely dressed and moderately attractive, and it was hard to imagine her married to a drunkard, but that's exactly the story she told.

According to Mary, they were high school sweethearts, just like Amy and me, and they were married in their early twenties. She said her husband had always been a drinker since the first day she met him, but that alcohol had never interfered with their lives. There was the occasional time when he would drink too much, and sometimes they would fight, but on the whole it was a good marriage. Then Mary said something happened, not overnight, but over a period of several years. Her husband began drinking all the time, and the two of them were often at odds, arguing over it.

"He wasn't the same man I married," she said. "He wasn't the bright-eyed boy I fell in love with in high school. He was now overweight and sweaty and unshaven; you would barely have recognized him from his high school photos. Then came the DUIs. He got three of them, and the court ordered jail time and rehabs. After his last DUI, they suspended his driver's license for a year, and I had to adjust my schedule to drive him to and from work each day. Finally, he was fired from his job. How they kept him on for as long as they did is still a mystery. Now we were living on only my paycheck, trying to pay all our bills with half the income we were used to. We've had to go to our parents for financial help, but even that hasn't covered all our obligations.

"Last year he said he was serious about quitting drinking, but since then he hasn't been able to put together a single month without relapsing. I told him I'd had enough, that I wanted a divorce, and that was when he asked for one last chance. So that's why we're here. This is his last chance, and he talked his parents into footing the bill for this program. I still love him, but there's no way I can go on living this way. I have my divorce attorney all picked out, and he's ready to prepare the papers. I have him on speed dial."

Mary didn't need the box of tissues. She wasn't so much sad as she was angry. While she was talking about her attorney being on speed dial, I leaned over and whispered in Amy's ear, "Don't get any big ideas." Amy just pushed me away.

The next family that got up to talk was a man with his three children. The man appeared to be a few years younger than I was, and his kids were all pimply faced teenagers. He spoke for the family and said they were all there to support the mom, who had a nagging problem with prescription pills. He listed all the medications he'd caught her with, and it was quite a list. He said this was his wife's first rehab; she'd been going to NA meetings for the past year, but they didn't seem to be working.

He went on to describe some of the embarrassing events that had led the family to decide she needed professional help. He said she'd forget to pick the kids up from school, and they'd have to get rides home from other parents or make the two-mile walk from the school to their house. He said she was once so stoned at her daughter's birthday party that she tripped while carrying out the cake and fell face-first into it. When the guests tried to give her a hand standing up, she became loud and unruly, and she was obviously so out of it that they had to send everyone home.

He also said she fell asleep once while cooking, letting a grease fire get out of hand that nearly burned down their kitchen. This was the last straw. He told the group he loved his wife dearly and that her kids all loved her as well, but they needed her to be a sober mom. The man's kids were listening as he spoke; there were two boys, and they remained expressionless, while his daughter started to cry halfway through the monologue and needed the tissue box.

I could go on with these stories, but you get the general idea. When it came our turn to speak, I let Amy do the talking. She did a good job of describing our family, the problems she'd had with me, and now the problem we were having with Danny. Amy, by the way, did not need the tissue box. Amy was never the kind of girl to cry easily in public. I have to say I liked that about her.

On the third day we got to meet all the addicts and alcoholics who had been the subjects of our previous discussions, and we saw them matched up with their friends and families. It was like some surreal Fellini movie, with all these different circus characters sitting in the same room, talking and laughing.

We got to see the nice couple's son, the one addicted to methamphetamine who was on his fourth rehab, the one who conned his own sweet grandmother out of her money. He was not at all as I had imagined. He was a clean-cut and handsome young man who could have been taken for a student body president or head of the debate team at any respectable college.

We also met Mary's husband, the overweight, sweaty, and unshaven alcoholic she'd been with since high school. He'd cleaned up his act, and his demeanor surprised me. He was jovial and optimistic, and he even shook my hand. If this was truly his last chance with Mary, he certainly didn't seem nervous about it. I wondered how he kept his spirits up, knowing Mary was just itching to pull the trigger on a divorce, knowing that she had her attorney on speed dial.

There was also the wife who nearly burned down the kitchen. You wouldn't have thought she was in rehab at all the way she carried on; she laughed and hugged her children, and then she floated about the room making small talk with the other families.

And then, of course, there was Danny, our own son, standing there and labeled as an alcoholic. He seemed so innocent, so out of place in this room full of deflowered Fellini characters. Looking at him made me want to cry.

Was Danny an alcoholic? Just the fact that I would ask this question proves that even a seasoned and admitted alcoholic like me can be blinded by denial when it comes to a loved one. I've never been a big proponent of group therapy or rehab facilities, but Family Week at Danny's rehab opened my eyes. I'll tell you what I learned on that last day about my son; I was educated and humbled. I learned that Danny had been drinking day and night for years, and that the amount of alcohol he'd been drinking was no less than I'd been drinking back when I was at my worst. I learned that Danny had been fired from his minimum-wage job at the sandwich shop over a year before for showing up drunk several days in a row.

He'd been supporting himself off credit cards he acquired by lying about his income, figuring out a way over the Internet to use the newest credit cards to pay the minimum payments on the old ones. I didn't even want to know what he now owed on these credit cards, because I was probably the one who would have to pay them off. I also learned that he spent very little time painting his art, and that he spent most his time in front of the TV. He spent his days on the couch watching talk shows, soap operas, and Dr. Phil, and he spent his evenings watching old movies and reality shows. He said his dream to become a painter had fizzled out years before; he just put random paint on canvases to make it appear he was still working at it. I should have been able to tell that the paintings he was showing me were frauds, but what do I know about art? I trusted him, and he was lying to my face.

Then came the news that hurt. He hated holidays and birthdays with the family, suffering through them, visiting us and pretending to be sober. He said we should've known better, that we couldn't even tell the difference between a drunk son and a sober son. "You were probably drunk yourself," he said to me. "It should take one to know one, don't you think?" I had no good answer for him. "It's been such a nightmare," he then said, and he started to cry. As soon as he started crying, Amy handed him the box of tissues. Then she started to cry, and he handed the box back to her. As for me, I was beyond crying. I told Danny I was so sorry. "I'm the one who's supposed to be apologizing," he said, but I knew he had this wrong.

When Amy and I got home that night, Miles was gone. He was supposed to leave a note on the counter whenever he went out telling us where he'd be and when to expect him home. Amy called his cell phone, but there was no answer. She hung up the phone angrily. She said, "This is getting to be more than I can handle."

"He'll be home," I said. "He probably just forgot his phone again."

"We should've taken him with us."

"You think so?"

"It would've been good for him."

"You're probably right."

"Did you have any idea about Danny?" Amy asked, referring to all the things he'd told us about himself in the therapy session.

"No, I didn't."

"He has looked sort of ragged the past few years, but I just thought it was an artist thing—you know, being so into his art, not getting enough sleep, and working all hours of the day and night on his paintings."

"Yes," I agreed.

"When's the last time he got a haircut?"

"I don't know."

"He needs to get a haircut."

"That isn't going to make him feel any better," I said.

"But it will make me feel better. I need to feel like we're getting somewhere, Lester. I can't live like this forever. Something has to change. It's been this way my whole life. First it was my parents and all their alcoholic friends and parties and nights on the town. Then it was you and all your problems, the bankruptcy, the binges, and the nights in jail. Now it's my son, that perfect little boy I gave birth to, locked up in that awful rehab facility with all those other addicts and drunkards. When is this going to end? I need this to be over with."

"I'm sorry," I said.

"I don't want you to apologize. I just want this nightmare to stop."

I asked Amy if she wanted to watch TV with me, and she told me she was going to bed. She said the week had worn her out. She just wanted to close her eyes and sleep, so I let her go.

CHAPTER 23

Pink Cloud

So what was it about this morning? Was it the proverbial clean slate? A new beginning? Was it that confident and big blue autumn sky with its cotton-white cumulus clouds and distant formations of birds?

I felt so good. I was on my way to Harry's, driving on the freeway, and the work congestion had just cleared up. I had called Harry first thing in the morning asking if we could get together, and he said to be at his house at ten. I would easily make it on time. A favorite song of mine was playing on the radio, and I tapped my fingers on the steering wheel, taking my time, navigating the morning traffic. When we spoke over the phone, Harry said to bring a light jacket, implying that we were going somewhere. It was a cool day, but where was he taking us? When I arrived at his house, he was loading a small cooler and a couple fishing poles into the back of his car. He was dressed in jeans and a T-shirt, not his everyday attire. "So what's up with all this?" I asked.

"We're going fishing."

"Fishing?"

"Yep," Harry said.

"Where are we going?"

"To the pier. Did you bring your jacket?"

"Yes," I said.

"Go in the house, in the kitchen. There's a thermos of hot coffee and a couple cups on the counter. Bring them out to me."

"Okay," I said.

I went into the house, got the items, and brought them out to Harry. He put them on the backseat beside the cooler. "I think we're ready. Let me lock up the house, and we'll be on our way."

We hopped in the car, and Harry drove us to Balboa Island, where we took the ferry across the bay. We drove to a public parking lot on the peninsula. We then carried our stuff out to the pier, where Harry picked a spot next to an Asian fellow who was seated comfortably in a fold-up lawn chair, already fishing. "Morning, Harry," he said.

"Good morning, Pedro."

"Brought a partner today?"

"This is Lester."

"Good morning, Lester."

"Morning," I replied.

"Catch anything?" Harry asked.

"Not yet," Pedro replied.

"What do you catch here?" I asked.

"Fish," Pedro said. Pedro and Harry then had a good laugh.

"I mean what kind of fish?"

"Wet ones," Pedro said, and they laughed again.

"Here's your pole," Harry said. "See what you can do with it."

"I'm not much of a fisherman," I warned.

"Neither are we," Harry said. "But we get lucky once in a while and pull a few up."

"Wet ones," Pedro said.

They both laughed again.

Harry and I dropped our lines down into the ocean, and we waited. Harry asked me if I wanted some coffee, and I told him yes. He poured me a cup and handed it to me, and then he resumed his stance at the edge of the pier, waiting.

"So tell me about Family Week. How did it go?"

"It was weird," I said.

"How so?"

"I'm not used to being on the sober side of the fence. I'm used to being the cause of all the angst, not the recipient. It was weird being in the room with all those parents, wives, and husbands of addicts, commiserating with them and trying to relate to them. And it was even weirder to see Danny there, not as someone I could be proud of, but as someone for whom I felt both pity and anger. I feel okay now, but I didn't feel so great when we got home. And Amy didn't feel any better."

"Rehab can be rough."

"Yes, it can."

"Did they hold lectures?"

"Oh, yes, and they had several speakers who talked confidently and scribbled diagrams on the whiteboard, passing out handouts at the end of their speeches. They told us addiction is probably a disease and that it needs to be properly treated as such. They explained how the addict is powerless, how it may have something to do with dopamine and synapses in the brain, how codependency is often a big part of the problem, and how they thought it could all be genetic and often hereditary. In short, they talked and talked the entire day, providing all sorts of information and conjecture. But by the end of the last lecture, we were no closer to putting our finger on the root cause of our loved one's problem than we were when we woke up that morning. The Big Book has it right when it says it's baffling."

"Yes," Harry said.

"Being there brought back so many memories. I remembered when I arrived at my first rehab, how drunk I was that night. I had promised Amy three weeks earlier that if I drank again, I would check myself into rehab. Sure enough, I did drink again, and Amy drove me to the only facility that had an open bed, a place in Laguna on Coast Highway in an old building that smelled of mold and human sweat.

"I called a friend of mine after Amy left and had him bring some vodka and Kahlua to the steps outside the entrance. We sat there drinking black Russians until someone inside the center got wise and chased my friend away. I then spent the next twenty-four hours sleeping in a cramped room on a very uncomfortable bed, in what they called their detox wing. What a joke this place was.

"Two days later there was an opening at Betty Ford, and I transferred there, where the rooms were clean, the grounds were nice, and the food was edible. I made some good friends at Betty Ford, but I have no idea where they are today. After I left, I did keep in touch with my counselor for a while, and he told me one of the guys I knew had died in a drunk driving accident just a couple weeks after being released. But like I said, I don't know what happened to the rest of them. Some of them might still be sober, but most of them are probably still drinking and using."

"Ah, a cynic!"

"No, just a realist. I don't think that many alcoholics or addicts ever get sober."

"But there are a few."

"I would like to be one of them."

"Like or will?"

"Yes, I *will* be one of them," I said, correcting myself.

"I enjoy fishing," Harry said. He paused a moment and then continued, "It's a lot like being a sponsor. Most of the fish just swim around aimlessly in the murky water, avoiding your hook, doing whatever it is that fish do. But once in a while you'll get a nibble, and every so often you'll get a hardy bite, and you can reel in the prize. Are you on my hook, Lester?"

"Pardon me?"

I have to admit that I hadn't been listening. I was staring at the water below, wondering if I would catch anything. I couldn't remember the last time I'd caught a fish. I mean, even during my vacation outings with Miles, I always came back empty-handed. With Miles it was a much different story; he could catch a whole bucket of fish with his eyes closed and his hands tied behind his back. It was uncanny how he could fish. No one else in our family was an angler, and I have no idea where he picked the talent up. I looked over at Harry. Just then, something tugged on Harry's line, and he began to reel it in.

"Did you catch something?" I asked.

"Let me see," Harry said, and he looked over the edge of the pier toward the water. Tangled up on his hook was a large hunk of seaweed. He reeled his line in, cleaned it off, and then dropped it back into the ocean water. For a while we just stood there, waiting to get an actual bite. It was not beachgoing weather, and the sandy shore was empty except for a few people taking strolls at the edge of the water.

When noon rolled around, we reeled in our lines and Harry removed a couple bologna sandwiches from his cooler, handing one to me. He also offered me a Coke, but I asked if any coffee was left in the thermos. The Asian guy named Pedro was still seated in his lawn chair waiting for something to bite. The sun was now high in the blue sky but partially blocked by a large cloud, and the seagulls were squawking nearby, probably wanting a piece of our sandwiches.

It was sort of nice, taking time off in the middle of the day like this, just doing nothing but fishing, eating, and thinking. It's funny where the mind goes, given a chance to wander.

I thought back to when I was Danny's age, when Amy and I had first moved to Southern California. We used to go to the beach often, coming here to escape the trouble we were in. My business enterprise had turned into a nightmare of the worst kind, with stalled projects, a mountain of past-due bills, and workers and subcontractors who were refusing to finish their jobs unless I brought their accounts up-to-date. My customers were furious, worrying about what had happened to the money they paid me and wondering if their projects would ever get completed.

One of the worst-off of these was a couple in Newport Beach, Gerry and Erin Baker. They contracted with me to do an extensive remodel of their home. I had ripped their entire house apart—roof and wallboard and wiring and plumbing lines—and I ran out of money shortly after the demolition. Their house looked as though it'd been hit by a tornado, and they were still trying their best to live in it. I had taken a large deposit on the job and used it to pay past-due bills on other projects, so I had no money to continue on with theirs. The Bakers were fit to be tied, calling me several times a day, working up a case against me with their attorney, and finally going to the police department and asking them to find out where all their money had gone.

The cops called me into their station, and I was interrogated by one of their detectives. He asked me to provide him with a complete accounting of how I'd used the Bakers' money, and I agreed to do this. But I knew there was no way I could provide an acceptable explanation, so I stalled the detective for several weeks. Meanwhile, my other projects were faltering as well, and I was making dishonest promises, bouncing checks, and giving my customers all sorts of lame excuses.

I did have one customer who was a very nice guy and very patient with me. His name was Abel, and don't ask me why, but he took a liking to me. I decided to try to get more money out of Abel by explaining how I had mistakenly underbid his project, and asking if he could please allow me to raise the price in order to get his job done. I brought him all sorts of phony cost breakdowns and copies of subcontracts and doctored check receipts to make my case, to show I was being honest. He agreed to the price increase and wrote me a very large check to keep his job going.

I deposited Abel's check in my account and used the money to pay back the Bakers, to get them and the police detective off my back. I remember celebrating this accomplishment at my favorite bar, getting good and drunk and reveling in the fact that I had escaped the claws of the Newport police. I wasn't even thinking about how I was going to finish Abel's job. God, what a mess. Abel showed up later on at my bankruptcy hearing, not so much to collect his money, since he knew I was broke, but more just to see me in person. "I trusted you," he said. What could I say back to this man? I just looked him in the eye and said, "I'm sorry, Abel." I'll never forget the look on his face.

Harry and I continued to fish.

"It doesn't look like we're going to catch anything today," Harry finally said.

It was now about three, and Pedro had gone home. Harry began to reel in his line and had decided to call it a day. I did the same, and we gathered everything up and walked back to Harry's car. We stowed away the equipment and cooler, and hopped in the car to drive back to Harry's house.

On the way back, Harry brought up his daughter. He said, "I called Alice last night."

"How'd it go?" I asked.

"Better than I thought it would."

"Did you ask about your grandchildren?"

"Just like you said. It was a great idea, Lester. She couldn't stop talking about them. There are two of them, you know. There's Robbie, who's seven, and Pamela, who just turned five. Alice told me all about their schools and preschools, their soccer games, and their many friends, and she described what they're dressing up as for Halloween this year. Robbie is going as a pirate, and Pamela will be a princess. She said they get a lot of trick-or-treaters in their neighborhood, so she always has to buy a ton of candy to be sure they don't run out. She said George will take the kids out to the houses this year, while she'll tend to the visitors at their own front door.

"I asked her if she remembered when she and her friends would go out trick-or-treating here in Newport in groups of five or six, trying to fill their pillowcases, and I asked her if she recalled her very first Halloween. Wow, I can remember that night so clearly. She went as Snow White in a costume Janice's mother made; her mother was a terrific seamstress, and she always volunteered her services for Halloween. We saved the costume, and I think it's still somewhere up in the attic, in a box."

As Harry went on about Alice and Halloween, I thought back to Danny's own first Halloween. He was four or five years old, and Amy and I took him out to a neighborhood of tract houses near our apartment complex. It was hilarious, watching Danny so quickly adapt to the tradition, running from one house to the next, getting free candy from complete strangers. He was dressed as Winnie the Pooh in an outfit Amy had picked up at a costume store. He was so unbelievably cute. One house we went to belonged to friends of ours, Bill and Carrie Sanders. When Danny rang the doorbell, Bill opened the door, holding a bowl of candy out to him. "Take a handful," he said, and Danny reached into the bowl, grasping as much candy as his small hand could hold. "What do you say?" Amy said to Danny, and Danny looked up at Bill seriously. "Close your door," he said. Amy and I still recall this and laugh about it every Halloween.

When we returned from our fishing trip, I said good-bye to Harry and hopped into my truck to drive home. A lot of people were getting off work, so the traffic was rather heavy. When I finally arrived at our house, it was close to five. The sky was dark, and it was especially chilly, so as I stepped into the house I lit the gas log in the fireplace. I got comfortable on the couch and turned the TV to a football game I'd recorded the previous Sunday. I liked recording football games so that I could fast-forward through all the commercials and just watch the action. The game was about half-over when Amy came home from work, and she asked me what I wanted for dinner. I told her to fix whatever was easy.

Miles wasn't home yet, being out with his friends doing whatever it is nineteen-year-old boys do with their free time, hopefully not getting into trouble. So it would be just Amy and I for dinner.

Amy was in the kitchen cooking when she asked me, "How do you think Danny's doing?"

"He's probably doing fine," I said.

"He'll be released in a week. We haven't talked about this yet, but he should probably stay here with us when he gets out."

"That'd be a good idea," I said.

"He can sleep in the guest room."

"I'm sure he'll be okay with that."

"I don't think he should go back to Laguna."

"I agree."

"I want him home with us."

I thought about this for a moment and then said, "We should talk to Danny. We should make sure he's on the same page."

"Yes," Amy agreed.

"I wonder how many months are left on his lease."

"I don't know."

"We'll have to move all his stuff."

"You can have your workers help."

"That's true," I said. "What do you think we should do with all his things?"

"Put them in the garage?"

"I don't think there's enough room. We'll probably have to rent a storage unit."

"Maybe," Amy said.

Were we getting ahead of ourselves? I didn't want our making decisions like this without getting Danny's input. After all, while he still seemed like a kid to us, he was a twenty-seven-year-old man. The next morning I called his rehab counselor and explained what we were thinking of doing, and I asked if it would be okay for me to discuss it all with Danny. He said, "Just a minute," and then he put Danny on the phone.

"What's up?" Danny asked.

"Mom and I have been thinking," I said. "We think it would be best for you to come live with us after you're released."

"What about my studio?"

"We think you should move out."

"Seriously?"

"We think it's for the best."

"So do I," Danny said.

"You do?"

"Yes, I do. I need to start over. I was hoping to move back in with you guys, but I didn't know if you'd go for it."

I was glad to hear this from Danny. It surprised me, but I was glad to hear it. It was good to know we were, in fact, on the same page. During the week following my phone call to Danny, I went ahead and moved his things out of the studio and set him up at our house. We were able to fit all his possessions in the garage without renting a storage space, and I hung some of his paintings up on the walls in the guest room to make him feel more at home. I worked out a reasonable agreement with his landlord, so we'd be let off the hook for the remainder of the studio lease.

I then called his phone, electric, gas, and cable TV services and asked them to forward the closing bills to our house. It was a lot of work, making this transition for Danny while keeping up with my other commitments, and the week went by very quickly.

I set my next meeting up with Harry for the day following Danny's release. We were to meet at Harry's house on a Wednesday evening. Danny was to be released on Tuesday, and Amy and I had to drive all the way to Riverside to pick him up. When we got there, he was waiting out front with his packed suitcase by his side, ready to go. He was all smiles, and after he said good-bye to several of the counselors, we piled into my truck and drove away. I remembered when I got out of my first rehab, what a crazy relief it was. I'm sure Danny felt the same way as we headed toward the freeway, knowing he had this difficult phase of his life behind him.

Danny was in a terrific mood. I was glad we had worked out his living arrangements in advance, and I told him how I'd set up the guest room for him and that I'd put all his extra stuff in the garage for the time being. He said he hadn't wanted to go back to Laguna, since it would remind him of his drinking. He told us he looked forward to coming home. "It'll be like old times," he said.

As we continued to drive, Amy asked all sorts of questions about the rehab program … about the people Danny had met, and about the counselors and whether they seemed competent and qualified. Danny was very talkative, and he answered all Amy's questions happily. I hadn't seen him in such a good mood in years. I commented on his good spirits, and Danny told me his advisor at the rehab center had told him he was on a pink cloud. I knew what this meant.

A pink cloud is that exciting feeling of optimism an alcoholic feels during the first months of sobriety. The body is beginning to function normally, and the head is clear and lucid. All the world feels like a wonderful opportunity. For some, it can actually be euphoric, not unlike that feeling they had when they took their first drink. I don't remember ever being on a pink cloud when I first got sober. I had too many legal and financial problems on my plate to feel optimistic, but all Danny had to worry about were the credit cards, and I think he knew I'd take care of them. It's no wonder he was so happy, and it made me happy to see him so energetic.

While we were driving, I asked him if he remembered telling us that he wanted to go back to school to study computer programming, and I asked him if he'd been serious about it. He said yes, that he was glad that I brought it up.

"Don't you remember when I first went to college, before I dropped out, I took a class in computer programming? It was the only class I got an A in, and I didn't even have to work that hard at it. I think I have an aptitude. Do you remember Colin Hardy, that friend of mine from high school with the curly hair and the limp? He had one leg shorter than the other, and you guys felt sorry for him because he couldn't play any school sports. Anyway, I ran into him in Laguna last year, and you know what he does for a living? He's a computer programmer for a company in Irvine, and he's bringing home six figures a year. He owns his own house and drives a brand-new Tesla, and he married a girl whose dad owns a chain of restaurants. To hell with all this painting nonsense; who wants to be poor for the rest of their life, trying on clothes at thrift shops and buying only sale items at the grocery store? I want to make something of myself."

"I think that's great," Amy said.

"Yes," I agreed. "You can always continue to work on your paintings in your spare time."

"I'm through with painting."

"Okay," I said.

"I'd be happy never to touch another paintbrush again."

When we arrived home, Danny carried his suitcase to the guest room. Miles appeared from the hallway and said, "Welcome back, big brother."

Danny seemed pleased to see him and asked, "So, how's the music coming?" Miles said it was coming along fine and told him if he came into his old bedroom he'd show him the music equipment he'd set up and play some of his recent songs. Danny said he would like that, and he proceeded to unpack his suitcase.

That was as much as I'd seen the boys talk to each other in years. For some reason the two just never were too friendly with each other. Danny had always looked at his little brother as sort of a screwup who was immature and not worth the effort of befriending, while Miles had always looked at Danny as unapproachable, too old to relate to, and somehow out of his league. But now here they were talking to each other like two old friends, and Amy and I both liked what we saw. It was certainly nice to have Danny back home. I felt energized and hopeful, like I was on my own pink cloud. Finally, I knew how it felt.

CHAPTER 24

Hank's Garage

That night after I climbed into bed, while Amy was already sleeping, I lay awake for a half hour thinking about the past few weeks. I realized that with all I'd had on my plate, I hadn't given even the slightest thought to taking a drink. I'd been thoroughly distracted from my obsession, and the very idea of getting drunk was actually repulsive to me. Had I made some sort of breakthrough with my sobriety? Was this what it felt like to be a normal and mature sixty-year-old man? I wanted to wake up Amy and tell her how I felt, but I decided to leave her alone. I would be meeting with Harry tomorrow, and I could tell him all about it then.

When I woke up the next morning, Amy was already out of bed. She was downstairs at the breakfast table, reading the paper and having her morning coffee. I walked down the stairs and stepped to the kitchen, where I poured my own coffee. I then sat at the table with Amy and reached for the sports section. "How'd you sleep?" I asked.

"I slept great," Amy said. "I feel so much better knowing Danny is back here at the house with us."

"Is either of the boys awake?"

"They're both still asleep. I think they were up late last night talking."

"It's good to see them getting along."

"Yes," Amy said.

"What's on your schedule today?"

"I'm going to work; then I'm coming home to pick up Miles. He said he wanted to come with me to the grocery store. He was rummaging through the refrigerator and the pantry last night, and he said there's nothing good to eat. He wants to pick out some food."

"I'm seeing Harry tonight."

"Yes, I know."

"I'm supposed to be there at seven. I should be home around ten."

"Are you two still working on the steps?"

"Yes," I said. "We have two left. We'll probably work on number eleven tonight; that is, unless we get sidetracked. You never know what Harry is going to want to talk about. Sometimes he talks and talks, and we don't work on the steps at all."

"I think Harry's been so good for you."

"There's no question."

"I remember when you came home from that noon AA meeting with his little business card. It had nothing but his first name and a phone number printed on it. You were wondering if you should call him, and I told you that you should. Do you remember that, Lester? Now it seems like so long ago."

"Yes," I said.

Amy folded over the newspaper and stood up. "I'm going to get ready for work," she said. Amy took her empty cup into the kitchen, placed it in the sink, and then walked up the stairs toward our bedroom. I added some coffee to my own cup, grabbed a cigar, and stepped out to the patio, where I sat down to smoke. I looked at our backyard, at all the work I'd recently completed. It was amazing how much I had done with my own two hands. The yard was starting to take shape, and all that was left to do was to plant the trees, install the sod, and buy some new patio furniture.

What a wonderful morning it was. The sun was rising into a hazy blue sky, the birds were singing happily, and there was a gentle breeze that blew my cigar smoke toward the neighbors' yard every time I took a puff. I thought about the backyard, and I could imagine us having parties this coming summer, cooking steaks on the BBQ, telling jokes and stories, and having some good laughs. This project was definitely one of my better ideas, and I patted myself on the back for it. Even Amy had to admit it was coming along even better than she'd imagined.

When I was done with the cigar, I went in the house and called Harry to confirm our meeting. I dialed his number on the kitchen phone, but there was no answer. It just rang and rang. I tried it again, thinking I might have dialed wrong, but I got the same result. I wondered where the heck he was. I always called in the mornings to confirm our meetings; he knew this, and he always answered. When I went upstairs to get ready for work, Amy had just finished putting on her makeup. I gave her a quick kiss good-bye, and she left the house. When I finally did get off to work, I had completely forgotten all about the fact that Harry wasn't answering his phone.

My mind was elsewhere, on my work. I had received a call while I was shaving from the carpenter at one of my jobs complaining about the door hardware I had dropped off to him the day before. The doors he'd installed were a special-order item, and very expensive. The carpenter had ordered and installed all of them, having had them predrilled for the hardware that was specified on the architect's plans. The owner, however, had changed the hardware brand and style, and not even thinking that the new hardware might not be compatible with the predrilled doors, I had picked it up from the supply house and delivered it to the job.

"The holes are all too big," my carpenter told me. "There's no way of installing this hardware in holes that are too big, and there's no way to make the holes smaller. We'll have to order and install all new doors." In my head I was calculating what this mistake was going to cost me in both dollars and lost time. I had originally told the owner that there would be no extra charge for changing the hardware, and I couldn't believe I'd done such a dumb thing.

When I returned to my office, I went ahead and placed the order for the new doors, and I asked the supplier to put a rush on them. If I didn't get them soon, it was not only going to cost me money, but it was also going to slow down my project. Well, that was one problem solved, but the rest of the day didn't go much smoother. There was a steady barrage of situations on my other jobs that required action. It was one of those days, not uncommon in the construction business, and I was busy putting out fires right up to around six, not even having time for lunch. After leaving the office, I stopped at a fast-food restaurant, and I ate a hamburger and fries in my truck on my way to Harry's house.

I was looking forward to meeting with Harry, since our conversations usually made me feel better about things, and I could've used a boost. I admired Harry for this, his ability to uplift another's spirits. I hoped someday to have the same sort of personality, so that others would want to be around me. I wondered whether other people looked forward to being with me at all. Did Amy enjoy being with me? Did my boys enjoy my company? I didn't know for sure.

When I arrived at Harry's, I parked in the street as usual, and the first thing I noticed was that a white Prius was parked beside Harry's car in the driveway. *Darn*, I thought. Had he made other plans? Was he working with some other alcoholic, having forgotten about our meeting this evening? Or did he have unexpected company? I now wished I'd tried harder to reach him on the phone earlier in the day, to confirm our meeting time. I hesitated on the walkway, thinking that maybe I should just turn back. But if he was with someone, maybe they were planning to leave when I arrived, and maybe he was, in fact, waiting for me. So I stepped to the door and knocked. I could hear voices behind the door, but no one was answering. So I knocked again, and this time the door opened. A woman stood in the doorway asking who I was.

It was Janice. I recognized her from Harry's pictures on the piano. She looked just like the wedding picture I'd picked up that day, except she was older. Her eyes appeared swollen and red as though she'd just been crying. "My name is Lester," I said. "I have an appointment tonight with Harry. But if you guys are busy, I can come back later."

"No, it isn't that," she said.

"Is Harry available?"

"Harry is …" she began slowly. "Harry is no longer with us."

"What do you mean?"

"Harry died. He passed away."

"You're kidding," I said.

"They took his body away several hours ago."

"What happened?" I asked.

"They think it was a brain hemorrhage. They say he's been dead for days. Harry and I were supposed to have lunch today, but he never showed up. I called him, but he didn't answer, so I came by the house to check on him. I found him on the bedroom floor."

"Who's there?" a man's voice said. He was standing behind Janice in the foyer.

"I think he's one of Harry's alcoholics."

"Invite him in," the man said.

Janice thought about this and then said, "Please come in." She stepped out of the way so I could enter the house.

"I shouldn't intrude," I said.

"My name is Kaleb," the man said, stepping forward and extending his hand for a handshake. I shook his hand.

"I think I should go," I said.

"It's up to you," Kaleb said.

"I should leave you two alone."

Janice smiled kindly as though I'd said the right thing. "What was your name again?" she asked.

"Lester."

"Best of luck to you, Lester."

"Thanks," I said.

Janice closed the door, and I walked through the darkness to my truck. Wow, what a shocker! So how did I feel? I didn't feel particularly sad or stricken by grief. And I didn't feel angry or resentful that Harry had been taken from me. I guess if I were asked to describe my feelings that evening, I would have to say I was stunned. I felt stunned but also remorseful. I was stunned that it had all happened so suddenly—one day alive and the next day dead—and also remorseful that I never had a chance to thank Harry for his time, for all he had done for me.

Some people have had a lot of practice with death, and they seem to know how to react. In my sixty years of life, I've had only two people die on me, my aunt Agnes and Amy's dad, Vern. I was not used to this sort of thing. I sat in my truck for a moment before starting the engine. "Son of a bitch!" I said out loud, and I pounded on the steering wheel with my fists. I then started up the truck and put it in drive to leave.

The next month would not go well for me. When I arrived home that night and told Amy about Harry, she seemed more concerned about my sobriety than she did about Harry himself. When I told the boys, the news barely registered. Neither of them knew much about Harry, and for them he was just some stranger, some friend of their dad who happened to kick the bucket. In fact, I was the only one in the family who'd been close to the man, and I found myself feeling angry, not that he'd died, but just angry at everything. Does this make any sense to you?

I was sullen and short with others at work. I didn't particularly care whether my customers were happy, and I was even less concerned about the well-being of my workers and subcontractors. Things that used to make me laugh, now just seemed dumb and trite. Things that used to make me feel love, now just seemed maudlin and pointless. Christ, what was I to do? Was this grief I was feeling? What would Harry have to say about all this? You know, I knew exactly what Harry would say. He would tell me to suck it up and be a man. He would tell me to be tough. He would probably quote that former televangelist Robert Schuller and say that tough times don't last, but tough people do. That would be just like Harry, to quote some religious nut to make an atheist's point.

Yes, I had to get ahold of myself. In AA meetings they tell you to turn all this stuff over to God, but in the real world it's so different. And I lived in the real world, didn't I? I didn't live in a fantasy universe created and ruled by a supernatural being. The answer lay in the truth, and the truth of the matter was that if I didn't toughen up, all Harry's work with me would be for naught. I needed to pick myself up and give it my all.

They say if you're feeling bad to just smile, that when you smile your mood will follow along with it … that there's something about activating the smiling muscles in the face that triggers those happy regions of the human brain. I didn't know if this was true or just gobbledygook, but I began to smile. And I began to count my blessings. And I began to recall all the things Harry had taught me while he was still alive. I can't say I was suddenly all giddy and riding a pink cloud again, but I was able to snap out of my monthlong depression, slowly but surely.

Then I had a great idea. I sat down at my laptop and began to type, recording notes on everything I could remember about the conversations I had had with Harry—every courtroom example he gave me, every analogy he came up with, every stupid joke he told, every bit of advice he provided. These notes would provide the basis for the book you are reading now. I didn't want to forget any of it.

While typing all these notes, I remembered Harry and I had never completed the last two steps of the program; we'd discussed only steps one through ten. Somehow, I needed to complete steps eleven and twelve without Harry. I suppose I could have guessed at them myself, but I wanted Harry's take. I needed to find another alcoholic Harry had sponsored, and find out exactly what he had said about these two steps. The problem was that I didn't know any of the alcoholics Harry had worked with over the years, or how to reach them. I decided my best shot was to attend the meetings Harry had gone to, and ask the groups if anyone there had been sponsored by him. Surely there would be someone, no?

So first I went to the noon meeting where Harry first introduced himself to me. When it came time to share, I raised my hand and explained Harry had passed away, which they seemed to already know, because there was no reaction. Don't ask me how, but word of death travels very fast among the AA crowd. I then asked if anyone in the group had been sponsored by Harry, and if so, would they please approach me when the meeting let out. That was all I had to say, and when I was done speaking, everyone applauded, as they do for anyone who speaks, no matter what they say.

When the meeting was over, believe it or not, my old religious friend Alex stepped up to me. Do you remember Alex? He's the soft-spoken guy who approached me months before to tell me Harry and I would eventually find God. Alex asked how I was doing, and then he told me he knew of a man who'd gone the full stretch with Harry, but who didn't attend meetings anymore.

He said the man's name was Hank and that he ran an auto repair shop in Fullerton. He told me the name of the shop was Hank's Garage, and that everyone there called him Mr. Hank. I thanked Alex for the information, and when I got home I searched the Internet for Mr. Hank, finding the repair shop and writing down the address. It was three in the afternoon, and I figured I had plenty of time to get to the shop before they closed. It was located in an industrial area, a large lot with a five-bay garage and some attached offices. The lot itself was surrounded by a chain-link fence, and there were all sorts of cars in various stages of repair. I found a parking space for my truck and walked to the reception area, where I discovered a young girl manning a desk and phone. "I'm here to see Hank," I said.

"You mean Mr. Hank?"

"Yes, Mr. Hank."

"Do you have an appointment?"

"No," I said.

"What's it about?"

"It's personal," I said.

The girl stared at me a moment and then stood up. "Hang on. I'll find him for you."

A short time later, Hank came into the room with the girl. "What can I do for you?" he asked.

"I'd like to discuss something with you, if you can spare a moment. It's about Harry."

"Oh?" Hank said. "Very well, follow me."

I followed Hank into his private office, and he shut the door. It was a dusty little room with a desk, some floor-to-ceiling shelves, and several hundred papers loosely strewn about. We both sat down. Hank was short, bald, and kind of surly, and his hands and fingernails were stained black with automobile grease. "Have you heard the news?" I asked.

"What news?"

"Harry passed away."

"Oh, wow," Hank said. "What happened?"

"I was told he had a brain hemorrhage. His ex-wife found him on the bedroom floor."

"Holy smokes."

"I've come to ask a favor of you."

"Okay," Hank said.

"Harry and I were working the steps right before he died. We went through all of them except eleven and twelve. I was wondering if you could fill me in on them. I need to know what Harry had to say."

"Eleven and twelve," Hank said, pondering.

"Would you be willing to do this?"

"I'm not a sponsor."

"I don't need a sponsor. I just need to know what Harry told you."

Hank thought for a moment and then said, "Why not? I think I can do that for you."

"When would you be available?"

"How about next week? I'm swamped the rest of this week. Can we meet somewhere for dinner?"

"That would be great," I said.

Hank and I agreed on a date, and Hank set the time for seven. He scribbled the information onto his calendar, and I logged it into my cell phone.

When I got home, I told Amy what I'd done, setting up this meeting with Hank to continue on with the steps. She said she was glad to see me getting back into the program, that she'd been worried about my mood since Harry died. I told her I decided that Harry would've wanted me to keep moving forward—that he would've wanted me to be tough, to be a man. Amy laughed at this and then said, "Oh, no, I mean that's good." I guess it was funny to Amy at first, the idea of me acting like a man.

Two days later, I came home from work in the early afternoon, planning to plant a few trees in the backyard. All the trees had been delivered, and they were standing in their plastic pots like ready soldiers. I found Danny in the family room, dressed in sweatpants and a T-shirt, watching one of those courtroom shows on TV. A half-empty quart of tequila was sitting on the coffee table, and my heart sank. I knew there'd always been a good chance of his relapsing, but I still felt terrible about it. "What are you doing?" I asked.

"Watching TV."

"I mean, why are you drinking?"

"Because I'm an alcoholic," Danny said. "Why do you think?" He reached for his bottle and took a big swig.

"What happened?"

"What happened to what?"

"What made you want to drink?"

"I'm powerless," Danny said. "Haven't you heard?"

"You don't have to do this."

"Like father, like son. Isn't that what they say?"

"Except I'm not drinking."

"Well, good. That leaves more for me."

I didn't know what to do. He was holding the bottle tightly in his hands, and if I went for it, I wasn't sure he'd give it up so easily. I didn't want this to turn into a physical struggle. I also knew from experience that it was very difficult to reason with alcoholics when they were drunk.

"Can I please take what you have left?"

"What are you going to do with it?"

"Pour it down the sink."

"You're going to waste this perfectly good tequila?"

"Come on, Danny. Hand it over." I reached out my hand, but Danny ignored me, taking another long swig, this time a very long swig. He then gave the near-empty bottle to me. "Thanks," I said.

"You can have what's left."

I took the bottle from him, went to the kitchen, and poured the leftover booze down the drain. Just then, Miles came in through the front door with a couple friends, and they entered the kitchen, probably wanting food. Miles saw the empty tequila bottle on the counter and his brother sprawled on the family room couch, and he asked, "What's going on?"

"Your brother's had a relapse."

"What's a relapse?"

"We can talk about it later. Now is not a good time for you to have friends over."

"But we'll stay upstairs."

"Please, Miles. I don't want them here. Not this afternoon."

"Okay," Miles said.

"Thanks," I said. "I'm sorry about this."

"It's okay. We'll find somewhere else to go."

The boys left the house so that Danny and I could be alone. I walked into the family room, where Danny was still on the couch. The booze he had just drunk so quickly was now hitting him pretty hard, and I could tell he was having a hard time focusing his eyes on me. "Come with me," I said. I wanted to get him to his room, to get him in bed so he could sleep it off.

"I'm watching TV," he said. His words were now slurred, and he was becoming incoherent.

"You're drunk," I replied. "You not even watching the TV. You need to go to bed."

"I only wanted a couple of drinks."

"I know," I said.

"I hadn't planned on drinking this much."

"Come on, Danny. Let's get up."

"Just a couple of drinks."

"Here we go," I said, and I pulled on his arm. I got him to his feet, but he fell back on the couch. "You need to help me out here, Danny. Try to stand up."

"Okay."

"I need to put you to bed."

"What time is it?"

"It's almost nine," I lied.

"Already?"

Danny was now standing. "That's it. Stay on your feet," I said. I swung his arm around my neck to keep him steady and upright. I walked him out of the family room, down the hall, and to his bed. He fell into the covers, groaned loudly, and then passed out. He was breathing heavily, as sleeping drunks do. I left the bedroom and closed the door behind me. I then went to the kitchen to get the empty tequila bottle, and I took it to the side of the house, where I dropped it in the trash can. I didn't want it in the kitchen wastebasket, where I would see it every time I went to throw something away. I wanted it as far away from me as possible, not because I thought it would trigger me to drink, but because it repulsed me.

I then did what any good father would do. I looked for Danny's car keys, just in case he woke up and decided to go somewhere. The last thing I needed was for Danny to be driving around town in his condition. I found the keys on the coffee table, and I hid them in a water glass in the kitchen cabinets. I then called Amy to tell her what had happened. She thanked me for calling her, and I could tell she was upset. But she had a lot of work to do and said she would talk to me about it when she got home. I called Miles on his cell phone and told him the coast was clear, that he could bring his friends back over. Danny was asleep. He said they were at his friend's house now playing basketball in the driveway, and that he'd probably eat dinner there and be home at about nine.

I would need to talk to Danny in the morning about his relapse, but what exactly would I say? What would Harry say if he were his son? How would I find the most effective words? Not that I'm an outstanding writer, but I've always been a much better writer than a talker, so I turned on my laptop and began to compose a letter to Danny. I would give it to him tomorrow, when he was sober:

> Dear Danny,
> I'm writing to you because you relapsed and I want to help. As for myself, I'm sober and I intend to stay that way. There's so much I could tell you about all the things I've learned over the past months from my sponsor, Harry, but I'll begin by explaining something he taught me that is very simple. I don't profess to know why you're an alcoholic, and I won't try to explain it. It could have to do with how you were raised, or it could be in your genes. Or it could be a combination of factors, like some perfect storm. But what's important isn't knowing why you're an alcoholic, but understanding why you continue to drink, knowing that you're an alcoholic. Do you understand this distinction?
> Harry would use the analogy of a man who can't swim jumping into a pool. It's a hot summer day, and the pool is cool and inviting, but if he jumps in the pool, he drowns. So if he does jump, is he powerless over water, or did he have a choice? We all have so many choices to make. We all have free will. I think I've told you before that I first quit drinking when I was about your age. I didn't go to rehab then, but I did go to lots of AA meetings. They taught me the same thing as your rehab counselors probably taught you, that as alcoholics we're powerless over alcohol, but is this true? Are we as powerless as they say? I don't think so.
> Years ago you met my aunt Agnes when you were a young boy, and I don't know if you remember her

very well, but she was an alcoholic like you and me. She stayed sober for over thirty years, and when I asked her what her secret was, she told me it was simple, that she just never took the first drink. It made no sense to me then, and perhaps it makes no sense to you now, but it means everything. Danny, I love you, but your relapse yesterday didn't occur because you're an alcoholic. It occurred because you decided to take that first drink. It was you who made this decision, not the alcoholism. You knew you couldn't swim, yet you decided to jump into the pool.

Well, that was it. The letter said what I wanted. I printed it out and folded it in thirds, planning to hand it over to Danny the next day. When Amy got home that night, I had her read it. She said she liked it. She hoped Danny would take it to heart.

The next day Danny slept in, so I didn't get to see him in the morning. I had to go to work, and I didn't get home until four. When I did get home, Danny was on the couch watching an old movie on the TV, but this time he was sober. "I have something for you," I said.

"What is it?"

"I wrote you a letter."

"A letter?"

"There are some things I'd like to say to you, and I felt I could best express them in a letter. Here, I want you to read this." I handed Danny the letter. He unfolded it and started reading. The expression on his face reminded me of the look my father would get when he read over one of my school report cards, curious yet serious. When he was done, his hands dropped to his lap. He said, "So basically, you're saying this is all my fault."

"I'm not blaming you for your alcoholism, but I am blaming you for the relapse."

"Wow, Dad."

"Do you disagree?"

"I don't know. I'll let you know later. Right now, I'm kind of in the middle of this movie."

CHAPTER 25

Both Hands

The restaurant where Hank met me was in downtown Fullerton. It was a cowboy-themed steak house with all sorts of western relics hanging from the walls and ceilings—old spurs, horseshoes, brands, and saddles. The waitresses all wore cowboy hats, tight-fitting western shirts with bolo ties, cutoff jeans, and girls' cowboy boots. I remember that the booths were upholstered with red leather, and the tables were topped with red-and-white checkered cloths. Every table had a big bottle of catsup and an even bigger bottle of steak sauce. The place smelled fantastic, like smoldering mesquite and sizzling slabs of beef, and the music system was playing old country western hits. "This is one of my favorite restaurants," Hank said.

"I like it," I said.

"Their steaks are terrific."

"I believe you."

"I'm going to order a porterhouse."

"I'm not sure what I'm going to get," I said, looking over the gigantic menu, "although the porterhouse does sound good."

"You can't go wrong."

"Yes, then a porterhouse it is."

"I always order mine medium rare."

"I appreciate your meeting me like this," I said. "What you have to say about Harry is very important to me."

"It isn't a problem."

"How long had you known him?"

"I knew Harry for six years. I'm a little over five years sober. It took me almost a year to get off the booze. How long have you been sober?"

"Less than a year," I said.

"How old are you?"

"I'm sixty."

"I'm forty-seven. I'll be forty-eight next month. Are you married?"

"Yes," I said. "For thirty-seven years."

"I'm divorced," Hank said. "My wife divorced me back when I was drinking. She told me she couldn't take it anymore. I drove the poor girl crazy."

The waitress showed up at our table, and we ordered our porterhouse steaks. Hank ordered a side of what they called cowboy beans, while I ordered a side of coleslaw. We both ordered dinner salads, which the waitress said she would bring right out.

"Here's to Harry," Hank said, holding his glass of water up to make a toast.

I clinked my own water glass against his and said, "Yes, here's to Harry."

"Holy smokes, I can't believe he's gone. I thought the old guy would live forever."

"It surprised the hell out of me."

It's funny how when alcoholics get together, they'll so often want to talk about their pasts. I think alcoholics feel compelled to identify with each other by telling old stories. It's a kind of twisted camaraderie peculiar to alcoholics, especially to those who are used to sharing about their lives in AA meetings. Hank was no exception, and he started way back when.

"Do you remember your first drink?" he asked.

"Oh, yes," I said.

"When I first met Harry, he wanted to know everything about me. He wanted me to start by telling him about my first drink. Most alcoholics can remember every little detail about their first drink. As for me, I was fifteen, a sophomore in high school. I was with a buddy of mine named Bobby Hartman, and his parents were throwing a birthday party for his brother, who just turned twenty-one. Since his brother was now of legal drinking age, Bobby's parents went out and bought several cases of beer, and they put the cans into several ice-filled coolers.

"We weren't invited to the party, since it was being held for twenty-one-year-olds. But we were hanging around prior to the party, and Bobby took six cans of the beer and hid them in his room. I asked him if he was afraid of getting caught, and he said no one would ever notice. He was right, and when the party started, we hung out in his room and drank the beer. Bobby popped open the first can, and I opened mine. I had never tasted beer before, and it was surprising. It had a strange and exciting flavor, and the carbonation tickled my nose. It wasn't easy getting the first can down, but the second and third were easier.

"Three beers are plenty for a fifteen-year-old novice, and the alcohol went straight to my head. I'd never felt so good in my life. Bobby and I had a terrific time hiding away in his bedroom, acting stupid, gossiping about other kids at school, and telling a few dirty jokes. I tell you, I've never felt so good since. It was one of those once-in-a-lifetime experiences."

"I know what you mean," I said.

"Well, for me that was the beginning of the end. I spent the remainder of my high school years chasing after that feeling every weekend night, drinking beer and hard liquor with my pals.

"When I graduated from high school, I got a job as a gofer at an auto repair shop, where the owner liked me and took me under his wing. I learned a lot from this guy, working as an assistant and eventually performing some of the repairs myself, and I finally became one of the mechanics. All this time I was still a weekend drinker. During the weekdays I was a hardworking and responsible employee, but on weekend nights it was crazy. After I turned twenty-one, my friends and I would go from bar to bar, drinking everything in sight. We'd be driving drunk half the time, and it was a wonder we were never pulled over by the cops. We'd stay out at night until closing time, always talking about picking up girls but never doing it. That is, until the night I came home with Suzy. Granted she was no Jennifer Lopez, but she was a pretty good catch for a guy like me.

"Don't ask me what attracted Suzy to me, because I don't know. When I first took her home to my apartment, I was so drunk I just passed out on the couch, and when I got up in the morning, she was still there. Later on, she told me that I had potential, whatever that meant. But I was impressed that she was impressed with me, and the two of us started dating. My drinking died down for a year or so, and we found other things to do besides barhopping. We'd go to movies, to concerts, and to the mall to window-shop. Those were good times, and I can honestly say I was pretty happy with myself for having snagged a girlfriend. She was a girlfriend, wasn't she? I mean, we always hung out together, and we kissed whenever we said good-bye.

"Well, one thing led to another, and the next thing you know we were married. Holy smokes, now I had a wife. Then I opened my own business, and I bought a house. I was on a roll, and it seemed like everything was going my way. That's when my drinking picked up again, at first in the evenings when I came from work—a few drinks to unwind, and then a few more, and a few more after that. Then the next thing you know I was demanding to go out with my old friends again and getting drunk every weekend. Suzy tried to slow it down, but it was more than she could handle. In no time, I was completely out of control, drinking twenty-four hours a day."

"I was the same," I said.

"You want to know what the weird thing is? All the time I was drinking so heavily, I remember nothing about Suzy. We were married and living in the same house, but I don't remember her, almost nothing at all. I may as well have been single."

Hank went on to tell me some stories about these drinking years, all the wild times he'd had and some of the stupid things he'd done. He told me how Suzy walked out on him and filed for divorce. He said he didn't care one way or the other at the time, that it was good riddance … probably the biggest mistake of his life. Then he told me about his drunk driving arrest and the night he'd spent in jail. The court ordered him to do community service and attend AA meetings.

It was in the meetings, listening to the stories of all the others, where Hank began to realize just what a disaster his life had become. He wasn't a happy-go-lucky drinker; instead, he was just a very lonely man with a huge drinking problem. He had a longtime general manager at his repair shop who had been in charge of things, keeping the business going, but he was about to quit. He didn't have any friendships, other than all those shallow relationships he had with the alcoholics with whom he had been drinking at bars. Suzy was gone, and he lived in his house all alone.

He said, "It suddenly hit me that I wasn't happy at all, that I'd been wasting years of my life. I experienced a moment of clarity, sitting at home drunk on my sofa and watching *The Price is Right*. I realized that given the direction I was headed, I would soon lose everything—the business I had started, my money, my house, and my health."

"So what did you do?" I asked.

"I continued to go to meetings voluntarily. I started sharing with the groups about my life. I bought a Big Book, and I read all the brochures. I listened to everything the others had to say. Then I had a second moment of clarity while sitting in one of these meetings—there was no way this program could ever help me the way it was structured. This whole idea of turning my life over to God was not something I'd be able to do."

"So you're an atheist?"

"Oh, no. I definitely believe in God."

"Then why the problem?"

Just as I asked this question, the waitress delivered our salads. She also poured us some more water. Hank thanked her and then went on with his story. "I believe in God, but not the God they describe in the Big Book. The God I have faith in has faith in me. This idea of turning everything over is ridiculous. I believe God has already given us the resources and tools required for us to fend for ourselves, and if we can't figure out a way to handle difficult circumstances on our own, then how will he ever be proud of us? I think God wants to be proud of us, no? We are, after all, his beloved children. We're all his children, each and every one of us—neurotics, liars, procrastinators, psychopaths, alcoholics, anorexics, the whole crazy lot of us. We were put on this planet to learn, grow, figure things out for ourselves, help each other, find our way around obstacles, and achieve success. Saying you need to reach out to God for help every time you get your rear end caught in a crack doesn't say much for your faith in his handiwork. As Harry would say, it's insulting.

"No, I'm the last person you're going to see insulting God. I brought this up at AA meetings several times, to the displeasure of those who disagree with me. But Harry didn't disagree. He introduced himself after one of these meetings, and he said he thought he could help me. He said, 'I can show you another way.' I wanted to stay sober, and I couldn't follow the steps, not the way they were written. So I gave Harry's way a chance. And now here I am, sober for five years. I've never been happier. I've never felt more confident."

"Did you know Harry was an atheist?"

"What's that got to do with anything?"

"I just wondered if you knew."

"It's beside the point."

Hank was barely done with his salad when the waitress came to take our plates away. He had spent so much time talking that he'd forgotten to eat. He asked the waitress to leave the salad to the side. Then they brought out our dinners, and I have to say my steak looked stupendous. It was large and juicy and smelled great. "Wow," I said. "This looks good."

"Anything else I can get you?" the waitress asked, and Hank and I said we were fine.

"So," I said to Hank, "getting back to the whole point of this dinner, what can you tell me about steps eleven and twelve? What exactly did Harry have to say?"

"Did Harry ever get around to telling you about the twins?"

"No," I said.

"It was one of Harry's court cases. He was hired by a pair of twins, Jason and Zachary Harrison, to defend them from murder charges for a car accident that killed a seventeen-year-old girl. The twins had very little money, but Harry took on the case for a small fee because it interested him. The girl's name was Sally Smyth, and she was driving on her way home from a friend's house when Jason and Zach ran into her. She was a good kid, attractive and athletic. She was popular at school, involved in sports, well behaved, and liked by kids and adults alike. Sally's parents were devastated by the accident, losing this wonderful daughter in the prime of her life. They knew she'd still be alive were it not for Jason and Zach.

"Let me tell you about these boys. They were identical twins, each twenty-two years old. Jason had been driving, and Zach was the passenger. Neither boy had been drinking; both were given blood tests right after the wreck, and their alcohol levels were zero. So what caused this accident? Jason said he'd fallen asleep at the wheel, but to the detectives on the case, something about this story didn't ring true. Certainly both boys wouldn't have fallen asleep at the same time, and if Jason had fallen asleep, wouldn't Zach have woke him up, or at least grabbed the steering wheel to prevent the accident?

"The detectives did some investigating into the boys' backgrounds, and they learned something interesting: they had had a reputation ever since they were kids of daring each other to do crazy and sometimes dangerous things. It was a game they were obsessed with, coming up with ridiculous dares and carrying them out, never mind the consequences.

"The detectives learned that when they were in elementary school, Jason had dared Zach to jump off their roof, and when Zach did so, he broke his leg and foot. They had learned this from a neighbor who had seen the whole thing take place. 'I heard the dare,' she said, 'but I didn't believe the boy would really jump.'

"Then there was the time in high school when Jason dared Zach to break into Mr. Ortiz's Spanish classroom at night and steal Mr. Ortiz's Mexican flag. It was a large national flag, hung high over the whiteboard. It was Mr. Ortiz's pride and joy, but when Zach broke the window to get in and climbed through the broken glass, he accidentally cut an artery in his leg. Blood was squirting everywhere, and Jason rushed him to the hospital. The doctor in the emergency room told Zach he was lucky not to have bled to death. The detectives heard this story from the school principal, who got the boys to fess up to the dare and then suspended them both from school for a week. 'I'll never forget those two,' the principal said. 'All that trouble just because of a stupid dare.'

"Then there was also the time after they graduated from high school and got jobs together working at a fast-food restaurant. Zach dared Jason to grind up laxative pills and put the powder into the hamburgers they were selling. Jason went to several drug stores and bought all the laxative he could get his hands on, ground it up, and brought it to the restaurant. He put the stuff into the hamburgers and passed them out to unwitting customers.

"The manager wouldn't even have known what happened, had not several customers returned the next day, complaining of food poisoning. One was a family of four, saying that they'd all got sick, all at the same time, and all right after having eaten the restaurant's hamburgers. What Zach and Jason didn't know was that the restaurant had hidden closed-circuit cameras covering the food preparation areas. The manager reviewed the tapes to see if he could ascertain anything unusual happening, and sure enough there was Jason pouring a white powdered substance atop the hamburger patties. When confronted with the video and a threat to call the police, Jason told the manager all about the dare and the laxative, and he and Zach were fired. 'Those two are nothing but trouble,' the manager told the detectives. 'It doesn't surprise me you're asking questions about them now.' It was clear something was wrong with these boys, and the detectives called them into the police station for questioning.

"The detectives interrogated the boys separately, and while Zach kept quiet, Jason spilled the entire story. Zach had dared him to drive thirty seconds without touching the steering wheel. 'I thought I could do it,' Jason said. 'It was only for thirty seconds. Zach was timing me with the second hand on his watch, and at first it wasn't a problem. But then the car started to drift, not to the right, but to the left into the oncoming traffic lanes. We were crossing the center line, and I asked Zach how much longer we had to go, and he said we still had fifteen seconds. Then we saw that girl's car, approaching us rapidly. I told Zach I didn't think we'd make it, but he told me she'd surely swerve out of our way. He said if I so much as touched the steering wheel, I would've welched on the dare. So I kept my hands off the wheel. We got closer and closer, and the girl just stayed in her lane. Maybe she was looking at her radio changing channels and didn't see us coming. Or maybe she thought we'd pull back to our side of the road. But she didn't budge an inch, and the next thing I knew we ran smack into her and spun off to the right, out of control. We demolished the whole driver's side of her car, and I was in shock. It was horrible. We never meant for anyone to die.'"

"So, what happened to the boys?"

"Harry worked out a deal with the district attorney. They pleaded guilty to manslaughter and were sentenced to terms in prison. I don't remember how many years."

"Why did Harry tell you this story?"

"Have you read step eleven?"

"Yes," I said. "I read it last night."

"What did it say?"

"Something about continuing to pray and meditate to understand God's will and seeking the power to carry it out."

"That's the one."

"What does that have to do with the twins?"

"Everything," Hank said. Then he looked down at his steak, which he hadn't touched since the waitress brought it out. "I need to eat this before it gets cold," he said, and he cut himself a big hunk and stuffed it into his mouth with his fork, closing his eyes and chewing. "This is great. So, how's yours?"

"It's very good," I replied.

"I love this place." I watched Hank eat his steak for a while, and we said nothing. Finally, he put down his fork and continued to speak. He said, "Harry called step eleven the maintenance step."

"The maintenance step?"

"Except instead of maintaining this unhealthy relationship with God, we look at our own recent actions and ask how we're doing. Are we keeping with the program? Are we working hard to stay vigilant? For every time we stray from the twelve steps, we're taking our hands off the wheel, daring ourselves to drive without direction like Zach dared Jason. 'You need to keep both hands on the wheel at all times,' Harry told me. So this is why he told me the story about the twins. It made sense then, and it makes sense to me now."

"I understand that, Hank," I said.

"It's Mr. Hank."

"Pardon me?"

"I prefer to be called Mr. Hank."

"Of course," I said.

We were done with our meals, and we never did get around to discussing step twelve. So I asked Hank if he was interested in having another dinner with me to talk about it. Instead, he took a paper napkin and wrote down an address. He handed it to me and said to meet him there Saturday morning. He would explain everything then.

When I got home that night, it was after ten. Amy was waiting for me and was excited to hear how things had gone. "So how's Hank?" she asked.

"It's Mr. Hank," I said.

"It's what?"

"He likes to be called Mr. Hank."

"So how'd it go?"

"Our dinner went very well. It was just like talking to Harry. It's like the guy never died."

"What did you talk about?"

"About keeping both hands on the wheel."

"What does that mean?"

I told Amy the things Hank had told me, including the story about the twins, and she said it all made perfect sense.

When Saturday rolled around, I was off to see Hank at the address he had written on the napkin. I plugged the address into my GPS, lit a cigarette, and drove through the morning traffic. The address was for someplace in South LA, not a great neighborhood, certainly nothing like the safe and sheltered housing tract where I had chosen to live in Orange County. What was Hank doing there, and why did he want me to come?

According to my GPS, the address was for a baseball field. It wasn't like the baseball fields near my own home, which were so well maintained by the city of Mission Viejo. This baseball field was neglected and dilapidated. The lawn was dry and full of bald spots, and the wood structures were splintered and bleached by the sun. The chain-link fencing and backstops had been damaged and peeled back by vandals, and no one had bothered to make any repairs. I stepped toward the backstops and spotted Hank with a group of boys at one of the dugouts. They were involved in a game against another team. Hank's team was up to bat, and when Hank saw me, he motioned for me to come over. Parents were in the bleachers, yelling and whistling, and one of Hank's boys was at the plate. When I arrived at the dugout, I asked, "So you're a coach?"

"Yep," Hank said.

"Why way up here in LA?"

"I'll get to that. Take a seat."

I sat down on the splintered wood bench and watched Hank coach the boys. They were an odd lot of kids, some of them kind of scary-looking and others more docile. One of the more docile kids wore a pair of thick Coke bottle glasses, and I wondered if he could even see the baseball. One of the scarier kids had a big bandage on his nose and a black eye, as though he'd recently been in a fistfight. Watching Hank manage these boys was pretty interesting. As a group they were kind of unruly, but Hank always seemed to be able to rein them in when their antics got out of hand.

Harry himself would have cringed to hear all the profanity being used in this dugout; I'd never heard boys this age cuss so much in my life. They were bullying each other, dissing each other, and pushing and shoving.

When the game was over, Hank gathered the boys around him to give them a speech. He told them that even though they had lost the game, he was proud of their effort. He then singled out a few of the boys and complimented them for what they'd done right. He talked about teamwork versus individual talent, and he even talked about life skills—what it took to make it in this world. When his speech was over, the boys ran off, still pushing and shoving, still cussing and teasing each other.

Hank said, "I'm glad you're here. You can give me a hand." I helped Hank carry the cooler and equipment back to his car. Once we had everything loaded up, he told me to follow him to a restaurant for lunch. We wound up at a small place in a run-down strip center, where we took a seat in one of the booths and ordered lunch. "So, why bring me all the way out here to watch a kids' baseball game?" I asked.

"This is my step twelve."

"It is?"

"Have you read the step?"

"Yes," I said. "It talks about carrying the AA message to alcoholics who are still suffering."

"Three years ago I got a call from one of my customers who told me there was an opening for a baseball coach here in LA. The season had just started, and the original coach had shown up drunk and got into a fistfight with one of the parents. He was discharged, and they were looking for a replacement coach, but they couldn't find anyone on such short notice. People weren't exactly lining up for the job, for coaching these kids can be a real challenge. Most of these kids come from broken homes, and many have parents who are practicing alcoholics and addicts. They're not bad people, Lester; there are just a lot of problems in these neighborhoods. Many of the kids lack direction and discipline, and they can be very hard to manage. My customer knew that I was a big baseball fan, and he asked me if I would be interested in the job. I thought of Harry and what he'd told me about step twelve, and I jumped at the opportunity.

"I volunteered for this job, but holy smokes, what a challenge it turned out to be. I've never had any kids of my own, so managing these boys was not at all easy. But by the end of the season I decided it was one of the most rewarding things I'd ever done. The parents were so pleased that they got together and asked me to coach the team again. I've been doing this now for three years, and I wouldn't trade it for anything."

"So what's this have to do with step twelve, with helping other alcoholics?"

"Harry said step twelve isn't just about helping other alcoholics. He told me that it's about helping, period. It's about reaching out and helping those in need, and in doing so, helping yourself. Harry said alcoholics need to love themselves in order to stay sober for any serious length of time, and as you may already know, there's no surer way in Harry's book to love oneself than to make the world a better place for others. So that's what I'm doing here."

"So, do you love yourself?" I asked.

"I'm working on it," Hank said. "Each day, I get a little better at it."

"Your team seems to like you."

"Let me tell you something about the way I coach. Do you remember the kid with the thick glasses? His name is Julian Rogers. At the beginning of the season his parents approached me, and they told me that the coach of the last team he was on barely played him at all. He would put Julian in the game only when the score was completely lopsided, during garbage innings when the winner and loser of the game had been established. They told him their son truly loved baseball, and that if I just gave the boy a chance, he would prove himself. Well, the truth was that their son was not a very good player, but he did want to participate. So I played him four to five innings each game, no matter what the score was. I had him playing in left field.

"In our game two weeks ago, we were ahead of the other team by a single run. It was the bottom of the ninth, and the other team was up to bat with runners on second and third. There were two outs, and the batter took his place at the plate. On the second pitch he whacked the ball deep into left field toward Julian. He ran like the wind to position himself, and he looked up to the sky. The ball fell into Julian's mitt, and then it fell from the mitt to the ground. The parents in the stands all groaned. Julian scrambled for the ball and then threw it with all his might toward home plate. Of course, the throw was off target, and the third baseman ran to get the ball. By the time the third baseman threw the ball to the catcher, the two runners had scored and they won the game.

"When the team all came back to the dugout, they were sorely disappointed, but one of the boys put his arm around Julian and said, 'Don't worry about it, Julian. That could've happened to me.' And one of the other kids said, 'Yeah, it could've happened to any of us.' I can't tell you what that moment meant to me as a coach, knowing that all my preaching to the boys about teamwork and supporting each other had actually paid off. We had lost the game, but for that moment in time, we had won the war. Yes, for that moment in time I loved myself for what I'd done with these boys."

"Harry would've liked that story," I said.

"Yes," Hank agreed.

The waitress brought our lunch orders. Hank had ordered a deviled egg sandwich, and I had the patty melt. We ate and talked more about Hank's baseball team until it was time to go. I insisted on paying the check. "I owe you at least this much," I said. When we went back to our cars, Hank shook my hand and wished me luck with everything. I told him how much I appreciated his time, and the two of us drove our separate ways.

Isn't it weird, I thought, *how some people come in and out of our lives?* Here was this fellow Hank, with his auto repair shop, baseball team, and clumsy, bespectacled player, serving as such an integral part of my sobriety, so very important to me. Yet he was someone

I would probably never see again, not ever. He was in and out of my life, just like that. You know, I made the drive from LA to my home in Mission Viejo without the slightest desire to stop at a bar or liquor store. That horrible trip to Tijuana ... do you remember that fiasco? It now seemed like it was decades ago, from another life as a different person. When I got home, I couldn't wait to tell Amy about my morning with Hank.

"You mean Mr. Hank, don't you?"

"Yes, of course," I said. "Mr. Hank."

CHAPTER 26

The Scorpion

It's now been two years since I first met Harry outside that noon AA meeting, since he first put his hand on my shoulder and handed me his business card. A lot has happened since that day, but you should know that I haven't taken a drink, not a single one.

Business has been pretty good these past two years. There's been no shortage of work, and I've been able to keep my three construction crews employed full time without many dead days. My customers are happy with me, and I've had only one who's been difficult to handle.

It was karma, I guess, that I got this customer, an eighty-one-year-old alcoholic who lived in Laguna Beach. His name was Donald Albright. He hired us to remove and replace some rotten decking at the front of his house, a job that was tricky and difficult, and required a lot more time than we anticipated. I put my best crew on the job, and the entire project took us about a month. Don was fine in the mornings when he was sober, and when I'd make my morning visits to his house, everything was roses. But by the late afternoons, once he'd had a chance to get a bottle of whiskey into his belly, he'd be calling me on my cell phone, ranting and raving about how long the project was taking … about how my workers were making disparaging comments to him in Spanish thinking he wouldn't understand … about how they weren't picking up their trash. It got to be pretty annoying, and I was very happy when we finished the job and I picked up my final payment.

A month after that, I received a long e-mail from Don, reiterating all his complaints about our performance, and then a month after that, he called me to do some more work. It was like he had a split personality, and to be honest, I felt sort of sorry for the guy. But when he asked for me to do some more work on his house, I lied and said we were too busy to handle it. I didn't want to work for him again. Alcoholics are such a pain in the neck.

As for our backyard, I finished that project about four months after Harry died. It came out great, and I took great satisfaction in the results. Amy, who'd been left out of the loop, seemed to appreciate all I'd done. It took her a little while to get used to it at first, but now every morning she has her coffee and reads the paper at the patio table, birds all singing around her and the sun rising into the big blue sky. I enjoy seeing this. It makes me feel good about myself to see Amy use the backyard.

Last year, we held several BBQ parties at the house, each held in the yard. At one party we invited some old friends and Amy's friends from work. At another party we invited Danny's new friends, all of them sober; there was not a drop of beer or hard liquor at the gathering. At the third party, we invited Amy's mom over for her birthday. Lucy didn't have a lot of friends in California, but a few of them flew in from Albuquerque. Lucy now lives in Mission Viejo, not too far from us.

Lucy moved back to California last year, wanting to be closer to Amy and her grandchildren. This made sense to me, since she no longer had Vern and was probably feeling lonely in the Albuquerque house by herself. You're probably curious to know if Lucy still drinks, and the answer is that yes, she does. She doesn't drink as much as she used to with Vern, but she can definitely still put the Scotch-and-waters away. This isn't to say she isn't supportive of Danny and me staying sober, and she's never encouraged the two of us to join her when she's boozing. But she has no trouble drinking in front of us. It's Danny and I who have the problem, not her, and she seems to have no intention of changing her lifestyle just because the two of us can't handle our liquor.

You know, when you first get into AA, there's a tendency to want to judge others, to say this person or that is also an alcoholic. I stopped doing that years ago. I keep my judgments to myself, and unless others admit they have a problem, I pretty much leave them be. So I leave Lucy alone and let her drink. She doesn't seem to be hurting anyone, and her life has not become unmanageable. I do sometimes drive her home from our house if she's been drinking, just to play it safe, but that's about as far as I go. She's a decent mother-in-law, and I leave it at that. I'm glad she moved back to California, because I think it's good for the boys to spend time with their grandma, even if she doesn't set the greatest example.

Speaking of the boys, they are both now enrolled in college. Danny is majoring in computer science, while Miles's major is undeclared. Despite Miles's distaste for school, I did give him the option of going to college or getting a job, and he decided on school. I think he made the right choice. I don't think he would have learned that much flipping hamburgers, stocking shelves, or bagging groceries other than learning to show up to work on time and do his job, and there will be plenty of opportunity for that later in his life. I guess I'm hoping he'll discover a career path in college other than music, for while I once was excited to see him chase his dream, I've come to realize that he should probably be more realistic. Is this wrong of me? When I see Miles, I see a lot of myself—the way I once was determined to be a famous writer, the way Miles now envisions himself as a successful musician. Is it wrong of me to be like my father, wanting my son to find a real job, wanting him to support himself?

It's kind of sad the way the dreams of youth can be extinguished, the way Danny gave up his painting and the way I gave up my writing dream. But it's all part of growing up, isn't it? Or is it? Maybe Miles will stick to his guns and actually become a famous musician, all this schooling be damned. Who knows? As Harry would say, sometimes it's best just to admit you don't have all the answers and leave it at that. So I guess when it comes down to it, Miles is still a work in progress. We'll see what happens.

If you're wondering if Danny has stayed sober, I'll tell you he's actually done a pretty good job. He's had three relapses since the last one I told you about, which isn't bad over a period of nearly two years. Right now he hasn't had a drink for seven months. He's doing well in school, and he's made some new friends. He no longer lives at home. Amy and I rented a small apartment for him closer to his college because we think a twenty-seven-year-old is better off living on his own. Danny had a girlfriend for about three months, a girl he met at school named Samantha. He brought Samantha over to our house for dinner, wanting Amy and me to meet her. Wow, what a dinner that was.

First of all, Danny warned us that the girl was a vegan, so Amy had to prepare the appropriate food. She didn't have any idea how to cook a vegan meal, but she did her best. I thought it was awful, but Samantha seemed okay with it. I have to describe this girl to you. She was several inches shorter than Danny, skinny as a rail, with thick black hair. She had tattoos all over her arms and neck of flowers and vines and flying birds. She wore a black tank top to show off her tattoos, black tights, and clunky black shoes. The weirdest thing about her wasn't her tattoos, however, but her piercings, through her nose and lips. It looked so uncomfortable to me, all that silver jewelry stabbed into the extremities of her face. It looked so primitive, so unsanitary. When she spoke, she had a strange feminine hoarseness, like the voice of a woman who spent a lot of time in smoke-filled rooms, maybe someone who smoked too much marijuana. But Danny said she was completely sober; she didn't believe in poisoning herself with invasive substances. She was the kind of girl who wouldn't even take an aspirin for a headache.

And speaking of aspirin, she had some very interesting views on medications. I don't remember how we got on the subject, but we began talking about cancer. Samantha told us that all the big pharmaceutical companies were making billions on cancer treatment medications. Doctors and hospitals were making a fortune as well, when everyone knew that a cure for cancer had been discovered years ago; according to her, the cure was being kept from the public so that all these corrupt individuals and corporations could keep making a killing off the disease. I'd read about this paranoid claim before on the Internet, but I'd never expected to hear it from one of our dinner guests. Amy and I were pleased to hear that Danny finally decided to call it quits with this odd girl. We couldn't imagine her someday being our daughter-in-law, raising our grandchildren.

You're probably wondering how my own parents are doing. I haven't been up to see them since my last visit, which I already told you about. I'm assuming the yard is in good shape and that the house is holding up. I've talked to them on the phone quite a few times, and they seem to be in good spirits. Dad still complains about his health, and his doctor has recently discovered some new ailments he supposedly suffers from. But I think if he'd stop going to this doctor, he wouldn't even know he had the ailments, and he'd probably be a lot better off. Doctors drive me crazy, but that's a subject for a whole separate book.

As for my mom, she's still a firecracker. She's still jetting around town in her car, and she said she got another speeding ticket a few months ago. She went to court again and argued her case before the judge. But this judge was younger, and he didn't buy any of Mom's complaints about law enforcement's disrespectful treatment of senior citizens. He found Mom guilty and ordered her to pay the fine. Mom called him an arrogant young whippersnapper. I laughed, because I hadn't heard anyone use that term for years.

So what about Harry's ex-wife, Janice? And what about Harry's daughter, Alice, and his two grandchildren, Robbie and Pamela? I haven't heard anything about them at all. I didn't expect to hear anything about them, but it's just kind of weird how they were so much a part of my life through my conversations with Harry, and then after he died, they just disappeared. I wonder what they did with Harry's house, all his books, and his car, and Alice's piano. Do you think they kept anything as a memento or remembrance, or did they hold a big sale, auctioning everything off and pocketing the cash?

I was never invited to Harry's memorial or funeral. I'm assuming they had something for him, but I don't even know whether Harry was buried or cremated. That was such a strange day, the day I went to Harry's house and discovered that he had died. You know, there are just a handful of days one truly remembers through a whole life—I mean, remembers with vivid clarity, like it just happened. I think that will be one of those days for me. I can recall what Janice was wearing, the way her eyes were red and swollen from crying, the way she held the door open for me, and the way that goofy-looking husband of hers insisted on shaking my hand. It was the only time I'd ever met Kaleb, and I didn't care for him at all. Drunk or not, it was no wonder Harry had tried to strangle the guy.

I miss Harry. He was one of a kind. He was a great teacher and a true friend, the sort of friend who honestly cared what happened to you. Some of his advice was hard for me to take, and some of it I soaked up like a dry sponge, but all of it was intelligent and well directed. I would have hated to have been a young district attorney facing Harry in court during the prime of his career. Harry could argue circles around anyone or anything, and I'm glad he was in my corner when I met him.

Harry once told me his variation of a well-known joke about a frog and a scorpion. I've heard this joke a hundred times, but Harry's version made me laugh. Harry said there's a scorpion who wants to cross a creek, and a frog swims by, and the scorpion flags him down. The scorpion says, "Can you give me a ride across the creek?" The frog thinks about it and says, "You'll just sting me halfway across, and both of us will drown." The scorpion says, "No, I promise I won't do that. You have my word." Against his better judgment, the frog agrees to carry the scorpion on his back to the other side of the creek. The frog swims in close to the shore, and the scorpion climbs on. The frog then begins to swim. Halfway there, the frog stops and asks the scorpion if he's okay, and the scorpion says he's doing fine. The frog then resumes his swim, and they make it safely to the other side. The scorpion hops off and thanks the frog for the ride. The frog says, "I can't believe you didn't sting me. I thought for sure we were both going to drown." The scorpion just smiles at the frog and says, "What, you think I'm stupid?" If you've heard the original version of the joke, you'll get Harry's punch line. If not, keep your ears open, and you'll hear the original version soon enough. Then you'll understand Harry and his view of free will.

For years I thought I was a powerless alcoholic, like a scorpion who couldn't change his nature. Now I see myself as a human being, with strengths and weaknesses, virtues and vices, morality and sinfulness, but most importantly with free will. What I choose to do with my life is up to me. Yes, it's a matter of choice.

Every morning I wake up, I step to the bathroom and look at my image in the mirror. I think of Harry's words, saying to myself, "Lights, camera, action." Then I brush my teeth, rinse out my mouth, and shave. Sometimes I can hear Harry's voice, like he's right in the room with me. It was all such great advice. Every bit of it. And thanks to my friend Harry, I truly believe my years ahead will be my best ever. Amy asked me the other day if I thought I would ever drink again, and I said, "What, you think I'm stupid?" That pretty much sums it up. That's my future in a nutshell.

CHAPTER 27

Epilogue

Unless you've been jotting down notes, you probably don't have a list of Harry's steps. Just in case you're interested, they're listed below:

1. Admitted that our lives had become unmanageable.
2. Came to believe that we and we alone could restore ourselves to sanity.
3. Made a commitment to take responsibility for our lives.
4. Made a searching and fearless moral inventory of ourselves.
5. Admitted to ourselves the exact nature of our wrongs.
6. We were ready to accept responsibility for our character defects.
7. We stopped making bad choices, and once and for all took responsibility for ourselves.
8. We made a list of some obvious people we harmed as a direct result of our drinking.
9. We let bygones be bygones, and chose to concern ourselves with the here and now.
10. Continued to take personal inventory and when we were wrong promptly admitted it.
11. We stayed vigilant, continuing to work the steps at all times.
12. Helped ourselves to love ourselves by reaching out and helping others.

You don't have to be an atheist to work Harry's steps, nor do you have to believe in God. These steps were written for every kind of alcoholic. The point is for people to take responsibility for themselves. Will they work for you? Of course, you have to truly wish to quit drinking in order to stay sober. But if you have this desire, and if you're ready to stop making excuses for your bad behavior, these steps might be helpful to you. I know they helped me, and if I didn't believe in them, I wouldn't have gone through all the trouble to write this book.

Are you an alcoholic? I wish you only the best, and I hope whatever road you decide to take leads you to a sober life. It's a wonderful thing for the alcoholic to be sober. I'm a sixty-two-year-old man, and the best years of my life are ahead of me … thanks to Harry, thanks to his audacity to rewrite the twelve steps, and thanks to AA.

Printed in the United States
By Bookmasters